Praise for the Novels
of Bob Reiss

THE SIDE EFFECT

BOB REISS

A DELL BOOK

THE SIDE EFFECT
A Dell Book / August 2006

Published by Bantam Dell
A Division of Random House, Inc.
New York, New York

ISBN-13: 978-0-440-24308-3
ISBN-10: 0-440-24308-4

Printed in the United States of America
Published simultaneously in Canada

www.bantamdell.com

OPM 10 9 8 7 6 5 4 3 2 1

For
Mrs. Manis, my English teacher
at Carr Junior High School in
Queens, New York. You started it, and I'm
forever grateful.

ACKNOWLEDGMENTS

Many thanks to Patricia Burke, T. A. Combre, Ted Conover, Richard Davies, Chris Earle, Josie Freedman, Phyllis Grann (who said think big), Clay Max Hall, Bill Massey, George Murphy of Key West, Esther Newberg, Jonathan Plutzik, Jerome Reiss, Wendy Roth, and Gary Schoolsky.

Also, I'm indebted to the very fine book *Mind Wide Open* by Steven Johnson, which was a source of valuable information on the functioning brain. My book is a novel. All mistakes are mine. But anyone wanting to learn more about the fascinating human brain should read Johnson's nonfiction gem.

ONE

The Chairman died the way he had lived: alone. Sometime between two and four A.M. on a muggy Wednesday in late July, while the rest of the New York City sweltered through the worst heat wave in history, 66-year-old James L. Dwyer walked into the bathroom of his East 58th Street townhouse, ingested a mix of prescription drugs, ironically manufactured by our own corporation, left a note on his study desk and convulsed into permanent sleep.

At least that's the way it seemed to the Filipino houseman who found Dwyer when he let himself in at four to prepare the Chairman's usual steak and eggs breakfast. Dwyer had always been a punctual riser.

The houseman, Aguinaldo, was a former Manila EMS attendant who checked for a pulse and tried CPR, but the body was cold, the color gone. He phoned me instead of the police.

"The Chairman always told me, if there's a robbery, or any reason to call the cops, phone Mr. Acela if you can't reach me. He said there might be important papers here. He said—"

Aguinaldo was starting to ramble, so I interrupted. I told him he had done the right thing. I calmed him enough so he could answer questions. "Was the front door locked when you arrived?" I asked.

"Yes, Mr. Acela."

"What about the patio door and the windows?"

Aguinaldo took some minutes to check. "All locked from inside except his bedroom window. That one was open by an inch, but it's on the third floor."

"Any furniture out of place, drawers open?"

"It does not look like a break-in, sir."

"Did you touch anything besides the body?"

"I read the note. But it makes no sense for him to do this. Did you read the *Wall Street Journal* article about his big deal last month? It called him Lucky Jim."

"Don't touch anything else. Don't phone anyone. I'll be there in half an hour."

I hung up and sat for an instant, stunned, in my den in Devil's Bay, Brooklyn, the boyhood neighborhood to which I'd recently moved back after twenty-six years away. The first-floor windows were open in my remodeled Cape Cod, and I could hear the sound of surf half a block away. I hadn't been sleeping. I'd been glued to my TV for the last few hours, watching the disturbing news from Washington. The President—a good and fair man—had resigned tonight, citing health reasons, handing the reins of power to his number two, a man known for extreme right-wing inclinations.

In fact, the summer so far had been marked by numerous sudden departures in the capital: a Supreme Court Justice; a crusading *Washington Post* editor; the head of the FBI, my old boss, another good man.

I shut off the TV, remembering the rest of what Aguinaldo had said.

A contract to come up with antidotes for chemical and biological weapons, sir. The Journal *called it one of the richest pharmaceutical deals in history.*

The shock was sinking in. I'd visited the Chairman just hours ago in his townhouse for one of our periodic late-night report sessions, and found him furious and drinking too much rather than confident, his usual self. It was not unusual for him to conduct business at home at ten P.M. I think he did it to have company.

I think I've made a terrible mistake, he'd muttered at one point.

And a few minutes later, *God help us all—the whole country—if I'm right.*

He stared at me and I'd had the oddest feeling that he could see inside me. Then he'd nodded as if he approved. *I can trust you.* He'd added, bitterly, *Not like some other people who I thought were friends.*

Because of this, and because scandals in the company three years ago—graft we'd dealt with in private—still left tensions, I discarded the idea of sharing the news with other officers until I saw for myself what had happened. I showered and shaved quickly, trying to clear my mind for what would be a long, grief-filled day. I'd be looking at the body of a man who had become a mentor late in my life, and might, with time, have become a friend. I'd be explaining to angry detectives why they'd not been summoned before me. I'd be briefing Lenox's acting CEO—a man I did not like—on what I found, as well as news reporters, depending upon how our publicity people decided to explain the ultimate indignity that a man—rich *or* poor—can inflict upon himself, his own death.

"Your reputation is like your soul," Dwyer had told me when he hired me away from the FBI. "You don't notice it when you have it. But lose it and go to hell."

I also remembered more of what he'd muttered

tonight, while pouring a double scotch. *They'd like me to disappear. Maybe I should.*

Had these been words of a man so distraught that he'd kill himself soon after, or a cry from a man in danger, I asked myself now.

I chose a somber summer-weight dark blue pin-striped Armani suit, a crisp white shirt and a somber tie in quiet cobalt. It would convey grief and power. I would need both today. I slipped into shined Bruno Maglis. My silver watch was a wafer-thin Rolex, my wallet Florentine leather. The haircut came from Madison Avenue, not Sal's Clip Joint on Duane Street anymore, not since I'd left government employ, and the black BMW waiting in my driveway was new, leased by the corporation.

I was 44 that night, at the peak of my success and the brink of disaster. I headed security for one of the world's richest pharmaceutical corporations. My ironclad contract guaranteed me two years of high income whether I lost my job or not. Hundreds of men and women—security guards, bodyguards, corporate investigators and even quasi-military protectors in Latin America—reported to me in three continents. I had the use of the Lenox Pharmaceuticals jet, and a company apartment on Fifth Avenue on nights I slept in Manhattan. My expense account was quadruple anything I'd ever enjoyed in the Corporate Crime office at the FBI.

I even had access to a luxury company condo in Venezuela, where I'd occasionally taken feminine companions, other type-A New Yorkers who understood the rules of our sun-drenched tête-à-têtes: to meet and enjoy the bed, to fly home and part as friends, to take on no personal obligations impeding our separate climbs and lives.

These days it was only at dawn and only rarely, in that brief period of clarity that precedes the rising sun, to be swept away by the day's distractions, that I'd started to suspect that I—Mike, for Michelangelo, as my now dead parents had dreamed of greatness for their only child; last name Acela, for the village outside of Naples from which my peasant grandparents emigrated—had transformed myself into a lonely man.

There was no time to think about that now. I poured espresso—my personal drug of choice—into a silver go-cup, and starting the BMW, flashed back to Dwyer's words on the day he interviewed me to replace Lenox's retiring head of Security. An accountant had come to the Chairman with suspicions of corporate malfeasance: fraud, dummy subsidiaries, links between executives and organized crime. Dwyer needed to know if the story was true.

"Mike, if you come to work here, you'll do whatever has to be done to clean us up, even if it means bringing down a Board member, even if that person is my friend. You'll run a private security force protecting our forty-eight thousand employees. Your jurisdiction will extend from our boardroom to our factories, loading docks, labs, computer records. But it will stop there."

"Meaning what?" I'd asked, suspicious but impressed with his quiet confidence. We'd been in his sun-drenched corner office at headquarters near Battery Park, in a new tower completed since the World Trade Center disaster. The Chairman was always a booster of the city in which he had grown up.

"Meaning that justice is private in our world. You'll have a free hand inside the corporation, but the rule is, *come to me when you find things out*. I'll fix them. Not the

FBI or the police. If you can't live with that, walk out now and I'll respect you for it."

"I won't break laws for you."

"No, but you'll bend them, just like you do for the FBI. You'll make deals to protect people and achieve greater good. At the Bureau you have the luxury of letting your superiors decide which suspect gets arrested and which gets a deal. Who gets protected and who gets prosecuted. Here, I decide. I choose how to keep the company strong. It's still justice."

"I'll report to you first," I agreed after a moment. "But if you ignore things I find out, I'll go my own way," meaning that my self-respect was not for sale. Only my ability. "The question is, can *you* live with *that*?"

He'd surprised me then—laughed at our bull-male posturing, poured two scotches and we'd toasted our devil's bargain, dangerous trust between strangers. A month later I'd come to Lenox and started collecting my FBI pension after twenty years on the job. Until then the Bureau had been the only place I'd worked since I was 18, a lucky summer intern chosen from thousands of applicants for two precious slots.

Within six months at Lenox I'd confirmed the stories the Chairman had heard. Our Chief Financial Officer had been fired and was still paying back monies he'd diverted. The Deputy Chief had "resigned" to "spend time with his family" and eleven million dollars had been chalked up to operating losses. They'd looted the company to pay for lavish lifestyles. But our stock had remained high, our investors had saved millions and no one outside Lenox—not the Justice Department Fraud Task Force, not the *Wall Street Journal*, not even the families of the fired execs—had ever learned the truth.

"Nobody screws with *my* company," the Chairman had told me back then. "I take everything that happens here personally."

Now I threaded the BMW through the zigzag streets of Devil's Bay, local name for the blue-collar enclave that had established itself over a century ago, at a time when rich New Yorkers bought their property in Westchester, not Brooklyn. The pipe fitters and bridge and tunnel laborers who built their shotgun shacks and saltbox brick houses here never dreamed that one day their oceanfront properties would turn prime, that as a new century began modern homes would begin replacing the old ones. An architect's glass tower, a Wall Street lawyer's restored Colonial, a screenwriter's California-style stucco-roofed ranch and swimming pool would replace the old one-story boxes.

Manhattan had discovered Devil's Bay.

Lights were on in a few older houses, where men and women were making breakfast, getting ready to head out for blue-collar jobs. The stars were out and the sky velvet over the flat Atlantic. The sickle moon rippled on the cattail-filled estuary of Devil's Bay—an old Depression-era rum-runner's cove—and glinted on a jet angling into JFK from Europe after a night flight, beginning its swerving missile-avoidance descent. Early morning, and the city was already hot with the kind of urban stickiness that marks the worst weeks of summer. As if a metropolis itself—even buildings—can sweat.

I headed onto the Prospect Expressway, toward Manhattan. Air-conditioning cooled the BMW, but in summer the heavy oxygen seemed harder to draw in.

I realized that I needed more information to help me analyze whatever I found at Dwyer's house. I took a chance on calling one person in the company who I trusted and who might help. Punching in numbers, I envisioned a white bedside phone ringing in a Tribeca loft apartment. I saw a petite, dark-haired woman lying on a baby blue pillow, and a lean, beautiful arm groping above an Appalachian patchwork quilt. Kim Pendergraph—Dwyer's personal assistant for twelve years—shared my fierce loyalty to him, and we had a special kind of friendship, the deep kind that exists between a man and woman who are attracted to each other but have never slept together, who have recognized some special quality in the other, one that they value over experimenting in bed. We'd dated. We'd pulled back before consummating our feelings physically.

"It's Mike. I'm sorry to wake you."

She started crying softly when I told her what had happened.

"I can't believe he'd kill himself, Mike. He's been acting angry lately. But Dwyer handles problems decisively. He doesn't run."

"No strange phone calls? Meetings?"

"Yesterday morning he walked out of his office and just stared at me for a minute, before he flew to Washington. He said he'd not valued the right things. It was odd."

Which is the way he looked at me tonight too.

"What did he do in Washington?"

"Testified before the Senate subcommittee looking into the antidote deal. And visited a small lab we own in Maryland. Naturetech."

"And after he got home?"

"I scheduled a dinner at the Hamilton Club with Schwadron and Keating," she said, naming two of Lenox's most powerful Board members, who were rumored to hate each other. "They're his kitchen cabinet.

He runs ideas past those two before he makes decisions. You know Dwyer. He never brings something before the whole Board until he figures out what he wants beforehand."

Are those the men he didn't trust?

"Did he mention any special reason for the dinner?"

"I had the impression there *was* a purpose, but he didn't tell me. Sometimes those three just catch up."

Fifteen minutes from the apartment now, I approached the Battery Tunnel. I saw Manhattan's towers across the harbor, lit and tall, cordoning off the southern tip of the island. This close to the heart of the city the air seemed to pressurize like seawater at dangerous depths. Maybe the huge buildings created the sensation, the pressing tons of brick and girder. Or maybe the mass of people out there, slumbering or stirring before dawn, actually thickened the atmosphere through sheer human presence. I couldn't see them but I could feel them and sometimes even sense the ones who'd come before. It's the Italian in me, I guess. The superstitious peasant inside the modern man. But I believe that human history has physical weight. That the air is filled with ghosts of desire and accumulated want, with all those bits of conflicting will colliding as they try to bend fate, time and love to personal control.

"Any problems with his family?" I asked Kim, referring to Dwyer's relationship—or lack of it—with his daughter, Gabrielle. I'd never met his last living relative, but the newspapers occasionally showed photos of the stunning beauty at a social event. The Wild One, the *Post* called her.

"They haven't spoken in over a year."

"Visits to doctors? Maybe he got bad news."

"As far as I know, he was as healthy as you," she said, her voice breaking again.

She agreed to keep the news to herself but made me promise to call and tell her what I found. In the end, Kim Pendergraph knew Dwyer as well as anyone, but no one knew him thoroughly. He had too many private places. And as I drove into the tunnel, that thought flashed me back to our final conversation on the day I'd been hired.

"One small favor," he'd said as I turned to leave his office. Despite his strong personality, which had earned him the nickname "General Dwyer" inside Lenox, physically he'd been unimpressive. He was bald and chubby and wore rimless glasses on his pale cheeks. His nondescript appearance was accentuated by shapeless gray suits of the finest Scottish wool. All the power was in his gray-green eyes, his calm voice. I'd done preliminary research on him before the interview, and knew that he was said to be unforgiving with his enemies, generous to friends, a Lenox lifer and a politically active right-winger who'd started his corporate education at age five, on the knee of his father, the former CEO. I knew he'd beaten bone cancer a couple of years back, and survived his wife's death. I knew that his daughter had stopped talking to him. And I knew that blows like these tended to remind a certain kind of man to pay more attention to his mortality and legacy, but I did not yet know if Dwyer was that kind of man.

"Now that you're with us, Mr. Acela, perhaps you could meet with our attorneys to advise them on what to expect from Liebenthal," he'd said, naming the lawyer heading the Justice Department Fraud Task Force, which at the time was investigating drug pricing for Medicare recipients. "Are they looking at us?"

"I'm FBI, not Justice," I'd said with growing fury, seeing suddenly why the job had been offered to me.

Dwyer had nodded. "Surely there's some cooperation between the Bureau and Justice. Perhaps you could make a call or two, unofficially. As a favor to me."

I'd told Dwyer angrily that our deal was off. I said that we'd misjudged each other. He should find another lackey. I knew nothing about the task force probe and wasn't about to use my connections to try to find out. In fact, had I known anything to start with about an investigation of Lenox, I would have never come in for the interview, I said.

I pulled open the door to leave but Dwyer had called me back and I'd seen relief in his face, which puzzled me until I came to know him better. "Forgive the crude test, Mr. Acela," he said. "If you'd accepted my offer I would have never hired you. A man who betrays his former boss will sooner or later betray his current one, I've found."

As things turned out, the task force hadn't even been looking into Lenox's activities at all.

Now I steered the BMW out of the Battery Tunnel and onto the West Side Highway. Traffic was building even at 4:51. Like me, most other drivers were alone. The eager or fearful ones, the ones who wanted to get a professional jump on the opposition, were trickling into their offices. A few yellow taxis cruised. Homeless people dozed in recessed doorways.

I turned right on 57th Street and headed cross-town. A traffic stoppage near Sixth Avenue halted me and reminded me that I wasn't a public servant anymore. In the old days I would have put the dome light on the roof and been waved through by police. But I was private now. I couldn't jail suspects or get subpoenas from judges. I couldn't enlist the aid of police departments or federal agencies unless I wanted to share corporate secrets with them, a bad idea, and one for which I'd be fired. The truth was, I could be arrested myself for committing excesses that my old co-agents occasionally overlooked among themselves when caught up in investigations.

With a flash of nostalgia I turned the car into the underground lot next door to the Chairman's townhouse, where he maintained a permanent parking space for his visitors.

Aguinaldo answered the front door, wearing an apron, holding a glass of Pepsi in his unsteady hand.

"Second floor," he said.

Treading up the winding, carpeted stairway, past photos of the Chairman with prominent friends—the head of the Metropolitan Opera, the new Director of the National Intelligence Agency, the owner of the New York Yankees—I had no idea of what had started in this house, no conception of the enormity of what had occurred on this hot July night, and of its implications for me, the corporation, the nation and even, without exaggeration, the entire sleeping world.

All I knew was that I must bat away grief and transform myself from shocked acquaintance into professional investigator. I must push away any emotion that might detract from the job in a home where I'd often reported to the Chairman, played chess with him, listened to his political diatribes and attended his small Christmastime dinner parties, late at night.

God help the whole country if I'm right.

"He's in the study," Aguinaldo said from behind me, sounding small and miserable. "I saw the body, but I do not believe I saw the truth."

TWO

Let me tell you a little about the pharmaceuticals industry. Just in 2005, legally sold drugs earned profits exceeding $118 billion in the United States alone, up from $99.5 billion in 1998, $90 billion in '97, and $53 billion just four years before that. As the Chairman told me once, the average Fortune 500 company increases profits in a good year by 7 percent, but Lenox, Merck and Pfizer—our pharmaceutical giants—make more than twice that.

"Which means when it comes to us," the Chairman liked to say, "there's no such thing as a bad year. Pharmaceuticals is the most profitable, fastest-growing legal business in history. Cancer rates don't depend on Wall Street. People around the world cry out for drugs every day to cure arthritis, malaria, glaucoma, flu. And those needs don't even begin to address our most profitable drugs, not disease fighters but the hair growers, mood changers, sex enhancers.

"Lifestyle drugs," the Chairman had said to me just last week with pride, reveling in any good news for drug companies. "Prozac to make you cheery. Viagra to help a fifty-year-old man perform like Valentino. Propecia to grow thick, hairy locks. Pharmaceuticals sculpt the world."

Well, our little profit-makers had killed him now, in his mahogany-paneled study, where he lay amid scattered pill vials beneath the wide staring eyes in portraits of Dwyer's ancestors: General Francis Dwyer, who had started Lenox in 1869, making cough medicine; Grandfather Louis Dwyer, who had taken the company international; Dwyer's father, who'd fought off takeover attempts from Bayer and Glaxo and taught his son, the Chairman had told me, never to lose control.

All mute witnesses. If only they could speak.

His robe had opened. His purple silk pajamas had slid partially down to bunch beneath his right buttock, and ridden up to pudgy mid-calf on the left side. His eyes bulged, now dull green, and the veins in his corneas stood out. His feet were blue. The body lay half on the woven Russian carpet, half on the polished teak floor. His features had frozen the agony of his last living moments. Dwyer's face seemed sharper, as if the cheekbones had risen or the skin had stretched. His lips were pulled back to show teeth and blood where he'd bitten through. The slight carrot tinge would probably identify one of the poisons that had killed him.

There was an overall rag-doll attitude to the musculature, as if the departure of will had left a heap of formless meat. No living person could lie with elbows and arms twisted at those angles.

Despite the central air-conditioning—the Chairman always ran it high in summer—the smell was awful, of urine, shit, half-digested food puddled and dripping down the bookcase, as if he'd spewn it across the room as he collapsed.

I kept myself from being sick. I hadn't worked bodies for a long time. I'd been a white-collar investigator for years, but—slipping on rubber gloves—remembered the basics from when I'd investigated bank robberies and kidnappings.

Chairman Dwyer's pajamas weren't ripped, as they might have been had there been a struggle. There were no scratches on his face or arms; no extra glasses or cups in view, as if he'd had a guest after I'd left; no sign that furniture had been moved; no impressions of shoeprints on the thick rug.

I checked his fingertips. No broken nails. No scraped-off skin or blood under his nails. I felt around his head. No injuries. I looked for bruise marks and found none.

The desk came next. In neatly typed letters, the pill vials there and on the floor named the lethal mix of chemicals that had probably killed him. The warning on the Chairman's blood-pressure medicine specifically said to avoid mixing it with the kind of sleeping pills he'd apparently taken. The date on the prescription was yesterday, so since the entire vial was empty, he must have swallowed over thirty capsules and washed them down with scotch from the empty Dewar's bottle on the Russian sea captain's desk.

I forced my eyes to the pathetically short note he'd left on his personal stationery.

I'm lonely.

Nothing about business or the problems and betrayals he'd alluded to tonight.

The signature and handwriting looked like his. The police, I knew, would check the silver pen and paper for prints. I was torn between the urge to call them now and the desire to protect Dwyer and Lenox if he'd killed himself. Besides, I was a good investigator.

That means it's hard to stop.

Working quickly, telling myself that I'd share anything

relevant with detectives, I went through the neatly organized drawers but found no damaging reports, e-mails or
notes lying around, although I was surprised to come upon
a stack of hand-printed betting receipts bound by a red
rubber band. The action was for little stuff: two dollars on
Golden Hoof at Aqueduct, last month; two dollars on the
Mets versus the Phillies at Shea, on the Dodgers over the
Marlins.

I didn't know he gambled.

I also found a list of stocks he'd bought last month.
Dwyer had purchased four shares of Compton Hotels at
two dollars and sixty-three cents a share. Two shares of
Deep Sea Marine at one dollar and seventy cents a share.
Two shares of Galvin Defense.

I frowned. *Why two? And why were the stock receipts
with the gambling slips?*

I pocketed the slips. No need for police or reporters
to find out about them yet, I told myself. But fifteen
minutes had now passed since I'd arrived here, and I
was pushing things by not calling the police. I'd verified
what Aguinaldo had told me. There had been no overt
break-in. But it was time to make a different phone call,
to get help.

On my cell phone I punched in the number of Danny
Whiteagle, a retired Air Force Intelligence agent who I'd
hired at Lenox as my number two. As I heard the phone
ringing in his Murray Hill apartment, I envisioned the
tall, thin, half Irish/half Mohawk, fifty-three-year-old
Iraqi War vet, with a small shrapnel scar streaking down
the left side of his long, toffee-colored, deceptively sad
face. He'd been a decorated hero, a captain in a drug task
force that had blown up illegal labs and arrested dozens of
GI crack dealers in the Philippines. A street investigator

with undercover experience, he'd married his childhood sweetheart and was the father of four loyal kids. He probably had about two hundred cousins walking the high-rise girders in New York.

"Why do you want to work for Lenox?" I'd asked him during our final interview.

Danny never smiled but loved jokes. "I get stock options. If there's a tie in the boardroom, I can tip the balance with my two shares," he'd replied.

"Can you give a hundred percent to a private company, after working for the military?"

"If you want the best man on point, the best at your back," he said, tapping the scar, "hire me and get a thousand percent. If you only need a hundred, find another guy."

Now Danny answered the phone, sounding wide awake.

"Let me get this straight," he said. "You were the last one to see him alive and you went back alone? I want your corner office when the police arrest you."

"Get over here. Help me look around."

"Boss, take the advice of someone whose family has been screwed by authorities for centuries. Get the cops on your side, fast."

"Danny, if he killed himself, there was no crime. If we find one, we'll report it."

He sighed with that sad, predestined attitude recognizable to Italians. "It's not a question of finding it. It's a question of them deciding we covered one up."

I kept up my search as I waited for Danny. I slipped last month's Verizon bill into my pocket to check the numbers later. I found no memos mentioning pending deals, no doctors bills or medical reports that might have pointed to a serious disease, no angry letters or notes suggesting a personal problem, none of the indicators I'd been taught to look for at a crime scene or suicide.

I couldn't get into his computer, not knowing his password, but as for his movements yesterday, his desk calendar confirmed that he'd been in DC, testifying and visiting a Lenox-owned lab.

Truth was, the death looked more like suicide by the second, whether I was willing to accept that as a fact or not. I was risking my job by not alerting the new acting chairman. I'd lessen the damage by calling PR now.

I phoned Sheila Oswald-Starke, our London-born vice president of Public Relations; a model-thin, gorgeous brunette and thirty-one-year-old who I'd dated briefly after coming to the company. She was one of those women who put everything—all her beauty and intelligence, charm and surface kindness—into making great first impressions. The truth seeps out later. We'd drifted apart with no regrets.

"I hope you haven't alerted the police yet, Michael. Not before calling me."

"I'll phone them now."

"No, you'll wait until I get there," she snapped. "You should have contacted me as soon as you heard. I have to assemble my people. The second the police know what happened, the press will too. Are you sure it was suicide?"

"I'm sure he's dead."

"The note didn't say anything about me, did it?"

"You?"

"One time, Michelangelo," she said coolly, as if Dwyer were alive and she were filling me in on her sex life in a bar. "And it happened two months ago. Besides, you have a thing with his secretary, don't you?"

"Her name is Kim, and I don't have a *thing* with her." People at the company always assumed that Kim and I slept together. "I like her."

"With people like us, 'liking someone' means we stick around with them for two months instead of one."

Despite my grief, her words reminded me why I'd never felt sorry when we stopped seeing each other. Sheila tended to ascribe to the world in general her own selfish views. I told her I'd hold off on the police and hung up, to find myself looking into Dwyer's open eyes in one of the room's matching mirrors, opposite antique pier glass cameo models from Kiev. Reflected, as in a centuries-old daguerrotype, was the once powerful man beside a corner of desk, a slit of red-bay bookcase, a bit of expensive wet bar, where I realized he'd left the glass I'd used earlier. With the twin mirrors reflecting each other, all of it—the portraits and silver bucket and tongs on the sidebar, the old ship's windup clock from the Czar Nicholas Russian whaler—were repeated endlessly as in an Escher drawing, an optical trick, growing smaller and more distant in a stylized infinity of death.

The sound of the doorbell downstairs meant that Danny was here, shaven, dressed in an already wilting summer-weight light-checkered jacket that swelled over his biceps, shoulders, starched white shirt and barrel chest. He rarely sweated but his scar looked whiter against his dark skin in hot weather. Incongruous thick lenses made his bronze-colored irises huge. For a big man, he moved quietly. He'd won the two-hundred-yard dash for the over-50 guys at Dwyer's last July 4th company picnic in the Hamptons.

"How did you get here so fast?" I said.

"Three thousand years of family experience waking up before dawn."

"Take the second floor. If you find anything, call me."

"You mind telling me what I'm looking for?"

"Anything that doesn't look right."

We split up. I headed for Dwyer's bedroom and bathroom.

I knew at some level, as I searched, that Danny was right about calling the cops. But I also knew that night, as my life pivoted in the balance without my knowing it, that the Chairman had judged my capacity for loyalty correctly. My allegiance was split between the company, Dwyer and whatever principles I'd dedicated myself to twenty-five years before, as an idealistic boy.

In my forties I had changed the way so many people around me had changed: the reporters who'd taken high-paying jobs as public relations people, the doctors who'd started their careers in poverty clinics and now wouldn't accept patients from HMOs, the lawyers who'd been fired up about justice and now applied that same passion to finding a loophole in the tax law for wealthy clients. The disillusioned who'd traded the possibility of love for mere companionship each night. All of us, I think, at some level wanted a second chance.

We had names for this evolution. We called it truth and our disenchantment reality. We were the late-night cynics at parties. Danny had grown older but kept his pure view of things, and was in the guest rooms while I searched the Chairman's bathroom.

That's where I found the vial.

I almost missed it. It was on the top shelf, behind his razor, a vial of Cipro antibiotic and a squeeze tube of sunblock number twelve.

But the label on *this* vial was hand-printed, not type-written. It had not come from a pharmacy. There was no prescription number on the vial, only instructions in blue Magic Marker: *"Take with water three hours before."*

Three hours before what?

There was no pharmacy or Rx number. No doctor's name on the vial.

I unscrewed the top and peered inside, to see a few greenish specks of an herblike substance resembling oregano or marijuana sliding around the bottom. It didn't smell like oregano or marijuana. Its vague chalky-salty odor reminded me of a beach.

I put the vial in my pocket, unwilling yet to risk the police sullying Dwyer's reputation by suggesting that he might have had a drug problem. I'd have the stuff ana-lyzed at Lenox's lab in New Jersey. It would probably turn out to be innocent. If it didn't, or seemed relevant to what had happened, I'd release the information then.

Then I went into the bedroom and found the covers thrown back, as if the Chairman had been in bed tonight. His reading glasses were on the night table. There was a ballpoint pen there too. I got on my knees and looked under the bed. I spotted a piece of paper that must have drifted down there.

It turned out to be a list, in Dwyer's handwriting.

BATTLE PLAN!
1) Tough it out!
2) Transfer S to bank first thing
3) White House? Naturetech?
4) Get disk to Mike tonight
5) Stay away from Eisner!

I stared at it, my heartbeat picking up. *Tough it out* were not exactly words you expected to hear from a potential suicide. But it was exactly what Dwyer would say. I envisioned the Chairman in bed, taking notes on his lapboard. Maybe he'd heard a noise downstairs. Maybe he'd gone downstairs for cold milk. Maybe—I had to admit—he'd changed his mind about the battle plan and left the room to commit suicide, and when he threw back the covers the paper drifted under the bed.

Get the disk to Mike?

What disk? I wondered.

Stay away from Eisner?

Who the hell was that?

I didn't know what "S" meant either, but I stared at the words *White House*. Hundreds of people work at the White House, and Dwyer had connections there. Had he meant to call a friend for aid? Or had he been identifying a source of his problem?

The doorbell sounded again. On the way downstairs I showed Danny the list in case he'd found anything related.

"I warned you," he said. "I didn't find anything mentioning this stuff. Great. The White House. You going to tell Sheila about the list?"

"She doesn't need to know."

"Plan to hide it from the cops too, Sherlock?"

Sheila, the Public Relations tiger, was here, along with white-haired Bob Czerny from Lenox's Legal Department. He planned to sit in on any police interview.

"I want to see the body," Sheila said with morbid curiosity. She looked sexy, cold and inaccessible in a tight, black calf-length dress, and high heels. Her lustrous hair was up in a bun.

"Women are lures," she'd told me once. "All of us know it. Some pretend we don't."

"It's better if you stay away from Dwyer," I told her now. "The police will be angry enough without finding out a whole parade of people went in there."

She looked disappointed, but the appeal to her professional side worked, as usual.

"Keating wants you in his office as soon as you're finished here," Sheila told me, naming Lenox's new acting chief executive, heir apparent and one of the two men besides myself I knew about who had talked to the Chairman tonight before he died.

They'd like me to disappear. Maybe I should, Dwyer had said. Had he been talking about Keating?

"Keating's not happy that you didn't call him," Sheila said.

"Nobody is happy today," I said.

"You're right," she said, backpedaling. "Examining Dwyer must have been awful for you."

She was eyeing me with curiosity, though, not sorrow.

I called the police.

Forget what you've seen in movies about the relationship between public cops and corporate cops. Hollywood depicts us on the bottom of the law enforcement ladder, brains-wise, power-wise, trustworthiness-wise. Scriptwriters call us rent-a-cops and their heroes give us a hard time. Remember the film *The Fugitive*? In that one, the corporate security chief turned out to be the killer.

But in real life, I'm a potential future employer to any middle-aged cop or FBI agent, the guy who can make their detective-pension years happy, keep their kids in college, help pay for a retirement condo in Myrtle Beach. So if they meet me during a case, they're about as antagonistic as a Pentagon general negotiating defense contracts. The general knows he'll be job hunting in the private sector within the year.

The detective's name was Berg, and he was respectful and professional, even when I handed him the list. Our interview went smoothly. Yes, Aguinaldo had called me when he found the body, I said. Yes, I'd searched the house, but that was my job, and I'd found no evidence of a crime. Yes, I had drunk scotch hours ago with the Chairman here, and used the glass in the sink, which of course will have my fingerprints on it.

No, the Chairman had given me no disk, even though his list indicated he'd been considering it. And no, I had no idea what Dwyer's "battle plan" had been about.

Berg tried his best not to look impressed when he asked about the White House reference, but clearly he was unnerved by it.

"I have no idea what the Chairman meant by that," I said.

Had the Chairman indicated anything about feeling depressed last night, about problems, or loneliness, Berg asked.

Dwyer had been angry but had not mentioned why, I said.

I lied to Berg when I told him that I'd removed nothing from the premises. I told the truth when I said I'd have no objections if he needed to follow up later on.

Our lawyer never objected to any question during the interview, although he was uncomfortable about the list, and by the time we were done, the Medical Examiner—the chief herself for a case this big—had probed the corpse and examined hands and feet and taken the body temperature. Blood samples had been labeled, photographs snapped. Detectives had dusted for fingerprints. Aguinaldo and Danny had been questioned in separate rooms.

"See? Nothing to worry about," I told Danny.

"Never is until too late."

It was mid-morning now, and as I walked to the front door, where Sheila waited for me, I could hear horns and traffic, frenetic Midtown outside, and see through the diamond-shaped window in the massive oak front door the heads of reporters massed outside and the antennae on their vans, raised like knights' lances waiting to skewer victims.

"By the way," Sheila said, "you look sexy in that suit. A death makes a person appreciate the better things in life. You and I had a good time, didn't we? I think about it often. Are you free tonight, for comfort?"

"I'm working," I said, thinking that *comfort* was never a word I'd associate with Sheila. But there was no denying the tingle in my groin.

"Oh, I don't mean early. I mean late," she said, brushing my beard affectionately with her palm.

"Not tonight."

She winked. "Give me a call when you drop the little secretary." As we reached the front door she composed her gorgeous face into an expression of grief that would have won her an Oscar.

"Remember, Keating wants you in his office," she said. "He said something about breakfast."

She opened the door and reporters began shouting questions.

"Is it true he had AIDS?"

"Will the Defense Department deal still go through?"

"Breakfast?" I mumbled to Sheila, unable to get the horrible smell out of my memory. "I won't eat for a week."

"Sensitive boy," she whispered. She looked as if she were about to burst into tears over the Chairman's death.

A reporter in the front shouted, "How come the Security Chief took so long to call the police?"

Other reporters wrote down the question, staring at me, frowning.

"I'll answer that," Sheila told me. "Not you."

Open your medicine cabinet and turn a pill bottle upside down. You'll see half a dozen numbers and symbols etched into the plastic. A triangle with the number 9 in it, for instance. A registered trademark that might say "NL," "SA," "GR." A date, the number 3 for March, for example, and 13 for, well, the thirteenth. The hieroglyphics identify the company that made the bottle, the date it was made and the factory where it was produced.

This is one of ours, I thought, eyeing Lenox's LX on the vial I'd taken from the Chairman's cabinet. I was stopped at a red light, at First and 47th, on the way downtown to see the new acting COO and chairman—Bill Keating—until the Board of Directors made his position official or moved him to the side.

On my cell phone I punched in the number of one of my most talented staffers.

"Hoot here," answered a young woman's voice on the other end. I envisioned the main Security office at Lenox, a large, sunny, third-floor room partitioned into cubicles, except for my walled-off corner office, overlooking the

Hudson River outside. In a rear cubicle I imagined a bony, 22-year-old third-generation Iranian American, dressed in classic East Village black, with a silver nose ring, a butterfly tattoo on her left wrist and a poster of the Jordanian singer Hamud Zayed on her bulletin board. A bottle of Mountain Dew sat at her computer terminal. She was addicted to the stuff.

I'd hired Shayla Hazzaz instead of pressing charges against her two years ago, when she'd hacked her way into payroll records and altered them so half a dozen workers on our loading docks—strangers to her—had started getting checks for $22,000 a week. She'd done it as a joke, picking recipients with birthdays in November, like herself. Two workers had alerted their foreman. One had bought a new Acura, which he was required to give back. Shayla had turned out to be a computer science major at Hunter, and a genius Danny had nicknamed "Owl" because of her round lenses. She'd changed it to "Hoot."

"I have a job for you," I said.

The way I figured it, if she wanted to pierce her nose with pins, wear thrift-shop clothes and listen to Mideastern music on headphones, it was fine with me. It kept her happy. Last year, *because* she was happy, Hoot had piggybacked her way into a Hong Kong computer system and uncovered a ring counterfeiting Lenox's antibiotic Kalpro and selling it as our brand. Confronted with evidence, the Chinese had executed the ringleader, a general, and closed down the factory in Shanghai. The Chairman had thanked Hoot personally. His only comment about her attire had been "How can she breathe with that thing in her nose?"

"Did Dwyer really kill himself? It's on the news," she said now. She talked like a teenager, fast.

"We'll discuss it later."

"Did he have AIDS? ABC says he did."

"I have no idea where that rumor came from."

"Hey! He's on the company med plan, right? I bet I could dig up his records."

I ordered her to stay out of the Chairman's medical files and read her the numbers off the pill bottle I'd found. I told her to find out which factory had made it. And who'd received it.

"What was in the bottle, Chief?"

"I'm hoping you'll tell me."

"What's special about it?"

"Just do it, okay?"

"You sound like my father," she complained. "It's people like you who *make* other people into hackers. It's the only way regular people learn the truth about things. Give me twenty minutes."

She hung up before I could reply, a linchpin employee in my little group of misfits.

Temperamental artiste, I thought, grinning. But like Danny, reliable, no matter how much she complained.

I phoned Kim as I pulled into my parking space underneath our offices, and told her about the scene in the townhouse but left out the part about the vial and list.

"He wouldn't kill himself," she insisted. "You probably think I'm fooling myself. People always say things like that after suicides. Like, *He wouldn't do it. We had a good marriage. Our finances were in perfect shape.*"

She sounded on the verge of tears.

"Kim, if he didn't do it, someone else did."

"All I know is, *he didn't*, and that's that."

"Have dinner with me tonight," I said, concerned about her. She was an emotional person, an honest woman of deep loyalties, who trusted her instincts in all things.

"I wish I were far away, Mike."

"I'll drive you to my house," I offered. "I'll grill steaks. We'll sit in the garden, walk by the ocean. I'll take you home after. Bring Chris if you want. He loves the beach. Stay over."

Chris was her son.

There was a delicate pause. "Dinner would be nice, Mike. Chris is staying at a friend's tonight. But it's not a good idea for me to stay," she said, drawing the line at our unspoken boundary, the one we took turns reminding each other about.

"Then I'll drive you home," I said.

"You're a good friend. I'll bring a bottle of Pinot Noir. Maybe we can figure out what happened in that townhouse. I'll make a list of anything odd that's happened in the last couple of weeks. I want you to keep working on this. Promise you will."

"I already made that promise to myself."

Two days later, running for my life, I'd regret the promise, but now, as I headed upstairs to see Lenox's temporary chairman, my encrypted cell phone chimed and I saw that Hoot was calling. It had taken my computer Einstein slightly over ten minutes to track down the vial.

"It was a cinch," she said. "It was part of a batch distributed inside the company. The records aren't detailed enough to show which exact project got the vial, but it was one of six. HR-103 to HR-109."

HR, I knew, meant "house research project," studies funded by Lenox without any partnership agreement with the government, a university or another company. All costs to be borne by Lenox, all profits to be shared with the individual researcher, depending on their contract incentive clause.

"Can you get a printout listing the projects?" I asked.

"Like I didn't think of that already?"

"Hoot, why do you make me ask for things all the time?"

She was silent for a moment, her acceptably mild form of authority rebellion. I heard her slurping Mountain Dew. The sigh that followed meant my little punishment for not assuming she was brilliant was through.

"Of the six projects, three were against cancer. Ovarian. Prostate. Bone. Those are at a lab on Long Island. Funds for HR-107 went to an NYU professor working on antidepressants. HR-108 went to an ethnobotanist in Venezuela trying to find medicinal plants down there. Eye disease."

I thought the stuff in the vial looked as if it had come from a plant, all right.

"That's five projects. You said six," I said.

A sigh. "Well, whatever the hell HR-109 is, its records—nothing about it—seems to exist in Research Department files."

"What are you saying? The records were deleted?"

Hoot laughed. "Maybe they were never entered. These days, with hackers like me around, if you want to keep something *really* private, store it on paper. All I know is, any computer records of HR-109 are either wiped out, stolen or locked up. So, like, what kind of incredible super-mystery secret project do you think HR-109 *is*, huh?"

THREE

The terrible phone call that changed my life—that led to my quitting the FBI and moving back to Brooklyn—came on a Sunday night three years ago. It was late October, a crisp, fall night, and I'd just returned to Manhattan from a weekend in the Berkshires with a girlfriend—a tall, beautiful, blond British advertising executive named Melanie Jaye.

Melanie had relocated to Manhattan from London to take over the Noelle Family Products account. You've seen her ads: the ones where loving parents powder smiling babies, hold hands while shopping, cook a Thanksgiving dinner for three generations of family.

"I satisfy the yearning everyone has for more love," Melanie had said as we'd driven up to the country on Friday night, holding hands.

The weekend would have been romantic, or at least relaxing, except that Melanie had spent half the time talking on her cell phone, fielding emergencies facing her staff.

While we paddled kayaks around a Massachusetts lake, for instance, past a riot of pumpkin- and flame-colored leaves, her voice had floated over the black water, saying, "Tell that fucking lawyer he signed a contract. If he walks, he'll owe the agency a million dollars."

While browsing in an old barn filled with antiques for

sale, her phone had chimed and Melanie had gone into a corner, but everyone in the place had heard her half of the conversation. "If you missed your fucking flight because you overslept, that's not my fucking problem," she'd said.

And over a dinner of lake trout and autumn vegetables at the Red Lion Inn, as candles flickered and our Pinot Grigio sat on ice, Melanie had growled into her little silver Verizon, "What do you *mean* the parents like each other? You think the audience wants to see them only *like* each other?"

To be fair, on our previous weekend away I'd been the workaholic, fielding calls from distressed members of my FBI team trying to talk our supervisor out of offering a plea-bargain agreement to an energy company exec.

The exec had swindled half a dozen states out of two hundred million dollars. When the plea bargain had gone through, my partner had called. "What's the point of working for the G? Even when we convict these guys, they land in prisons with tennis courts, not barbed wire."

Anyway, on Sunday afternoon, as Melanie and I drove home on the Taconic Parkway, it had been clear to us that the luster was off a romance that had never been more than a casual romp to start with. There were no hard feelings. The weekend had been the prelude to one more bloodless breakup that served as transition to the next interesting partner in line.

Nobody got hurt. Everybody stays friends. So why, I'd wondered, does this bother me?

"Let's have dinner in a couple weeks and catch up," she'd said when I dropped her off at—appropriately— not her apartment but the ad agency, where she had work to do.

But thirty minutes later, after leaving my rental car at Avis and walking to my Chelsea loft, I'd answered my phone to hear a different kind of female voice: upset, drunk, crying. I did not recognize the voice but it had the Brooklyn accent I'd grown up hearing in Devil's Bay.

"They told me not to call," she sobbed.

"Who did?"

"They said leave it alone. But some people spend their lives paying for one mistake, while others walk away from trouble scot-free, don't they, Mike?"

"It's not right," I agreed, grabbing a pad, assuming the call related to a case.

"You messed up her life and now she's dead."

And even then I thought it was a case. After all, FBI agents spend their lives "messing up" people's lives, if those people happen to be ones we arrested. Maybe someone I'd arrested had died in prison, from suicide, fight or illness. It wasn't unusual for family members or lovers to blame the agency at those times.

"Pam should have called you years ago," the voice went on. "She never should have let you get away with it."

The name did it, combined with that accent. I still didn't understand why I was being blamed for anything, but I knew who the victim in this story would be, and I filled with dread for her. I saw a small, dark-haired girl in a black bikini, sunning herself on the beach, by the Atlantic. I saw myself rubbing Coppertone oil onto her tanned shoulders. I remembered her heart-shaped face inches away from mine, as we made love in the finished basement of her parents' home in Devil's Bay.

"She was driving through the intersection," the voice was saying. "The truck hit her car sideways."

Pam Grano had been a neighborhood girl who I'd had

a crush on in high school, but never dated until the summer when I was finishing up law school, slated to start work at the FBI. We'd run into each other when I was home visiting my parents. Our time together had been brief and passionate, and I'd missed Pam when I'd moved to Washington. I'd written and called her, and we'd made plans for her to visit. But one day she'd simply told me she'd met someone else.

"You walked away from her," the caller said now.

I remembered a smiling, happy girl who loved to bike and jog and who'd wanted to coach girls' soccer. I remembered how in tenth grade I'd first noticed her on the girls' track team, liking the way her ponytail bounced when she ran. Six years later, the first time we'd made love, on the beach, our moans had mixed with the surf sounds and the low drone of planes overhead. We'd lain together afterward, watching the jets, like romantic rockets, taking passengers to faraway destinations we had never seen before.

"You're her sister," I said. "Tia."

"She was dead on arrival."

I remembered Tia, all right, an even prettier girl who, for some incomprehensible reason, had even then spewed forth anger at her parents, boys, friends she claimed had betrayed her. Tia had been bitter at 23 and right now the rage seemed worse.

"Men don't care whose lives they wreck," she said.

"Tia, I'm sorry. This has to be awful for you. But I don't understand why you're blaming me."

"A *real* father would have been driving that day. But Pam had to do everything with that boy herself."

"A father?" I said, my voice sounding suddenly small and far away to myself.

"Your son was cut to pieces. He bled to death. Pam was taking Paul to football practice. You never had anything to do with him his whole life."

If there's one emotion that law enforcement people deal with regularly, it's shock—from victims who've had their lives shattered, criminals who have been caught, family and friends on both sides in a courtroom. Every life has shocks in it, terrible surprises that can cripple or empower. I'd been shocked when my parents died, and when a good friend of mine, another agent, was killed in a shoot-out.

But some shocks are so unexpected that they realign the universe, reorder pasts and futures, create their own trajectories for altered lives. To learn that your child is dead has to be the worst shock in the world. To discover that you never even knew he existed until that moment was, for me, in some ways, worse.

My head was swimming. My blood flow seemed to have stopped. I remember seeing a cockroach crawling on the floor of my apartment, and that a siren outside had seemed impersonal, far away. The window sash had looked crooked. The weekend I'd just returned from— my date in the Berkshires—seemed a mockery of meaningful life.

"She never let us tell you about Paul," Tia was saying. "But she's not here to stop me now."

In her grief I couldn't argue with her. But in my shock I thought, I'd had a *son*?

"When is the funeral, Tia?"

I lay in bed that night surrounded by the trappings of my successful life: subscription tickets to Lincoln Center, receipts—reimbursable by the Bureau—from Peter Luger Steak House in Williamsburg, and La Dolce Vida on the

East Side, where the sauces could give a healthy man a heart attack from sheer joy. There were tailored suits in the closet by Armani, and ticket stubs from Yankee Stadium. Yes, I had a great life. If you don't have a family, an FBI salary, when you throw in the Corporate Task Force expense account, goes far enough in the Big Apple to make you think you're someone else.

What did my son look like, I thought. *Did he like base-ball? Did he do well in school?*

On the day of the funeral I dressed in black and steeled myself against the reaction of her family. I took the subway to Brooklyn instead of opting for the quick way in and out, a cab. The F train swayed over elevated tracks I'd traveled as a teenager on weekends sometimes, on my way into Manhattan, Dad having again canceled whatever trip we'd planned to a ball game, museum, Chinatown.

I could never be mad at him, though.

"Mom's feeling sick," he'd say on those days as I heard her retching in the bathroom, or heard her wheelchair creaking around on our wooden floors.

"I can't go with you today," he'd say. "Here's a twenty. Have a good time."

As a boy I'd helped take care of her too, most afternoons after school. Getting medicines. Wheeling her along the ocean. Reading to her. She loved novels about the FBI.

I want to be an FBI man, like in these books, I used to think while I washed bedpans or sat with her watching television.

"Go away to college," she'd say. "Far away. You've done more for me than any ten other people. And don't get saddled taking care of a sick person in life, like your father did. Choose your wife carefully."

And I would think, *I'm not going to get married.*

Oh, I'd call each week after I left, and come back to visit at Christmas, at Easter. And when I was based in New York, each Sunday I'd send a car service to bring my parents into the city for shows. I sent them on cruises. I spent hours with Mom in hospitals. But for years, Devil's Bay made me smell ammonia, bedpans, Lysol.

Heading to Pam's funeral, all these memories came back as I rode my time machine, the F train, and transferred to a bus for the rest of the trip to Devil's Bay. I stood across from St. Mary's church, watching mourners stream in. I recognized a few old friends, and my parents' friends, who looked stooped, thinner, older.

I waited until they were all inside before entering. I sat in a back row, feeling watched by the statues in the alcoves, by the saints. I was unable to make myself go up front yet and look at Pam's body, unwilling to peer into the larger casket beside it, containing, I'd confirmed by then discreetly, my 16-year-old son. Would I see my own features on the face inside, I thought, if I did?

When the whispering began, and the head-turning, I steeled myself for a visit from Tia or her father. Then I saw Pam's dad get up from the front row and start toward me up the aisle, with a familiar heavy gait that I remembered, the walk of a physical laborer.

I gathered up my coat, stood to look in the coffins and leave.

But instead of asking me to go, the old hod carrier took my arm. "Come down front, Mike," he said. "The father sits with the family."

"You want me with you?"

"Tia shouldn't have called you. She's always been an angry person. What she said wasn't right. It's not the way the family feels. I knew you'd come."

I repeated, stunned, "With the family?" and felt a warm sensation forming in the corner of my eyes.

"We held a family meeting when Pam learned she was pregnant," he told me later, as we drank beer in the basement where I'd first kissed his daughter. "Mike, you were always a kid I liked. Hardworking. You looked after your mom. Who could blame you for wanting to get out? You hadn't had a childhood. Pam understood that."

"That's why she never told me?"

Mr. Grano shook his head. "No. No one's that noble. I asked her to be honest with herself, asked my daughter, 'If you weren't pregnant, would you *want* to marry Mike and spend your whole life with him? No other man, ever? Because don't think a baby will make you feel differently.' And she answered that she didn't know. She was too scared. Well, I'd seen plenty of bad marriages screw up parents and kids both, so me and Millie told her we loved her. We didn't give a damn who the father was. We said, '*Only* tell Mike if you're ready to share a life with him.' Our concern was for Pam and our grandchild, not you, Mike. So I hope *you'll* forgive me."

I walked out of the house and to the beach. When no one could see me, I broke down crying with grief. I'd arrested felons. I'd shot a man once as he tried to kill me. But I stood bawling like a nine-year-old over a child I'd never known and a life I'd run away from as I remembered the rest of Mr. Grano's words.

"She had a full, loving life, and so did Paul. Don't feel like you failed her. That's what Pam would want me to say, no matter what my other daughter thinks."

When I returned to the house I realized the family had kept the secret of my fatherhood from the whole neighborhood. Tia glared but never spoke to me. And I saw that never, not for an instant, had my son felt unloved. He'd been surrounded by family.

My old high school pals had come over: Ritchie Hahn from the Wildcats; Sal Aslekios; Marty Fox, now a cameraman at NBC; Steve Kasanjian, still half blind, still cracking stupid lightbulb jokes, still with his old girlfriend Marisa, except now she was his wife.

They embraced me, but I wasn't part of this place anymore. I'd grown up in a different direction. But what was I? A playboy with an expense account? A public servant who made deals with felons? A man trying to stay a boy?

The job offer came from Lenox soon after, after I'd given up my apartment and bought the fixer-upper in Devil's Bay. I'd started working on the place on weekends. I'd planted a tomato garden like my father had. I'd split into two people, the public man, powerful, sought after, respected; and the private one, who had seen enough of his future to suspect he was on the back side of a mountain, climbing down from heights he once had aspired to reach.

I was too old for love now. I'd accepted that in my heart.

But sometimes, on the street or driving in my car, I'd catch myself watching parents with teenagers Paul's age; going shopping, or just sitting and saying nothing. Other cars became dioramas of other futures, moving museums.

I liked working at Lenox. I was grateful that it kept me busy. I liked the oddballs I'd hired, like Danny and Hoot.

I'd liked James Dwyer and now he was dead.

* * *

Bill Keating kept me waiting for an hour and a half outside his office as he fielded calls from shocked Board members, major stockholders and overseas execs. Chairman Dwyer would have told me to come back later if he was busy. Keating's style was to let you know every minute that he was boss. I sat on a couch and checked by phone on various Security projects. I scanned the morning *Times* and was shocked to see that student protests at Berkeley and University of Oregon had exploded into violence last night after the new President was sworn in and proposed stricter national security measures. Funds for social programs and roads would be cut. Monies would be diverted to the police, Immigration, the military, Homeland Security.

"With a new President comes new priorities," a White House spokesman was quoted as saying. I winced at the photos of crowds being gassed by police, of clean-cut kids being herded into arrest vans.

"Sorry you had to wait, Mike," Keating said haggardly when I finally walked through the door at eleven. Normally Keating looked boyish, but he seemed genuinely depressed and shocked, older than his 37 years. He was an ex–Princeton wrestling champ, and he still had the build, but his body was going soft at the edges. The face was angular and the eyes light bronze. The hair was thick, light brown, neatly brushed. Occasionally a small tuft dropped over his forehead and Keating involuntarily jerked his head left to move it out of the way. He was a weekend sailor at his house in Rye, and as it was summer, he had the tan.

"I just got off the phone with the Police Commissioner. They're calling it a suicide."

I frowned. "So fast?"

Keating scanned a report on his desk, so I couldn't see his eyes. "I'd call it professional of them," he said, waving me into a chair. "Apparently things were cut and dry at the scene and the lab. No reason to think anything else. And grief aside, Mike, it's best for Lenox to get this off the front pages as soon as possible."

I told Keating about the list I'd found. "That doesn't seem so cut and dry to me," I said.

"The police have a different point of view. Tell me, Dwyer's note said he planned to give a 'disk' to someone named Mike. Is that you?"

"If it is, I never got it."

He regarded me more directly. "Let me know if something shows up. Frankly, that list referred to some sensitive issues that we'd rather keep private. Not your concern." He shook his head. "I wonder why Dwyer did it."

"I thought you might have an idea, sir."

"Why me?" Keating asked, reaching for coffee and not offering any. The office was big and sunny but typical Lenox—no frills—at Chairman Dwyer's insistence. Walnut furniture. Eggshell blue carpet. Paintings of Lenox facilities in France. Functionally comfortable. "We give the stockholders' money back to them," Dwyer liked to say. "If you want a Degas in your office, buy it yourself."

"Well," I said, having decided to lie and keep Kim out of it, "the Chairman mentioned last night that he'd had dinner with you and Tom Schwadron."

"*You* saw him last night?"

Keating seemed startled by the news.

"I had a drink with him at his house."

"His home." The idea of my socializing with Dwyer

struck Keating as odd. He was the kind of man who would invite someone like me—an ex–FBI agent—to a company cookout, but never to a more private birthday party or wedding; the kind of upper-management guy who'd eagerly ask about old FBI cases. Kidnappings and bank robberies sounded exotic to him. But his attitude otherwise—the way he asked questions or lectured me—implied that he knew more than I did as a general rule.

I lied again, remembering Dwyer's reference to "Naturetech" in his note. "He asked me to check security at one of our labs."

"Well, you and I will schedule a briefing in the next few days. I want to know everything you've been working on. Meanwhile, if James told you about our dinner he must have mentioned we were celebrating the Washington deal."

"He did, but I wondered if he also mentioned anything that might have been bothering him?"

"No. I told the police that." Keating sat back and I could see him collecting himself. He'd answered me automatically, as if I were a cop, and now he seemed irritated by his own cooperative response. "But you're not an FBI agent anymore, Mike. That's the larger issue we need to discuss. Thanks for going to his house. It had to be hard for you. It took presence of mind. But you should have alerted me right away."

"I didn't want to wake you until I had the facts."

"That's not your decision."

He was right to chew me out, and he did. He said he expected from now on to be phoned instantly in an emergency. He said he knew I'd had a "good relationship" with the Chairman and he was to be treated the same way. He understood my loyalty to Dwyer, but if I was going to have a problem transferring it to him, he wanted to know now.

"Every team needs a captain, Mike."

"I understand."

"I don't want to make a bad day worse, but once the news broke I started getting calls. I can't be waiting for you to decide to tell me things. The captain needs information. The captain deals with the big picture, not pieces. If a team member doesn't tell the captain everything, everyone suffers. Stockholders. Workers. You."

"It won't happen again."

"Good. Let's move on. *Did* you find anything besides the list I should know about, whether or not you mentioned it to the police?"

When I told him about the gambling slips he frowned and said, "Two dollars?"

When I brought up the odd substance in the vial, Keating's frown deepened and he thought for a moment. "What's the point of sending it to the lab?" he asked.

The answer seemed obvious. "To find out what it is."

"We just went over this. You're not the police." Keating sipped his coffee. I wondered if he did this to give himself time to think. "Look, if the Chairman liked to bet occasionally, or needed something extra to help him sleep, who needs to know? Any chemicals in his system would have showed up during police analysis. So leave his personal business alone. For God's sake, Mike. I've spent the morning reassuring people that there's no bigger problem out there."

"It might be evidence."

"Then you shouldn't have taken it," Keating said. "But you wanted to protect him and Lenox, so don't stop now. It'll be tough enough for Gabrielle," he said, naming Dwyer's daughter, "without her reading some article about James having a drug problem. You know how reporters exaggerate. And how much are we talking about anyway? Two dollars? Two grams?"

"The vial came from Lenox," I argued. "So how do we know for sure there's no bigger issue here?"

Keating's wave indicated that to him the vial was insignificant. "There are twenty million Lenox vials in circulation and a thousand places anyone could pick one up. It's a nine-cent item, Mike. My wife stores vitamin C tablets in them when we take a trip. And last time I checked, we don't distribute anything that doesn't come in pill, tablet or liquid form. Do you have the substance? You must have it with you. Let me see it. You came here directly, right?"

I gave it to him and he opened the vial and sniffed it.

"Smells familiar, but what is it?" he said. "Leave it here, with me. In fact, let's put an end to this right now."

He dropped it in his wastebasket.

But his eyes narrowed and he reached for his phone when I told him about the missing computer file on HR-109. He punched in a number from memory, and as he started speaking I realized he'd called Lenox's head of Research, Ralph Kranz.

"Ralph? Bill Keating," he said, passed on my story, waited, listened, said, "I'll tell Mike" and hung up.

"Kranz says it's standard when a project shows promise to delete it from the general file and move it to a more secure location. He's furious because your people shouldn't have been able to get into any file at all, and he wants whoever did it to show him how he got in."

"She will, sir."

"And to promise it won't happen again."

"What *was* HR-109?"

Keating seemed about to shut me down. He sipped more coffee and patted his lips with a napkin. Then he said, "It looked like it was going to be a nice anti-arthritis drug until it failed tests. After we closed down the project the file should have been returned to general. Kranz will correct the oversight. But next time you want something from him, ask. I can't blame him for being hot."

"Sir, isn't it better that our people found a flaw, not a hacker?"

"Not unless it was an authorized test."

But Keating softened because, after all, I had a point. "Mike, you've done a terrific job at Lenox, the way you cleaned house. I like you. But the people you drove out still have friends here and they don't like your methods. James protected you. I'd like to assure your critics that your cowboy days are over. I want to keep you on the team. Confidentially, the folks who resent you even found a loophole in your severance agreement. They've gone to James from time to time to ask him to fire you without pay."

"I'm your man, sir," I said, thinking, *I drove those people out? They stole millions.*

"We'll leave police matters to the police, then?" he said.

"Absolutely."

"Find anything else at the house?"

"No, sir," I said, slipping my hand into my pocket and intentionally dropping my house key to the rug, where he couldn't see it.

I walked out of his office, counted to five and walked

back in. Sure enough, he was on the phone, and I heard the nervous words "I'm telling you, Eisner . . ."

Stay away from Eisner, the Chairman's list had said.

Spotting me, Keating jerked the receiver away from his ear in the involuntary reaction of someone caught doing something wrong. It took a fraction of a second for his surprise to turn to rage and back to blandness. With practiced liars, infinitesimal tells are the best you get.

I believed I'd just seen guilt in his face.

"Dropped my key, sir," I said, making sure the vial remained in the wastebasket. "Here it is."

Keating still held the phone as I left. In the hallway I passed workmen carrying drills toward Dwyer's office. It was necessary to get to his papers, but the sight left me feeling sick.

Back in the garage I sat in my car in the muted underground light and tried to make sense of things. I'd never liked Keating. Now Dwyer had died and Keating had threatened my job if I looked into it. Keating had claimed he was "interested" in why the Chairman had killed himself. But then he'd tried to stop me from finding the answer.

At that moment I understood just how far from the Bureau I'd traveled. I remembered the promise I'd made to Dwyer, which had convinced him to hire me. *If I tell you something and you don't do anything about it, I'll take care of it myself.*

Well, Dwyer was dead now, but my promise was not.

I called Danny on my cell phone and asked him to meet me at La Guardia Airport. I needed a witness to what I planned to do for the rest of the day, for lies I planned to tell.

"Where we going?" Danny asked.

"Washington."

I was jeopardizing my job but did not yet fathom greater danger. That changed twenty minutes later when the death threat came.

FOUR

The threat began with a prim and proper woman's voice coming over my car phone as I drove to the airport.

"Michael Acela?"

I envisioned an executive secretary—someone like Kim—on the line, at Lenox.

"Yes."

"Please hold for Chairman James Dwyer."

Had I been holding a phone instead of talking into a head-mike, I would have dropped the receiver. Then my shock changed to rage.

"What is this? Some joke?" I snapped.

"I can't hear you, sir. Speak up."

A warning horn blasted on my right, and I jerked the wheel left—narrowly missing a collision. A white Chevy Suburban roared past on FDR Drive, its driver shoving his middle finger at me. In my anger I hadn't realized I'd drifted into his lane. I was passing the rent-subsidized towers of East Harlem, heading toward the Triboro Bridge and La Guardia Airport in fast traffic, on my way to Washington, where I hoped to visit Naturetech and find Tom Schwadron, the other member of Lenox's Board who'd dined with the Chairman last night. Cars swerved right and left ahead, avoiding a two-car fender bender. The East River churned past on the right.

"Hey, Mike," said a new voice in the earpiece now, a man's voice, chuckling. "You like riddles?"

The voice held false heartiness, not friendship but mockery, control. Young guy, I pictured. Late twenties or early thirties. He was having a fine time on his power trip.

"Who are you?"

"Wait for the riddle, because I know you'll like it. What's the difference, Mike, between an FBI agent and an *ex*-agent?"

"The ex won't follow Bureau guidelines when he finds you. The ones about not using physical force."

The caller made a blooping sound like a quiz show buzzer. "Sorry," he said. "The answer is, if an FBI agent gets killed, law enforcement is all over it. But if an ex-agent has an accident or, say, commits su-i-cide, nobody follows up at all."

He was trying to scare me but I only grew angrier. I checked caller ID on the seat panel, but saw it was blank, not even showing an OUT OF AREA on the screen. Considering the sophistication of my unit, that meant this call probably came from another specialized phone.

"You know my name but I don't know yours," I said, straining to pick out background sounds that might give a clue as to the caller's location. No luck.

"I'm Master of Ceremonies," the guy said. "Regis Philbin. Bob Barker, man."

No accent, I thought. And he's not law enforcement, at least not officially. LE guys don't make the sort of threat he'd just made. So scratch police, Justice, FBI.

"You were at Dwyer's house," I said. It was a question.

"Mike, you're not playing by the rules. The MC asks the riddles, and I know you'll like this one. What's green, comes in vials, and looks like . . . *marijuana!*"

Startled by his knowledge, I almost missed the left-hand exit looping up toward the Triboro Bridge. Fast-moving traffic hemmed me in, bumper to bumper. If one car stopped short, ten would pile up. I turned the AC off to better make out background noise on the call, but all I got was static.

"I need more details," I said.

"I don't think so."

"Give me a hint."

"It's worth big prize money to the contestant who gets it right and sells the disk. The one Dwyer gave you."

Easing through the E-ZPass booth, I chose the over-pass highway to the Grand Central Parkway into Queens, the rushing cars around me a stampeding herd. We were in an industrial zone, the buildings were smaller than in Manhattan. I passed factories, a rail yard, a large gray-stoned cemetery. I knew from the Bureau that opener phone calls often set a relationship. The longer I kept this caller talking, the better my chance of controlling things.

"I always wanted to win prize money," I said.

"Who doesn't?"

"Oregano," I said. "Is that the answer?"

His pause told me I'd irritated him with levity, and he came back at me with a flatter, pissed-off tone.

"You lose the washer-dryer, Mike."

First clue, I thought. *You have a temper.*

"Before we try again, Mike, let's tell the folks at home about today's contestant. Mike lives alone in Devil's Bay, Brooklyn. He has a wall safe in his bedroom and a photo on the dresser of his parents. No living relatives. Two hundred and eighty thousand in munis at Weber. Mike loves his tomato garden and takes long walks at night on the beach, alone. He has a sweet little girlfriend, Kim

Pendergraph. Aren't you afraid she'll get mugged? Or *you'll* walk into the ocean one night and drown accidentally, or kill yourself and leave a pathetic note about loneliness?"

"Kim's not my girlfriend."

"Then you wouldn't care if something happens to her."

"Who told you about the list? How did you get into his house?" I asked, hoping the caller would like to brag. That he'd give me any useful tidbit of information at all.

"What kind of FBI guy are you if you have to ask? Let's talk about what Dwyer gave you."

"I'd rather meet in person for this kind of thing. Anyplace you want."

The car in front of me braked suddenly and I jerked the wheel left, by reflex. The BMW responded superbly, rocketing into the next lane, except I'd had no time to check for traffic. I braced for collision, held my breath. Horns erupted around me. But there was no impact. No car had been there.

Then, in the infinitesimal beat of time before the caller resumed speaking, it hit me. *He'd paused when I veered around the accident earlier, and he'd stopped talking just now when I hit the brake.*

Clue number two.

He's behind me. Now.

"You don't want to meet me," the voice said as I glanced in the rearview mirror. All I saw were hundreds of cars back there, reflecting moving light. "So cut the shit, Mike. Answer now unless you want to move into the penalty round."

I switched lanes and tried again. The looming cab of a semi truck blocked my vision. Traffic was too heavy to allow me more than a fraction of a second to glance back.

The sheer volume of vehicles shielded anyone following me—if I was right and someone was even there at all.

"Last chance," the voice said.

Did Keating call this guy? Keating is the only one I told about the vial. Or did he know beforehand?

"I changed my mind. Go fuck yourself," I said, and hung up, remembering the old FBI field rule. *An angry adversary makes mistakes.*

Or was I making the mistake? I didn't even carry a gun with me. I never needed it on the job, and kept it at home.

I called Danny and told him to forget about the airport. I told him where to go instead, fast.

Flushing Meadows Park—only five minutes from La Guardia—was the site of the old 1964 World's Fair, which my parents had visited the last year Mom had full use of her legs. Dad took me there before a day game at Shea once, where we watched four complete innings before an emergency at home pulled us back. "Mom and I saw the wonders of the future at the fair," Dad told me that day, nostalgically. "The monorail, which still hasn't been built. The electric house, which was supposed to cost pennies to operate, and free us from energy bills. Ha! The hospital of the future, where doctors would cure all diseases, so people like Mom would never get sick."

Now, with the World's Fair long dismantled, the park occupying its former grounds was visible from the highway, its principal feature the Unisphere, the huge steel globe that had symbolized in 1964 the peaceful world of the future. "Another prediction that didn't work out," Dad had said.

I parked in a near-empty lot off the Grand Central Parkway. I locked the BMW, trying to look distracted and fearful, like a guy who'd gotten a death threat on his phone. I figured that the man who'd called could not possibly have known I'd been originally headed for the airport. If he was still behind me, he'd assume I'd been on my way to the park all along.

Everyone at Lenox was sure Kim and I were lovers, I thought, walking out of the parking lot. So was the caller from Lenox, or had he just talked to someone there?

In the brutal heat I strode purposefully along empty walkways, past empty benches, empty meadow, copses of oaks. Flushing Meadows Park remained a barely used expanse of green stuck between highways. No one lived near it. You had to travel to reach it, and weekdays, few people did. The air was thick and humid, causing objects over a hundred yards off to ripple. The city was liquid. Perhaps all the tar and steel would melt into one mass of urban lava: part old Chrysler, part Trump Tower, part Statue of Liberty and a bit of the old Van Wyck.

My rage was rising. The caller had threatened Kim, and me, and had almost claimed outright that Dwyer had been murdered or driven to suicide—all related to the grainy substance in the vial and a missing disk.

I kept my head down, as if preoccupied. I did not look around. After all, no one was supposed to be behind me. Right?

I heard the *whoosh* of traffic from Grand Central, and a boat horn from the nearby Flushing Bay marina. Pausing beside a municipal trash can, I reached in and picked out a discarded *New York Post*. A pro following me—even a stupid one—would think *dead drop*, as I tucked the paper beneath my arm.

I felt a wave of annoyance at the Chairman.

Couldn't you just have told me exactly what you wanted?

I sat on a bench, unfolded the paper and scanned the top headline. This was a later edition than the *Times* I'd read earlier, and the protest news had been replaced by a breaking story. *Marines Stomp Bomb Plot.* Based on information gathered from captured terrorists, US raiders had pulled off a surprise attack on a Global Jihad stronghold in the Mideast, arresting top leaders, uncovering plans for attacks in Philadelphia and San Francisco, and blowing up a chemical weapons lab.

Colossal blow to enemy, a subhead read. *Brilliant intelligence work cited.*

The article quoted the Director of National Intelligence, responsible for personally ordering the raid. "We got lucky," said Richard (A. J.) Carbone, reached at the Hamilton Club in New York, Dwyer's Club, where Carbone was scheduled to speak on strategic defense in the terrorist age.

In the photo Carbone looked proud and confident, just like he did in the picture I'd seen at the Chairman's home. Too bad Dwyer wasn't alive to read this, I thought. He'd been rabid on the subject of homeland security since the 9/11 attack, when two Lenox account executives at a conference in the World Trade Center had died. Certainly the upcoming speech was the kind he would have attended.

I had no chance to read more. My cell phone chimed.

"I see him," Danny said. "White. Mid-twenties. Lean but muscled. Marine Corps tattoo on the right forearm. Detroit Tigers cap and sunglasses, and a black guayabara over his jeans. Gun's under the shirt in back."

"The woman?"

"I don't see a woman. Move around, Boss. Let's see if he follows or she shows up."

I snapped the phone shut and folded the newspaper. I strode purposefully toward the Unisphere, as if whomever had just called had told me to head that way. Beneath the huge globe I stopped and pivoted as if searching for someone. I snapped open the cell phone irritably. I pretended to punch in a number, pretended to listen, closed the phone. Then I walked quickly around the back of the sphere, which would force anyone behind me to reposition themselves to watch.

As I shielded my eyes and looked out toward the parking area, I noticed a guy by a tree, to my left, in a baseball cap. Then my phone chimed again.

"No woman," Danny said. "And the bathroom's empty. Hit it, Boss."

Heading toward the small, brick public restroom, I finally spotted Danny on the grass outside, alone. He'd changed into raggy khakis, soiled sneakers and a stained white T-shirt. He looked as dazed as a drunk. There was an upright paper bag beside him, with a glass-necked bottle poking out. Danny took a drink, probably of water.

Old undercover trick. Always keep clothes changes—separate costumes—in the trunk of your car.

Inside the bathroom I smelled Lysol. I really needed to use the urinal. I positioned myself at the corner stand, farthest from the door, and finished quickly. I zipped up my trousers but continued to stand in place, waiting.

A minute passed.

Three.

Maybe this wasn't going to work, I thought.

Five minutes went by but nobody entered, and my phone didn't chime, which meant Danny still had the guy in sight, and Mr. Short Attention Span was still out-side, probably wondering why I hadn't come out, or who I was meeting.

At eight minutes my phone chimed once and stopped, and a second later I heard footsteps and saw the shadow at the entrance and heard the snap of heels on tile. I smelled aftershave. I felt a presence beside me, at the next urinal. He was checking to see if I was in here with some-one, and he wasn't going to let me ID him from his voice.

"You hit forty," I said, without looking at him, to draw his attention from Danny entering the bathroom, "and you need twenty minutes to take a piss."

When Danny hit him from behind the cap fell side-ways. The face went slack with surprise before the mouth slammed into the urinal. He groaned, and I punched him in the kidneys. He arched backwards. Danny pulled the automatic from his belt. I saw it was a 9mm Glock.

"The difference between an FBI agent and an *ex*-agent is, the ex-agent can do things like this," I said. Danny kicked the guy's legs out from under him. He went down, head bouncing on tile. One shoe was off. I saw a hole in a front sock, and a bit of very white skin. The big toe was dirty.

Normally I'm not a violent man, but I learned a long time ago in Devil's Bay, when someone threatens you, hit first, hard, so hard the guy won't come back.

"What happened in Dwyer's house?" I demanded.

"You're fucking with the wrong people."

I leaned closer. "Who sent you?"

Our attack had taken seconds. The guy was breathing hard, gasping. Blood ran from his nose and mouth and a deep gash in his forehead, which would need stitches. Without the cap he looked older, in his mid-thirties; his face was long, and shiny with pain, and had been darkened by sun to a tea brown. His hair was short and thick on the sides, ocher-colored and balding at the crown. The blue in his eyes matched the faded ink on the tattoo adorning his right forearm. USMC.

"Who told you I have the disk?"

"No wallet," Danny said, turning his pockets out. "Or ID." He knelt and slipped the bottle out of his paper bag. He pressed the guy's fingers to the glass.

"Nice thumbprint here, Custer," he said. "Index next. What a cooperative fellow you are."

I ratcheted down the rage coursing through me. It would distract me. Plenty of time to let it out later.

"What was that stuff in the vial?" I said.

The guy wasn't using his cheery MC voice anymore. He was belly down and he sounded muffled, like someone in a dentist's chair, with a probe in his mouth. "Your mother."

I slammed the heel of my shoe into his back. But he wasn't going to tell me anything. He was hard. He forced out, in that chewed-up voice, "Whatever you do to me is nothing compared to what they'll do to you. Give it to me. For your sake and your girl's."

Danny rose and kicked him in the stomach when he tried to get up, and he rolled up into a ball, trying to cover himself, but the blow cost us time. The guy couldn't talk now, as he struggled to breathe.

"What," I said, feeling as effective as a broken record, "is on the goddamn disk?"

In the distance we heard sirens, getting louder.

Danny cocked his head, frowning, eyeing the wall in the direction from which the sound was coming. I envisioned two or three squad cars racing toward us along the parkway.

"It's not for us. Nobody could have called them," Danny insisted. "They must be answering another call."

The guy smiled up at us, through blood.

"*She* called them," he said.

Which got us moving. There was no time to see if he was right. It wasn't the kind of end to this confrontation I'd envisioned, but neither was jail. "If I see you again, you'll have the accident," I told him, but let's face it, I was turning to run, which diminished the force of any threat considerably.

He gasped as we ran. His words floated after us.

"You won't see me next time, Mike. Neither will Kim. Traitors like you everywhere are going down."

FIVE

"Traitors?" I said.

"Don't ask me," Danny said. "Wait for the print results."

The Delta Shuttle to Washington is probably the most reliable air service in the United States. Every hour, flights leave the old Marine Terminal at La Guardia for the half-hour flight to the capital. Even with new security precautions in place, jets go out like clockwork.

We'd bought fresh clothing before flying, because, after all, showing up at airports with blood on your shirt is a bad idea if you want to be allowed on your flight.

"Of all the things he could have said, Danny, why that?"

We'd also ordered a bonded courier from a private fingerprinting service to meet us at La Guardia and pick up the sample Danny had taken. I used the service usually when hiring people for sensitive security work. Worzak Security was discreet, and would run the prints against military and law enforcement databases, to let us know if applicants had criminal records. Applicants always signed releases permitting us to run the checks.

In this case, no permission slip had been signed. And Worzak, another ex–FBI agent, hadn't asked.

"I want these results as fast as possible," I'd told Worzak over the phone.

"Is tonight soon enough?" he'd replied.

Now Danny pulled my thoughts back to the present, as the plane banked toward the capital. "Tell Detective Berg what happened," Danny suggested.

"We have no proof. We beat *him* up, not the other way around."

"Give Berg the vial."

"Keating threw it out."

"Tell Keating?" Danny mused, looked out the window at the runway coming up, and said, "Forget I brought it up."

"Danny, I made a mistake dragging you into this. When we land, turn around and go home."

"Boss, once they threaten you, you have to keep going, whether or not things turn out the way you want."

It was sunny in the capital, furnace-hot, with the kind of indolent heat that only a city built on a swamp can offer. The Diamond cab's air-conditioning worked fitfully. The dreadlocked driver listened to NPR, where the news concerned Lenox. Public interest groups were charging that the Pentagon deal had been concluded without proper competitive bidding, and had cost taxpayers too much.

"Forty million dollars too much," one Senator said.

As we pulled up to the Senate Dirksen Building, where today's hearings were being held, I was on the phone with Kim, who'd been working on funeral arrangements, trying to reach Dwyer's daughter. I filled her in on what had happened, but left out the part about the vial and disk. It was safer for her not to know. But I had to tell her about the threat against her. God bless her, she got mad.

"That *proves* that the Chairman didn't kill himself."

I heard a harsh grinding noise like drilling in the background.

"It doesn't prove anything."

The note was in his handwriting, unless it was forged, or written under duress, I thought.

"You promised you'd keep going, Mike."

"Even after the threat against you and Chris?"

I told Kim to send her son away for a couple of weeks, and said I'd assign a security man to stay outside her apartment. She grew quiet as the reality sank in. But then she said, "Anyway, I may be leaving soon."

"Quitting Lenox?"

"Moving back to Vermont from New York."

I didn't like hearing that.

"Keating said I'm out, Mike. I can work for someone else and keep my salary. But he'll change everything for the worse. God, he personally supervised the workers who broke into the Chairman's safe. I hate it."

"Do you still want to come for dinner? I should be home by eight."

"Even more than before. I can use a few drinks. I'll put Chris on the train to my mom's this afternoon. Call when you're finished in Washington. But if you're tired, we'll do it another time."

"If you can stay up, so can I, Kim."

Danny remarked as I hung up, "You ought to see your face when you talk to her." We were walking up the marble steps of the Dirksen Building. "Take the girl out."

"We're friends."

"You say that like it's a disease, not a basis for more."

"Your boss is telling you to mind your own business," I snapped.

"You mean like *don't* watch your back against the guy

with the tattoo? *Don't* help you kick the shit out of strangers in bathrooms?"

I started laughing. I couldn't help it. I felt as if I hadn't laughed in weeks.

We went through the metal detector in the lobby, along with a half-dozen journalists heading for the hearings. That's where I knew I'd find Tom Schwadron, the other Lenox Board member with whom Dwyer had dined last night.

Danny started in again on my personal life as we waited for the elevator. "You live alone."

"Look, I know you mean well."

"I like you, Boss. You're honest. You think about things. But your personal life sucks. You don't want to be a neighborhood guy but you are, don't want to be button-down but you are."

"I thought Sigmund Freud was Jewish, not Mohawk."

"Jews are the lost tribes," Danny remarked. "So maybe he *was* Mohawk."

His eyes widened over my shoulder as I heard the elevator door open and turned and looked into Gabrielle Dwyer's face. A blast of sensuality hit me. I'd seen photos of her at Dwyer's house, and on Page Six of the *Post,* but they failed to capture the raw allure, the shock that some women can deliver through mere appearance, the near-perfect way she fit together as she strode toward me without recognition. We'd never met.

Beneath a cream-colored calf-length dress, pumps, matching jacket and silk blouse—a conservative outfit for the allegedly wild child—slim legs rose up into lean hips and below apple-sized breasts. Her face was cupid-shaped, with a round chin, button nose and lips that had the slightest pout.

Then her black eyes met mine. She seemed startled for an instant, but she couldn't have recognized me.

"Ms. Dwyer?"

The eyes widened. The gait slowed. There are some women who can erase the rest of the world from view when you meet them. Up close she looked even better. Her cheekbones were high. Her tanned skin looked as perfect as her posture. The jet black hair captured natural light and, tight to her head, dropped into a long braid that reached the small of her back. The whole effect was of constrained wildness. I was aware that other men in the lobby were staring at us, aware of collective energy and envy directed our way.

I thought, *Why is she here, not in New York?*

"I'm Mike Acela, Ms. Dwyer. I work for your father. I'm sorry about what happened last night."

She stood looking at me for a beat too long, but the death must have dazed her to start with. Then she said, "I just heard," which was odd because hours had passed since Dwyer's death broke in the news. As next of kin, she should have been called by police. She added, "I don't have a cell phone. I was in Middleburg, at a spa. Tom Schwadron just told me upstairs. I'm headed for the airport."

Why was she meeting Schwadron? I thought.

"Did Keating send you to find me, Mr. Acela?"

Ah, the pretensions of the rich. Or perhaps it's their experience. Run into them a thousand miles from home and they assume they're the reason you've come. But I loved her voice. My throat had gone dry at the sight of her, and I felt a small itch start in my groin. I hadn't reacted to a woman this strongly since I was a teenager.

"Actually, I'm here to talk to Schwadron too," I said. I

felt awkward around Gabrielle Dwyer. "We're all at your disposal at Lenox. Your father spoke of you with love."

A lie. He'd never spoken to me about her at all. But I told myself I wanted to ask her about her father. She was an heir. Heirs are always suspects. Her observations about Dwyer might help me figure out what had happened. But I couldn't force people outside the company to sit for interviews anymore, couldn't even pursue an investigation *inside* the company without infuriating my new boss. So I'd decided to spend the next few days starting conversations by passing along the Chairman's "kind words" about people.

Even Keating wouldn't take umbrage at that, I hoped.

"Love?" repeated Gabrielle Dwyer, head cocked, voice cooler. Her perfume—a faint musky scent—seemed to fill the lobby antechamber.

"I had drinks with him last night," I said. "He talked about you."

"You're *that* Mike Acela. The Security Chief."

"Yes."

"The one who came in and soon lots of top management started resigning."

Yep, I thought. Back then Danny and I had planted illegal bugs, tapped phones, bribed secretaries and even broke into the Chief Financial Officer's house to confront him with evidence. Freed from the constraints of traditional law enforcement, we'd accomplished in two months what would have taken the FBI years, if they would have been able to finish an investigation at all.

"All strictly legal, Ms. Dwyer."

I hadn't realized she was reaching to touch me until I felt the coolness of her fingers brushing my wrist. The touch was a jolt.

"You just lied to me, though."

Her eyes locked onto mine.

"My father said nothing about love."

I felt myself reddening. I searched for a reply. I said lamely, "I wanted to make you feel better."

"That's a presumption to assume you could, and that you'd know how to do it. My father didn't love," she said with either flat candor or suppressed rage. "But he picked up strays who would be loyal. Kim Pendergraph. You, maybe. People who would love *him* without incurring obligation, not the other way around."

"I liked and respected him, Ms. Dwyer."

"Then that makes one of us, I suppose," she said as if I'd insulted her, which, I realized, I had.

She seemed trouble and troubled, and she turned and, with a scissor-legged clip that angry women have perfected, snapped her way across the lobby. I caught up to her outside, midway down the marble steps. She was waving for a taxi. When I stepped in front of her, she dropped her hand.

"I'm sorry," I said. "I pretended to understand what you're going through."

At least she didn't pick her arm back up, or walk around me. So I tried again.

"I lied because I hoped to talk to you about your father. I'm not sure the story the police are putting out— about suicide—is true."

Her face seemed a jumble of competing emotions, of anger and confusion. Whatever nerve I'd just touched had been rubbed raw long ago. My words represented one more father problem coming at her at the end of a long infuriating line. "That's beside the point for him now, wouldn't you say?" she said.

But she stayed in place, and that told me she was listening.

"I know I was wrong before," I said, letting her see my real emotions, "but at the Bureau I learned that family members usually want to know what really happened. I don't know if it's out of grief or curiosity. I only know that closure eases their minds."

I was taking a chance by revealing more than I should. But after the clumsy way I'd started things, I'd lose the opportunity to talk to her if I didn't offer something back. In truth, I'd later admit, I didn't know if she might really help me or if I just wanted to see her again.

You'd think that by the age of 44 a guy would have his sex drive under control.

Forget it.

"What did the police say when you explained what you think?" she asked.

"I need to find out more before I talk to them."

"How did Keating take it?"

"He threatened my job if I started looking into it."

"And you're *telling* me this? I'll be speaking to Keating, you know. Today. I could pass it along."

"Instinct," I said.

"There are all kinds of those."

"Your call, then," I said, remembering that Kim had once told me that the fights between Gabrielle and Dwyer had been long and painful, and clearly they'd left bruises. Now the estranged daughter was making some fundamental decision about me. I had a feeling that with this woman, people got only one chance usually—at talk, at friendship, at everything.

Some people are like that, overly experienced or overly afraid.

I also remembered the words of the man who had followed me. *She called the cops.*

Who, I wondered now, was "she"?

"Is that suspicion I see in your face, Mr. Acela?"

"That's what I do," I said, letting her know that she was right.

Believe me, when someone that beautiful stares into your eyes, five seconds can last a long time.

"You won't learn anything from me," she said.

"Then our talk won't last long."

Her expression subsided back into the cool mask. "Are you going back to New York tonight after you pass on more of my father's fabricated memories to Tom Schwadron?" she asked. "He'll believe you, by the way. He'll want to. He's needier than he looks. Don't let him fool you."

"Yes, I'm going back."

"There's a restaurant named Al Dente near Cooper Union, in the East Village. Meet me there at eight."

I remembered Kim's grief, and how much she'd need to talk tonight. "I have a meeting," I demurred. "Would tomorrow be convenient, at any time you want?"

"For you? Yes," she said, starting to walk past, a taxi having pulled to the curb for her.

"I'll cancel the meeting."

"Don't worry, Mike. The food's good at Al Dente. You like veal? Or do you feel sorry for the little calf too?"

I watched her get into the cab, admired her sleek posture and smooth movements, and the way her legs disappeared before the yellow door shut. After she left, her perfume lingered. The air pressure was back to normal by the time I reentered the lobby, and when I was in the elevator, minutes later, Danny said flatly, "You're going to cancel with Kim?"

"For business."

"Yeah, but what kind?"

Then we rode upstairs to tell more lies, and I hoped I'd be better at it the next time around.

SIX

"Big companies make big targets," the Chairman used to say. "For lawyers, politicians and reporters wanting to take away our control. They charge us with overpricing drugs, making them impossible for the poor to afford. They say we've stopped making malaria killers because the profit margin's too small. They want to tell us what to make, what to charge, who to sell it to. But if we come up with a drug, we should control it. It's our right."

"Sir, admit it, lots of people can't afford many drugs," I'd argued back once, over an evening drink.

"Everyone wants to help the sick, my friend," the Chairman had replied. "Do you know how much I personally donate to leukemia research every year? But last time I checked, nobody helps Lenox if we go out of business or our stock plunges, and you and I lose our jobs."

"That's what Tom Schwadron explains in Washington?"

"Tom meets with Senators and folks at the White House. Thank God we have a man like that on our side."

Now Schwadron said, "*You* saw Dwyer last night, after we did?" He looked as surprised as Keating had when I told him, so unless he was acting, Keating probably hadn't called his rival after I'd left.

Danny and I sat sipping Snapples with the great convincer in a break room in the Dirksen Building. The subcommittee he'd been monitoring was in recess, and the room was comfortably fitted with leather chairs, potted palms, a coffee table piled with *Time* magazines. We were alone, although down the hall, dozens of reporters waited for the hearings to restart.

Schwadron seemed shocked by Dwyer's passing, hollow-eyed at the loss of a friend.

I'd never actually met him until now, and he was impressive, one of those WASP Clark Clifford types, a tall, lean, youthfully white-haired power broker originally from Connecticut; Virginia Law, Purple Heart winner in Korea, ex-POW, former Ambassador to Saudi Arabia, still vibrant at 71 and striking-looking in his crisply tailored gray Brooks Brothers suit and signature bow tie, today colored maroon.

"That list you told me about referred to a couple of problems the Board is handling. What was Jim's message for me?" he said.

"The Chairman seemed upset. I guess he knew he was going to kill himself," I lied. "He said, 'When you see Tom, tell him how much I value him.' I should have guessed what he was planning. Hindsight's 20/20, I suppose."

"You can't blame yourself. *Did* he say what upset him?" Schwadron leaned forward, fixed his gray eyes on me.

"The dinner with you and Bill Keating."

Tom Schwadron, Esquire, leaned back and frowned. He was one of Washington's highest-paid attorneys, according to the *Washingtonian* magazine I'd read last week.

The magazine had shown a photo of him in his office, with its view of the Capitol. Schwadron had been at his desk in the picture, and the entire machinery of government outside had seemed part of his view, accessible at his whim, or so the article implied. Then again, Washingtonians exaggerate almost as much as Hollywood people, I've found.

I pushed a bit harder. "He mentioned a research project. HR-109."

"Research?" Schwadron continued to look stricken, but that didn't necessarily mean anything more than that Dwyer had been his friend. He shook his head. "We didn't talk about research."

In fact, if Bill Keating had been Dwyer's protégé, Schwadron had been the confidant, Kim had told me once. Schwadron was close to Dwyer's age and they shared a generation's predispositions. Add the Washington influence and Schwadron looked to history for guidance, while Keating chose the marketplace. Schwadron opted for diplomacy in situations where Keating advised combat. Schwadron's legendary confidence came from a belief that he could convince almost anybody of anything. Keating's from the wolf inside him, eager to attack.

Now Schwadron sighed. "At my age you lose people regularly," he said, shifting eye contact between Danny and me, including both of us in the conversation. "But to take your own life. I've never understood that."

"The dinner . . ." I tried again.

"Yes, yes, it upset all of us."

If that's true, Keating lied when he said it was a celebration.

"Tough decisions," I said.

"They're all tough."

"Three hours," I prompted, using the old interrogator's technique of suggesting that you knew more about a subject than you really did. I'd referred to the time period scrawled on the vial I'd found.

Schwadron looked into the distance and nodded. "Three hours can change the world."

"I know."

"Pearl Harbor," he said, "9/11."

"Terrible days," I agreed, alarmed by the references. How had he reached them in relationship to last night? And what could they possibly have to do with a drug company?

But then Schwadron's eyes slid back to me and his distant look changed to thoughtful. Fishing expedition over, I knew. He reached for his Snapple. It was quiet in the break room, an island of privacy for staffers or guests who needed to rest between committee sessions. He said, "You came down to Washington just to see me?"

"Oh, no, sir. Danny and I have to check out a lab in Maryland. As long as we were flying into DC anyway, I thought you'd like to know what he said."

"That was thoughtful. James said you were like that."

"We ran into Gabrielle Dwyer in the lobby."

"Poor girl. She actually hadn't heard about his death, and I had to tell her," he said, confirming what she'd told me. "She's a dinosaur. No e-mail, no cell phone. Sometimes I think life would be saner for everyone if those things hadn't been invented. I was actually going to try to repair the rift between James and Gabrielle. Now it's too late. Never let fights fester with a loved one, Mr. Acela. Gabrielle is terribly shaken up."

"Actually, she seemed angry."

"No one in that family shows their real emotions. Maybe because they run so deep."

Schwadron glanced at his watch and rose. Break time

was over, but even in dismissing us he had a benevolent, fatherly air, of patience, experience, regard. He said, "You know, Mr. Acela, I thought you did a great job three years ago. You helped avoid a scandal. But with Dwyer gone, things may get rough for you in the company."

Which was what Keating had said, but Schwadron put a different spin on it. "Bill Keating is not your biggest fan."

"I'll be fine, sir."

"I suppose you'd prefer that I not mention to him that you were here."

"I would never ask you to do that."

He nodded approvingly, and I had the impression he'd known I'd been questioning him but didn't mind. "You impress me, Mr. Acela. You have a likable, professional manner. If you ever decide you need to switch jobs, feel free to call me." He gave me his card. "My private number. I'd be happy to put a word in for you in Washington. People here are always looking for good private security. It wouldn't be hard to find a matchup you'd like."

"That's generous of you," I said, feeling out of my league, wondering if I'd just been offered a favor or a bribe. Everything this man said seemed to point in several directions at once.

He smiled. "Well, the lions are waiting, Mr. Acela, back in the coliseum. If you don't choose what to feed them, they get their own ideas about what to eat."

"Can the Senate really force us to cancel the Chairman's deal?" I asked. I didn't care whether they did or not. I wanted to appear like a good employee.

"Oh, everyone forces someone to do something," Schwadron said with a wry grin. "And in Washington, every issue comes down to one word, every time."

"What word, sir?"

"Why, I thought you knew. Control."

We left and Danny frowned at me. "Pearl Harbor?" he said. "You say three hours, he says 9/11."

"I didn't like that either."

I thought, what could it mean?

The afternoon business sections were filled with news about Lenox. The Board had moved swiftly to confirm Keating as Dwyer's temporary replacement, and Keating had apparently spent half the day reassuring reporters that the company was in solid shape. No scandals were brewing. No drugs were about to be recalled. Our finances were terrific. The stock had even regained two points since this morning.

Drug Boss Commits Suicide! read the banner headline in the late-edition *New York Post,* above a photo of Dwyer.

Special Section Inside: The Stresses of Corporate Work, Five Ways to Ease the Load, read an insert on the front page of the *Daily News.*

"You can't blame me for what happened here yesterday. I just followed the Chairman's orders," said the small, neat, mustached man behind the desk, across from us.

At three, we were in rural Maryland near Gaithersburg, at Naturetech, just off the I-270 laboratory/research corridor north of Washington, as if this were a standard surprise security visit unrelated to Dwyer's death. I had no idea what I was looking for but hoped something here might give me an idea of what had upset the Chairman last night.

Danny and I occupied the office of Chief Scientist Dr. Raymond Teaks, surrounded by his family photos: Teaks coaching boys' soccer, Teaks coaching girls' basketball, Teaks the devoted father and family man, who had just acknowledged having some problem here yesterday.

We said nothing, hoping he'd volunteer more. We projected an air of polite accusation. It didn't work.

I prodded Teaks. "What's *your* interpretation of what happened yesterday? Who *should* we blame?"

"Oh, no," Teaks said, standing up. "Fool me once, shame on me. Fool me twice?" He smiled neatly. "You want the tour, gentlemen? This way. But if you want to know about yesterday, call Chairman Keating himself. Those are my instructions. Would you prefer to start in the building or on the grounds?"

"Grounds first. So," I ventured, "are you functioning at a hundred percent capacity today even after yesterday's problem?"

He nodded proudly. "Why not? There was no damage. Just the . . ."

He broke out laughing and shook his head. "You're smart. Come along," he said.

The grounds were grassy and rolling, a converted polo farm that abutted a county park on one side and farms and a Sat company on the others, Teaks explained as we walked. The double fences—one electrified and one barbed—were hidden from the main building by woods lining the periphery of the property. A guard post was visible by the main entrance. The orange brick one-story facility was set on a small rise and built in three spokes like a wheel without a rim. Each spoke was a corridor extending out from a common lobby. Wing A housed administrative and security offices and was the only one with windows, Teaks said. B contained storage areas. C, the most secure, had the labs, and a loading dock outside.

Inside, we found A and C wings protected by Lenox's usual CCTV cameras and motion detectors. C wing offered veterinary operating facilities and recovery rooms filled with cages, all empty at the moment. The animals were actually housed before surgery in B wing, to calm them. So animal experimentation went on here.

"What are you working on?" I asked Teaks as we reached the steel door leading to the labs. I tried to figure how to divert the conversation back to yesterday.

"Mostly cancers," he replied. "Naturetech was acquired by Lenox because of our work synthesizing natural compounds. We have contracts with private collectors in South America who hunt down potential cures in rain forests and coral reefs. We dry the plants or reef poisons and mix the residue into compounds. We test the compounds against diseases. If one shows promise, we figure out how to synthesize it in our lab. If you can't synthesize it, the natural supply runs out, and quickly if the plant is rare. Or the host country demands a big share of profits. But once we've synthesized a compound and can make it on our own . . ."

"Lenox gets all the profits," I finished.

Teaks sighed and looked into the distance, imagining successes, probably. "The dream is that we'll come up with the next rosy periwinkle. That little plant upped the cure rate on childhood leukemias from twenty to eighty percent, and became the backbone for treatment of Hodgkin's disease."

Dr. Teaks used a key card to unlock a steel door and we entered a long, artificially lit lab where brownish liquids sat in beakers and white-coated scientists measured drops of compounds into test tubes and onto microscope slides.

"Here," he said, touching a two-liter tube filled with mud-colored liquid, "is a nice brew of Venezuelan cycads—the oldest living plants found in the Orinoco Basin—and filtered water heated to ninety-four degrees. According to some Indians along the river, this will cure what *they* call death pain in the belly, and *we* hope will turn out to be a cancer. So over *there*," he said, pointing to a glass cabinet spotted with "biohazard" stickers, "we check for results."

Danny and I peered through the glass to see shelves lined with small rectangular dishes the size of tape cassettes. Each dish was lined with circular plastic wells half an inch deep. Growing in most wells we saw a pinkish, fuzzy substance that looked like mold.

"Stomach cancer," said Teaks, eyeing the stuff as if it were no more dangerous than a fried egg sandwich. "We drop in the compound at varying strengths. We monitor the dishes to see if the cancer dies or keeps growing. So far, our 'death in the belly' plant shows no result against prostate cancer, breast, bone, and leukemia. You have to test each compound against different cancers, because it might kill one kind but leave fifty others alone."

"What other experiments do you do here?"

"Excuse me?" Teaks fingered his mustache. I think he'd realized I was trying to push him again.

"You said *mostly* you work on cancers. What else?"

"Autism," Teaks responded as I tried to imagine the source of yesterday's problem here. There could be a dozen answers. A theft. A blunder. A failure.

Teaks was saying, "We're testing a couple of drugs that affect the limbic system, especially the amygdala, the part of the brain that humans use when we try to understand one another in simple social situations. How schooled are you in neuroscience, Mr. Acela?"

"As much as the average person."

"Well, autistic kids just can't read other people. You smile at them and they have no idea what it means. They actually have to take lessons to help them understand a smile. Their brains don't interpret the simplest social clues. We're experimenting with a couple of possibilities to—how do I say it—help them out, chemically."

"In the brain," I said.

"Neurofeedback. FMRI scans."

"And that's it? Cancers and autism?" I was frustrated.

"Yes."

"Ever hear of a project called HR-109?"

He looked genuinely confused. "No."

"I see you're doing surgery on animals here."

Teaks nodded and picked at his neat mustache again, and I wondered if I'd pinpointed the source of his earlier discomfort. He probably got the animal question at dinner parties all the time. "If a compound shows promise, we have to test it on animals before moving to humans. But you'll find our paperwork proper. Maryland is scrupulous in its testing laws, and rightly so." He sounded defensive.

"Any animal activist problems, Dr. Teaks?" Maybe *that* was what had happened yesterday, but either way, I would do this security inspection the right way in case Keating checked up on me later.

Teaks looked relieved. "We're off their radar, thank God. Nothing like those poor British labs who have to deal with the Primate Liberation Front. Those nuts are terrorizing researchers, threatening lives. Besides, we bring our chimps in at night, through a back entrance. I feel sorry for the animals," he added, as if regret would make up for the experiments. "I make sure we sedate them, keep them comfortable, but in the end, Mr. Acela, we're injecting them with lethal diseases, or cutting them up."

Dr. Teaks rapped superstitiously on a wooden table. "As for security, Naturetech is quiet as a cemetery at night. The labs are sealed, even if someone gets into the building. And guards go through bags each night when our scientists leave. I told all this to Chairman Dwyer when he was here just yesterday, God rest his soul."

We studied the security system blueprints and left Teaks in his office—which he didn't like but could not overrule, under company policy—and used the blueprints as an excuse to go poking around on our own. We checked locks, security panels, cameras. I intended to cover my ass by writing a full report on Naturetech's security system, to make my trip here look legit. We buttonholed staffers, but clearly they'd been ordered not to discuss work with strangers. They always referred us back to Dr. Teaks, with an embarrassed smile or shrug.

"He's holding back, but about what?" Danny said. "I keep remembering Schwadron's crack about Pearl Harbor. Surprise attack."

"I didn't like that either."

"You're thinking terrorism?"

"Well, chem or biological weapons," I said. "Teaks says they don't do that here, but he wouldn't be allowed to tell us if they did, not without permission."

The labs were clean. The ventilation system secured. There were no big tunnels for water or wiring and no easy exits to the roof. As we checked the alarm system, an intercom announcement summoned us urgently back to Teaks's office. We ignored it.

The mechanical room, with its coolers, gas lines and air-filtration equipment, looked to be in top shape.

We'd spotted no files, labels or reports that made mention of HR-109.

"Attention! Attention! Will Michael Acela and Daniel Whiteagle please report to Dr. Teaks's office immediately!"

"This is just like high school after I broke into the cafeteria," Danny said, "and got caught eating space pops."

I'd canceled dinner with Kim and told her I'd drop by her apartment after a "business meeting." I'd made sure she'd have security outside her apartment tonight. I'd left a message for Hoot to see if she'd discovered yet what house research project HR-109 was. No reply.

"Attention! All Naturetech staffers! If you know the whereabouts of Michael Acela or Daniel Whiteagle, please call Dr. Teaks!"

Danny and I entered the animal holding area in B wing, to find five primates—three baby chimps and two long-limbed spider monkeys—looking sleek, fed and drugged in cages. The closest chimp watched us with terrible yearning in its eyes.

"I hate that we cut these guys up," I said, sounding like Teaks, I guess. "But my mom was sick for twenty years. I'd rather an animal died if it saved human lives."

Danny looked tired. "Do you think Schwadron knew about the surprise attack on you?"

"That's a stretch."

I heard running footfalls outside in the hallway, heavy ones that might come from boots. Except none of the people I'd seen here wore boots. The footsteps were coming closer. Naturetech seemed to be experiencing another problem today.

The most alert-looking chimp stood up in its little

cage, its brown eyes locked on mine. It stuck out its hand as if seeking contact. I imagined more knowledge in those eyes than I'd be comfortable with him having. I wanted to touch the hand and comfort him but had no idea what injections this animal had received, what disease it might be carrying.

Out in the hallway the footsteps ran past the door.

The chimp mewed as I turned away, trying to regain my attention. I said, "Did Schwadron offer a bribe or a favor back there, do you think?"

"What's the difference?"

"And what does he want back?"

"Only love from you, I'm sure," Danny said. "Maybe he was really blown away by you after six whole minutes. Some people make terrific first impressions."

"It's not smart to wise off to your boss."

"Or what? You'll fire me? Do that and I'll call you up on discrimination charges and won't follow you into bathrooms anymore."

"Ah!" announced Teaks's voice from the doorway. "*Here* you are, gentlemen."

He looked decidedly unhappy entering the room, flushed and urgent, and I was shocked to see the reason why. Three soldiers walked in behind him. A lieutenant and two specialists. The specialists had sidearms out.

"May I see your ID, sir?" the lieutenant asked. He was young, blond, and looked efficient and suspicious.

Instead of complying, I shot back, "This is company property. What gives you the right to demand IDs?"

I knew that Chairman Dwyer never would have consented to this had he been alive.

Teaks stepped between us, sweating openly now and eager to defuse a confrontation. "Please, Lieutenant, let me explain to Mr. Acela. Lenox just called. The army is apparently going to be helping out with security here."

"Taking over," the lieutenant corrected.

"To protect cancer research? Or the chimpanzees?" Danny asked.

"To keep unauthorized visitors out," the officer replied politely, but with a steely tone, producing an access roster that listed the names of all personnel permitted on the property today. I looked it over. Of course, I wasn't on it. I'd never been frozen out of security work at one of our own facilities before.

"This is outrageous," I said. "What happened here yesterday?"

"Take it up with Chairman Keating," Dr. Teaks said, hustling us from the room and toward the exit. His staffers were going about their normal business. But in the lobby I saw that my Security guard at the badge gate had been replaced by a soldier. Outside, in the driveway, I saw more Lenox guards getting into their private cars and leaving the grounds. Soldiers had taken up positions at the entrance gate, and a soldier with a German shepherd walked the front perimeter fence. The lieutenant and Dr. Teaks walked Danny and me to the gate, where a taxi waited.

Dr. Teaks shook my hand as if ending a normal visit.

"It's hard to believe that Chairman Dwyer killed himself," he said, as if he'd just remembered he should have said it earlier. "Terrible. Awful thing. It's like the whole world is going to hell."

Ninety minutes later, in the Delta Shuttle again, at twenty thousand feet, Danny counted possibilities on his big fingers as he summed up.

"One, *soldiers*. Something happened at Naturetech yesterday and Teaks was ordered not to talk about it. Two, Keating or Schwadron lied about the dinner. Then Keating threatens to fire you. Schwadron offers a job. Three, the lovely daughter wants to meet you later. Her dad died and she wants *you* there. Not a friend. Not a lover. *You*."

"Meeting was my idea, not hers."

"Meeting *tonight* was hers. And any one of these people could have sent that psycho who threatened to kill you and Kim. Who was the woman he mentioned, the one who placed the call to your phone? Hmmm?"

"You're running out of fingers."

"I don't want to depress you, Boss, but you destroyed evidence giving it to Keating. You have no proof the vial ever existed. And if it turns out Dwyer was murdered, your fingerprints are all over his house."

"No wonder no one complained when I quit the FBI."

The captain announced we'd soon be landing, and we were in the terminal twenty minutes later, passing beneath overhead monitors showing CNN—and a caption reading, "Another resignation in Washington"—as I checked phone messages and we headed toward the short-term parking lot. The first message stopped me in my tracks.

"This is Major Carl Eisner of Defense Intelligence," a blunt-sounding voice said. "Please call me as soon as possible about a matter of mutual concern."

"A major," I said, my pulse picking up. Eisner had used the old law enforcement trick of intentional vagueness to throw me off balance, which frankly was not hard to do at the moment. I remembered the Chairman's warning to himself. *Stay away from Eisner.*

"That's the guy who Keating called the second you left his office," Danny said.

I erased the message.

"I want to know more before I call him back," I said.

"Wouldn't it be great if you could push buttons and make people disappear too." Danny sighed, and stuck with me like a bodyguard as I walked to retrieve my BMW. Apparently, I saw from glimpses of other overhead monitors, the latest resignation had come from a Republican Senator and moderate swing vote on the Senate Foreign Relations Committee. She'd been fighting allegations of campaign funding improprieties and had given up and quit.

"You want to get down on your knees or should I do it?" Danny said when we reached the car.

"This is so paranoid." But I spread a handkerchief on the ground and looked under the chassis. Old FBI maxim: If you're afraid of car bombs or just tracking devices—or simply imagine the possibility—never wash your car, so you can see fingerprints in the dust coating. And keep the driver's door open when you turn the ignition, so if a bomb goes off you'll be blown free.

Cheery thoughts for the terrorist age.

"Tomorrow we start carrying guns," I said.

"Cancel Gabrielle. See Kim," Danny advised as I straightened up, having found nothing.

"I told you, Danny. It's business."

"Kim spent all day reconstructing Dwyer's schedule. She knew him better than anyone, better than his daughter. So why isn't seeing *her* business too?"

"I don't think I'll get another shot at Gabrielle."

"That's what I mean." Danny sighed and held out his huge hand. "Give me your house key."

I had it out already. In light of all that had happened today, he would check my home while I dined with Gabrielle. He'd sit outside in his car a while, watch the house, then knock on neighbors' doors and ask if there had been any strangers or repair vans on the block today. Eventually he'd let himself in and check phones, bookcases, night tables. I'd do the same thing when I got home.

"Don't break anything," I said. But I was calmer. The confrontation at Naturetech seemed farther away.

"Let's see who shows up at your house while you're at dinner," Danny said.

"Gabrielle doesn't know where I live, Danny."

"She had an innocent air."

I told Danny to get an independent backgrounder on Naturetech, and a list of spas near Middleburg, and confirm that Gabrielle had been there last night. Then I gave him the security alarm code at my house, and told him the location of the keypad, on the left side of the front door, over the umbrella stand.

"Hey, those numbers are Kim's birthday," he said, grinning. "What a coincidence."

"Go to hell," I told him, and got into my car.

What is it about friendship between a man and a pretty woman? Everyone thinks it's impossible to maintain, but they're wrong. What's so hard about going to ball games with a woman, palling around with her, even if she's good-looking, helping her if she's in trouble the same way you'd help any friend? Being an adult means being able to control your urges, and enjoy friendship with a female without unbuckling your pants.

It's not like I'm seventeen years old, I thought as the cell phone chimed. I was driving across the Triboro Bridge in heavy traffic, toward the lights of Manhattan.

"It's Hoot," she said, sounding upset. "Those assholes won't let me go home until you come to the office. All because of HR-109."

"What did you find out?"

"Nazi bastards. They are so mean!"

I told her to slow down and tried to calm her. I asked who was keeping her in the office and learned that Keating had chewed out Ralph Kranz, head of Research, after Hoot had penetrated his department security. Hoot had walked Kranz through gaps in his system. Instead of appreciating it, Kranz had gotten mad.

"He made fun of my nose stud in front of everyone," she said. "What is it about people? If you have the mental facility of a pea but dress nice, everyone thinks you're a genius."

"I'll be there soon. Did you get the file?"

"What do you think, I burned it?"

I left a message for Gabrielle Dwyer at the restaurant— her home number being unlisted—saying that I was in New York and would meet her a little late. Traffic eased on the FDR and I made the trip downtown in twenty minutes, but I'd been up for a long time without sleep. I was tired, and had no patience with Kranz.

I hate executives who take frustrations out on subordinates—or waiters, toll takers, janitors, messengers. Clearly Ralph Kranz had been embarrassed by the security lapse. But there was no need to humiliate Hoot.

I found her alone in a conference room, sullen as a

teenager sitting through high school detention, and looking like one in her black jeans, black T-shirt, black Converses and black socks. The nose stud was silver and so was her lone pendulum earring. Her black glasses accentuated the owl look. Despite her tough words on the phone, the faint sweat smell told me Kranz had been chewing her out and she was hurt. Hoot had the brain of Einstein and the heart of a kid.

"Here's your stupid file," she said.

I started to open it but Kranz walked in, a small man in his late thirties with a puffed-out chest. He was a balding, pear-shaped, white-shirted Napoleon, the kind of management guy who lords it over subordinates and assumed he and I would never show differences, no matter how vast, in front of Hoot. To him, we were of a class, like parents who were not supposed to show disagreements before children. Even if two management guys tried to disembowel each other in private, in public they were supposed to pretend—Kranz felt—that management is always right.

"I'm sure you had no idea how your people dress when you're not around," Kranz started off, pretending to give me an out when really he was implying that I lost control of things the minute I left the office. By lecturing me in front of one of my staff, he figured he was demeaning me.

"Sloppy in dress, sloppy in mind," I said. "That kind of thing, right?"

I had little patience for this after all that had happened today. I'd hated office politics at the FBI too. Kranz's voice dripped with insincere camaraderie. "I'm sure you'll agree that there's a certain image to be—"

I cut him off by turning to Hoot.

"Next time someone besides me orders you to do things, you don't have to listen. You work for me."

Hoot sat up straighter.

I added, "You didn't have to stay here. You could have gone home."

She looked from my face to Kranz's. Then she smiled. It was a nice smile.

Kranz looked stunned, and I felt sorry for anyone who worked for him. I told him, "Ralph, Hoot was hired to keep hackers out of our system. She found a hole in your system, so she's done her job. Apparently you haven't done yours."

"She's . . . she's supposed to ask before running a test."

"That's your security plan? Hackers ask permission and you say no?"

Hoot snorted with laughter and Kranz went purple. "There's no need to talk to people like that," he said.

"That's my point."

I terminated Kranz's game by telling Hoot it was time to go. We left him standing in the conference room, stunned, humiliated, furious.

"Sorry I got you into trouble," Hoot said in the elevator. But she looked thrilled, so I figured, What's so bad about making one more enemy today if it keeps up department morale?

"Next time, ask," I ordered, mindful of Keating's orders. "But you did a good job." I opened the file finally, riffling through the other projects to get a glimpse of HR-109, and realizing that after all the trouble I'd created getting this, there was no way of knowing if the file even had anything to do with the Chairman's death.

"It's about a fish," Hoot said, looking over my shoulder as I noted the name of the project's creator, a freelance scientist named Asa Rodriguez in Key West. "Isn't that funny? A whole project on one tropical fish."

A fish would be studied at Naturetech, I thought.

The elevator door opened. Hoot and I walked out into the lobby, alone.

"A fish?" Apparently Lenox had given Asa Rodriguez a small grant to search for some fish. I couldn't even pronounce the scientific name of the thing.

"It has a drug in its spines—y'know, for protection," she said as I looked over a sketch showing a small sleek fish with a riot of crimson spines on top. "Except the poison halts arthritis too, not just kills the fish's enemies. Well, that was the theory. It didn't work. Isn't it weird where medicines come from?"

In her relief, Hoot was rambling. "I guess if Native Americans could find medicines in forests, Lenox can come up with drugs from coral reefs too."

My eyes fixed on the name of the lab where the arthritis trials had been held.

"Naturetech," I said. "Shit."

How come Dr. Teaks said he'd never heard of HR-109?

I had a headache. I hadn't eaten. I was tired, and reaching for connections, trying to find threads.

At any given time, I knew, Lenox is funding—fully or partially—over a thousand searches for new drugs. Less than one half of one percent of these projects work out.

Could a rare fish be connected to Dwyer's death?

The ticking in my head grew louder as questions multiplied. *Could HR-109 still be active, which is why the file was missing, and why Teaks lied?*

I knew that a company that came up with an arthritis cure would make billions annually, and so would investors and scientists who would share in the profits.

But why would troops guard an arthritis project? It makes no sense.

I went down to my car when Hoot walked off, and checked my messages again. Carl Eisner had called two more times, sounding increasingly angry.

"You really should call back," he said in the last message, which sounded more like a threat.

Well, I'd call after I read more of the file. As I opened it, eager to learn the details of HR-109, I had a vision of that chimp in the cage in Maryland, reaching out to me. A doomed creature—maybe one intentionally given a terrible disease—seeking comfort and contact and touching only cold bars.

Of course, Gabrielle Dwyer called at that moment, before I started to read.

"It's eight-twenty. I'm at the restaurant. I'm tired and it's been a bad day."

She didn't sound tired. She sounded sexy. Pouty. Beautiful. Maybe it was the memory of that braid, I thought. There was something about that long braid: the soft shine of it, the tight way it hung down so far that it brushed the swell of her ass. I wanted to touch the braid and untie it. I wanted to see what her hair looked like when the braid became undone. Just her voice had restarted the vibration inside. Everything about that woman appealed to me—at least physically.

Oh, Michelangelo. Drawn to fire again.

Reaching to start the BMW, I told myself I'd read the file after dinner. If I wanted to ask Gabrielle questions and get real answers, I'd better hurry. It was clear that she was not the patient type.

But, distracted by the thought of her, I'd missed

quick-approaching movement to my left. My key wasn't in the ignition yet and the men—at least two, I saw—were close, and now I heard the slap of running footsteps on the right side too.

You won't see me next time, the man who'd followed me this morning had said.

I fumbled for the key, trying to get away, but I was too late, too slow, and a voice at the window shouted, "Freeze! You! Now! Freeze!"

I saw the gun before I saw the man behind it. He looked as scared as I was, standing feet planted, both arms out in G shooter style, and it sank in that he wore a dark rumpled suit, not an expensive one.

Feds.

The voice saying, "With one hand, slowly, unlock the door."

My heart sounded louder than the swoosh of the door opening. There were three of them in all, a blond and two dark-haired guys. Beyond them, as far as I could see, this level of garage was deserted.

"Out of the car," the blond ordered, and now I recognized the voice from my cell phone. It was Carl Eisner, the man who had claimed to be with Defense Intelligence.

The face I looked into was blocky and thirtiesh, freckled, a Midwestern face, freshly shaven and blunt-featured below a crew cut, but it was also worn, lined prematurely, filled with harshness that accentuated the sense of menace coming from this man.

"You're tough to find," Eisner said, rifling through my glove compartment as a second man pulled me from the car and the third man popped the trunk.

"Get out of there. What are you looking for?" I said, hearing from my own mouth words I had always before associated with suspects, not law enforcement.

"Leave your expensive car here," Eisner sneered. "You're coming with us."

SEVEN

The unmarked townhouse was on 26th Street, near the Hudson River. The private two-car garage made Eisner's black Ford disappear. The remodeling job inside included hermetically sealed doors, carpets to mute footsteps and bulletproofed, soundproofed windows, probably thanks to the new Patriot Act. The I-room where I faced Eisner across a small walnut table was bare, and painted a soft gray "comfort shade" that FBI psych consultants in the nineties had recommended to relax suspects. The air-conditioning vents would hide the mikes and camera. The track lighting was bright and hot.

"Explain it again, Mike. Why spend so much time at Dwyer's house before calling the police?"

"To make sure nothing damaging to the company was lying around. It's my job."

"It's important to keep the company safe, you mean."

"I couldn't save him."

Eisner nodded. "It was especially important to protect Lenox this morning, after such a terrible event."

"That's what I've been trying to say," I said.

Eisner leaned toward me. He'd not advised me of my rights, not handcuffed me. He was a large man, all bone and muscle. He had the sunburned face of a farmer and the shoulders of a linebacker. His hand wrapped a coffee mug that said BEST UNCLE. The cords in his wrist stood out.

"I'm more interested in what you're not saying," he said. "Where's the disk, Mike?"

"Disk?"

"As in: 'Put S in the bank. Avoid Eisner. Give Mike the disk.' "

The blood drained from my face. "The police gave you the list?"

"I ask the questions. You gave up that right when you went private. You handed in your credentials, Mike, exchanged them for that nice BMW we left behind."

"I never even saw any disk."

He made a derisive sound in the back of his throat. "Then explain why you didn't notify your new chairman of the death, and why you went romping off to Washington afterward."

His hair was thick and crew cut, the sideburns out of style. His posture was iron. The blue eyes were flat and bright and remained absolutely focused, in a permanent squint, as if he'd spent too much time in the sun or as if anger so saturated his personality that it had drawn in his synapses. Large nose. Small ears. Stubble patch beneath his round chin, as if his mind had been elsewhere when he shaved.

"I didn't go 'romping off,' " I said. "My job was done at the Chairman's house. I have other duties too."

From his accent, I placed this man from a Rust Belt state, Ohio or Pennsylvania, where factories were failing, cities deteriorating, unemployment lines filled with embittered third-generation Poles and Serbians whose grandparents had moved halfway around the world, only to watch their children lose work.

I hadn't called Lenox to tell them I'd been taken here, hadn't demanded a lawyer. If I did—if Eisner even allowed it—Bob Czerny would show up, demand to sit in and instruct me on when to respond to questions, when to shut up.

I didn't want to shut up. I wanted answers too.

"Why is Defense Intelligence so interested in the suicide?" I asked.

"Is that what you insist it was, Mike?"

"Why are you interested in a drug company?"

"A small matter. A forty-million-dollar overpayment to Lenox. Presto, change-o, public money disappears!"

"Eisner, if I were trying to hide things, why would I give the police the list?"

"Because you knew he had a similar one in the safe in his office. You knew your name would come up either way."

Eisner held up his palms. "Hey, I'm just one ignorant guy. I wasn't there. *You* were. You were in that house twice last night. Didn't you get what you wanted the first time around? That detective—Berg—thought you took something. He said you hesitated when he asked."

"I didn't take anything."

"Maybe you didn't mean to. Maybe you put it in a pocket by *accident*. Lots of times people put things in pockets absentmindedly and find them hours later."

"I guess when you spoke to Keating today, he told you the disk you want wasn't in Dwyer's safe."

Eisner smiled. I had the feeling he could sit here for hours, losing no energy, waiting for a crack in my composure—a slip, a tell, a bead of sweat rewarding his doggedness by running down my face.

"Let's go back to last night. Don't you think it odd for Dwyer to invite his head of Security to his home at night, unless it was something urgent?"

"Not with him."

"Both you guys aren't married . . ."

"Don't even go there."

"Well, ten at night, Mike. You said you were at his house for ninety minutes, Mike. An hour and a half strikes me as a long time to get instructions from your boss, Mike."

"I told you. He likes to talk. The disk you think I took, does it have anything to do with HR-109?"

The briefest flare lit Eisner's irises and then subsided, and I saw myself reflected in his eyes, small and straight-backed and looking tougher than I felt.

"That woman who works for you—Hoot—she's Iranian, isn't she? A Muslim?"

"I'm not going to honor that with an answer."

"And that assistant of yours, the big Mohawk, has cousins in AIM, the subversive Indian movement."

"And your ancestor tried to overthrow King Leopold in 1205 in Belgium, I bet."

Stay away from Eisner, the Chairman wrote. *Well, I'm not telling him a damn thing.*

"Time," Eisner said, leaning forward, still ignoring my query, but if he had no knowledge of HR-109, he would have asked about it. "Like this morning. You leave Keating's office and need two hours to make a twenty-minute drive to La Guardia. The shuttle to Washington leaves hourly but you don't go right off."

"I made phone calls in the airport."

"Then you reach Washington and go straight to Na-turetech to conduct a security check," he said in a tone that told me he knew I'd lied. "No side trips. Right?"

"Right."

So he didn't know about my trip to the Dirksen Building.

Eisner said, "But Dr. Teaks said you arrived at Naturetech almost two hours after landing. It's a forty-minute drive."

"I got caught in traffic."

"Because of an accident or road construction?"

I shrugged, knowing he would call the DC and Maryland police and check any story. "Traffic just stopped and then started moving again, out of the blue."

Eisner lifted his mug but didn't drink. "I bet you have a taxi receipt for the trips, though. For reimbursement. The receipts will have times. I never met an exec that doesn't keep receipts."

"I forgot to ask for one."

He smiled without warmth. "You're forgetting a lot. I hope your company provides Alzheimer's medicine to employees."

"I was upset about Dwyer. Normally I get receipts."

"Well, maybe you don't *need* receipts anymore because you have so *much* money of your own. Maybe you pay all these little expenses yourself. That disk is worth a lot to people. You a patient man, Mike?"

"At the moment, no."

"I ask because if I were the one called in the middle of the night by my boss, I'd be angry. I mean, you're in the middle of a fun evening. Restaurant. Girlfriend. Getting laid, Mike. Then suddenly the damn phone rings and you have to drop everything. The great chief wants to chat."

I wanted to punch that face.

"It wasn't like that."

"He was a talker, you said. He calls when he feels like it and you rush over and he talks. Hell, Mike, I'd quit a job like that. I'd have resentments, is what I mean."

"What gives me resentments is guys in parking lots with guns. Guys suggesting I'd sell my company's secrets."

Eisner lifted his mug and upended it so his neck muscles moved, and I had the feeling, hearing the liquid go down, that there was no pleasure in consumption for him. The drink was merely fuel, like gasoline going into a car. With this man, nourishment powered rage.

He said, "People cause their own problems and blame someone else. All you had to do was call me back. But you were stuck in traffic, doing nothing, but still too busy to pick up a phone."

"All this because I didn't call back?"

"You're an ex-Fed, Mike. You know what it means to ignore a call."

Gabrielle Dwyer must have left the restaurant by now, I knew. I wondered how I could find her. I needed to talk to her.

"Did you and I ever meet before?" I asked with real curiosity. "In Washington? Is there something I'm missing? Because I'm getting the feeling this is personal with you."

He slammed the mug on the table.

"You know," he said, "last year I had a man in this room, in that very chair. A guy like you, ex–Air Force Procurement who'd gone private, become a weapons shipper. Taken Uncle Sam's training and made a side deal with a Saudi to slip half a dozen stolen shoulder-fired missiles onto a ship bound for Tunis and the Blue Jihad. By the time I finished with him he was crying, swearing he didn't know where the missiles were going. He said the Saudi told him the destination was South America, the Saudi insisted the missiles were going to a legitimate government, to be used for self-defense. I believed that part because I know that's how guys like you live with yourselves. You sell out and convince yourself that no one will be hurt because of things you do."

Eisner had surprised me. He sounded like he meant it. He'd gotten to me also but not in the way he thought. I remembered the bugs I'd planted at the Chairman's insistence, three years ago. I'd told myself back then that breaking the law for Lenox was for the greater good, that no innocent people would be hurt. I still wondered about it sometimes, though, if I'd gone too far.

I may ask you to stretch the law again, the Chairman had said last night. Why?

"That man is in Leavenworth," Eisner continued, misinterpreting my discomfort, "along with half a dozen other turncoats I've tracked down. Ex–Justice Department. Ex–Homeland Security."

"What is on the disk that you think I stole?" I asked him. "Lenox's formula for sunblock or chewable aspirin?"

"I could be wrong. But your prints were all over that house. You were the last one to see him alive. You disappeared for hours today, and frankly you don't seem to have a record of loyalty to people you work for."

"Who are you to question my loyalty? And I'm *not* the last one who saw him alive," I said, locking eyes.

Eisner pushed back from the desk and stood up. There was latent force in the man, and I wasn't about to accept his words at face value either. I even wondered if it was possible that he'd sent the ex-Marine who'd followed me to Flushing Meadows Park today. Maybe that guy was *still* a Marine. Eisner wasn't going to cow me into talking to him. I'd do it when I was ready, if it was right.

"Just a theory," Eisner said. "He lets you in, so the house alarm was never triggered. You press your Sig Sauer—the one you have a license for—to his head and offer him a choice. Hand the disk over or else. Then write a note, chew some drugs, go to sleep without pain."

"You need to work on your people skills," I said. And then I tested him. "Or maybe you were the one looking for that disk last night."

His rage was immense, and it infuriated me. I'd seen agents sour on suspects at the FBI, get a bug for a suspect, decide on misguided instinct or misread evidence, or for personal animus or even a bribe, that a particular person was going to take the blame for something. And that agent would bring the full might of the Bureau to bear on the target, and ruin lives, careers, families, years.

It happened rarely but it happened. And now I saw in this man's face a shiny, driven certainty that I recognized, abhorred and feared.

I'm going to check you out too, I thought.

I said, "I was home, sleeping. You like checking times? Check the time I drove back to Brooklyn, and paid the toll on my E-ZPass. Check the time on your watch now, because this interview is through."

"Wait."

We were standing, eyeing each other like wrestlers about to lunge, and suddenly I wondered if he had the power to keep me from walking out of this room. Defense Intelligence can do things to suspects I'd never been permitted to do at the FBI. Under the newest Patriot Act, Congress has given Intelligence agencies unprecedented peacetime powers. I wondered if Eisner's men were outside, ready to stop me in the hall.

But he surprised me again. "My people don't believe me yet, not yet, but I'm authorized to offer a deal."

I flashed to the man who had followed me this morning

and made an offer for a disk too. Did he work for Eisner? I wondered again.

"How much?" I said.

"Amnesty."

"The Chairman was my friend," I said, reaching for the knob, wondering if it would turn.

"You'll go home free. Tell me everything you know. But now. Right now. One-time offer only."

I pushed the door open and saw an empty hallway.

"What does Defense Intelligence care about arthritis?" I said.

"Arthritis," he said, moving toward me, coming so close that I could feel the heat off his body and smell the dry-cleaning chemicals on his shirt. "You know, I'm glad you didn't take the deal. And I forgot to tell you, your passport's on the watch list, so if you're planning on traveling, stay out of the international terminal. It won't do you much good."

I couldn't believe how normal the night looked when I walked outside finally.

I couldn't believe the city looked the same. But I knew it wasn't the same anymore.

Oh, Mike, we've been worried about you. Danny and I have been trying to call you."

Five minutes later I was on my cell phone, in a cab, heading back to Lenox to get my car. I was talking to Kim Pendergraph, trying to keep the anger from my voice. Now that I was alone I admitted to myself that Eisner had terrified me. It was ten-thirty. Gabrielle Dwyer had long ago left the restaurant. The maître d' didn't have her home number but Kim might know it. Her iPod contained most phone numbers the Chairman had used.

"Danny's here," she said. "He said Defense Intelligence went through your house. They had a warrant."

I closed my eyes and felt the hard bumping motion as the cab hit potholes. I imagined Eisner's guys opening drawers in my home, unzipping cushions, planting bugs in phone lines, tromping through my tomato garden outside.

"Did they do damage?"

"Danny said they left it like they found it, but they took away your gun, for tests, they said. Danny refused to get out until they were done."

In a way, I was grateful Eisner had done this. As my sense of violation grew, fury drove my fear away.

"Kim, do you have a home phone number for Gabrielle Dwyer?"

There was a pause, and her voice grew cooler. "Why?"

I told her Gabrielle had been my scheduled "business meeting" earlier. I said I'd run into Dwyer's daughter in Washington and she'd promised to talk about him tonight.

"Love that braid," Kim said softly, using a tone—a special woman's tone—perfected to verbally disembowel opponents. "That's her nickname in the secretarial area. Nose up. Back straight. Princess Braid."

"I told you, it was supposed to be a business dinner."

Kim gave me the number. Then she said, slightly contrite, "Have you eaten? I made lemon pasta. There's plenty left."

I got through to Gabrielle's answering machine and started leaving a message. "Sorry I didn't show up. I had a run-in with Defense Intelligence—"

Instantly I heard a click on the line and her real voice: quiet, intense, intrigued.

"About my father?"

"They're looking at what happened to him."

"I don't understand. Defense Intelligence?" She sounded rattled. Concerned.

"That's what I'm trying to figure out too. And why the army's taken over security at one of our labs near Washington. I couldn't call you earlier. Kim Pendergraph gave me your number."

Over the line and in the background I heard cool saxophone tones. Coltrane was playing "You Are So Beautiful." I envisioned Gabrielle on a couch, barefoot, in a sleeping gown. Her braid was undone. Lights were low. Her hair fell freely over her shoulders and framed her face in black. The hair rose and fell with the swell of her breasts.

Abruptly, I could smell her perfume in the cab.

"How about breakfast tomorrow?" she asked.

"Sure."

"Nine A.M.?" She gave me an address in the East Village, off Broadway, near Cooper Union. "Do you like bagels and scrambled eggs, Mike?"

"Who doesn't?"

"With onions and cheddar cheese? Hot coffee? Orange juice?"

I was surprised she was going to cook it, surprised to hear solicitousness in her. She was worried, all right. This was a softer voice from the one I'd heard in Washington. At least I had something for which to thank Carl Eisner.

"I'll bring something sweet," I said.

When I hung up, the phone felt warm in my hand, alive, and I saw the driver's eyes on mine in the rearview mirror. Something in my voice had drawn his gaze. Driving strangers around, maybe he listened to their voices the way other people tuned in to talk radio. Maybe he tried to guess life stories based on accents, cadence, smiles, mood.

The driver's eyes drifted back to the West Side Highway. But I could see in the rearview mirror that he was smiling. He was thinking, I just heard the voice of a man imagining a woman in his arms.

Then self-preservation kicked in and I told the driver that I'd changed my mind about our destination. With Eisner's people watching me, or waiting at the garage, I was not going to retrieve the BMW tonight, and I was not going home.

I told the driver to head toward City Hall.

Go left, turn right, change lanes *now,* I told him. I didn't see any vehicles following, but that didn't mean they weren't good at it, weren't there.

I had the driver drop me near the Brooklyn Bridge, four blocks from Kim's apartment.

"Nice night to walk over to the Heights," I told him, and started off on foot toward the bridge's pedestrian path, making sure no one was behind me.

After the cab turned the corner, I counted to twenty, then reversed myself and walked west. No cars turned around.

K im Pendergraph had bought her Tribeca loft the way she did most things in her life, sensibly. At least that's the way she'd made decisions since giving birth to her son, Chris, as a 19-year-old single mom, a decade and a half ago. Three years back she'd purchased the 1,600-

square-foot space on Reade Street at an insider's price when the old rental was converted, borrowed money interest free from the Chairman, splurged to make the purchase and never looked back.

Walking up Reade Street, I felt a jolt of alarm when I spotted a broad-shouldered silhouette in the recessed doorway of a closed pizza shop opposite her building. Then a hand waved from the shadows. A face moved into the lamplight.

It was one of my security staff, guarding Kim.

An old-style cage elevator carried me to the fourth floor and opened directly into her apartment. I walked into a high, tin-ceilinged loft, with polished pine floors, faux Doric columns, and a wall of meshed-glass windows looking out at a penthouse roof garden on a converted spice factory across the street.

"You look pissed off, Boss," Danny said.

Kim had created smaller "rooms" inside the big one by arranging furniture. Twin brown leather couches faced each other over a pine coffee table stacked with *Atlantic* and *Time* magazines. Woven multicolored Appalachian throw rugs brightened the floor. Three comfortable-looking sitting chairs were arrayed in one corner, where another coffee table displayed photo books on bicycling and skiing, Kim's hobbies. The exposed-brick east wall supported one long floor-to-ceiling bookshelf, packed with volumes and photos of Kim and 15-year-old Chris: at the zoo, the planetarium, on a hiking vacation in Costa Rica, at the Chairman's summer home in the Hamptons, which he loaned to them for a week each July.

"Have some wine," Kim said, putting a goblet in my hand.

The bedrooms were glassed-in and visible from the

rustic country-kitchen area, where Danny, Kim and I sat at a Mexican pine table minutes later eating her lemon pasta, tomato and mozzarella salad and drinking oak-flavored Oregon Pinot Noir. Kim spent her bonuses on this place.

"Did Eisner mention that he was with Keating for an hour this morning?" Danny said. "He comes out and he's after you. His guys asked me if you belong to any political organizations. If you travel overseas a lot. If you're in contact with anyone you used to investigate."

"We have eleven factories overseas," I said, disgusted.

Kim said, "He asked me about Hoot and Danny. There's extra lemon in the pasta, the way you like."

She was in denim tonight, as usual, denim shorts and a long-tailed shirt. She had a petite, delicate-looking ex–ballet dancer's body. Small hands. Small nose. Small breasts. Her hair was cut close, low at the nape, high at the forehead, glossy brown with a hint of rust. Her eyes were the pale blue of New England ice. At home she almost always wore lots of thin silver bracelets from Arizona or New Mexico. And her lithe way of moving drew male glances on the street. Barefoot now, she kept her Vermont farm girl's calm, an appealing ability to seem at home with whatever rhythms dominated nearby space.

The effect was of someone in quiet control, always at home, always open to new experiences.

"Did Eisner or his guys say anything about HR-109?" I asked.

"No."

Kim shook her head. "I never heard of it either. But tell me what you know, Mike. I hear things sometimes."

I tasted the lemon pasta. The linguini was flavored with the zest of citrus, freshly grated black pepper, heavy cream and ultra-fine sea salt and fresh Romano cheese. It was a meal to make problems go away for a little while.

When I told Kim that HR-109 was supposed to fight arthritis, she nodded, but it was just her way of processing information. When I mentioned the name of the researcher, Asa Rodriguez, she sat up, excited. "I remember him! He came to the office a few months back!"

"*Dwyer's* office?" I asked, surprised. In the company hierarchy, a freelance researcher is lowest of the low.

Kim nodded. "He walked in off the street. The guard called up, said a researcher was here and wanted to talk to Dwyer. Everyone knows about his open-door policy. If you have a company ID, sooner or later you can usually get in."

"Why did Rodriguez visit the Chairman?"

"He looked like an old hippie," Kim said. "He'd flown up from Key West on his own dime. His project had been canceled. His story was amazing. I mean, a drug from a fish?"

"Did Dwyer see him?"

"I remember them all," Kim said, half standing and reaching for a pitcher of ice water. I couldn't help but admire the tight movements of her ass. "A guy from the loading dock. A secretary. People take advantage of the open-door policy all the time, but I'm the one who decides who gets in. I hate having to turn people away."

"I know," I said. Kim could ramble sometimes, and she spoke of Dwyer as if he still lived.

"I didn't turn *him* away. He was *insistent*. He said there'd been a mistake on his project and he didn't care if Dwyer was busy. He'd wait and not bother anyone. *Just give me ten minutes with him,* he kept saying. He was forceful. He came back the next day and brought a sand-wich. He waited for two days."

"Did he tell you what the mistake was?" I asked, my curiosity rising.

"I remember he said he got interested in finding new drugs because he's allergic to about a thousand things. He quit NIH because his department head was pompous. He had a theory that—"

Danny broke in. "Kim. Please."

Kim leaned forward, eyes bright, happy when helping people.

"It's astounding, really," she said over the rumble of a passing truck outside. "You know how sometimes Lenox finds drugs in rain forests?"

I sighed. I ate. You couldn't rush her.

Kim was a walking encyclopedia of pharmaceutical information. She had an eager love of knowledge that I've found in self-educated people who never went to college. "Pilocarpine, against glaucoma," she said, "comes from the jacaranda bush in the Amazon. Glaziovine, an antide-pressant. The bark of the Oregon yew tree can cure ovar-ian cancer."

"Get to Asa Rodriguez," Danny begged.

"Well, he'd been freelancing in the old National Can-cer Institute search for cures in rain forests and coral reefs. Any poison that a plant or animal uses for defense might turn out to kill disease too. When the project lost funding, he kept working by himself. He had a theory. See, he lives in Key West, where treasure hunters found that old galleon, the *Atocha*. Remember? They looked for fifteen years and brought up four hundred million dollars of treasure."

"What does treasure have to do with medicine?" Danny broke in.

"I thought Indians are supposed to be patient."

"Where'd you get that dumb idea?"

"Maybe *you* want to tell the story."

"Stop it," I said. "Both of you."

"Sorry," she said. "Well, Asa said the man who found the *Atocha* did it by flying to Madrid and poring through old records from the fifteen hundreds, to figure out where the galleons sank. Asa figured he'd try it with *medical* records. He got a grant to check logs that Columbus brought back from the Caribbean. His idea was to see whether any Caribbean tribes—the ones the Spanish killed off later—passed on knowledge of medicines from the sea."

"Good idea," Danny said thoughtfully, rubbing his cheek. "My great-grandmother used to pick this weed on Long Island. Whenever my brothers and I got a sore throat—"

"Oh, now *you* want to tell stories," Kim said, grinning.

Danny laid his big hand on her small shoulder. He said, "I'm telling you, Mike," meaning that I was a fool for not loving this woman.

"Telling him what?" she asked.

"Go on," I said.

"Secrets," Kim sniffed. "Asa flies to Madrid, and sure enough, he digs up references to a fish that, when you grind up the spines, is supposed to cure pain in the hands. He figured that meant arthritis. He got a grant from Lenox, just a couple thousand dollars, to try to find the fish."

"Which he did," I prodded, fascinated.

"After four years. He found it in some newly discovered coral reef but didn't say where. He processed the cartilage according to the instructions and sent the residue to Ralph Kranz, for tests."

"Kranz," I said dryly, the ticking in my head growing louder. "I hope Asa went to Harvard, or Kranz wouldn't pay attention to him. Did Asa tell you what the residue looked like?" I envisioned the substance I'd found in the vial.

"I didn't ask."

"You're doing great," I said, but Kim frowned. She thought she'd missed something important. I asked, "What did Kranz do with the stuff?"

"Tested it, but it had no effect," Kim said, confirming what Bill Keating had told me this morning.

Disappointed, I asked, "But if it didn't work, why did Asa fly up to see the Chairman?"

"Because when Lenox canceled the project, Asa made another batch and tested it on locals in Florida. Kranz had tried it on animals. Asa found human volunteers."

"You mean it worked?" Danny asked, looking up sharply.

Kim shook her head. "It still didn't cure arthritis, but Asa said it had a side effect. *That's* why he wanted to see Dwyer. I never saw anyone that excited in my life."

My heartbeat picked up. She reached for her wine and Danny and I said in unison, in the silence, *"Side effect?"*

So many huge pharmaceutical finds, I knew, had started out geared one way and shown beneficial side effects. Viagra had been tested as a drug to reoxygenate blood. Minoxidil, which regrew hair, had been a side effect. Aspirin, the Chairman had told me once, would be a prescription drug if invented today, because it helps prevent heart attacks, not just lower fever.

So now Danny and I sat back and both felt the excitement that comes when the threads in an inquiry start combining, entwining, forming themselves into a picture.

"What kind of side effect would Defense Intelligence be monitoring?" Kim asked, frowning.

I grew alarmed, remembering the soldiers at Naturetech, and the Chairman talking about how his "mistake" could change the world.

"Biological weapon," I said. Just the words made me nervous. "That would freak them out, all right. But if Asa tested it on people in Florida, why didn't we hear about them getting sick down there, or dying?"

"It was hushed up," Kim proposed.

"Or it's an antidote," Danny said. "Lenox's contract with the Defense Department is to come up with antidotes. But if it's an antidote and Asa Rodriguez tested it on people, they would still have to be sick first. You don't think he intentionally spread a disease, do you?"

Kim shook her head violently. "I can't imagine the Chairman going along with that. He wouldn't do it. And if the drug was a weapon or antidote, why did the Chairman have it in his bathroom? What would be the point?"

Nothing about this makes sense, I thought.

I asked Kim, "Did Dr. Rodriguez show up before or after the Chairman closed the deal with the Pentagon?"

"A couple months before."

"What the hell *was* that stuff?"

"Pearl Harbor," Danny said, and the words sounded chilling now. "Schwadron said *Pearl Harbor.* I'm going with weapon or antidote. They're afraid someone stole it.

That's what's on the disk. Maybe Eisner's on the level. Maybe Dwyer had it in his medicine cabinet in case there's an attack."

I asked Kim the big question.

"What was the side effect?"

Her face fell. "He'd only tell Dwyer. They met, and called in Kranz. We put Asa up at the Plaza for the next three days. Then he went home. I bought the ticket."

"Drop it, Boss," Danny advised. "This is beyond us, and we both know what'll happen if the Feds come down on us. Defense Intelligence can lock you up forever if they're even suspicious. Stick you in prison and forget you exist. We did our best. The Chairman would be grateful. Cooperate with Eisner. Get him off your back."

"Cooperate how? He already knows about the list. He's sure I stole the disk, and for all I know, *he's* involved. Or Keating is. I'm not telling anyone anything until I know more."

Stay away from Eisner.

It was like Dwyer was in the room, cautioning me but holding back secrets. An essential part of the mystery was missing. The part the Chairman had called his terrible mistake.

"You're out of this, Danny. I'll go to Key West by myself to see if people have been getting sick there. You stay with Kim. I'll find Asa Rodriguez. Alone."

EIGHT

My dead son came to me that night in a dream. It had been happening more lately. Maybe a shrink would say I was imagining different paths in life, or lost possibilities. I rarely saw his face during visits. He manifested himself more as a talking shadow or disembodied voice, a sense that I'd turn a corner or open a door and he'd be there. Usually I sensed his presence before seeing or hearing it. Always the dread, loss and failure he inspired was the same.

"Dad! They're wrecking the garden!"

I was in my home in the dream, stepping around wreckage left by Eisner's people, sick and angry as I eyed the detritus of their violations: my FBI plaques trampled on the floor beside my rifled bookshelves; my wallet open like water wings on my desk, stripped of ID but not cash, as if Eisner were telling me that I'd sold off my legitimacy to the Chairman. The empty holster—his confiscation of my Sig—had crippled my ability to defend myself. Pill bottles lay scattered on the floor, but instead of pharmacy labels, each showed Dwyer's list glued to their front.

Stay away from Eisner! the label said.

Through the open window, my son's voice rose in fear. He sounded 10 years old tonight, but in other dreams the age varied.

"Let go of me!"

I moved too slowly to help. My muscles worked in

disproportion to my need. It took forever to take a step, as if I were running under water, and when I opened my mouth to call to him I found to my horror that my vocal cords were paralyzed. I couldn't even let him know I was there.

"I didn't live my life in a wheelchair," my son cried. "So why blame me?"

Transported by dream, I looked down from my bedroom window at my son being dragged through my garden, by the man I'd beaten up in Flushing Meadows Park. The cleats of Paul's soccer shoes cut tomato vines in half. He was small and helpless against the man's power, shaggy blond and wearing a dark blue soccer uniform with script that read, "Wendy's Pork Sausages," like a kid I'd seen kicking a ball with his dad in Verrazano Park last week. He pummeled the man's thighs with his fists. His attacker barely noticed.

I couldn't see Paul's face, as always, only a vaporous oval where it should be, as if a camera was out of focus, or a cataract was my eye's object instead of a face.

I suppose Paul came to me in different forms because I'd never known him. He'd manifest himself as whatever cameo approximation of filial love I'd noted while out that day. He might be dressed like a boy I'd seen at Lenox's father/son picnic, or a boy who'd passed on a bicycle. He might be the kid I'd noticed leaving a clothing store with his parents, wearing a small knapsack on his back.

And now, from my perch, I watched Paul's abductor drag him toward a car in which sat the dead Chairman, except his eyes were open, his face upturned, his unblinking stare fixed on mine, as if he was trying to tell me something, but I didn't know what it was. Soldiers stood near the car.

I had to keep my son from reaching the car but knew it would be impossible.

And then the man from the park was standing beside me in the bedroom at the same time he was outside, opening the door of the car. I wanted to scream. Hands pulled the boy in, while the soldiers did nothing. It was like seeing an animal disappear into a snake.

The man said from an inch away, in Eisner's voice, "I'm glad you didn't take the deal, Mike."

I woke on Kim's couch, with dawn streaming through her windows. The sheet was moist with sweat, the dream's panic a lingering drumbeat in my chest. The rumble of trucks below mixed with the sounds of horns and sirens. The day's reality began to dent the horror of the dream. I smelled coffee brewing and padded to the butcher-block counter, to find a note beside a souvenir I Love Vermont mug.

"Went running. Help yourself to coffee. Your clothes are in the dryer."

You went out alone? I thought, my fear for her skyrocketing higher than the siren sound.

Danny was gone, having returned home at midnight. I looked out the window—as I had in my dream—and my heart dropped as I recognized the Lenox security guard just standing down there—a new guy for daytime, sipping coffee, leaning against a pole, a fool in a beige suit doing nothing when he must have seen her run off alone.

Furious, I grabbed my cell phone and called the Security emergency desk. I had them punch my call through to the man downstairs. I watched him lazily flip open his phone as I pulled my pants on, cradling the set with my chin.

"Connors," the guy answered drowsily, like he needed more caffeine, his drug of choice, to wake up.

"It's Mike Acela. She went *running*. Why are you just standing there?" I barked.

He knew he'd made a mistake but he tried to talk his way out of it. "She said it was all right with you. Since you're here anyway, I figured . . ." he added, trailing off, not wanting to get personal with his boss. But the meaning was obvious. If Kim and I were lovers, and I was in her apartment, then he had to accept what she told him.

"She ran west, toward the river," Connors said, trying to make amends.

"Get a taxi. Go south along the running path. If you see her, bring her back here. I'll go the other way."

"I'm sorry, Mr. Acela."

I finished dressing and took the maddeningly slow cage elevator downstairs. I flagged a cab right away, as empty ones passed every few seconds in this neighborhood after dropping fares off at City Hall. I told the driver to get to the West Side Highway, turn right and stay in the curbside lane. I told him to move as slowly as traffic allowed. After all, the running path was across six lanes of traffic. I didn't know what Kim was wearing and lots of people were out running at six A.M.

This nightmare was real. I surveyed the joggers and power walkers along the Hudson. Early morning was popular with athletes during summer because the heat would skyrocket later, making breathing difficult. Six fucking o'clock and there had to be over a hundred type-A runners out here.

There! I saw her, alone, moving at a brisk clip.

Relief flooded me. But then I saw a familiar-looking man thirty feet behind her, loping along easily, in jogging clothes too. His jaw was bandaged and the baseball hat was different, but the build was right. It was the man from Flushing Meadows Park.

She had no idea he was there, of course. Kim looked cute and oblivious, moving at a respectable clip among the joggers, her only protection at the moment. Kim in matching green shorts and Reboks. The guy in military gray and a tank top, not even exerting himself, waiting for his opportunity. The guy like some predatory big cat behind a deer.

My taxi would pass them in a second, across the highway, and I could get out and run across to intercept her. But suddenly the cab stopped. The light had turned red. Kim and the man pulled ahead, moving quickly away.

"Run the light," I ordered the driver.

"You want me to lose my license, man?"

More joggers were now between us. And then I saw a sight that froze my heart. Kim turned off the path and was sprinting back across the highway, back to the city side. She'd be heading to Seymour's Bagels for a sesame-seed special with butter and lox. She was completely unaware of the figure behind her, crossing the road too.

I pushed the door open while the light was red. I threw a bill—I didn't see the denomination—on the front seat as I leaped out. The driver yelled, "Hey!" as car horns blared and I charged across the intersection. Kim had disappeared onto Laight Street, a block north. The man reached that corner too, and then he was out of sight as well. I was in good shape, but wore leather shoes, not sneakers. The soles slipped on the sidewalk as I ran.

Fear for her gave me energy. I heard the air pumping and my grunts and the scuff of my shoes. I pushed a man carrying a briefcase out of my way. I almost tangled up with a dogwalker. I rounded the corner—terrified that she'd be gone—and caught sight of her halfway up the block where she'd apparently stopped to jog in place and talk to a different dogwalker, a friend.

The guy behind leaned against a parked van, thirty feet back.

Kim started running again. So did the guy.

I was losing breath. Kim's friend, a redheaded woman, reacted fearfully to me as I charged toward her. She backed away. So did her tiny dog. She fumbled in a purse, probably for protective spray.

"Kim!" I shouted.

She was too far away to hear, and horns were honking on Varick. But the man heard, slowed and turned.

"Kim!"

Horns blared, but she heard me now too. She stopped. Turned. She and the man eyed each other. He was only five feet behind her. . . .

The guy spun, waved at me and sprinted north.

When I reached her, she'd turned white. "That man . . ." she said, staring off toward Varick Street. There was no way for me to catch him.

"He was the one from the park, Kim."

"But Mike . . . he was . . . How did you get here?"

I answered harshly. "You don't go running alone. Not for now. My guys will go too."

I took her arm, relieved at the realness of her beside my dream, the smoothness and the faint vanilla smell that came off her even if she was sweating.

Kim looked like she needed to sit down, so we leaned

against a parked cab. She started hyperventilating. She said, "I run each morning. I figured nothing would happen in . . . in daylight."

I put my arm around her shoulders. She leaned against me and shivered as if cold, but it was shock. "I overreacted," I said. "I didn't mean to snap. I didn't explain things before. I was worried about you."

She looked like she was five years old.

"Don't apologize for caring, Mike."

B y eight-fifty I was in a different cab, heading toward Gabrielle's apartment, when my cell phone chimed. I'd left Kim with Connors. I'd been mentally reviewing questions to ask but it was hard to concentrate. I was shaken at Kim's near-miss. But still the thought of seeing Dwyer's daughter released some powerful chemical in my blood.

"It's Danny. How was Kim's couch last night, Boss? Lumpy? Lonely?"

"I'm not in the mood," I said.

"Then I guess it was both. Worzak got back to us on the prints from the park." Danny whistled. "Rabbit team," he said.

I told the driver to turn down the radio as Danny started the recitation. "Oliver Lee Royce. Age thirty-four and originally from—ready for this?—Beverly Hills. Bad genes, bad upbringing, who knows what his problem is. Maybe his ICM agent parents dropped him on his head when he was a kid, or made him watch too much Fox TV. Anyway, he joined the Marines, all right. Secret Ops. Comes home from Afghanistan with medals and kills a lawyer outside a bar near Lejeune. The guy insulted the Detroit Tigers."

"Then why's Oliver out?"

"He claimed self-defense. The only witness who could prove otherwise picked up a blonde at a street fair, took her home and was found dead the next morning of a heart attack, but he's only thirty. Woman's gone. No description. No prints. Total vacuum job on the apartment, like she was never there. Not one damn pubic hair, his *or* hers. The autopsy lists natural causes. Ollie goes free."

"The woman who called me," I said.

"Oliver's married to Abby Hayes Royce, also from sunny California. Worzak ran their Social Security numbers, and guess what? Several trips to Amman on tourist visas. Two to Uruguay. Two to Bahrain. Tourists in Bahrain, huh? They're clean except for one other arrest of Oliver, in Buffalo, for beating up an airport security guy who gave him a hard time. He found the guy's home address, rang the bell and broke three ribs. Positive ID. Charges dropped without explanation."

"On an *airport* security beef? Do I sense the long finger of the G protecting its own?"

"These days our happy couple owns a string of lap-dancing places near sunny Camp LeJeune."

"Cash business. So who do they work for, Danny? Are they freelance, G or both?"

"Worzak doesn't know, but he heard a rumor about Abby."

"Good old Worzak."

"She was enrolled in pharmacy school when Oliver was in the service. She's a chemist. Perfect rabbit team. Ollie does the hard stuff. Abby the soft. When it's over they fuck like bunnies. I hope they never have kids."

My head hurt and my questions were multiplying. As the cab reached the Cooper Union area, I said, "What *was* that stuff in the vial?"

"You're the one who gave it away."

"Danny, if you want to get ahead in a company, it's a bad idea to constantly remind your boss of his mistakes."

"Is that the secret? I knew I was missing something. You were right to hand it to Keating."

I sighed and told Danny to go to the office as if today were normal, and tell anyone who asked that he had no idea where I'd gone.

"Don't do it alone, Boss. Worzak ran Oliver's IQ. The park screwup was a fluke. He probably figured you for a rent-a-cop. He won't make that mistake again, and she's as bad as he is, or worse."

"He went after Kim this morning. I scared him off."

I told Danny to concentrate on ongoing projects: a check on one of our lab managers in Los Angeles suspected of falsifying product test results, and an industrial espionage case in Caracas, where two top executives had been hired away by a German firm. The German had promptly announced the development of a new AIDS drug similar to the one Lenox was testing.

I promised I'd call Danny if an emergency arose.

"White man's promises. Good till the moon falls from the sky, the oceans dry up, or thirty days, whatever comes first."

"Keep Keating away from me."

"Yeah, I'll use my vast powers. By the way, have you dined with the ice queen yet? Five bucks says she doesn't touch a frying pan. She looks like the gourmet takeout kind to me."

"Make sure someone good is watching Kim. Transfer

the guy who was there this morning. And make sure the new people know how to jog, fast."

I phoned Hoot as we pulled up to Gabrielle's building, and reached her as she was heading for work. She was thrilled when I told her to turn around and call in sick today.

"Great! There's a sale at Uranus!"

"You're going to work from home. I don't want anyone looking over your shoulder. Got a pen? Look up anything you can find on an Oliver Lee Royce and Abby Hayes Royce."

I spelled the names and gave her their Social Security numbers.

"Royce is a former Marine. Abby might have gone to pharmacy school. Also, get me anything, in legitimate databases only, on a Major Carl Eisner of Defense Intelligence. No hacking. I don't want you to trigger a security firewall."

"I'm better than that," she grumbled, but asked, "Social Security number?"

"I only have the name. Cross-reference Eisner with the Royces and with Keating. Credit check on Eisner too."

"That'll take, like, hours."

"After that, do a general search on a Lenox lab called Naturetech, in Maryland," I said, fishing. "And its chief scientist, Raymond Teaks. Send everything to my special e-mail address, the encrypted one."

Hoot asked exactly what I was looking for, and whether it had anything to do with the Chairman's suicide.

"Just do what I asked, please. Also look up the Florida Keys and diseases. I want to know if there have been cases of some new sickness there over the last few months. Especially near Key West. Anything odd at all."

She said I was requesting tons of material, more than I imagined, and if I gave her a better idea of what I needed, she could work computer triage, eliminate unnecessary references, send pertinent ones along.

"Does this relate to HR-109?" she asked.

"Maybe."

Hoot said she hated being out of the loop. I was just like her father. I didn't trust her.

"If that were true, I'd never ask you to do this," I told her. "Don't tell anyone I did, for your sake, Hoot."

I didn't actually cook breakfast. It's from Petite Fromage," Gabrielle said.

I cursed Danny the wiseguy under my breath and kept eating. The omelet was delicious, flavored with melted asiago, truffles and portobellos. The sesame rolls were hot, the kiwi slices rimmed the plate, the home fries were crisp and brown and flavored with basil and olive oil, my peasant's palate said.

The coffee came from Petite Fromage also, by way of Jamaica's Blue Mountains. The Danish came from Mike Acela, by way of Hot 'n Crusty Pastry, across the street.

"Can I take the Fifth if I don't like a question?" she asked, smiling.

"No."

Gabrielle's braid was tied, tight and long, and it fell over her shoulder. Her white tank top showed off tanned arms and a flat belly. The waist of her skintight jeans was visible above the tabletop. Her long legs were tucked beneath her on the straw-backed chair. When she'd answered the door, I'd seen she was wearing white strap sandals, and that her toenails were a coral color, like a blush.

"The funny thing is, Mike, when you told me Defense Intelligence was asking questions, I thought my father would have wanted you to answer them. He'd sell his soul to keep government regulators away from Lenox, but when it came to defense he was the original patriot. If he could have figured out a way to help them, he would every time."

The two-bedroom apartment was smaller than I would have imagined for a rich girl, brownstone building instead of doorman, rustic instead of modern, hardback books and a PBS DVD collection—*The Civil War, The Story of Climate*—and the dog on the floor was a pound mongrel, a retriever/collie named Audrey instead of a high-priced designer model that substitutes for children in the apartments of the single, disposable-income crowd.

The door to her bedroom was closed. I couldn't help but wonder what it looked like in there.

I started out by saying that I could be wrong about her father. His death might turn out to be exactly what it looked like.

"With him, nothing was."

"I don't want to give unrealistic expectations."

"That's not the way you came across yesterday." She looked into my eyes. The tingle started in my groin.

I explained that I was going to ask about subjects that might seem irrelevant, that in an investigation you went at things directly and obliquely at the same time. The direct part came when you tried to pin down times, purchases, phone calls, evidence. The intuitive part meant asking questions about a personality, hoping it would provide a clue.

"Do you want to know right off why I doubt he killed himself?" she asked. "He wouldn't have used Lenox pills. A gun, gas, even drugs from another company. But using a Lenox product would be like committing suicide twice. There was never self-hatred in my father. He lacked the self-knowledge for that."

"You said yesterday that he couldn't love anybody."

"Is this relevant?"

"I told you, I don't know."

She seemed to draw into herself. The kitchen was small and lemon-colored, with hanging pots and ferns at the open window. A eucalyptus smell wafted in from the back garden. A single strand of white pearls touched her throat. I liked the way her lips moved when she spoke.

"Do you get along with your parents, Mike?"

"I did. They're dead."

"Do you miss them?"

"Yes. But," I remembered, "my mom was sick for years and it was," I said, struggling for the right words, "a terrible kind of relief when she died. I hate that I feel that way. I hope it never affected how I treated her."

She broke off the tiniest bit of sesame roll. "Are you always this honest with people?"

"I have a feeling that if it's not a two-way street with you, it's not worth the time."

"I like an intuitive man. Okay, then. I . . . I used to think when I was little that the way he acted with me was my fault. That I was the reason he never came home at a decent hour, never took vacations with Mom and me. I felt I'd displeased him. If he happened to mention something disapproving, how I dressed or did homework, if he gave any hint, I'd throw myself into changing. I'd work hard. Then I'd watch the clock to see if he came home earlier, and whether he'd talk to me, not just read reports."

"He was a workaholic."

"An avoidaholic. It wasn't until I grew up that I realized he didn't like anyone being close. It had nothing to do with me. What's the quote? Children begin by loving parents. After a while they come to understand them. Rarely, if ever, do they forgive them. He didn't sleep around on Mom, didn't mind paying bills. He simply hated the idea of anyone depending on him emotionally. So he buried himself in work or politics and surrounded himself with admirers who had to go home each night. He'd lecture them about politics and reputation. Finally I wised up, gave up."

"Because of a specific event?"

"Because a specific event made the pattern clear. I sat with Mom when she died, at home. Her eyes kept going to the bedroom door. She'd spent her life waiting for him, and *still* the look was there. Pain and hope. I promised myself I'd never let someone do that to me again."

"That's a bad story."

She shrugged. "I didn't wish hurt on him. I just didn't see why I had to pretend we had a relationship. Pretending has a big price, and it always comes at the back end of things, not the front. Do you know the real reason I think it bothered him that we didn't speak?"

"It embarrassed him in front of other people?" I said.

"I like intelligence in a man," she said.

"What don't you like?"

"Intimacy."

We fell silent, eyeing each other. It was a real mutual interview, I realized, and with shock I understood the look she'd given me in Washington. She was attracted to me too.

"I can't help you with questions inside the company," she said. "Not with your mathematical part. But if there's one thing about my father and motivation, it's that he was a sucker for adoration from strangers. If he made mistakes, I'd imagine it was because he never let people know him, so he couldn't know them back."

"You're harsh."

"I'm accurate."

"You didn't touch your omelet."

"I'm rarely hungry mornings," she said, and smiled. "But I'm ravenous at night."

E ver hear of a research project called HR-109?"
    The dog studied our faces, stopped every few feet to look back on its walk, tilt its head, apply doggy logic to my presence. "Audrey's not used to sharing me," she said. "You've broken her comfortable routine. And I told you, I'm the wrong source for the company. No to HR-109."

"Did your father ever talk about the Hamilton Club? He dined there the other night. And Keating and Schwadron are members."

"It was his kind of place. You can't get in unless you're nominated, and you can't be nominated unless you've achieved something. Birth doesn't count. Money doesn't count. People like us, he called the members. People who should be running things without having to deal with quotas and restraints. Those are his words."

I said, surprised, "Blacks? Women? What quotas?"

"It was about talent. He couldn't care less about color but he believed talented people should be left alone. He hated laws establishing rules for his elite. He said America was dumbing down and our best politicians catered to mobs. He made me read a story by Kurt Vonnegut once: 'Welcome to the Monkey House.' Do you know it?"

"No." The dog turned and gazed from my face to Gabrielle's, as if it wanted to hear the story also. Then it was distracted by the smell coming from a deli. I guess we were all thrown off by physical urges today.

"It was science fiction, in the future. Society was set up so average people would never feel bad about themselves. If you were a great athlete, for instance, and could run faster than other people, you had to wear weights to slow you down. If you were a terrific singer, they'd put implants in your throat. Handicap Laws, they called it. Anyone with talent was rendered average."

"Sounds like a boring place."

"To him it was hell. What's that old quote? Politics is the refuge of the emotionally crippled? Dad would rant about quotas and restraints. Why do you want to know about the Hamilton Club?"

"I'm fishing," I said with real frustration.

We resumed walking and I recognized threads of what she was saying in memories of the Chairman. Late at night, over scotch, he'd gone on about politics while I sat in his study, happy to be considered a confidant.

Pathetic. I hadn't, in the end, even been that.

We reached her door and both fell silent. I imagined some nice things that might happen if we went inside. The day was scorching. The apartment would be cool and private.

"I have a flight to catch," I said.

"And I have to get to school."

Neither of us moved, though. She'd surprised me again. "Are you a teacher or a student?" I asked.

She laughed. "I'm at PS 2, tutoring in a reading program for slow kids. I guess I'm the opposite of my father. He would have taken away their books and given the extra money to the more talented ones."

"That's extreme," I said.

"Extreme people," she said, "can be the nicest in the world one-on-one. And you seem surprised that I work. Did you think I go to spas all day?"

"I just thought teachers had to be at school by eight."

The braid hung over her right shoulder, and there was a thin sheen of sweat above her lip. Seeing her long fingers on the leash made me envision them touching me.

"I'm not a real teacher. I just help out under a program funded by the Reading Foundation."

She laughed again, an open, appealing sound.

"Which is me. I fund the program. I *am* the program."

Our awkwardness reminded me of the ending of a first date, when you're unsure whether or not to kiss the girl. You'd think these questions don't occur to men in their forties, that some things get permanently resolved in life.

Ha.

"If there's anything I can do," I said, "call."

"If you're back from your travels by Saturday," she said, meaning two days from now, "take me to a fundraiser."

I must have blanched, because she said, "Is that bad mourner behavior? Well, originally I wasn't going. But it's a special party, Mike. Being there might help you. Two of your prime suspects will be there and you'll catch them off balance. They'd never expect to see you."

"I didn't mention any suspects."

"Silly me. I must have misread you in Washington when you said you'd been threatened if you looked into things."

I envisioned a fund-raiser at the Metropolitan Museum maybe, or on one of the big yachts that often hosted such things in the harbor. The Forbes yacht, perhaps. Donors steam past the Statue of Liberty, munch hors d'oeuvres and scribble checks to the Cancer Society. They write the event off tax-wise when the government comes around.

I said, "Keating will be there?"

"He's the star. It's probably his biggest social event of the summer, the annual chili cook-off between him and Schwadron, at Keating's home in Rye. Just a hundred or so of the more influential people in Keating's life—anyone he's trying to impress, anyone he's working with on a big deal, anyone he'd like to know better or who can make him richer—sprinkling on onions and sour cream, lying on his private beach, washing down chili with champagne and Lone Stars. Keating and Schwadron could kill each other over who makes better chili. I haven't gone in years, but I just changed my mind, if you'll take me."

I altered the venue in my mind from black tie to Gatsby beach party, the yacht becoming a sloping lawn, the tuxedos changing to green Lacoste shirts, the gowns and stiletto heels to Prada sandals and Gucci sunglasses. I put Gabrielle Dwyer on the private beach. She looked breathtaking in a black one-piece bathing suit.

Attraction's first phase involves making excuses for the

other person. She wasn't acting like a daughter in mourning, but like her dad, I told myself, she must keep emotions to herself. She was holding them in or refusing to deal with them. Or she was sharing them with close friends, strangers to me. Otherwise her grief would crash down on her later. I'd seen it sneak up on people at the FBI.

Her behavior was odd, therefore, but not *wrong*.

Besides, in my mind and on that beach, she rolled onto her belly on a blanket, and I saw the soft swell of rump, with bits of white sand clinging to it, and the way the sun tanned her flanks and changed, quick as Dr. Jekyll, into shadow where her flesh brushed hot sand.

"I can't wait to watch Keating's face when he sees my escort is the Security man," she said. "You can bring up subjects you'd never be able to talk about otherwise, especially when he starts drinking. You'll get a pocket view of Keating's money-grubbing world. But I warn you, Keating and Schwadron make killer chilis."

She smiled. In her eyes I saw challenge.

"Those two will rip holes through you if you don't watch out."

I kept thinking about Tom Schwadron's words about Pearl Harbor and 9/11. I kept seeing soldiers replacing my security team at Naturetech, in my head.

Cancer research, my ass.

From a pay phone I called SunGo, that season's new low-cost Florida airline, and checked walk-on fares and flight times to Miami. I planned to buy a ticket at the last minute, not to reserve one.

Just like terrorists do, I thought, remembering lessons at the FBI. Eisner would love finding this out.

I found a nearby Chase Manhattan where, using my bank card and photo ID, I withdrew three thousand dollars in cash from my personal account from a teller, bypassing the ATM machine. ATM withdrawals show up instantly to federal law enforcers tracking bank activity. Counter transactions require several hours before registering on the screens.

Eisner, do the Royces work for you? And why didn't you ask me what I was doing at Naturetech yesterday? Because you already know what's there? Did you send the soldiers?

Back outside, I fought off the urge to go home and walk through my house, to check damage after yesterday's search. I couldn't risk going anyplace that might be monitored.

So instead I walked into a candy store and bought a long-distance phone card, good for two hours of talking on almost any pay phone in the US. My old FBI supervisor Barney Birnbaum's Miami phone number was in my Palm Pilot, but I hadn't called him in over a year. I hoped that my retired friend still lived in the same home.

"Lifeguard station," answered the familiar rasp over the line, meaning the old curmudgeon was in his backyard by his little pool, probably smoking smuggled Cubans, probably sunning his leathery 72-year-old frame, probably drinking cranberry and lime juice, with a Tim O'Brien novel on his potbelly and his ex–biology professor wife, Francie, puttering around her tropical garden nearby.

When I identified myself he said, "Ah, the nation's finest ex–investigative agent."

When I told him what I needed he said, more slowly, "Sure I can lend you a car. Francie ripped her Achilles tendon in a sand trap and can't work the clutch on the

Maxima. What's wrong, Mike? Problem with your credit cards? Can't rent a car?"

"You don't want to know."

"Actually, *you* don't want to tell." He sighed. "What flight are you on? I'll pick you up. Come for dinner. You can talk about security work and I'll tell you about my fucking colon. Then go rob a bank or whatever you plan with the car. Only do me a favor, hit a pole during the getaway so I can collect insurance. That lemon never worked right."

I'd become so paranoid in the last two days that I actually hesitated about giving him the flight information.

"No time for dinner?" Barney said, sounding disappointed. "Drop by for a quick drink."

He was lonely, I realized, old and, from the sound of the colon reference, sick. I told him I'd love to come. I said I'd call back with my flight number when I knew it. I warned him that I couldn't stay late because I had a long drive ahead of me.

"Mike, I can't walk more than two hundred yards anymore without having to sit down, but I can still drive like a pro. Do you need help?"

"You were a great supervisor," I said, moved by his unquestioning loyalty. "I was happy working with you."

The clerk at the SunGo counter was glad to take my money. Steamy Florida is not exactly a destination of choice for New Yorkers in summers, and the SunGo gate at JFK was practically empty except for a few scattered passengers—none of whom appeared to be going on vacation—waiting to board the one-twenty P.M. flight.

I sat beneath the CNN monitor during a long delay and tried to figure out the best way to approach but not alarm Dr. Asa Rodriguez. I was half aware of the hour's big interview, with pretty *Washington Star* columnist Alicia Dent, who had broken several stories recently resulting in resignations, most notably the President's. In the last two months she had also publicized one Mississippi Senator's abortion, one gay affair between a powerful Chicago Congressman and an aide, and one instance of kickbacks on a CIA computer contract.

"An astoundingly accomplished record," the announcer said. "What's the secret of your success?"

I was distracted by the loud voices of two men behind me, pissed-off journalists complaining about Alicia Dent.

"My secret is good gut instincts," she said.

"She's so lucky it could make you puke," the jealous *Times* reporter behind me said.

I wanted to tell him that there was nothing to worry about, that luck changes, that the Chairman had been "Lucky Jim" in the *Wall Street Journal,* and dead on the front page only days after that.

But the boarding call finally sounded and we filed onto SunGo's 757, where I stepped over the cute blonde seated—in an almost-empty plane, of course—in the middle seat, and I strapped myself in by the window. The plane accelerated down the runway and tilted upward. The city dropped away and grew smaller and browner, and sunlight glittered off two million flame-colored windows below.

"Business trip or pleasure," said the voice beside me, and turning, I realized that she sounded familiar.

"You shouldn't have beaten my husband." I felt the light touch of long fingernails on my forearm. "It made me so mad," the woman next to me—Abby Hayes Royce—said.

NINE

"You know what I love about airplanes?" asked the woman beside me, who Danny had said was a professional killer. "You need trust to fly. You never know who you'll sit next to: new friend or new problem. You're strapped in at thirty thousand feet and can't walk off if you change your mind."

No one else sat within rows of us, I realized. The woman added, "You put your life in the hands of strangers. If that's not trust, what is?"

She was tall, even sitting, and athletic, with toned arms, superb posture and a baby-faced, wide-eyed look in her toffee-colored eyes. Her cheekbones were high and prominent, her jaw round, with a dab of baby fat at the tip. Her ash blond hair was thick and perfectly cut in a squarish top, giving it a tamed appearance, wildness under control. The two top buttons on her turquoise blouse were open. Her cleavage swelled but I kept my eyes off it.

Her presence in the middle seat blocked easy exit to the aisle.

"Abby Royce," I said, my voice steady but my heart galloping. The plane seemed suddenly warm.

What's that story Danny told? The witness in her husband's trial took her home and had a heart attack. She's a chemist. Watch her hands.

They were under an airline blanket.

"I told Oliver you were smart," she said, looking approving that I'd known her name, as if by doing so I'd confirmed her fundamental appraisal of me. "I told him to try straight negotiation. But he likes games. Humor's an overrated quality in a man."

"It can be annoying at times," I said.

Believe me, there are so many ways to introduce foreign chemicals into a human body. Between my years at the FBI and my time at Lenox, I'd learned enough to make my blood race now. Certain secretions from frogs, for instance, or from a rare Venezuelan caterpillar, dabbed on human skin will be absorbed into the blood and induce heart attacks or strokes. These natural killers come from South American jungles. Lenox imported them for research. Anyone with a license could.

Her hands shifted under the blanket, sliding closer to me on her lap.

All she'd have to do to transmit a poison was to "spill" a drink on me, or touch my skin to dab on whatever drug she'd smeared on a Band-Aid or rubber thumb glove.

"I'm going to move across the aisle," I said, getting up in violation of the glowing seat belt sign. "We can be more comfortable that way."

Her hands stayed under the blanket as I stepped over her knees. I told myself she'd not make a move yet, not before we talked. She would want the disk from me, and would need to give me time to get it.

"*Cosmo* magazine goes on and on about men with humor," she said as I strapped myself in again, and she moved to the aisle seat on her side, to be closer. "It's not jokes I need."

"How did you find me?"

"Oh, you were so rattled by that near-miss with your girlfriend. You were watching Oliver."

I felt sick. "You were there."

The brown eyes twinkled. "*Svelte* magazine says it's bad to involve yourself in another couple's problems. By the way, do you have the disk now? It was smart to give the vial to Keating, but we both know you have the disk."

"So Keating called you."

"If you want to think that."

"What if I said I don't have any disk?"

She settled back. "Like I said. New friends. Plenty of time." But beneath her blanket her hands drifted fractionally closer to the aisle.

I tried a different tack. "Can I assume we're talking about HR-109?"

She considered. "Assume what you want."

"What's the side effect?"

"I couldn't care less."

"How much are you offering?"

"*Glamour* magazine says it's better to let the other person go first in negotiations, to get a better deal."

Some predators attack when sensing fear or body heat. Abby watched my eyes and I watched the lumps under her blanket. I tried to remember if I'd seen rings on her fingers when I'd sat down—jewelry that could cut—but realized I'd been observing the luggage crew on the tarmac outside, not her.

"Oliver needed stitches," she said as if my beating him up had increased whatever penalty she'd exact if negotiations failed. But then she made her proposal. "Four hundred thousand in any currency, jewels, whatever you choose. Or wired anywhere you want."

"Only four?"

"*Glamour* said in negotiations one side makes the first offer and the other's supposed to counter. Go ahead."

The plane leveled out. The sky was blue, the clouds puffy as in fairy tales. No other passengers sat within rows of us, and the flight attendants were occupied at the front end of the plane, rolling a refreshment cart down the aisle.

I said, to keep the conversation going, "What's to prevent you from trying to kill me after I sell it?"

"Nobody wants another death at Lenox, if possible."

"Do you have any idea of the real value of HR-109?"

"I couldn't care less."

"What's to stop you from selling it yourself once you get it?"

She sighed, growing impatient with my questions. "Even if I did, what difference is that to you? But believe me, I wouldn't stay protected that way. I'd live the rest of my life like you, looking over my shoulder."

I envisioned Eisner, Keating, Schwadron, my rogue's gallery of suspects, all of whom had the recourses to hunt down an employee who betrayed them. "Then your boss is pretty powerful," I said.

But she was finished responding. "Look, arrange some clever safeguard to protect yourself if you're worried. From the way you've been sneaking around, you've not sold it yet. Let's get this over with. I want to take Oliver home. He doesn't do well in big cities."

"Hi!" a cheery female voice broke in, with a southern accent. "Can I offer you two a drink?"

We looked up at the grinning flight attendant, a middle-aged Asian American who held out packs of salted peanuts as if they were fine truffles.

"Water, no ice," said Abby politely.

"Nothing for me," I said, keeping my hands free, remembering the way the worst topical poisons worked. A short time after coming into contact with one, the victim would start to feel feverish, or suffer joint pain, stomach cramps, chest pains. He'd start to choke. Then would come the hammer blow in his chest.

The stewardesses rolled away the cart.

"Talk about mistakes," I said, trying another tack and hoping Abby would turn out to be as vain as her husband. "Whomever killed the Chairman acted too soon, I guess. Never got the disk that they went to his house for."

She sipped water and put the empty cup on the seatback tray beside her, closer to the window. She *was* wearing a ring, I saw now, a thin silver one with a blue stone on it.

"Oh, they got it. But Dwyer apparently made a copy. You have it."

"But—"

"No more questions. Let's talk about you, Mike. Paying cash for air tickets. Lying to Defense Intelligence. Five hundred thousand. You'll sell to somebody, so why not now, to me?"

She held out the hand with the ring on it, across the aisle, to shake hands, as if we'd made a deal.

"Where's your husband?" I said. *They work as a team,* Danny had said. And clearly they'd been together both times that Oliver had shown up.

She closed her eyes and pushed her armrest button. She eased back her reclining seat. Her eyelids kept moving, even when closed, so she was thinking. She looked as peaceful as a five-year-old.

"See what I mean? You're looking over your shoulder already," she said.

I made a terrible mistake, Dwyer had told me two nights ago. Now I asked myself for the hundredth time, *What was it?*

As I involuntarily glanced toward the other passengers, she turned slightly in her seat, in a way that brought her hand closer to me, on the aisle-side armrest.

I stood up to get away from her. Moving into the aisle, I told myself that had I been in the Bureau I could have had the captain call ahead and arrange for agents to meet us, to question her. But SunGo didn't have seat-back phones for private citizens. And there was no one for me to call.

Then her eyes opened and her hand—not the one with the ring on it—fluttered toward me. I grabbed her wrist before she could touch me. She was quite strong.

"Good reflexes," she said. "Oh, you heard *that* story."

Looking down, I saw a flesh-colored Band-Aid covering the top of her index finger. It could have been just protecting a cut. But it could have been something more.

"Six hundred is my real, actual final offer, Mike. Going . . . going . . ."

"Tell Eisner I'll think about it," I said, watching her expression. I tried, "Tell Schwadron."

"Let go of me," she said. "Or are you going to make a scene?"

Had she just tried to kill me? Had she realized I had no intention of doing business and actually tried to murder me on a plane? It seemed impossible. You'd think, I told myself, that if someone just tried to end your life, you'd at least *know.*

The arrival-gate lounge was packed with passengers

waiting to fly north and escape the heat. Faces and bodies careened close. Boarding calls echoed, adding to the general feeling of anarchy on the ground. The air-conditioning system must be powerful, I thought, because the terminal was freezing. But then I noticed that no one else seemed to mind, and an itch started up in my throat.

Where is Oliver? He could have beaten me to Miami if he came in on a private jet, or even one that landed on time.

I found a pay phone in an alcove while I watched Abby recede briskly into the crowd, never looking back. I would have to turn my back on the crowd while I punched in numbers, but I preferred not to use my cell even though it was encrypted.

"I'm outside the terminal in the car," Barney said, answering on the first ring. "Have a nice flight?"

"Change of plans. I can't go home with you. Take the car to the Palm Reef Hotel and park it in the rear lot. Leave the key on the driver's-side front tire. I'll reimburse you for your cab ride home."

"What the hell is going on, my friend?"

"Just a precaution."

"You want me to send someone to walk you through the terminal? I still have people I can call."

"I'll be fine."

"You sound congested. You sick?" Barney asked me. "You seemed fine this morning."

"Little cold," I said, hoping that's all it was.

I checked my messages and found two from Danny, one each from Kim and Eisner, one from Keating's fussy secretary, Theresa, ordering me to call Keating, a bad sign. The departure lounge was emptying as flights left.

The fewer people around me, the safer it would be to move. I used the pay phone again while I waited, calling Danny first.

"Ready for this, Boss? Eisner's guys went through my apartment this morning after you left. And Kim's."

I coughed. I remembered Abby's fingernails brushing my wrist when I sat down on the plane. I pictured the seat divider that had separated us at the beginning of the flight and recalled something else. I'd never seen her put her hand on the divider, but I'd rested mine there. She'd had time before I sat down to dab a chemical on top.

Danny said, "Also, Eisner was in with Keating for an hour. Kim went into the waiting room and heard them shouting. She couldn't make out the words."

So Abby'd had two opportunities to infect me. And we'd been in the plane for more than enough time for a chemical to start working by now.

But she hadn't even started negotiating yet. She'd have to know, if the negotiations worked, that I'd need time to get the disk. She wouldn't have tried anything until negotiations failed.

Danny said, "Keating's looking for you and he doesn't sound happy. The Board confirmed him as temporary chairman this morning. *Sieg heil,* Boss. Lenox's Third Reich begins."

When I told him what had happened on the plane, he said, "I decided to keep Kim with me from now on."

When I told him to take precautions with his own family, he said, "I already sent them away. And I started carrying my gun."

Eisner had taken my gun, and there was no way to get one in Florida, not if I wanted to move fast, I thought.

* * *

I called Keating and found Theresa the gatekeeper—barometer of her boss's mood—distant on the phone. Keating kept me waiting and I coughed again.

Keating demanded when he came on the line, "Why did you visit Naturetech yesterday?"

"Don't you remember, sir? I told you the Chairman asked me to check security at one of our labs. Why'd the army move in, sir? Believe me, we can handle any problem there."

Keating ignored the question. He sounded enraged.

"Where are you calling from, Mike?"

I hated to say Miami, but his caller ID would show my area code. I said, "We've had some thefts from warehouses in Dade County. I want to check out the situation in person."

"That won't be necessary. Come home."

With a disembodied feeling, I saw what was coming. But the way he did it involved more skill than I'd credited him with.

"Mike, I just learned that you actually tapped phones at Lenox three years ago. *Executives' phones!* Dwyer kept notes in his safe and they showed a wide pattern of abuses. It won't be necessary to come in. We'll clear out your office. Pick up your stuff in the lobby, tomorrow."

My head was throbbing. Had Chairman Dwyer actually kept records to give himself leverage over me? Or had Keating known about it the whole time? Was he lying? I couldn't believe half the people I talked to anymore.

"You won't find the disk in my office," I told him.

"Excuse me?"

"You were going to fire me all along," I said. "You just waited for the Board to confirm you as chairman."

He softened a bit. "I understand your anger, Mike, but I can't tolerate this sort of behavior. I'm disappointed in you. I expected better of someone who came from the FBI."

"But, sir, the Chairman knew everything I did," I said, pretending to beg, needing to maintain access to the company if I was to find out what had happened to Dwyer. What was happening to me and my friends.

"*I'm* the chairman," Keating snapped. "Your IDs have been invalidated. Your key card is turned off. Our lawyers advised me to go to the authorities. But I'm thinking we'd rather keep this in-house, and maybe, Mike, even figure out a way to retain your severance package, if you want me to try."

Which meant, make waves and lose money. Make waves and face prosecution on wiretapping laws. But slink off and get a lump sum payment equal to your salary for two years.

Yeah, slink off and maybe one day my housekeeper will find me dead on the floor too.

I tried to sound meek, needing Keating to think that I'd come straight home and that I was beaten, harmless. "Could you possibly give me a recommendation for another job, sir? I only did what Mr. Dwyer asked me to do."

Keating went silent, as if considering it, which he wasn't. The silence went on.

"When the dust settles, perhaps."

"If I could just come in and explain in person."

"It's better to leave things this way. I'm sad, Mike. I thought better of you. I had no idea you broke the law."

I'm getting a fucking cold. That's all, I told myself. *And if it isn't a cold, there's no time to get to a hospital. The air-*

port infirmary will be worthless. Doctors would never pin-point what I have anyway. Go to Key West.

The gate area was clear now and I started moving. I wondered suddenly, *Did Abby infect me with HR-109?*

I halted. Was it possible? After all, I was on my way to Key West to see if people there had been succumbing to some new disease or condition—the possible "side effect" of HR-109, a discovery important enough to cause the army to seal off our lab.

I stopped at a newsstand and bought Lenox-brand aspirin and throat lozenges. At a fountain I drank down a couple of aspirin. Loyal Mike Acela. Paying money for his company brand.

Concentrate on something else. Your job.

But I had no job.

I decide when I stop working on this. Not Keating.

I monitored faces and clothing, trying to pick out Oliver Royce or whoever Abby would have watching me. I had to go to the bathroom anyway, so I found one, washed my face, checked my tongue, which looked gray, came out and made sure none of the faces I'd seen earlier were still there.

How about clothing? Did I recognize a shirt, color combo, hat, slouch, way of walking?

Nope.

Almost at the security station now. I knew that any-one waiting for me would have my photo, so there was no need to pick me up until I left the gate corridor and entered the terminal proper, with its larger crowds. Even in calm times between fleet departures, Miami's airport is a semi-madhouse. A watcher could be waiting at the lug-gage pickup or the doors to the street, both places where

I used to station myself when I was at the Bureau, assigned to surveillance.

Abby's people or Eisner's . . . were they the same? . . . would be idling at a choke point, where foot traffic from many directions converged.

Entering the terminal, I passed the funneled mass of humanity backed up at the security checkpoint. There were many more people to keep track of now. I noticed a trio of soldiers eyeing travelers heading for departure gates, approached the soldiers and made up a story. I said another passenger on my flight—a drunk—had threatened to attack me outside the terminal. I asked if one of the soldiers would mind walking me to a cab.

"Don't worry, sir," a soldier said confidently. "Nothing will happen to you while we're here."

Outside, the sun was high and bright and the heat seemed to erupt from the buildings and sidewalks, as well as burning down from overhead. Traffic was congested. Idling cabs lined the curb. The soldier waited with me until it was my turn to get into a taxi.

"See, nothing to worry about," the soldier said.

In the cab, I looked back as we drove off, to see lots of traffic—cars, vans and limos behind us. I had my driver pull over before we left the airport. I waited a few minutes and no other cars pulled over too. But when we started off again, I spotted a green Taurus that had passed us earlier, parked on the roadside ahead, hood up, driver on his cell phone, watching me pass. It wasn't Oliver Royce.

I couldn't tell if there was anyone in the passenger seat of the Taurus.

My driver watched me in the rearview mirror, "Mister, you sick? You look like shit."

"Summer cold," I said.

* * *

The green Taurus hung back but I spotted it twice on the way into Miami, changing lanes, dropping back, easing up again. When I told my driver what I wanted him to do about it, he eyed me in the rearview mirror as if I were insane.

"My girlfriend's brother is certifiable," I explained, offering him a fifty-dollar bill over the seat. "I sleep with his sister so he follows me around, threatens me all the time, says I better marry her. She's thirty-six years old, for Christ sake. Not a kid."

"If you slept with my sister, I'd do the same thing," the driver said.

Cubans.

"I'll marry her," I told him. "I just need more time."

"Sure." He stuffed the bill in his guayabara pocket.

He stayed in the middle lane, drove at a steady speed all the way into Miami, intentionally making things easier for whoever was behind. I watched the Taurus in the sideview mirror, not wanting to let its driver see me looking back. We stayed this way for twenty minutes, during which my fever lifted, thanks to the aspirin, I guess. We came up on an exit ramp for 7th Street. Might as well try now, I thought.

"Signal that we're getting off," I said.

"I know how to get off," the driver said.

The Taurus stayed sixty yards back, easing right, signaling now, with two cars separating us as we reached the 7th Street ramp. Up on 7th Street, the opportunity I hoped for came almost immediately. A big semi tractor-trailer truck wedged between the Taurus and us.

"Now!" I said.

The driver hit the accelerator and made a hard right at

the next corner. We spun onto a narrow street lined with small one-story houses. I was already lying down. As my driver swerved to the curb, I kicked the door open but stayed inside, out of view.

The driver got out and stood up, and from where I lay I could see the upper half of his body, see him shaking his fist in the direction of the nearest yard, acting his part perfectly, screaming curses. Shouting that I'd run off and not paid the fare.

Then I heard brakes squeal behind us and the quick sound of car doors slamming, and the slap of footsteps running off in the direction in which my driver had yelled.

A moment later, the driver looked in at me as he shut my door, grinning.

"*Idiotas.* They ran off 'after' you," he said, breaking into laughter. "Two of them. One had a bandage on his face."

Was it Oliver Royce?

We drove off, buddies after that.

He dropped me at the Flagler Hotel, two blocks from the Palm Reef. When he drove off I walked into the Flagler and out a back entrance and strolled to the lot where Barney had hopefully left his car. I sucked a throat lozenge. My throat felt raw.

The ignition key was where it was supposed to be. The tank was full. Barney's scrawled note on the front seat said, "I meant what I said about this lemon. Crash it and destroy evidence of my illegal intent—i.e., this note."

But the car worked fine.

An hour later I was driving south on US 1, the old main north-south highway, a stop-and-go road leading to Key West. Traffic was light. The only car to stay behind me for any appreciable distance was a Hertz rental van with a family inside. In my rearview mirror I saw Mom, Dad and two kids eating burgers and singing songs.

The sun was dazzling, the heat immense and humid, and the farther south I drove the emptier the vacation highway looked, the motels closed in summer, and the restaurants, the palms slumped and the Atlantic Ocean, when I glimpsed it, was turquoise and flat. The window was open. Heavy somnambulant air saturated the car. Pinkish-black thunderheads towered to the south, building up energy, floating bombs.

I need to contact Hoot before she finds out I was fired.

I gassed up at a 7-Eleven and bought a Cuban mix sandwich and a Coke. Eating while I drove, feeling somewhat better, I hit the seven mile bridge while listening to the radio for news. I flipped channels and stopped on a talk show when a familiar-sounding voice said, "Some amazingly skilled interrogators and new techniques helped our forces overseas identify the terrorists and capture them."

The guest turned out to be National Intelligence Director Richard (A. J.) Carbone, Dwyer's old friend. "In fact," he added confidently, "if our security people had an even freer hand *inside* the country, we could make the United States a lot safer from terrorism. Fortunately, our new President realizes that you cannot err on the side of safety."

The show's host agreed but added, "That sounds like a broadside at our civil libertarians, sir."

"Too many of them don't realize civil liberties are for

people who deserve them, not for those with destruction in mind."

"Let's change subjects," the host said. "You were a good friend of former Lenox Pharmaceuticals Chairman James Dwyer. Do you think his suicide had anything to do with accusations that Lenox overcharged the Defense Department by over forty million dollars?"

Carbone sounded offended. "Jim Dwyer was probably the most moral man I ever met. And whatever drove him to take his own life will turn out to be personal, not business related, I'm sure."

"Then you don't think Lenox profited excessively."

"That's not my area of expertise."

I'd passed Key Largo and Islamorada. I passed Marathon and, closing on Key West, spotted the NEW! INTERNET! sign by a new roadside strip mall on Big Pine Key. It was the only shop open, and had a half a dozen motorcycles out front—a crowd in the summer. I pulled in and went inside. I paid, occupied a corner terminal, and hoped Hoot would be at her computer, back in New York, accessible through an encrypted chat room she'd set up.

The place was filled with biker types treating their kids to computer games.

Hoot was home, and clearly had not yet gotten the news that I was no longer her boss, or she would have asked about it. She typed back, "With all work here, where else be?"

Impatient always, Hoot bypassed prepositions when on the Internet, and answered questions in single words.

Had she found any cases of a new illness, or outbreak of sickness in the Florida Keys? I asked.

"No."

Had she found anything on Oliver Lee Royce and Abby Hayes Royce?

The only new fact I learned was that Abby owned a business importing herbal medicines from South America.

Great.

"How about Major Carl Eisner," I typed, listening in the background to tinny bleeps, laser blasts and characters screaming on computer games. The biker parents stood in front of the shop, drinking beer.

"What want?" Hoot sent back. "Mortgage? Home address? Many speeding tickets Reston, Virginia."

Did Hoot have anything of a military nature on Eisner? About what exact work he did?

"Defense Department firewall."

I cursed under my breath. I'd specifically ordered her to stay away from barred-access files. There was no telling what kind of traps Defense Intelligence set to identify people trying to break into their files.

She added, "Newspaper articles, though. Wife killed."

It was classic Hoot to save the important stuff for last and make me beg for it. I typed back, "Tell me."

From the cryptic words appearing in front of me, I gathered that Eisner worked for DI's contract oversight group, which looked for fraud in military contracts, usually ones involving strategic materials.

Which means HR-109 might indeed be a weapon.

In Seattle, according to the first newspaper article Hoot had found, Eisner had arrested a former US Army sergeant working for a Defense contractor for trying to sell missile parts to Iran. Eisner had testified in court that the man was a "traitor who deserved the death penalty."

An earlier *Washington Post* article, dated five years ago,

was even more interesting. *Husband of Dead Captain Reinstated with Full Honors.* The article went on to explain that Eisner's wife—an Air Force captain and helicopter pilot—had been killed in Iraq in an attack first reported as a missile strike. But Eisner the bird dog had investigated on his own, discovered the missile story was a lie and gone to his superiors with a theory that the copter blew up when a faulty experimental weapons system exploded.

He'd been transferred and then discharged when he pursued the case in defiance of orders. He had linked the bad parts to a kickback scheme that had cost the Air Force three million dollars and had fitted a whole fleet with substandard weapons.

Eventually two dozen people had been arrested, including Eisner's immediate superior.

I sat back, staring. Eisner sounded like a passionate advocate of honesty in the military, a man I might even admire under other circumstances, not someone who would hire professional killers.

But the story was five years old. In five years a man could change.

"What about Naturetech and Raymond Teaks?" I typed.

"Two hundred hits. B-o-r-i-n-g."

I sighed and asked Hoot to send what she had when we were done. Finally, still pretending to be her boss, I asked for a general rundown on the two companies in which the Chairman had purchased two shares of stock. Galvin Defense and Deep Sea Marine. I had not thought to do this before because the purchases had been so tiny.

A pause. She'd be pissed off, getting more work.

"Someone at door," she typed.

"Don't answer."

But she'd gone off. Waiting, I sucked a throat lozenge, growing more uneasy.

"Are you back?" I typed after a couple of minutes.

No answer. The cursor throbbed on the screen.

"Hoot?"

Words appeared now. "I am back, sir. A deliveryman was at the door. What specifically do you want on Galvin Defense and where are you?"

I felt a stab of dread. Whomever was typing was using complete sentences, plus, Hoot had never called anyone "sir" in her life.

I sent out a nonsensical question about a nonexistent case. "Did you find anything on the Ohio counterfeit labeling operation? You were supposed to check yesterday."

"Sorry, I'll get on it," whomever was sitting at Hoot's desk replied.

I broke the connection, cursing. I called the police in New York and told the emergency operator I'd been talking to Hoot when suddenly I'd heard a scream before the phone went dead. I was sweating again, but not from fever. I told the operator to dispatch a squad car to Hoot's apartment, fast.

"Your name, please?"

"Carl Eisner," I said. I spelled it. "E-i-s-n-e-r."

I prayed nobody was hurting her. I prayed it was Eisner's people with her, not Abby's. Abby's would be worse.

I hung up and called Danny, using the phone card, and told him what had happened. I'd sworn to keep him out of things, but that was impossible now. Someone had to check on Hoot and Kim.

"Just keep going," he said. "We need answers, and

maybe they're in Key West. I'll call your encrypted line if I learn something."

"I may have made a mistake," I said, sounding like Dwyer, "by not giving everything to the cops. You were right."

"You did fine, Boss."

"I'm not your boss anymore."

"Honorary title, then."

He was right too about finishing the trip. I went outside and got into the car and continued south, heading toward the edge of the country, seeing swamp on both sides of the road, feeling my world falling apart, compressing and changing, and I told myself to concentrate. Distraction is the enemy, my old instructors used to say.

TWELVE MILES TO THE PIER HOUSE, a billboard said, as I saw a navy copter flying toward its base near Key West.

Then I rounded a corner and saw a line of cars, and I began to sweat more heavily.

A military roadblock lay ahead.

TEN

The first time I ever tried to shoot a man was from behind an FBI roadblock. It was a year after I graduated from Quantico, and I'd been flown with other agents to North Carolina, where we hunted for a terrorist named Mohammed Hassan.

Hassan was a Pakistani immigrant, a worker in a Scotchman convenience store in Wilmington and ringleader of a group, we'd learned, that planned to ram a speedboat filled with explosives into one of the navy ammo carriers—ocean-going ships—that loaded up at Southport on the Cape Fear River and supplied US forces around the world.

On the afternoon of the shooting I manned one of several roadblocks we'd set up along a network of dirt roads near Town Creek, a blackwater river half an hour from Wilmington. Hassan's country home was there. He'd been using it to meet with the other plotters and finalize plans for the attack.

But Hassan had been tipped off that we were looking for him. He'd stolen a red pickup truck and was on the run.

What I remember most about that afternoon was the sense of rage and anticipation that filled me as I waited behind an FBI Humvee, watching for rising dust ahead, which would signal an approaching car. The agents and police officers around me were young and eager, and every one of us felt violated by the terrorist's plan. We were armed with shotguns and pistols, and protected by Kevlar vests. We wanted to be part of the team that caught Hassan. But after hours of waiting, the flies and mosquitoes were biting in clouds, and the scorching heat and swamp stink made our irritations worse.

Anyone driving toward us would see the roadblock, I knew. But what they wouldn't see were FBI snipers hidden in trees behind them, in case they tried to run or opened fire.

Just when we were ready to give up, a dust cloud appeared and became a fast-moving pickup. But the pickup skewed sideways when the driver spotted us and slammed on his brakes. He skidded toward a ditch. He backed up. I heard a shot. An agent screamed, "He's shooting!"

And all hell broke loose.

Our fusillade sent birds flying and made the pickup shudder. It lurched forward and sagged and slowed as bits of metal flew off it. Tilting sideways, it rammed into a stump.

The tires had been shot out.

Then Hassan was out, running through high grass toward the piney woods. He twisted when the first shot hit him, jerked halfway around and started hopping, but still he ran. Struck again, he spun and fell sideways into the grass.

"I got the son of a bitch," cried the agent next to me, but it was impossible to know who had hit him.

When I reached him, he was on his back, cuffed and crying, smaller than he'd seemed in his photo, skinny, bald and bespectacled, with an expression of raw terror on his face. Blood drenched his pants. I smelled shit on him, and piss. He'd vomited all over his white button-down Scotchman logo shirt.

Hassan cried out, "I did not do it. I love this country. My cousin is the one you want."

I didn't believe him. None of us did. Innocent men do not steal trucks. So I'd been surprised to learn during the trial that Hassan had not been armed that day. The opening shot had been fired by a sniper.

And I'd been more surprised to learn, five years later, when Hassan was released from prison by a judge, that he *had* been telling the truth. His cousin had been the one plotting to blow up the ammunition ship, and had implicated Hassan to give himself time to get away.

While I'd been manning the roadblock, the cousin had slipped out of the country into Canada. A year later he was blown up in Lahore, while making pipe bombs in his home.

Now, inching closer to the Florida roadblock, I remembered Hassan and the crazy desire I'd felt that day for an excuse to fire at him.

Ahead, two army Humvees formed an inverted V on the southbound lane. Soldiers had their weapons out. As cars squeezed through, their drivers were ordered to keep going or pull over to the side. I saw a red Focus there, a blue Jetta, green Civic, old overloaded white Buick Electra. Clearly the vehicles weren't cause for the stoppages.

The drivers were.

It was too late to turn around. I could only hope that the soldiers ahead weren't looking for me. I told myself I'd done nothing wrong and there were a dozen other reasons they could be here: terrorism or drug related.

Six cars to go.

I flipped radio channels, hoping a local broadcast would reveal the purpose of the roadblock.

And now I saw two soldiers taking licenses from drivers who'd pulled over, and bringing them to a Humvee where someone else ran computer checks. Still other soldiers walked the line, peering into backed-up cars. Young and tense-looking, they occasionally spoke into neckmikes, telling their officers about the people they saw.

Four cars to go. With a sinking feeling I realized that all the drivers who had been pulled over looked like middle-aged, dark-haired, white males. None had passengers in their cars. They were alone.

I reached the vehicular triage point and tried to appear curious. Glancing up into a corporal's aviator sunglasses, I saw myself reflected back. The soldiers would be working from a photo, sketch or profile, I knew, as I had while manning roadblocks for the FBI.

"Would you mind pulling over, sir?" asked the man at my window, unemotionally.

"What's the fuss?" I asked, trying to sound like an innocent, put-out tourist. My throat had gone dry.

"Terrorist alert, sir. Pull over and take out your driver's license, please."

I joked, "Hey, do I look like a terrorist?"

He didn't smile, didn't frown.

I asked, "How come you're not blocking the road to Miami, just the one south? Aren't there more targets in the other direction?"

He stared at me, deciding if I was mocking him.

Then he took off the glasses. "Why don't we let the people who know more than we do make those decisions, sir. You know what the President says: If we inconvenience a thousand people to catch one bad apple, we've all had a good day."

I pulled over and watched a soldier with a handheld reflector walking the line, peering at the underside of a low-slung Electra with peach-logoed Georgia plates. Another soldier rifled the trunk.

I held my breath as a female soldier brought my license to the Humvee. Moments later she returned it to me.

"Thank you, Mr. Acela," she said, mispronouncing my name with a hard *c* instead of a soft one.

"Have a good stay in Key West," she added.

The roadblock got smaller in the rearview mirror. I approached Key West, passing billboards for restaurants, hotels, sunset cruises, dive trips. Between the troops behind me and the gauntlet of happy ads, the place seemed schizophrenic. Peaceful refuge or terrorist target?

My cell phone chimed. I checked the incoming number.

Eisner was calling. I wondered if he was tied into the roadblock computers.

Find Asa Rodriguez fast, I thought, letting the phone chime.

Energy in the United States has always dispersed itself toward the edges. We were settled by people who moved to solve problems, restless seekers predisposed to striking out toward far shores. The sense when approaching our borders is one of wildness, uncertainty, opportunity. Peacefulness lures with redefinition, openness with the illusion that you can change your life. Lands-end houses our unhappy, our restless, our different, our reborn.

Kim had provided Asa Rodriguez's home address from her records. I got a map at a Texaco station and located the house within minutes, maximum amount of time necessary to get anywhere in Key West. Asa lived on a small curvy residential street lacking sidewalks, dotted with brightly painted converted cigar-maker shacks and abutting the back side of the island's airport. At least I hoped it was the back side of the island's airport, because the twin-engine Cessna roaring in behind the high, vine-covered chain-link fence across the street was either crashing or landing as I pulled over in front of Asa's house and a pile of discarded rattan furniture. I got out of Barney's car.

A new black Yamaha Virago was parked outside, with a license plate that read HERS. A sign said the house was scheduled to be remodeled. The yard was fenced off but the gate open. I strolled up the walk, past a riot of co-conut palms, ferns, sour orange trees, bamboo and epi-phytes, toward the open door, hearing an old Cream album playing from inside. Nineteen-sixties rock.

"Hello?" I called out, standing in the doorway, look-ing into the living room. It was clear I was far from New York City if people left their doors wide open.

I smelled the sweet odor of marijuana. All the furni-ture in here looked new. New leather couches. New big flat-screened plasma TV. Pricey Iranian carpet. Clearly Asa Rodriguez had been spending money lately.

I also saw a large bubbling fish tank—stocked with tropical fish—and a teak bar lined with dark rums. The bookshelves displayed knickknacks, not books. Conches. Bobble-head dolls. And a dozen framed photos of the same man and woman—a time line of their relationship, spanning decades. No kids.

"Anyone home?" I called.

I saw the couple as 20-year-olds, newlyweds, with sunflowers in their hair, outside a steepled church. I saw them as thirtyish longhairs, in khaki uniforms and sunglasses, working as deckhands on a sunset cruise ship. I saw them as graying 40-year-olds, marching in Key West's Fantasy Fest dressed as Neptune and a mermaid. I saw them as scuba divers, and I saw the man in a glassed-in porch research lab, possibly the back of this house. He'd been a freelancer, all right, doing research during off hours from work.

"Can I help you?"

The woman had come out of a back room, slim, leathery and barefoot, about 50 now, or aged prematurely by the sun. She wore khaki shorts and a black T-shirt. The hempy odor grew strong at her approach.

"Is Asa here?"

She answered with friendliness, without bothering to ask who I was.

"He's where he usually is evenings. The Blue Conch."

"Is that a bar?"

"On Caroline, near Duval, next to Tel Aviv T-shirts. Third stool from the right. Give him a message. Tell him Ray Teaks in Maryland keeps calling. Tell him to turn his cell phone on."

My sense of being close to answers picked up. I got back into Barney's Maxima and headed for Key West's main drag, a strip of shops, restaurants and bars. I'd visited the island several times over the years on vacations, so I knew where to go. Even in summer I passed a smattering of strolling tourists, the usual barefoot locals peddling big basketed bikes, more tourists on rented scooters and a drunken Pulitzer Prize–winning novelist I recognized from TV.

Everyone on Duval Street looked more relaxed than I felt.

The Blue Conch announced itself with—what else—a blue neon conch in front. At the bar, the third stool from the right was empty, so I occupied it, hoping Asa would come over when and if he showed up. The place was almost deserted, with rotating ceiling fans, hanging fishnets, old license plates on the walls and photos of local divers, including Mel Fisher, Key West's famous treasure hunter, who'd found the $400 million sunken *Atocha* in the 1980s. Fisher's neck was wrapped in gold necklaces in the shot, bounty from the sea, like Asa's fish.

"Barbancourt and Roses," I ordered from the lone, amiable-looking bartender, "two parts to one. Where's Asa?"

He grunted. "I heard he had engine trouble. He left the *Eureka* on one of the finger piers behind the Turtle Kraals. He'll probably be in later, after another fruitless day of searching for his damn fish."

He was a fat, pale, bearded man in a floral-print shirt, and he spoke with a Boston accent. But what caught my attention was the way he kept rubbing his right hand with his left. The knuckles, which looked uninjured, seemed to hurt him quite a lot.

"Injury?" I said, hoping I'd gotten lucky, and his pain would help me now.

"Arthritis." He made a face as he worked a thumb into his knuckles.

Bingo!

"My sister has it," I lied. "She used to play competitive tennis. Now she can barely hold the racket." I shook my head in sympathy. "Looks painful."

"I can't remember when it didn't hurt."

I sipped my drink. He seemed content to talk, and there weren't other customers to take him away from me. *Go slow,* I thought. "I understand there are some great new medicines in the pipeline," I said, knowing this from Lenox. "My sister said NIH is testing a promising possibility, but to get into the sample group you have to win a lottery. That's how many people applied."

The bartender nodded unhappily. "I didn't get in."

I asked casually, "What about Asa's stuff? Did you try that?"

The guy got a dreamy smile on his face. But he kept rubbing his hand. "It didn't work either. I had high hopes when Asa told me it came from Indians. Indians are in tune with the natural world, you know."

"If you don't mind my asking," I said, puzzled, "why are you smiling if the drug *didn't* work?"

"Seven thousand bucks," he grinned, "that's why. During the month I was in Asa's group I went to the Indian Casino and cleaned up in poker. Normally I can't play for shit. That night?" He crooned, "You gotta know when to hold 'em . . ."

At any other time this would have struck me as a good story, but I was more interested in the drug. "Pretty damn lucky," I said to keep the conversation going.

His grin broadened. "I couldn't lose."

"Sorry the drug didn't work."

His face fell. "I'd trade poker luck for a drug that works any day," he said, rubbing his knuckles. "All Asa's did was give me a rash on my back. And a headache."

"What sort of rash?" I asked, interested now, knowing that the effect of biological weapons often starts with a rash, burning eyes, shortness of breath.

He shrugged. "Just a rash. It went away when I stopped taking the drug. Some guy flew down from the company that worked with Asa and asked ten million questions about that rash. Did my throat close up? Did I run a fever? What the hell was his name? Mintz? No. Kranz! Ralph Kranz!"

Kranz was here? I thought, surprised.

The bartender said. "I gotta serve another customer."

I hadn't seen the two blondes come in. I nursed the Barbancourt, feeling the rum spread through me. The bartender forgot me as he joked with the girls at the end of the bar. To get him back, I signaled for another drink.

"The lady in the halter top asked about you. She's interested, my friend," he said, pouring, smiling.

"Did anyone else in Asa's test group get sick?"

"Huh?"

"Did other people get the rash too?"

He seemed surprised that I'd ignored the blonde, so I toned down my eagerness. "It's just that whenever I hear about an arthritis drug, I try to find out more, to tell my sister," I said.

He glanced at the girl and shrugged, as if to tell her, "I tried. He's not interested."

Then he put his elbows on the bar. "We didn't socialize. But there was this one guy, Dick, from Big Coppitt Key. He came in here once with Asa. What was his last name? I'm bad with names. Some bartender, huh? Wait! It was Dick Milenko. A major in the Army Reserve, he said."

"See?" I said. "Mister Memory."

"My dad's like you. Always calling me if he reads a magazine article on arthritis. Your sister's lucky to have someone in her life who cares."

I thanked the bartender and overtipped him.

"Aren't you going to wait for Asa to show up?"

"I'll be back," I said.

I looked through the phone book by the pay phone and found a Dick Milenko listed on Osprey Lane on Big Coppitt Key.

Back in the car, I headed north. It took less than fifteen minutes to reach Big Coppitt, a small island lying well south of the army roadblock. I asked a man peddling a bicycle directions and less than a minute later pulled into a horseshoe-shaped driveway fronting a well-lit, two-story stucco home set back from a palm-lined road. A magnificent old banyan tree sat in the front yard. A new black Bronco occupied the crushed-shell driveway. Its rear bumper sticker read "Army Reserve."

When I rang the bell, I heard chimes.

The door opened. Bright light framed the tall, handsome man who peered out at me, fit-looking and in his late twenties, I judged, with broad shoulders, a neat mustache and a haircut just on the long side for a military guy, even in the reserves. The eyes were pale brown. He wore blue jeans and a short-sleeved matching shirt with a Rebok logo.

"Major Milenko? I'm sorry to bother you at this hour. I took a chance you'd be home. My name is Mike Acela. I work for Lenox Pharmaceuticals."

I held out my wallet, showing my now canceled company ID.

He frowned politely. "I don't want to be rude, but I'm packing, Mr. Acela. I have a flight to Riyadh out of Miami at six-thirty A.M. I'm an engineer for Pratt. We're replacing some old engines on the Saudi Airlines 767s next week. And by the way, I'm a lieutenant colonel now."

"I know it's late, sir, but at Lenox we've had a breakthrough with the drug you tested. I hoped I could ask just a couple questions about it before you go."

"Interviews are never limited to a couple of questions, and I told your Mr. Kranz everything. No fevers during that test. The headaches went away. He must have asked a thousand questions."

I nodded as if I knew this. "But did he tell you we think we fixed the problem with the drug? It works now."

Milenko paused. A hopeful expression replaced the put-out one on his face. I felt guilty lying to him but added, "In fact, we plan to test the new batch on the same groups, that is, if the same subjects want to try again."

Milenko tilted his head, very interested now. "I really can't spare more than a few minutes. I always tell myself not to put off packing until the last second. I always forget."

He stepped back to let me in.

Based on the half-complete state of the living room, I pegged Milenko for a recent divorcé or man who'd just split up with his live-in lover. Indentations on the blue shag carpet marked spots where furnishings had been removed: a couch, a sitting chair, a coffee table. I saw an empty alcove in the wall unit, big enough to hold a 24-inch TV. I also noticed a couple of bright rectangular spots on the coral-colored walls, where I supposed paintings or posters had hung.

Milenko said, "All I have is iced tea. Want some?"

No plants. No pets. No photos of anyone besides Milenko in uniform—showing the major in Baghdad beneath a huge street poster of Saddam Hussein, and standing

"More than that," I said, remembering that the *Wall Street Journal* had called the Chairman lucky, that the Director of National Intelligence had called the Intelligence work in the Mideast lucky at first, and later on the radio he'd talked about breakthroughs in interrogation techniques.

I also remembered something that the Chairman had told me on the last night I saw him, something I had not attached extra meaning to until now. *It is hard to fight an enemy who has outposts in your head.*

I'd assumed at the time that he meant betrayal inside the company.

The stories I heard tonight are coincidence, I told myself now.

But was it possible, biologically feasible, that a chemical could somehow enhance a person's mental abilities so much, it would be mistaken for luck at first—before people understood what was *really* happening? Of course, if such a thing *were* possible, I saw, the ramifications would be staggering. In finance. Politics. Love. War.

That would have burdened the Chairman, all right.

I also remembered something that old Barney Birnbaum had once told me, at the Bureau. "The greatest failures this agency ever committed happened because agents refused to believe evidence in front of their faces, because it didn't fit in with preconceived notions."

But I was letting myself get carried away even considering this. All I'd heard were two unconfirmed stories.

You need more information. You're grasping at straws.

I heard Lieutenant Colonel Milenko sigh. "I said my story had nothing to do with the drug."

I needed to find other people in the group and ask more questions. Pulse hammering, I asked Dick Milenko if he knew whether anyone else who had taken HR-109 had contracted a rash or fever. I needed more names.

"Mildred didn't."

"Mildred?"

"Mildred Orsichek's the only one I know. She didn't mention any fever. She moved back to Shaker Heights. I haven't talked to her in months. Have you?"

"I've had trouble finding her," I said.

"No prob. I have her number." He left the room, was gone a few minutes, and came back with a slip of paper.

"Remember," he said as I left, "if you've worked the kinks out of the drug, I want to be in the first group to test it. My joints get worse every year."

"I promise," I said, hating myself for encouraging hope in him. I told him, "We'll call you when we know."

I stopped at the first pay phone I found—back in Key West—and called Shaker Heights, Ohio. An elderly-sounding man answered Mildred Orsichek's number on the second ring. It would be an hour earlier in Ohio: ten P.M.

"Is Mildred there, please?" I asked, my heart racing.

"She's having a bad evening. She's in bed."

I told the man I was a reporter for the *Cleveland Plain Dealer*, researching a feature story about . . . I was going to say "arthritis testing," but suddenly heard myself say, instead, "cognitive science."

"Huh?" the guy said.

"Luck," I said, for lack of a better, faster way to explain. "I'm working on a story about people who have had good luck."

Let's get this nutty idea out of the way, I thought, *and get back to real science.*

I said I'd heard Mildred had an interesting story about luck. Would the man mind asking her to come to the phone?

"Who told you she has a story?"

"Dick Milenko, in Florida." In case Mildred refused to talk to me, I asked the man, "Does her story have anything to do with a rash?"

He hesitated. "Oh, that rash. She loves that story. And the money's come in handy, with her arthritis bills and all."

"The money," I said. My hand was wet.

"Let me go see if she feels like talking," he said.

I held the phone and waited, hearing my own breathing. I heard a dog barking over the phone, and a radio talk show playing. Minutes went by. Then I heard the man in the background. "Don't rush it," he was telling someone. "Millie, catch your breath."

The phone scraped on the other end and I heard labored breathing. She sounded old and sick.

"This is Mildred. You heard my story?"

"Only that you *have* a story."

She had to catch her breath, and then the tale came out between wheezes. She belonged to "a group of old ladies who dabble in the stock market. We take turns researching companies in which to invest, which is easy to do if you have lots of free time."

"By the way," I asked. "When did this happen?"

She mentioned the period during which she'd been in the test group taking HR-109.

Then she said, "It was my turn to pick stocks, so I studied the Internet, annual reports, the *Wall Street Journal.* I also attended the board meeting in Florida of Poseiden Energy, in which the group had already invested, quite heavily.

"Well," she added, "I'm not sure exactly *why*, but I had this *feeling* that those men up there were *lying*. I went up to the chairman afterward and introduced myself, and the feeling got so bad that even though the stock was shooting up, I made the girls pull *all our profits* out that afternoon. Three days later, the chairman was indicted. The bottom fell out. We would have lost tens of thousands of dollars."

"But you didn't," I said.

"No," she said. "That's my story. I also tried the lottery that month, as usual." She laughed. "But I didn't win. Only with stocks, and only when I actually went to the meetings and got close to the management people myself. My friends said I guessed their intentions. I was just lucky."

I t was eleven-twenty now. I felt as if I'd been up for days. But I drove back to Caroline Street and walked into the Blue Conch, my head swimming. Asa Rodriguez would know the *real* story of HR-109.

But the third stool from the right was still empty.

Disappointed, I seated myself again.

Three out of three, I thought. *Is it possible?*

Waiting for the bartender, I considered the phone message to Asa that his wife had asked me to deliver.

What does Dr. Teaks want to talk to Asa about?

I also considered Kranz coming here and interviewing people in the HR-109 group. Kranz had spent lots of time asking about rashes and fevers. But he wasn't stupid, just obnoxious. If the side effect truly related to some breakthrough involving heightened mental skills, he would have misled the interviewees and asked about other things first, as I had.

"You just missed Asa," the bartender said, coming over. "Oh! Wait! He's coming out of the men's room now."

I turned to see a tall, thin, weathered, long-haired man wearing baggy cutoffs and a stained white T-shirt—recognizable from the photos at his house, and not exactly Lenox's average-looking scientist—walking slowly out of the bar without looking back.

"It's your lucky night," the bartender said. "I thought he'd gone home."

I followed Asa Rodriguez out onto Caroline Street, trying to figure out how to make the approach. I heard piano music—a Michael Franks tune—coming from a two-story house with an open-air balcony. Rap music blasted from a pink Mustang driving by. I heard a steel grate going down as a man closed up George's Bar, and saw a couple arguing on the corner of Ann Street.

"I bet you *slept* with her," the woman screamed. "Tell the truth! I'll know if you lie!"

I didn't want to startle Asa but didn't want to risk losing him either. I couldn't assume he was going home, and considering events recently, I preferred to grab an opportunity when it came up. I hoped he'd slow down at a shop window or stop to unchain a bicycle or unlock a car. Or maybe he was walking back to his docked boat. I could stroll up casually, pretend to recognize him and try a don't-I-recognize-you-from-Lenox line.

He turned right off Caroline onto Peacon, a one-way lane through this historic quarter, wide enough to accommodate only one car at a time. It was deserted at this hour, and the homes were dark. I watched him walk behind the side of a small bungalow, and from the tinkling sound realized he was taking another piss.

Here we go, I thought.

Then I heard the musical chimes of a cell phone from his direction, the first eight notes from "Margaritaville." I halted. Clearly his phone had been switched on, and a moment later I realized he was one of those people who raise their voice loudly when talking on cell phones. From where I was standing, his words were quite clear.

I heard, "I *knew* it was the amygdala. The answer *had to be* in the limbic system. And the effect gets *stronger* if you heat the sample longer, Teaks."

Then he snapped, "Well, if I weren't so allergic to the damn stuff, I would take it myself and fly up there now."

And then, after a pause, "I don't care what the contract says. I never would have signed if I thought you people were going to—"

Teaks must have cut him off. Asa Rodriguez listened and then said, angrily, "I don't care who threatened me. If I want to tell the fucking newspapers what's happening, I will."

He hung up.

I waited as the shadow—Asa Rodriquez—detached itself from the wall and weaved back toward me, less drunk-looking now, more disturbed.

He nodded vaguely at me. Key West is a friendly place. People aren't scared of being mugged on the street. They say hi to strangers even when upset, even at night.

"Asa? Asa Rodriguez?"

He halted, trying to place me. He came closer in the dark. There was no one else on the street.

"I work for Lenox Pharmaceuticals. I'm a friend of

Kim Pendergraph's. Remember me? We met in the Chairman's waiting room when you were in."

He froze. Of course he didn't recognize me.

"Mike Acela," I said, holding out a hand. But his reaction shocked me. He backed away, terrified.

"Oh, God," he cried out. "You! Don't hurt me!"

Sneakers pounding, he began to run.

"I just want to talk to you!" I called after him.

But he ran faster, disappearing around the corner onto Caroline.

Nothing is easy today, I told myself. I started to run too.

Big mistake.

ELEVEN

I wanted to ask him so many things, like whether a rare fish, ground up, could actually bring victory in a battle. I wanted to ask what he'd just threatened to tell the newspapers, and if he knew the Chairman's mistake.

"I'm not who you think I am," I called.

Mostly, I wanted to know who had warned him to run from me.

Or is he running because he was involved in the Chairman's death?

But instead of asking anything, I was doing a bad job of chasing him. He was skinny but fast, his sneakers and shorts better suited to sprinting than my loafers and khakis, the clothing of the man I'd masqueraded as all evening, a New York exec on a tropical job.

He disappeared around the corner of Simonton, and I pounded after him, past houses and closed shops and display windows filled with mannequins wearing Mangrove Mania T-shirts, bathing suits, sarongs. He was heading for the waterfront. The bartender had said Asa docked his boat behind a bar called the Turtle Kraals. I remembered drinking there years ago, but had no idea where it was.

I called out, "I just want to talk," rounded the corner of Front Street and the harbor lay ahead, black and flat and filled with docked boats. Half a mile out, past a breakwater, was a long, low fog bank. Red and green running lights marked speedboats racing toward shore to beat a thunderstorm. Lightning flashed inside a vast cloud hovering over the fog.

To the right, down a long boardwalk, Asa Rodriguez fled past ticket booths for sunset cruises, a reef environment relief gift shop, a waterside labyrinth of construction gone wild—overbuilt and overextended like every other square foot of shore. It was a twisting, packed maze of bars, docks, ramps, steps, public phones and sleeping drunks. Buildings and boats blocked views. Hemingway's tropical hideaway had long ago evolved into hippie haven and more recently been converted into condo central for the fourth vacation home and cabin cruiser crowd.

Running, I recalled, more as a flash of collective memory rather than concrete thought, all the times the Chairman had bragged to me about Lenox projects, to lengthen life, reduce cancers. "Miracles," he'd say, "once considered the province of heaven. God's outstretched palm holds a Lenox pill."

I also remembered Asa saying the word *amygdala* into the phone, and that Ray Teaks in Maryland had explained it was the part of the brain on which Naturetech worked.

I exercised regularly at a gym, but I wasn't accustomed to running in thick, tropical air. The only edge I had came from the scientist's sprinting style of landing hard on his heels, so even when he was out of sight I heard the *thwack* of footfalls.

But the footfalls stopped abruptly and I halted also, trying to listen for him as I caught my breath. I leaned against a pole plastered with advertisements for charter fishing trips at Garrison Bight. I envisioned the man ahead, heaving, cocking his head to hear if I was still coming.

I called out, "I need to talk about HR-109."

No answer.

I started running again, past bar after bar. I almost crashed into a railing as the boardwalk ended. No, I saw, not ended but made a sharp left, and I was vaguely aware of a sign overhead, in the dark, under the closed entrance to still one more bar.

TURTLE KRAALS, it read.

Pelicans lined the roof, staring or dozing, ghostly in the dark.

No Asa in sight. A sump pump was running loudly nearby, making hearing footsteps impossible. Looking out into Key West Bight, I saw a complete fucking Rube Goldberg–like maze of docks: floating docks attached to fixed docks, fuel docks, B docks, docked boats stretched away, dinghies, outboards, inflatables, cruisers. It was more crowded than Grand Central Station out there. The air smelled of gasoline and fried fish. Where the hell had Asa gone?

What did that bartender say Asa named his boat?

Thunder exploded over the harbor. My shirt stuck to my back from sweat.

I headed for the nearest pier as a rubber Zodiac boat detached itself from the one farthest away and droned into Conch Harbor. A bare-chested figure steered in back.

Shit. It's him, I thought.

But I realized the man wasn't Asa. The hair was too short, the hunched shoulders too wide.

Stepping onto the closest dock, I smelled the incoming storm's electricity on the wet cool breeze.

I hoped Asa was on one of these boats, maybe trying to start it, maybe on a cell phone whispering to Keating, or Kranz, Eisner, Schwadron, Teaks, whomever had told him my name. If I were Asa, afraid and alone, I might also be reaching for a weapon, a kitchen knife or, I realized, remembering that he was a diver, a speargun.

I wish I had a weapon too.

I called over the rhythmic hammering of the sump pump, "Whatever you heard about me is wrong!"

No answer. Now the sweat was in my trousers, running down my legs.

Find a hotel, I told myself. *Try to talk to him tomorrow, in daylight, when he's not frightened.*

But considering the speed with which things were falling apart for me, whatever I intended to accomplish would have to happen tonight.

I stepped onto the second dock in line, paused at each tied-up boat, peered down, checked names, figured I'd remember Asa's boat when I saw it.

I saw a small dredger, the *Yo Mudder,* and a sailboat, the *Away We Go,* and a small Azimut, the *Just Say Yes.* Those weren't the right names.

"What's the damn side effect of the drug?!"

Thunder roared, closer. Lightning sizzled over the bay. Mad with frustration, I thought, *Just give me a minute and I can get some answers.*

Stars winked out as the fog bank approached.

Then I reached the last pier and the fog engulfed me. The ambience changed from balmy South Pacific to cold South London in seconds. It was impossible to see more than twenty feet away.

I reached the last boat, a small cabin cruiser, and saw its name, *Eureka,* in gold paint. *That's it!* The first raindrop hit. My eyes moved over the gunwale and I spotted the body lying beside the open cabin door.

Lightning strobe-lighted the still life below me in green: green fiberglass boat, green skin, green water.

I went green myself.

It was Asa, all right. The face was turned away from me, but the stringy hair and baggy shorts were the same.

The guy in the Zodiac must have done this. Was it Oliver Royce?

I climbed onto the boat as the rain broke into a torrent. I slipped and almost fell on something slick on deck, but kept my eyes on the door to the cabin, in case someone hid inside. I poked my head in and, in another lightning burst, got a split-second glimpse of a floating lab: stone countertops, metal cabinets, Bunsen burners, posters of tropical fish.

The door to the head was open. Nobody here.

Outside, the rain fell hard and cold and I leaned over the body, smelling a sweet/rancid blood-and-shit odor. Christ. When I turned over the body, his head tilted back too far. The neck looked broken. His eyes stared, wide open. I found no pulse in the throat or wrist, and probing, located a knife wound in back, between the third and fourth ribs on the left side.

One clean jab, the way a trained Marine would do it.

Tiny bubbles of oxygen—the froth of departed life— dissipated at the right corner of his lips.

I tried CPR anyway, just in case. I pumped his chest, did mouth-to-mouth. Rain flooded out of his throat. It was too late to save him.

Sitting back on my heels, for a moment I even wondered whether my coming here, my trying to talk to him, had caused his death. Or had it been his threat to Ray Teaks over the phone?

Don't touch anything else, I told myself, watching my shoeprint in blood washing away. *You cannot work this alone anymore. Call the police.*

That's when the nausea hit me. At least I managed to throw up over the side, and not contaminate the crime scene any more than I already had.

I groped in my pocket, pulled out my phone, but in a flash of lightning spotted a plastic Baggie sticking out of Asa's pocket—the kind of bag in which people carry marijuana.

My hand seemed to reach for the baggie by itself. Sure enough, I saw a half-teaspoon's worth of oreganolike substance inside. Hunched over the bag to keep the rain out, I opened it and sniffed. I smelled the salt-sea odor again.

Every second you don't call the cops works against you.

But I was overwhelmed at some level, split into two people: the dazed citizen who'd stumbled on a murder, and the trained investigator at the scene. The citizen told himself to call the police. The investigator was trying to figure out the crime scene—and frankly, was reluctant to give away another sample of HR-109.

Still holding the cell phone, I remembered the bartender telling me that Asa had been looking "fruitlessly" for his fish today. It made no sense. Hadn't he already *found* the fish?

Finally I gave up, and started to punch in 911, but at that moment a flashlight beam switched on, startling and blinding me, coming from out on the water, ten feet away.

A friendly male voice cried out, "Hey, Big Asa! What are you doing standing in—"

I hadn't heard the boat glide up, between the noisy thunder and the sump pump, but now I saw two figures behind the beam—a man and woman, from their silhouettes. And with dread I knew what *they* were seeing. Not the friend they'd expected, but a stranger covered in blood.

"*You're* not Asa," the guy said.

I talked fast as the beam dropped to illuminate my bloody hands. "I found him like this. There was a guy. A Zodiac . . ."

"Oh, *God,*" the woman cried as the beam froze on Asa.

The man gasped. "What did you do?"

All three of us started shouting at the same time.

"It wasn't me!"

"Brian, get out of here!"

"Martha, call the cops!"

The world filled with noise and confusion: thunder, pumps, rain, screaming. The guy must have turned his throttle up, because his boat leaped forward, churning out toward open water. He probably figured that boating through a lightning storm was safer than staying near me. From the woman's silhouette, I saw she held her cell phone, and was punching in numbers I should have finished dialing myself, before the couple showed up.

Her call will go through before mine. Key West is a tiny island. The cops will be here in minutes. Either contact them now or get away fast.

In the fraction of a second during which I processed my options, I felt them as urges rather than logical choices. An innocent man—from the police point of view—would stick it out, tell the story. But the police would find Asa's blood on me, and my prints on the boat, unless they washed away. And plenty of witnesses around town would assure them that I'd been searching for Asa tonight.

Plus, I'd lied to people about working for Lenox. I'd misrepresented myself as Asa's friend to the bartender. I was a suspect in the Chairman's death back home.

And what did I have to support my side? Just a name—Royce—and an unsubstantiated story about a man in a Zodiac, who I hadn't even actually seen on Asa's boat.

I picked up my phone and hit *9*.

You can convince them. Stick it out. Once you run, you're a fugitive.

I punched *1*, and another *1*.

If even one person saw you chasing Asa, and they come forward . . .

I heard a siren.

I ran.

I can't count all the times over the years that I've advised suspects claiming innocence to trust the FBI. Put your faith in me, I'd tell them. Mike Acela is a human lie detector. Basically, ninety-nine percent of the time, the system works.

"Truth is the best protection," I'd assure them in jails, at their businesses, in their homes as they sat with family, trying to decide whether to talk to me or not. I'd really believed my words. I'd been so earnest that I'd convinced suspects to cooperate lots of times.

Well, things look different when you're running and don't personally know the investigators as friends. The rain burst down in a fusillade. The docks were empty. I tried to retrace my steps to the car, knowing I had a few minutes to move it before police converged on the area, and cursing myself for parking in front of a meter outside the bar where Asa had last been seen alive. I'd even left a piece of paper on the front seat on which I'd scrawled Asa's name in thick Magic Marker, and his address and the name of the Blue Conch. If I didn't get the car out of there before morning, it would start collecting tickets. A smart cop would notice the car and wonder why no one moved it. He'd see the note. He'd track down Barney, who would say I'd been acting funny, scared, secretive.

Friendship among ex–FBI agents—when it comes to protecting accused murderers—only goes so far.

I heard another siren, coming toward me from a different direction. I tried to fix my position by remembering the map in the car. Key West was six miles across, the Turtle Kraals on the north, the eastern spit running into a narrow bridge toward the mainland. Being a tourist destination, the city can afford a larger-than-average police force, I knew, and top-of-the-line access to criminal databases. The cops are out in force at night, when drunken visitors become unruly. They don't need a lot of time to mobilize.

I imagined a police dispatcher sending out my description, provided by the couple in the boat.

He's six feet tall with dark hair and a beard. His white short-sleeve shirt and khakis are covered with blood.

A cinch to spot.

Get the blood off, I told myself. *Hide. No, get the car while you can, because there's no one out in this storm to see you. Leave the island before a roadblock goes up at the bridge.*

How far from the car was I anyway? How many minutes had I spent chasing the scientist from the bar?

My footfalls sounded loud as I reentered the maze of

shops. Between the storm, my shock and my unfamiliarity with the island, finding my way back seemed impossible. The rain was blinding. I had no layout in my head. I'd paid little attention to the route I'd run while coming here. I'd been concentrating on Asa, not the way.

I almost crashed into a bicycle rack. Had I passed it before, or had I passed a different rack? I almost ran into a real-estate guide dispenser. I didn't remember seeing the little tattoo parlor or "chapel by the sea" before, or the plate-glass window behind which a mannequin stared out at me, in a diving suit and goggles. In a flash of lightning I saw—reflected—just how *much* blood covered me.

I can't go back to the car like this.

I spun and ran back and reached the boardwalk. The sirens sounded closer as I pulled off my shoes and jammed them tightly into my pants at the waist.

Now I saw headlights coming, and flashing red lights. So I jumped into the sea.

The water was deep right off. I was a decent swimmer, not stylish but strong. I glanced back, heading out along the docks. The rain made the shore seem farther away already, but the lights there gave me a fix. The police would not hear me swimming. There was too much other noise for that. But I heard a big power boat coming, and thought, *Coast Guard,* and saw a bright searchlight beam a hundred yards out, aiming diagonally toward the piers and Asa's boat as the patrol headed in.

The beam swept past me, missed me by fifty yards.

My clothes weighed me down. I swam harder, under the boats and docks, up and down, using shore lights—homes, bars, headlights—to stay parallel to the island, but the current pushed me seaward. The outgoing tide got stronger.

Something bumped my feet.

Shit.

I kept swimming.

It bumped me again, harder.

Jesus, I thought. Don't be a shark. Don't be something big and hungry.

I forced myself to stroke steadily, to imagine something harmless and curious down there, a turtle, or dolphin, or piece of half-sunken wood.

Whatever it was, it was gone.

After what I judged about twenty more minutes—in the strong current—I turned back toward shore, muscles aching. I aimed at a dark patch between two sets of streetlights, hoping it would be a lawn, a strip of private property owned by people who were asleep—or even better, away in summer.

I hit bottom and pulled myself ashore, ran across a small strip of beach onto Simonton Street, passed a couple of old warehouses and reached the backyard of a remodeled two-story stucco bungalow. I saw a trio of upside-down kayaks on a wooden rack, seagoing models with paddles and life jackets beneath them, and a couple of Adirondack chairs and a picnic table beside a propane grill. The rain still pummeled me but was letting up. I considered stealing a kayak, carrying it back to the water, but I had no sense of direction out there, and the current had been getting stronger. I was cold and my muscles ached. I lumbered toward the bungalow and its rear deck, huge satellite TV antenna and wall of glass in back.

A lone light burned in the kitchen, which looked empty of people inside a sliding glass door. But I spotted a pile of dirty dishes by the sink. This family was not away.

Then a dog started barking inside the house. A large animal, from the sound. A German shepherd appeared at the glass door of the kitchen, snarling, framed in light.

I hurried around the side of the house but realized no more lights were going on. No one inside was reacting to the crazy barking. Perhaps the owners were out.

And when I practically ran into hanging wash left in the rain, that confirmed it. If anyone were home they would have taken in the wash before it got soaked.

The dog had moved to a side window, but the barking was muffled, as the window was closed. I didn't think neighbors would hear it. On the line hung clothes for a family: men's stuff, women's stuff, kids' stuff. I used a sopping towel to wipe my head, face, arms. I checked the towel in a flash of lightning and found it clean. The rain and my swim must have washed the blood off my skin.

But the blood on my clothes was still there.

I took a short-sleeve button-up floral-print shirt off the line, and cutoff shorts that felt snug but fit. I whispered thanks to the homeowners as I unpinned tennis sneakers off the line. They were small for me also, but, with the laces undone, I wedged them on too.

"ROOOOOOOOHHHHH," went the dog, throwing itself against the window, enraged.

I transferred my wallet, keys and cell phone to the new clothes, and the plastic Baggie I'd taken off Asa. I stole a soft-billed cap off the line. DOLPHINS, it said.

I heard no sirens anymore, just the soft slap of rain. Back at the docks, I figured, the crime scene would be cordoned off now. The police would be checking shops, shore and boardwalk. They'd be shining flashlights into trash cans and Dumpsters. They'd be driving the streets, looking for anyone matching the description they'd been given. They'd have an artist or e-sketch officer working on a rendition.

Perhaps by now the first quick sketch was complete—if the couple on the boat had returned.

I figured I was a quarter mile from the Blue Conch, and now I was going to force myself to walk back to it and make another stab at getting the car. I took along my rolled-up discarded clothing. I couldn't leave it there for anyone to find. It would have Asa's blood and my DNA on it. Even dim-witted cops could track me from the clothes if they ran my DNA against federal databases.

FBI agents are required to have DNA profiles on file.

So I tucked the clothing under my arm and started walking. At the front of the house I peeked out at the street. It was nice and quiet, narrow and lined with small homes, overhung with banyan and ficus trees. The homes were dark. I saw no headlights, heard no engines.

I opened a green trash can, stuffed the discarded clothing in the garbage bag inside and retied the bag.

It was so quiet, I heard insects droning and leaves dripping.

Walking back toward Barney's Maxima, watching for headlights, I had a little time to think.

If I can reach Miami I might be safe. I didn't tell anyone my name tonight except for Dick Milenko, and he's heading for Saudi Arabia early tomorrow. He may not hear about the murder before he leaves.

My hope rose until I realized that even if I *did* get away, back in New York Lenox would soon get news of the murder of one of its top freelancers. *When Keating knows, Eisner will, unless they know already because they're responsible. They'll ask for the suspect's description. They'll send my photo to Key West. The cops will show it to the people who saw me.*

I felt sick. Trapped. But there was nothing left in my stomach to eject.

Get off the island. Figure out what to do after that.

Keeping to side streets, soaked and disoriented, I tried to work my way back toward the car, tried to fight off despair. It was hard to imagine things getting worse. If the Royces didn't kill me—or the police didn't arrest me—Eisner was out there. Chairman Dwyer's "mistake"—whatever it was—had unleashed deadly forces. I realized that even if I got out of Key West, the only way for me to prevent my death or eventual arrest was to identify the real murderer and the reason two men had now died.

Finding the answers wasn't about doing a duty for Chairman Dwyer anymore. It was about saving myself and my friends.

And then there was that nagging other question. Because Dwyer had said the whole country was in danger.

What the hell does that drug really do?

I spotted headlights coming and hid alongside the nearest house. The headlights cruised past. They belonged to a pickup truck, not the police.

I was shivering but did not know if it was from the swim, exhaustion or fear. I longed to check into a hotel and take a hot shower. But the police would be canvassing guesthouses, checking ledgers, giving my description to the men and women behind the front desks.

Minutes later I found myself back on Caroline Street. The neon sign above the Blue Conch was turned off. The drizzle continued but the fog was gone. I saw a young tourist couple on the street, strolling, arms entwined, oblivious to the rain and to me as they collected romantic memories to bring home after a trip.

A hippie-looking man pedaled by slowly on a bicycle, the tires sending up sheets of spray. He looked as if he couldn't care less if it was raining or not.

At least people are out. One more block to go.

And with a surge of triumph I spotted the Maxima, but just then a police car rounded the corner fifty yards ahead and rolled toward me.

I slowed but resumed speed, picturing myself as the officers inside the car would: a bearded man strolling toward them with the right build for their suspect, but dressed wrong. A man walking in the rain.

Why didn't I leave the fucking car alone?

For the first time in my life, I felt the meaning of the expression *my skin crawled.* But the cops rolled past. I saw pale faces looking straight ahead behind rain-streaked glass. I felt weak with relief.

By now my hands were shaking so badly it was hard to get the key in the slot, and when I got inside I ripped up the note on the front seat. The rain picked up again as I found the map of Key West and drove off, taking side routes, heading toward the island's far side—the bridge to Cow Key and Miami.

I took Eaton Street past the cemetery, an old cigar factory and rows of converted cigar-maker shacks—now tidy, high-priced, brightly painted homes. I passed a grove of mahoganies and smelled night-blooming jasmine in the rain. I rolled over the overpass above a harbor called Garrison Bight, and CHARTER BOAT ROW, a sign said.

I never passed another squad car but took comfort in

the fact that even at this hour cars were out. In Key West, people move around all night. In minutes I was on North Roosevelt, coming up on the ramp to US 1 and the bridge, feeling better until I spotted blue flashing lights—the roadblock—up on the approach.

Heart pounding, I drove past the turn onto US 1 and stayed on Roosevelt, the main road ringing the island, with its hotels, restaurants, shopping malls.

But I couldn't just keep driving around. Sooner or later a squad car would pull up beside me. I couldn't park and sleep in the car unless I wanted to risk waking with a flashlight beam in my face.

In impulse I turned into a mall containing an all-night Walgreen Drugs. As I appraised the risk of going in, a Subaru with Mississippi plates pulled up and five drenched-looking college-age kids got out. They'd been caught in the rain also. They filed into the store.

I walked in behind them, so the clerks might assume we were together. Inside I moved fast, gathering up a towel, souvenir Key West T-shirt, cheap windbreaker, power bars, OJ, sunglasses, razors, blond hair color, scissors, a woman's compact and two packs of disposable diapers.

The Mississippi people split up, gathering supplies separately. Walking to the cash register, I called across the store at them, "Meet you in the car."

"How old is your baby," the clerk asked me at the register, ringing up the Pampers.

"Little Tom? Five months," I said. "He goes through diapers as fast as three other kids combined."

Ten minutes later I found a spot that seemed a decent risk for leaving the car while I looked for somewhere to sleep. It was walking distance from US 1, on Duck Avenue, a residential road. Several other cars were parked along the curb, and there were no signs posted restricting hours when parking was legal.

The rain had stopped. The air was cool. I took everything I'd bought from the trunk except the Pampers. I'd bought them so the clerk would remember diapers, not hair dye.

On foot, carrying the plastic bag, I headed deeper into the tree-lined residential neighborhood, past small homes, some with stucco walls around the garden, some with boat trailers out front, some, the more cheaply made, raised on cinder blocks or with trellises or bushes hiding crawl spaces beneath.

I have to sleep.

More than a few homes seemed to be locked and shuttered in summer, their occupants away. Some homes had screened porches, but if the owners were away, the porches would probably be locked. Anyway, they were usually in plain view.

At the first shuttered house I approached a floodlight went on, triggered by a motion detector. I got away fast.

At the second, I found a good-sized crawl space behind a row of bushes, but the ground under the house was muddy and smelled of garbage. When I started to crawl in anyway, I heard an animal hissing.

So I got out of there too.

My third try was luckier. The house was shielded by thickly packed trees and had an outdoor shower in back. I hoped it would work tomorrow even though the home was locked. The building occupied slightly raised ground and was dry underneath. I heard no animals when I crawled in.

Save the dry clothes for tomorrow.

Ravenous and wet, I ate the power bars and drank the orange juice. I pulled out my encrypted cell phone and flipped it open. It was so expensive it was supposed to be waterproof. I was gratified to see the light come on, even after my swim.

I called Danny's e-set in New York. At two-thirty A.M., he answered on the third ring, drowsy, but as usual, annoyingly wry.

"Let me guess," he said. "You're in a waterfront hotel, sipping rum. You're buzzed. You figured, wake Danny."

"What happened to Hoot?" I said.

"Her landlady told me two men showed up with Defense Intelligence IDs and took her away."

"Did the landlady actually see it?"

"She saw the car leave."

"Did you talk to Eisner?"

"Me? I was fired. You, me, Hoot. Keating washed his hands of us. Kim quit."

I felt a stab of fear. "Then who's watching her?"

"She's at my place. I've got cousins outside, guarding my building. Nobody gets in unless they see. What about you? Find out anything useful from that scientist?"

"Someone killed him," I said, "before we could talk."

I didn't add that the police were hunting me. That would have made him culpable for aiding and abetting. But I told him it looked like HR-109 might have nothing to do with biological weapons at all. It was possible—unconfirmed but conceivable—that the drug might somehow powerfully enhance the way people processed information, work on the brain to heighten cognition in warfare or business, the ability to intuit other people's inclinations. Their lies. Their truths.

He said doubtfully, "You mean like *mind reading?*"

"More like intentions. Not thoughts. Believe me, I know how far-fetched this sounds."

"No shit," he said. But he didn't object. He took my speculations seriously. After a pause he said, "If that's true, no wonder the army sealed the lab. No wonder DI is going nuts. The last thing you'd want is for terrorists to get hold of something like that. In fact, the last thing *I'd* want is for *anyone* to have it except me."

"But it seems impossible," I said, pulling out the plastic bag, turning it upside down, watching the little grains rolling around inside.

"Coffee makes you more alert," he said.

"I'm not talking about being more alert. I'm talking about a drug that can—it sounds crazy—help you find a terrorist. Know if your wife is lying. Christ, it would change everything. How can a drug do that?"

"Maybe it can't. You're asking me? But I know who we can talk to. My cousin Lou is a powerful medicine man."

I sighed. "Someone more qualified might be more helpful."

"He's big in the field."

"A *medicine* man?"

Danny said proudly, "Lou holds the McDermott Chair in Cognitive Science at NYU. He turned down offers from Harvard last year. He's a pioneer of brain study. FMRI scans. Biofeedback. He was runner-up for the Nobel Prize. He can explain the brain to us like Joe Oz talks about Fords."

"Why didn't you just say he's a doctor?"

"If a doctor isn't a medicine man, who is?" Danny said. "Open your mind."

I had to remind myself amid his jokes that Danny was

unaware of the true state of things in Key West. I told him to set up a meeting with the "medicine man."

"He's very busy," Danny said, but it was a taunt.

"I'll see you tomorrow," I said, looking around my hiding place, praying my words would come true.

"Boss, The Weather Channel showed some big storms down there. Stay dry," he said, and I knew Danny meant more than that. He meant take care of yourself. "Stay dry," he said again.

I felt sorry to lose the connection when I hung up. I was alone, under a stranger's house, trapped and sought by police in one murder, possibly being set up to be charged for another in New York.

Strangers had threatened to kill me. My job was gone. *Stop feeling sorry for yourself. Get some sleep.*

I spread out. I used the Walgreen's bag stuffed with new clothes as a pillow. At least the ground was warm.

As I lay there I again held up the plastic Baggie I'd taken off Asa Rodriguez. I opened it, sniffed it. I remembered the instructions on the Chairman's vial.

Take three hours before.

A small shard of streetlight angled in and glowed on the plastic. I thought, *If there's one thing I could use right now, it's brainpower, or whatever the hell helped Dick Milenko win his war game, and an old lady sell stocks. And if it helps out with plain old luck, I'll take that too.*

Why not, I thought. Why the hell not?

I upturned the bag and ate all of it.

Time to test 109 myself, I thought.

TWELVE

I opened my eyes to squint into bright floodlights. The glare was painful, but I couldn't raise my hand to shield my eyes. My body refused to sit, and with movement gone, like a blind man who hears more acutely, my other senses grew keener. I smelled rubbing alcohol, formaldehyde and tart, ammonialike urine.

But it was the familiar scent of Le Homme aftershave that made my confusion turn to fear.

Light classical music wafted down from speakers beyond the floodlights, as rhythmic and soothing as a hypnotist's voice. I recognized the tune even in my disoriented state. It was Debussy's *La Mer*, the Chairman's favorite. He loved to play it on his CD at home.

"Ah, Mike."

A face jutted into view above, its lower half covered by a blue surgical mask. Inquisitive eyes peered down at me, and I recognized the nasal New England intonations of Keating's voice. He wore a loose surgical gown.

"He's awake," Keating said, leaning closer. "Guess what I'm thinking, Mike. Monkey see, monkey guess."

I turned my face away and my fright turned to terror. Steel clamps bound my wrists to the operating table. My hands were long and covered with black hair, my knuckles double-jointed, my fingernails dirty yellow, my biceps powerful and hairy, and I smelled fresh urine as the warm trickle ran along the inside of my thighs.

"Their brains are like *ours*," lectured Ray Teaks, moving into the bright light. His gloved fingers drew back the plunger on a small hypo. "I won't hurt you, Mr. Acela. I'm a sensitive guy," he said.

Teaks half turned to address a small group of observers behind him, civilians and soldiers from the roadblock. Teaks told them, "The chimp knows I'm lying. He ate the grains."

"Let me go," I said.

"Hey! The chimp's talking!"

"I won't tell," I promised.

"You're damn right you won't," Keating said as the crowd drew close, a human noose of bad intentions, bad expectations. Gabrielle was there, in a tight black mourning dress, biting into a cherry Danish. Danny shook his head sadly as if I had disappointed him. Schwadron wore a surgical mask, but I recognized the friendly crinkle at the corner of his eyes. Eisner saluted like a toy soldier, in uniform. And I spotted Kim beyond them, a small figure in the corner, trying to push close, trying to flash me a warning that I did not understand.

"I chose badly," I said, but I wasn't talking about my investigation.

The crowd bent closer, their faces distorted like those of relatives leaning into a baby's crib.

"Every pet needs an owner," Schwadron said. "I offered you a new owner. But you said no."

I heard the grinding of an electric motor. I tried to fight but the clasps held tight. Abby Royce stood over me now, wielding a surgical drill. Light sparkled like water on the whirring blade as Oliver reached down and gripped my head to keep it steady. His grin showed broken teeth.

And then the faces began changing, becoming my parents, my old FBI friends. Gabrielle and Kim stood beside each other now, Gabrielle's naked arms extended as if to embrace me. Kim gripped the shoulder of a small faceless boy, who had been, in other dreams, my son.

"Give me the disk," whispered Keating, putting his arm around Eisner's shoulder.

"Don't pay attention to *them*. Look at me instead," Gabrielle urged as the blade touched my hairline.

The screaming of the drill grew louder. An enormous pain sliced into my skull.

I shot awake—gasping, heart pounding. My headache was splitting—a wedge of pain driving into the top left side of my skull, where the blade had made contact in the dream. I ran my hands over my head. Instead of bright light above I saw the wooden slats of a house, but I still smelled alcohol and Keating's aftershave, and the faint electrical burning from the drill.

It was the smell that made the house unreal. Nightmares fade when you wake from them, but this one was different. My heartbeat wasn't slowing. My breathing stayed harsh. I told myself I was in Key West, under a house and by a garden. But some other part of my brain—a wholly different system of analysis—insisted that all I saw around me was a lie.

I knew I was being operated on now, *knew* I was under anesthesia and Abby was cutting into my skull.

Wake up.

The headache grew worse, spiked down into my neck, gripped the area between my eyes.

I crawled out into the sunlight and stood shakily, fighting pain. I took in the backyard, ficus trees, outdoor shower, white fence.

This is real. The operation was the dream. The nightmare is over.

I ran my hands over the trunk of a lemon tree, reached up and plucked a fruit and put it to my nose and breathed in the citrus odor. I bit into it, let the tart juice help clear my head.

Slowly, my heart was calming.

A dream. A terrible dream. A nightmare fueled by a drug, I thought, crawling back into the confined space beneath the house to retrieve my supplies.

Great, I thought. I wanted intuition. I got hallucination.

Is that the best you could do? I asked 109, in my mind.

I sluiced the sweat off in the outdoor shower, appreciating the shock of cold water. I hung the little mirror I'd bought and—with scissors and razor—removed my beard. I toweled dry. I trimmed my haircut, rounding it off. Without the beard and with the new haircut, my face looked less angular in the mirror.

Add the sunglasses. The model I'd chosen would accentuate a rounder face too.

New clothes on. But I skipped applying the dye, deciding not to risk doing it badly. A good cop can spot a bad dye job half a mile away, and during a manhunt a bad dye job screams, "Look my way."

God, what a dream.

Peering out from the property, I saw that the street was deserted. I strolled out and began the walk back toward the bridge to see if the roadblock was gone. The sky was blue, the sun low and yellow in the east, over the water. All signs of the storm were gone.

My watch told me it was 8:38 A.M.

Drive to Miami. Fly home. Try to figure things out in New York before the police find out who you are.

It was a race.

Walking closer to US 1, I saw with relief that the approach was open. But craning northeast toward the causeway, I felt a barb move into my belly. Beyond the MARATHON, 45 MILES sign, I spotted a line of slowly moving vehicles. The roadblock had been downgraded to a slowdown. Traffic rolled through a gauntlet of squad cars as officers peered into each vehicle as it passed.

Why are they still here?

I turned and headed back to the Maxima, which I found parked where I'd left it, on quiet Duck Avenue. I got inside and started the engine. I turned on the radio and found a local station right away.

"Key West Police Chief Rick Follett said this morning that there's been no identification of the man who last night murdered Chief Follet's brother-in-law. Possibly the same man who came to Rodriguez's home yesterday evening."

Oh, shit. That's why the roadblock is still up.

"Follet said no motivation has been established for the killing so far. Asa Rodriguez's wallet was found at the scene, filled with money, so robbery is out. Police found fingerprints, which have been sent to the FBI lab in Miami."

My headache was getting worse.

"Mrs. Tanya Rodriguez has offered a ten thousand dollar reward to anyone having information leading to an arrest.

Extra patrols are out and the attacker's sketch has been posted widely. Meanwhile, City Council members have asked the chief to end the bridge slowdown, but Follett said he will keep it in place.

"He said, quote, 'Any politician that doesn't like it can kiss my ass.'"

I rifled the glove compartment, hoping Barney would have aspirin inside for the headache. No luck.

I noticed as I closed the compartment that I had contracted a bright purple rash on the back of my wrist. It was only two inches in diameter, but it itched like hell.

So I got the rash and the headache. But it was the other part I wanted, the damn sixth sense. Wouldn't it be funny if the drug has no effect at all?

I knew I better get moving, not sit in front of a house. There were no good choices here, only gradients of risk.

If I tried to wait for the roadblock to lift, I might be identified before I could reach New York and do more investigating. But if I moved around I risked being spotted from police posters, or by someone who'd seen me last night. And there was always the possibility that the clerk from the drugstore had seen a poster and told the police about the clothing and shaving equipment I'd bought.

Try to rent a boat.

I rechecked the map of Key West and made my decision. I started the drive back toward Garrison Bight and Charter Boat Row, to see if charters were operating in the summer. If they were, other tourists might be hiring them today.

With over ten thousand people on the island, the police couldn't be watching all of them at the same time.

I drove with the window open. The air felt hot on my face. Four-lane Flagler Avenue was flat and spotted with cars showing license plates from all over the country. Red traffic lights blinked like LED security cameras. Sunlight was bright as the floodlights in my dream, and—even with sunglasses on—pooled into shimmering lakes on the road. Palm trees and roofs of small homes rose above stucco walls and chain-link fences. I passed a Dion Gas & Fried Chicken place, Budde's Office Supply, the Little Havana strip mall.

I was less than two miles to the Bight but the blocks seemed longer than I remembered. I heard a siren and saw a red pulsing light in the rearview mirror overtaking me, and heart hammering, I pulled over. An ambulance, a white blur, rushed past. Minutes later at a stoplight a busload of children halted beside me, and dozens of small faces fixed on mine. The kids shouted and pointed. They pulled at their mouths, making faces. The driver looked over and shrugged, as if to apologize for their behavior.

Then the smile turned to a frown. The light changed and I drove off.

It got worse. Noises started up in the wheel well. Something was wrong with the car. The noise sounded like rocks in the wheel, hitting metal. It was so loud that pedestrians stared.

Damn.

I pulled over by the Patriot's Plaza shopping mall, a block-long row of storefronts—Winn-Dixie, Pier 1 Imports and Boog's Sporting Goods. I considered abandoning the car but the idea of walking long distances in plain view seemed more risky than trying to fix the car's noise. Forcing calm, knowing that fear is a mind killer, I opened the trunk and got out tools. I hoped that removing the hubcap would reveal a few stones there—and the solution would be simple.

The rash had spread up my forearm now.

I had good luck, though. There *were* stones in the wheel well, and I dropped them in the gutter. I put the hubcap back on and stood up just as a police cruiser passed by, its occupants having decided not to help me out.

But then the squad car made a right turn at the nearest corner, which meant it was either driving away or circling back for another look.

Walk away for a few minutes. See if they come back. What if Asa's wife described the car to the police?

Leaving the Maxima, I strolled into Boog's Sporting Goods—keeping my eyes on the plate-glass window and the street outside.

The police car did not come back.

I bought a fishing rod and tackle box, some lures, some extra line. What kind of fisherman would I be if I showed up at the docks empty-handed?

My cell phone chimed as I picked a *Key West Citizen* off a stand near the cash register and waited in line. Caller ID told me Gabrielle Dwyer was phoning.

I flipped open the unit to answer but was almost physically halted by a sudden powerful thought—almost a scream—in my head.

That man is a thief.

The words—they weren't actually *words* so much as a sensation of certainty—flooded into me with such force that I snapped my head around, shocked.

I found myself looking at a man striding up to stand behind me in line, a small scraggly guy in a Bulls basketball shirt, faded stained jeans and Converse high-tops. He held a Publix shopping bag and a new baseball he intended to buy. He looked about twenty. He glanced into my eyes and must have seen something he didn't like there, because he frowned and cocked his head. He glanced behind him to see if I was looking at someone else.

He shifted stance. And he averted his eyes.

What the hell just happened in my head?

A moment later the man casually turned and walked back into the aisle, away from the line. I followed his movements in the security mirror mounted above the cash register.

The man stopped by a display of expensive fishing reels in the back of the store. He glanced at the mirror at the front of the store, watching me in it, checking if I was looking back. He reached into the shopping bag.

He put the reel that he had stolen back on the shelf.

Holy shit, I thought, astounded.

"That'll be one hundred and eighteen dollars," the clerk behind the cash register told me, smiling.

I must have seen him out of the corner of my eye shoplift the reel. I must have been distracted, so it took a while to register, I told myself as I paid.

The man in the basketball shirt was hurrying out of the store now. He glanced back at me with something like fear in his eyes as the door closed behind him.

"Here's your change," said the man behind the register. "I hear the tarpon are running. Good luck."

How did I know that man stole something?

"Everyone can use luck," I said.

I went back to the car and unfolded the paper. My heart was a snare drum and my headache had subsided into a dull, steady pain.

Maybe it was the way he was walking or the way he glanced into his shopping bag that triggered my intuition. Sure. That was it. Not any drug.

I was so off balance, it took me a second to realize that the police sketch of me dominated the lower front page.

Police Seek Killer in Key West.

The likeness wasn't wrong, but it wasn't exact either. I'd noticed one constant in police sketches over the years, and it was the sense of incipient menace that the artist always conveyed—the shadowy brows, heightened stares, the feral quality to the face. Have you ever flipped through Wanted sketches in a post office and seen someone who looks like they're going to a party? Or mowing a neighbor's lawn as a favor, which—admit it—even hardened murderers do?

Nope. It's like, in the sketches, you walk around with your face screaming guilt to the world.

So now I saw that the *shape* of my face was right, sort of, the spacing between the eyes correct, and the high forehead, and the strong chin corresponded roughly to the shape of the beard I'd cut off. But the hair was flatter, probably because it had been wet when the couple on the boat saw it. And the eyes had that sullen intensity marking cop sketches around the world.

Or maybe I'd really looked like that when I was standing over the dead man last night.

In short, the sketch was enough to make a good policeman pause if he saw me, but it wasn't enough to make him shout, "There he is!"

I scanned the article. Asa's wife had confirmed that a man fitting my description had been looking for him last night, which meant the cops knew I'd gone to the Blue

Conch, and that meant the bartender would tell them he'd sent me off to talk to Dick Milenko.

And Dick Milenko had seen my Lenox ID. Even if he was abroad, he'd probably be reachable by e-mail or phone.

There was no reference to Lenox so far, or HR-109.

GETOUTOFHEREGETOUTNOWNOWNOWNOW!!!!

It wasn't words this time in my head but a screaming sense of danger flooding every muscle in my body. I jerked up, turned on the ignition but drove off slowly, resisting the urge to slam my foot onto the accelerator. I waited to hear a siren but nothing happened. I had no idea where the sense of danger had come from, but the force and certainty in the intuition far exceeded anything I'd ever felt.

Only then did I glance in the rearview mirror, to see a small boy staring at my receding car. He held a leashed beagle with one hand, a newspaper in the other. He was looking back and forth from the newspaper to the car.

This had been the second time that the sense had gripped me in the last ten minutes. Both times the surge had come out of nowhere. Both times it had almost been a voice shouting in my head. Both times the feeling had caused my headache to spike.

I must have seen the kid from the corner of my eye, I told myself. I had not registered his presence consciously. But unconsciously I'd known to leave.

Or is it possible . . . conceivable . . . that you're actually picking up intent? Which is the specific effect you were testing for.

In my head, I still saw the fright on the face of the thief in the sporting goods store.

And the little boy, looking at the newspaper . . .

My certainty had been so powerful. . . . .

Don't leap to conclusions, I thought.

The phone began chiming. Gabrielle was calling again, from her apartment, and if she'd tried to reach me twice in a few minutes, the reason might be urgent.

This time I answered, told her to hang up, leave her apartment and call me from a pay phone.

Eight minutes later she called back. When I heard what she had to say, the rash on my arm started itching.

"Your father sent you a *package*?" I said.

"Turns out he *did* send the disk to you, Mike."

I t came by private messenger. With a note."

"Read it."

"It says, 'Gabby, if you've received this, I'm in prison. . . .' "

"Prison?" I said, dumbfounded.

" 'In jail or disappeared, which means I've been arrested under the Patriot Act but not charged. You and I have no relationship to speak of, so no one will think I sent this to you. Keating and Schwadron made a deal behind my back with another so-called friend in Washington. My old pal A. J. Carbone. The disk will explain. Do *not* try to open it. Get it to Mike Acela, our Security Chief. Do *not* go to the police. Do *not* talk to Major Carl Eisner, who may contact you and try to scare you into cooperating with him. Do not tell *anyone* in Lenox that you have this. Trust Mike completely. He'll do right.'

"I don't understand," she said.

I was baffled that he'd so completely underestimated the danger he was in. I was gratified by his confidence in me, but disturbed by the cold instructions to a daughter with whom he did not speak. The Chairman I'd known was considerate. But Dwyer had put his only child in danger because of the disk. There were no words of love in the note. Only dismissive marching orders and certainty she'd obey.

"Now you understand him better, Mike. He must have figured Eisner would rifle your house for the disk."

"Well, he trusts you if he sent it to you," I said to give her back some measure of respect. Reading that note to me must have been humiliating.

I heard a snicker from Gabrielle. "Pretty pathetic, isn't it, when the people you turn to for help are an estranged daughter and a hired hand. What's on this disk?"

"We'll open it when I get back."

"You need passwords to get in. Questions for you. Like, 'What's your favorite piece in chess, on some yacht?' What does that mean?"

I flashed back to a weekend cruise with the Chairman in the Caribbean where I'd functioned as bodyguard and companion. Dwyer and I had gone off on a seventy-foot Azimut the company owned. We'd sat up nights over chess while he talked about Lenox, asked my advice on policy. It was flattering to be consulted, whether he took my advice or not. I'd beaten him with clever use of my rook. It was a nice memory.

"Here's another question. 'Who hit the big home run?' "

Another great memory. He'd invited Kim, Chris and me to attend a Mets game in the company box at Shea, on the third-base line. I remembered us screaming with excitement when Mike Piazza hit a grand slam over the center-field fence, and the giant mechanized apple went up and down, and the stadium went wild.

Gabrielle said, reading my emotions, "When I was little, if he wanted me to do something, he'd remind me of presents he'd given. It was one more way to exert control."

I was tiring of the Byzantine father/daughter dynamics. I asked, "I gather you tried to open the disk?"

"Wouldn't you? Tell me the passwords. I'll go home and do it and call you back."

I considered it. Any new information would help me, and I wanted badly to know it. But I hesitated out of loyalty to Dwyer. Ah, Italians. Loyalty is our best quality and our worst fault. Had Dwyer had a good reason to not tell her things?

And then she said, "By the way, where *are* you, Mike?"

Now the logical part of my mind warned me not to tell her too. A misstep could cost lives.

"I'm in Tallahassee," I lied. "We'll open it together when I get home."

Silence. Then, "You won't tell me?"

She's already ignored his instructions. What other instructions would she ignore? The one about not talking to Eisner? Or not going to the police?

"We'll figure it out," I soothed, "when I get home."

I heard a slow deepening in her breathing. The nutshell history of a woman whose armor would never be strong enough to fight off problems with an overpowering dad.

How well do I really know her?

"You're just like him," she said.

"Gabrielle . . ."

"You and him. 'Help me, trust me. Then go fuck yourself, because I'm not going to give anything back.' "

"That's not what I meant."

She said bitterly, "I could hand the disk to Keating."

Words that—despite my doubts—made me mad.

"Look," I said, "we can assume by now that your father was murdered. I told you when I met you that I'm not *supposed* to trust. This is about a lot more than you and your father. Would you trust *me* with *your* life?"

I knew people did not talk to her this way. I didn't know how she'd react. I held my breath. But when she spoke again after a long pause, it was with sadness.

"He's pulling your strings, Mike. All those personal memories? It's no coincidence those are his passwords. He plays with people. He's dead and still doing it. People fall for it all the time. You're falling for it now."

"You might be right," I admitted. "He's Svengali and I'm the dumb security guy. But we'll do it his way. We'll assume he had a reason. I meant what I said earlier, we'll open it together. If I didn't trust you, I'd never do that."

I heard her breathing flatten out as if I had given her barely enough hope or respect to calm her. I was in a minefield. It wasn't only a question of getting the disk.

I flashed to Asa Rodriguez, lying in the rain.

"Okay, Mike," she said in a colder voice. "I'll wait for you. I don't have a choice."

I gave her Danny Whiteagle's number and told her to call him and tell him everything. I told her that she was in danger also now that she had the disk, and that Danny would protect her.

"My father cared more about a piece of plastic than you *or* me, Mike. The story of his life. It's not just childish resentment, and that's what you'll find out in the end. I guess everyone needs to find out for themselves. This will turn out to be about *control*. It always is."

Which made me remember Schwadron saying the same thing in Washington.

I wanted to jettison my doubts about her but couldn't yet, not if I wanted to be prudent. I wished I could read her mind. Haven't you ever wanted that? With someone you love or fear, or will have to battle? Every adolescent's fantasy, right? Having a portal into thoughts.

But right now it seemed to me that her voice held more resignation than frustration. The residue of her life of resentment hung between us, but her rage had also been evidence that there existed a repairable link.

"I'm on my way," I said. What was one more lie, right? I saw now how crucial it would be to get into Keating's party tomorrow. It was the only place I might get a chance to confront him for any length of time, the place where, Gabrielle had said, I'd get a pocket view of his world.

I told her, "We'll talk to Keating, and Schwadron. Maybe even Director Carbone will be at that party."

And with that there was a pause on the other end, and in a softer voice Gabrielle said, "Then you haven't heard."

"What happened?" I said, the premonition of even more disaster a hollow thumping in my chest.

"He resigned today. Alicia Dent broke the story. Something about a long-term married girlfriend. Twin daughters on the side. Our new President won't tolerate that kind of behavior."

"He's gone?"

"He left the country already. He's going to Europe for a while. The President will nominate someone new."

I hung up. Something huge and terrible was happening. It was the thing the Chairman had unleashed. It was conscious and malevolent and after people I loved. And I *still* wasn't sure yet what it was or who was behind it.

And on the personal level I wanted to be close to Gabrielle and see what my intuition told me about her, not just about a disk. I wanted to stand beside the woman and look into her exquisite face, and see if I understood more when under the influence of Lenox's new find, the chemical washing the synapses of my brain, the one that had helped a major play war games. The one that had failed to alert the Chairman that he was about to die.

Garrison Bight turned out to be a large oval harbor on both sides of a two-lane overpass. Long parking lots flanked the overpass, and the charters went out from a series of slips along a concrete walk protected by an open-air tin roof, with its leaping Marlin logo and line of pigeons standing dumb in the sun.

A few slips were empty. Some boats were being cleaned. A handful of customers—a family, two fat men holding fishing rods and six-packs—looked like they were negotiating prices with guides. I steered the Maxima into a parking lot. It had no posted rules announcing hours for parking. Maybe I could leave the Maxima here for a few days, I thought. But an ad taped to the side of a public phone—beside a police sketch of me—gave me a better idea.

The eyes in the sketch watched me as I checked the Yellow Pages and wrote down the number I needed.

You make a decision and then you live with it, my father used to say. You make your choice and do your best and don't kick yourself if things don't work out.

I casually strolled down the walk toward the fishing guides looking for customers, the deckhands fixing engines.

One sign said, CAP'N NICK MURPHY. HALF-DAY RATES! Another sign said, BONEFISHING, A SPECIALTY.

Boats rocked gently. Kitty-corner across the channel rose an indoor garage-style boat-storage facility, four stories high, open like a warehouse, with boats stacked in elevator slips like cars in New York high-rise parking lots. In the water below, gasoline streaks floated in rainbow colors past the slips.

And suddenly the voice in my head went off like a siren again, a booming warning that seemed unrelated to anything I saw.

DANGEROUSDANGEROUSDANGEROUS . . .

I didn't run, though. That would have drawn attention to me. I didn't give in to the fear, but sat down at the edge of the walk and—in an open area between boats—calmly opened my tackle box. I affixed the spinning reel to the rod, and a silver lure to the line. I was a fisherman. I was relaxed. As I worked I let my eyes again take in the row, looking for something I'd missed.

That's how I spotted the two men, on one of the boats, talking to a captain. The smaller man was averting his head as if he'd just been looking in my direction. The larger one was occupied with the talk.

The men weren't in uniforms or even suits, but the clean-cut look and big frames, the short haircuts, the intent way they leaned in toward the captain, the authority in their posture, the compliance in the other man's, told me enough.

I had not seen an unmarked car in the parking lot, with its telltale tall antennae. But detectives use their own private cars too, especially if they're on extra shift and all the official cars are in use.

The man who had just glanced my way—the balder,

shorter of the two cops—stared out at the water as if engaged in thought.

This was the third time in an hour that the surge of powerful intuition had hit me. I wouldn't say I was used to it, but I'd stopped questioning its accuracy when it came. It wasn't an actual voice, of course. It was more like a clear message, packing the power of super-logic, to be ignored at my peril, a vivid certainty that was as forceful as any truth I'd ever acknowledged to myself.

Why didn't I get any feeling when I spoke to Gabrielle?

Where did the sensation come from? That was to be discussed later, with Danny's scientist cousin if I could reach him. Now I just accepted what I was receiving.

It might help get me home.

As for the cops, they weren't eyeing me now, weren't interested in me. They'd walk over if they were. No, the sense I'd gotten was the type I'd feel upon spotting a pack of feral dogs, and needed to figure out how to get past them without making them overly aware of me too.

I started to get up to leave but the smaller man treaded toward me. I sat back down, not wanting to give him a close-up view of my size and build. I kept my face averted as the footsteps closed. I felt the thud of his approach.

Then he was past me, his receding steps like lessening pings on a radar set. My headache subsided. The second policeman was still on the boat ahead, which put cops on both sides of me now. But the odd part was, I'd noticed that all my fear seemed associated with the smaller man, not the larger. As if the danger came from one cop, not both, even though two were here.

Test the feeling. Use it. You have to stand up sooner or later.

The small man was out in the parking lot now. He got into a car and started the engine, waiting for his partner to join him, I suppose.

I rose and, tasting salt in my mouth, continued up the walk in the direction of the larger cop. I wondered whether a few grams of ingested chemicals would actually warn me in time if I was making a mistake. I drew within four feet of the bigger plainclothes detective. But still I felt no blast of alarm.

And then, as I passed, I heard the captain tell the cop, "Frank, she'll come back. You'll apologize to her. You'll make up. My daughter loves you."

The cop is distracted, I realized. *He's somewhere else.*

I walked right past him, having let intuition guide me.

Holy shit, I thought. It works when you're close up, not over a phone.

After that it was easy. Ridiculously easy.

I rejected the first fishing guide I spoke to after talking with him for five minutes. I'd chosen a sloppy-looking man on a shabby boat, figuring that he'd need money and be more open to schedule changes once we got out on the water. But when I talked to him I got a strong sense that he couldn't care less about money, and that for whatever reason, he preferred not to take out a customer today.

So I left him alone.

The second guide I found operated a pricier boat, better kept, but speaking to him I had a clear, strong sense that he was desperate for a customer. I don't know if he really needed money that much, but my gut told me to hire him.

So hire him I did.

Then I excused myself, went back to the car, left the spare key atop the right front tire and made a phone call to Key West's AAA-Driveaway, which normally hired drivers to take cars far north.

Minutes later as I chugged out into Garrison Bight on a half-day charter, I reached into my pocket and pressed the button on my cell phone, making it chime. I pretended I was getting a phone call from my "wife," who was on Cudjoe Key, where our Kia had broken down.

"Call me back after you talk to the mechanic," I said.

I told my guide that I wanted to try fishing for tarpon on the northeast side of the island. Twenty minutes later we were rocking in the Gulf of Mexico when I made the phone chime again.

"The mechanic said *how* much? That's ridiculous!" I snapped.

My guide was looking at me. He'd heard the whole thing.

I went back to fishing. When I got a third call from my distraught wife, ten minutes after that, I told the captain I was going to have to cut our trip short and that I needed to get to Cudjoe Key, fast. I asked if—for another fifty bucks—he'd mind ferrying me there and dropping me off so I could confront the mechanic who was trying to rip off my wife.

"No prob," he said. "You want me to stick around and take you and your wife back to Key West, Mr. Johnson?"

"Nah, we have a dinner up there, friends. Keep the money for the charter, of course. Next time I'm in Key West, we'll go out for tarpon again."

Dropped on Cudjoe, I walked to a small strip mall, which I remembered from the drive down. Barney's Maxima was in the lot, key on the front tire, credit card receipt from AAA-Driveaway in the glove compartment. It had cost 180 bucks to get someone to drive it here and get a ride back to Key West. For that price, no one had questioned my story about needing the whole day to do business in Cudjoe, needing to have the car ready to drive north when I was done.

Three eventless hours later I dropped the Maxima off at Barney's house in Miami, and by eight P.M. I was back in New York City, walking off the SunGo flight as if returning from a normal business trip. The jolt of intuition had hit me once more, on the plane, when I had a sudden certainty that my flight attendant was fantasizing about having sex with me. I'd figured the feeling was untestable, but then as I left the flight, she'd slipped me her phone number scribbled on a card.

Now the rash on my arm was subsiding, and I wondered if that meant I would lose the heightened alertness brought on by—I now fully believed—HR-109.

How long does this stuff work before you need more? I thought, calling Danny as I left the terminal.

"Hi, Boss. I've been following the Rodriguez murder on the *Key West Citizen* website. Helluva sketch of the suspect. Pale. Black beard. Six foot one. Any idea who that might be? Because they figure they'll ID him soon."

"Where are you?"

"Mohawks," he said, and the code word told me he was in trouble too, at a safe house. I envisioned one of his cousin's homes, in Rockaway, a seaside neighborhood in Queens. He'd taken me to a party there once. The cousin collected Mohawk artifacts: arrows, a dugout canoe, even one of the five original tribal conference stools. The basement was a museum.

"Eisner's on the warpath, so to speak," Danny said. "He's tearing up the city looking for you. Kim's here. So is Gabrielle. They know what happened in Key West, and I'm not sure if they want to kill you more because of each other, or because you haven't told us what really happened down there. But as the great warrior said, Boss, 'You who are about to meet two very pissed-off women, prepare to die.'"

THIRTEEN

"So Keating knew all along what was in that vial," said Danny. "Throwing it in the trash can was an act."

"My God," breathed Kim, staring at the computer. "You told us what the drug did to you, Mike. But to actually see it confirmed in a report!"

The owners of the house were on vacation. Danny had posted half a dozen relatives as guards outside on the block. They couldn't stop Eisner, who would come with a warrant this time, but they could stop the Royces if they showed up.

The four of us were alone in Danny's nephew's bedroom, a paneled basement hung with the innocent trappings of teenage yearnings: a blowup poster over the single bed of the Olympic superstar Michael Phelps; a sepia repro shot of the Chief Bigfoot ride on the 100th anniversary of the Pine Ridge Reservation massacre, showing four modern-day Native Americans on horses; a magazine cutout of sexy actress Julia Dunn, star of the new film *First Lover*.

Kim occupied a Windsor chair on my left at the desk, dressed in denim as usual, and Gabrielle stood on my right, in white, arms folded, face tense. Danny was a large presence behind me. The jokes about my clean-shaven appearance had stopped.

Fascinated, we stared at the screen, at words written

by a man who'd thought he was going to be arrested, not killed.

"Mike," Dwyer had typed, "I made a decision to limit sales of a new drug to appropriate people: Homeland Security, responsible CEOs, Defense authorities and police."

"Appropriate?" said Kim. "What the hell does that mean?"

"Quiet. Let me read."

Dwyer wrote, "I've been betrayed by people who want to wrest away our God-given right to control our own product. That's my prerogative. Not theirs."

"I told you," Gabrielle said softly. "Control."

Dwyer wrote, "This disk will tell the story. It's a copy of the one I took from Naturetech—along with several pounds of HR-109, the entire natural supply. By taking it, I've ended any chance Lenox has to synthesize the drug until I regain control."

"*That's* why the Royces broke into his apartment. To get it back," Danny broke in.

"Will you all shut up." I finished the message. "Read these files. Whatever you've been told about me is a lie. Behind my back friends made a deal to oust me and share control of 109 with the government. They'll lock me away under the Patriot Act and claim I'm a danger to national security. Get the disk to our lawyers. Use it to force National Intelligence Director Carbone to free me. We'll show those bastards they can't take 109 away from Lenox, and from me."

"Carbone can't help anyone anymore," Danny said.

"Poor Mr. Dwyer," said Kim. "He thought he was going to be replaced."

"He was replaced, all right."

I had confirmed to all of them when I arrived—from concern for their safety—that I was being sought for the murder in Florida. I'd said I'd take the disk and be on my way. But Danny had stopped me. "Why? Did you do it, Boss?"

"What do *you* think?"

"Then if you're not charged, how are we aiding? You're staying, unless you want to change your story and admit you did it, you psycho freak."

Now my heart beat strongly as the disk's table of files came up on screen. Memo from Keating. Memo from Schwadron. Synthesis formulas for HR-109.

"Go to Keating's memo," Kim said.

"No, Schwadron's," Gabrielle said.

The women were cool to each other, I'd noticed. But I thought Danny's decision to keep them together for safety was a good idea.

Keating's memo appeared on the screen and we leaned forward, reading.

"It's a decision tree," Kim explained. "Dated right after Asa first came in. When Dwyer faced big decisions, he had people he trusted analyze the consequences. Tell him what might go wrong if he took different paths."

Keating had advised, "*Jim, I disagree with your decision to sell Enhance outside the company. I urge you to keep it for Lenox upper-management only, guaranteeing us unparalleled advantages in business, government and employee relations. Let's use this miracle for ourselves.*"

"Son of a bitch," broke in Kim hotly. "Selfish, greedy bastard! He wanted *not* to sell it!"

No wonder Asa was upset, I thought.

"Enhance," mused Gabrielle. "The name tells the

story, doesn't it? Do you really think Keating or Schwadron had my father killed over a drug?"

"Why don't we keep reading and find out more," I said.

"So long as a limited natural supply exists, and as early synthesis failed, why share?"

"So that's what Teaks is doing at Naturetech," Danny said. "Trying to make it in the lab before the natural supply runs out."

"I thought Indians value silence," I said.

"Racist," Danny said.

Keating wrote, *"Imagine the chilling consequences if a drug enabling anyone to recognize a liar—actually read people's intent—was available to the public. The legal and moral problems would be overwhelming. A husband believes his wife is cheating on him. He buys Enhance and confronts her. Confirming that she is lying, or simply believing it because he took the drug, he murders her and blames 109 in court. Or imagine that a terrorist uses Enhance to evade authorities and kill thousands. If we don't limit the drug's use, Lenox would be liable."*

"Holy mother of God," Danny gasped. "He's right."

"Dwyer faced one hell of a choice," I said, talking to myself now, remembering how the drug had helped me elude the police.

"In short, benefits outweigh liabilities only if we keep strict control."

"That Keating," Gabrielle said, flushed and lovely. "Always worried about the other guy. To think I thought badly of him. And who decides who gets this marvel? Keating, that's who."

"Two classes of people," Kim whispered, horrified,

envisioning it. "The enhanced ones and the others. My God! It would be like that novel, *Walden*!"

"*Walden*?"

"It's about the future, where people are divided into two classes. Average people are force-fed a drug called Soma. That way leaders can control them."

Gabrielle shook her head as if this were ridiculous. "Keating and my father didn't want to force-feed this drug to anyone. They planned to withhold it."

"For people like them."

Gabrielle smiled. It struck me that she and Kim had just switched positions. Kim was attacking the Chairman. Gabrielle was defending.

"That's a little paranoid, don't you think, Kim?" she said. "Like science fiction? Besides, I thought you loved everything that Daddy did."

"Heart transplants used to sound like science fiction. Why is it so difficult for unimaginative people to see the truth until it's too late?"

"I resent that tone," Gabrielle snapped in a way that told me the issue went beyond Dwyer. "And you sound like an old Communist. Listen to yourself. 'Average people'?"

Kim had turned red. "The Chairman said it in his note. 'Appropriate members of society'! You think that means a mechanic? Think, Gabrielle. You go for a job interview. Your new boss took the drug. The IRS has it. Or management during a strike. Or in an election, except only one side has it because it's controlled by 'appropriate' people. It's disgusting! People would go through life knowing that someone else has a way to know what they're thinking, but they wouldn't have a clue what goes on in that other person's head."

Gabrielle rolled her eyes. "People who earn a couple

hundred thousand dollars a year, dear, don't all share the same thoughts."

"Don't call me dear."

Danny broke in, truly puzzled. "But what the hell is Lenox *supposed* to do with it? Destroy it? This is incredible! No wonder Keating fired us. He didn't want the secret to get out."

"He didn't want us to figure out he fought with the Chairman, and maybe helped kill him," Kim said. "They're all just a bunch of oligarchs fighting among themselves."

"Are we going to finish this or conduct a philosophical debate?" I asked.

I read the end of the memo, chilled by possibilities.

"Selective distribution is not illegal unless it violates the Civil Rights Act, discriminates on the basis of age, sex or religion. The bottom line is, privately controlled, Enhance will make Lenox powerful and rich."

"You mean it will make Keating that way," Kim said.

"Click on Schwadron, the great compromiser," Gabrielle said. "Want to bet he had a totally different, equally selfish idea?"

Schwadron had written, *"Old friend, a man is lucky if once in his life he is called on to make a decision that will impact the world for better or worse. You will be remembered for the way you handle this new miracle drug, which I suggest we name Oblige. . . ."*

"Ass kisser," said Gabrielle.

"Oblige?" said Kim.

"As in 'noblesse oblige.' As in the obligation for the powerful to take care of everyone else," Gabrielle said, and eyed Kim more thoughtfully. "Maybe you weren't so wrong after all," she said more softly.

"*My friend, you must allow the government to safeguard our precious gift. You know my fondness for old sayings. Well, Emerson said, 'Government must not be gentle. It has, of necessity, in any crisis of the State, the absolute powers of a dictator.'*

"*Harsh words for a harsh time, when the innocent are endangered by the few. The terrorists we cannot see. The white-collar criminal with a smile on his face who brings a corporation to its knees. But once we synthesize Oblige, Lenox will have a tool to assist those who protect society. Our police and legislators. Our civic and military leaders.*"

I stopped reading when I heard the scrape of a chair behind me. Kim had pushed away from the table and stood up. Her small fists were clenched, her breathing had gone shallow. Passion turned her face red again.

"Liar," she said. "He's such . . . they're *both* such liars! They just want it for themselves but they act so pious. Civic *leaders*? He means himself. Quotes? *I'll* give you quotes, and they're about freedom of thought, Mike. Because that's what this drug is about. Either give it to everybody or give it to nobody. Otherwise, whoever has it will use it against the rest."

She looked glorious at the moment, suffused with passion, and not the sort that comes from personal disillusionment, like Gabrielle's, but from self-knowledge, a solid set of beliefs.

Kim recited, "'The opinions of men are not the subject of civil government.' Thomas Jefferson said that."

"He did?" Gabrielle said, impressed.

"'The mind is the expression of the soul, which belongs to God and should be left alone by government.' Adlai Stevenson."

"Did you major in political science?" Gabrielle said.

"I never went to college," Kim said, embarrassed by it, but honest.

And she read, I knew. More than anyone I knew. She read everything: books, magazines, newspapers. And she remembered what she read.

She looked around at us, embarrassed at her outburst. Then she sat down, flushed, breathing hard.

"I get carried away," she said.

I said, reasoning slowly, letting Kim's warning, the part about using the drug *against the rest,* reach me . . . pulse hammering as a new, terrible possibility entered my mind, "The resignations in Washington. If the wrong person took the drug, someone with access to important people, if they were fishing for dirt, looking for a way to damage someone, all they'd have to do is sidle over at a party, or arrange an interview for the press."

"The news stories! The *President*! You think those people were driven out?"

"I'm saying *if.* I'm probably getting carried away, but *if* you took the drug and *if* you wanted to get at someone, well, you just ask them questions, right? And wait to see what your intuition tells you about their answers. Any problems with money, Mr. Secretary? Anything in your past that you'd like people not to know? Bribes? Affairs? Tax evasion?"

"Is it *possible*?"

"If the drug truly works . . ."

"It could tell you *where* to look for secrets. Once you know where to look, it gets easy. You'd learn them all in the end," I said.

I put my arm around Kim. She shook it off.

"You," she said angrily, "keep scrolling. See what else Schwadron says."

What's the matter with you? I thought. But my rash was gone. Without 109 in my system I had no idea what she'd meant. I turned back to the screen and Schwadron's report.

"Oblige is a strategic weapon. National Intelligence will seize it when they learn it exists, as they would any deadly tool. They cannot allow the wrong people to use it.

"In short, the government will sooner or later control Oblige, so I urge you, while you have the chance, to negotiate a deal that will give us a little control too, and some substance for ourselves. Oblige can keep America safe by harnessing the human mind the way a nuclear bomb harnesses the atom. Let's share it with the proper people in a way that will keep our nation and corporation strong and rich."

The memo ended. The technical file, which came up next, was a lot of numbers and potential synthesis formulas. I didn't understand them. But perhaps Danny's cousin at NYU could explain.

I said, sitting back, shaky, "So Keating and Schwadron disagreed how to handle the drug while Naturetech raced to synthesize it. Keating wants it for Lenox exclusively. Schwadron wants it for Uncle Sam too. The Defense contract must have given some to Washington. Then what happened?"

"Washington wanted it all," Danny said, "when they saw how well it works."

I remembered the words the Director of National Intelligence had uttered on the radio yesterday, about "new interrogation techniques" that had helped pinpoint terrorists.

"They tested it in the Mideast," I theorized. "Then demanded more. Maybe Dwyer refused because it would have concentrated too much power in one place. Maybe he just had a bug about control. So Keating and Schwadron made a deal to oust Dwyer. Dwyer finds out. He steals the sample for leverage. He goes to dinner with them, confronts them."

Gabrielle shook her head. "But if the drug is such a miracle and my father used it, how come he thought he was going to be arrested, not killed?"

"Maybe the drug's not infallible," said Kim.

"Or maybe whomever ordered the death did so *after* the dinner," I said.

I felt tired and confused, and disgusted by the greed in the memos. I added, "Or whomever did it was someone else, not Keating or Schwadron. Someone in Washington."

"Eisner?"

"We don't know. And we can't rule out personal reasons. Or the resignations."

Then Danny broke out laughing, which I found extremely irritating. He laughed harder. Gabrielle asked, "Going to share?"

Danny wiped his eyes. "We have our heads on wrong," he said. "We're so dazzled, we're not seeing things right. You want *personal?* Okay, imagine 109's not a miracle drug, but six hundred million dollars' worth of heroin. Stop thinking about our suspects as if they're public servants or ideologues and start thinking addicts, drug lords. Dwyer *takes* the stolen supply *home*. He goes to dinner and *tells* people he has it. Hours later he's murdered and 109 is gone. Gee, what possible personal motivation could there be for murder with a stolen miracle drug in his desk? And a formula that any government, drug dealer or rival company would pay hundreds of millions of dollars to buy?"

"And Asa threatened to tell the newspapers about 109," I said. "So he was killed too."

Kim asked, "How would the betting slips you found in Dwyer's apartment fit into this, Mike?"

"I figure Dwyer tested 109 himself early on by betting on ball games, where it didn't work, because that involves luck, and on stocks, where he personally knew people in the companies, and probably talked to them. So the drug worked in those cases."

"And Eisner?"

I shrugged. "Eisner got involved when the Defense contract looked too large. *That's* how *he* learned of 109. Eisner could be working for anyone."

I sighed. My head hurt. "But we're guessing. And what about the Hamilton Club? Does that figure in? Dwyer, Keating, Schwadron, Carbone . . . all members."

"Well," Gabrielle began hesitantly. We turned to her.

"I'm not an investigator," she began.

"Go on."

"I'm not sure I even believe all this, even with the disk."

"What were you going to say?"

She sighed. Her mouth was red and wet and her eyes were dark pools. She said, "I have an idea about the Hamilton Club. It would fit in if you understood how my father thought. People worth knowing. That's why he joined those stuffed shirts. To him they were people who *deserved.* Like Kim said before."

"So?"

"So, if the drug is real, I can imagine my father at the club, dining with Director Carbone, for instance. Old friends. Well, Carbone's in charge of anti-terrorism operations overseas. He's got staff interrogating prisoners in the Mideast, right? But they never know who's lying to them, who's telling the truth."

"Always the problem," said Danny, the ex–Intelligence officer, rubbing his chin in thought.

"So imagine him sitting with Carbone, listening to Carbone's frustration, feeling guilty because HR-109 could help keep America safe and—"

"And he told him," I said. "Because *not* to tell would make your father responsible in his own eyes if something bad happened later."

"Right."

"And the secret starts spreading. Friend to friend."

"*People like us.* That's the key to my father. He was big on social responsibility, but he'd need an excuse if he was going to do something selfish, like keep the drug for himself and his friends."

"Things start going out of control," said Kim. "Carbone wants more than Dwyer wants to give. End of friendship. Not to mention, *Carbone* is gone now."

"So what do we do?" said Danny. "Give the disk to the police?"

I shook my head. "It doesn't prove any of this. It doesn't prove I didn't kill anyone. And if the cops get it, they'll do what they did with the list. Give it to Eisner."

"The press?" suggested Kim. "Put everything on the Internet?"

Danny snorted. "Yeah, a secret formula for the whole world to try to figure out. You want to trust reporters with your life, Mike? Or be the guy who handed 109 to the Islamic Jihad?"

"Danny's right," I said. "Maybe I'll learn something at the party tomorrow. Gabrielle, you said everyone Keating does business with will be there, right? I have to get in."

"If you're not arrested before that."

Danny yawned. It was now two A.M., and we were all clearly exhausted.

"Well, my cousin will see us in the morning and hopefully explain how the drug may work. We'll sleep here tonight. Gabrielle, take the upstairs bedroom. Kim, you sleep here. Mike and I will sack out on couches in the living room."

Outside, in the night, we heard a siren coming closer.

We froze as the siren approached the house, but it faded. Danny and Gabrielle went off to get linens from a closet, leaving Kim and me alone.

"What was the drug like for you, Mike, when you took it?" she asked.

I sat on the single bed, beneath the boy's poster of the Olympic swimmer. Innocent heroes. "Things were clear."

"You want more of it?"

I thought about what she'd asked. I didn't like the answer. "In a way."

"You know," she said, sitting beside me so our thighs brushed. "After you told Danny about the killing in Florida, we went on the Internet, and got the whole story. What did you think? We'd abandon you?"

"I didn't want to get you in more trouble."

She leaned close and I thought she was going to kiss me, but her face had that sadness in it again.

"All we did tonight was make guesses," she said.

I opened my eyes and the red numerals on the clock read 4:55. I could tell I wasn't going to fall asleep again. A quarter moon was visible through the window. Danny snored softly on the couch across from me, under a thin blanket, out of which stuck his big feet.

I was careful not to wake him as I dressed and carried my shoes into the foyer. I slipped out of the house, into the sticky semidarkness of predawn. I heard the surf a block away. It reminded me of my childhood. The houses were dark, and the moon low over slanted rooftops. Several figures were visible sitting on stoops up the block.

Danny's home guard.

I walked on the beach a while. It looked clean, at least in the darkness. Mesh trash cans tilted like half-drunk sentries as I gazed across the pale expanse of trucked-in sand, toward the Atlantic. There was a tar smell from the boardwalk behind me, and a city-sea odor, the ever-present hint of diesel fumes that seemed to tinge each molecule of air. A bright funnel of moon shimmered on wavelets. I saw a green set of running lights out there, probably from a trawler heading for the fish market.

At that moment the ocean seemed severed from the city, not an expanse connected to the metropolis, but one that tantalized you with possibility, a horizon different from your own. I'd stood like this as a teen, back in Devil's Bay, when I couldn't sleep, and dreamed of change, wanting something that I thought would be better, bigger, richer, more.

Now, in my forties, I was still looking out at the ocean, gazing with longing toward a spot where things disappeared instead of becoming clear.

"Mike?"

She'd come up quietly, softly, her feet bare in the sand. She wore an open zip-up hooded sweatshirt over her small shoulders. Her hair looked shiny. Her eyes were big.

"I'm sorry I was mad before," Kim said. "I wasn't angry at you."

"It would have been okay if you were."

"What are we, Mike? Friends? Is that it? I'm not putting this on you either. I promised myself a long time ago, after Chris's father, no serious lovers. Just good friends. Sex and friendship. Keep them separate. You tell yourself that your past doesn't affect you. That you're stronger than it. You lie."

"I know. I tell myself the same things."

"I'm not saying this because of Gabrielle either. She's actually quite nice. I regret that crack about Princess braid. She seems to . . . like you. And I wasn't mad because you didn't tell us early on about Key West. I was mad because you got to take the drug and I didn't. Isn't that crazy? Because I was afraid that 109 helped you see something in me that I couldn't know in you."

"I saw sadness in you. But I wasn't on the drug."

She nodded and stepped closer to the surf, farther from me. I saw the back of her head now. Not her face.

She said, "But is that because something ended? Or never was?"

I moved closer. I smelled soap on her. I put my hands on her shoulders. She relaxed enough to lean against my body. I felt the length of her against me. I put my chin on her head. She pulled my hands forward and around her chest, so I could feel her small breasts, but not in a sexy way, in a human way. This much we'd done before, but things seemed changed now. Maybe it was because there was nothing to be taken for granted. Maybe it was the ticking clock. Something in her righteous fury at the house had drawn me to her in a new way, something clean and uncomplicated that showed strength and commitment. I don't know if that's enough. But it's a lot.

We were kissing suddenly. Her body fit perfectly into mine, and her hand gripped my hair. Her smell was fresh and the kiss went on a long time before we broke apart.

We stood that way a while, unmoving. A narrow slit of orange glowed in the east, at the surface of the water. The brightness spread upward in beams as we turned to walk back toward the house.

There, lights were on. Windows were open. Gabrielle stood on the second floor, looking out at us as we walked up. I couldn't see her expression. She turned away.

In six hours—at noon—I was scheduled to escort her to Bill Keating's chili cook-off, where Schwadron would be present too, where I'd find my main suspects, at least on the New York end. I had a feeling that I'd get no second chance to see these people in the same place again.

When we got inside, I smelled coffee and bacon. The radio was on. The day would be hot. Danny came out of the kitchen with an apron on. It said, THE GRILLMEISTER! He took in Kim and me with a glance, but was wise enough to show no emotion. He told Kim, "Eat up, Boss. We have to get over to NYU, fast."

"I thought I was the boss," I said.

He grinned. "I call everyone boss. My kids. My wife. The baker. I am but a humble servant of all."

"What's the rush?" Kim said. "The party at Keating's isn't for hours."

"I checked Key West on the Internet. As of four this morning, the police were close to locating a man in Saudi Arabia who they believe talked to the killer and may know his name. Dick Milenko's the guy you told us about, right?"

I'd known this would happen. I'd hoped for more time.

"That's the rush," Danny said. "Once Key West has the name, so do the Feds. So does Keating. It's over."

"Or would you rather not go to the party, Mike?" said Gabrielle's voice, and I turned to see her coming down the stairs like a debutante. She was dressed all in white. White flowing summer dress. White strap sandals. White pearl strand at her tanned neck. And her hair free for the first time, glorious and unrestrained as I'd imagined, blue-black as it fanned over her shoulders in a waterfall. She looked smashing. She changed the room.

"Will you run, Mike?" she asked. "Or stay?" She hadn't asked it like a mere question. It sounded like a test.

"Run?" I said. "Where would I run?"

My enemies were multiplying.

I wished I had more 109.

FOURTEEN

"You are looking at the brain's limbic system, and the amygdala, which controls intuition."

An hour later, fascinated, the four of us sat in professor Whiteagle's 14th-floor study above Mercer Street in Greenwich Village, in a three-bedroom apartment, faculty housing for NYU. The apartment faced south, toward the spires of Lower Manhattan, and the gap in the sky where the towers of the World Trade Center had stood. Danny's cousin was 37, lean, fit-looking and slightly bowlegged, like an athlete, with a black braid that matched the color of his squarish glasses. His brown and green cotton shirt hung over black jean shorts, and his feet sported Reboks. A book called *Our Brain* lay open on his desk, amid a clutter of potted houseplants, scientific papers, journals, university leaflets and scattered computer disks.

I'd listened to plenty of biology lectures as a college student, and in forensics classes at the FBI. I don't think I'd ever been as interested in one of the lectures as I was right now.

"For a long time scientists thought the brain operated as a single functioning unit," Professor Whiteagle said, flipping pages in *Our Brain*. "But more and more we've found that different parts war with one another. Maybe that's what keeps the brain sharp."

He held out the book to show a diagram of the brain. "The limbic system and neocortex are cases in point. The limbic system's amygdala controls the *emotional* brain. The neocortex controls the *logical* brain. So if you're taking a multiple-choice test in high school, for instance, and you get an intuitive feeling that answer A is correct, that's your amygdala talking. And then, a few minutes later, when you start to question your choice and second-guess your answer, that's the neocortex chiming in. Odds are, if you change that first answer, you made a mistake. Everyone has had that experience, of intuition being right but being overridden."

The sketch he displayed showed the familiar three-quarter circle shape of a human brain, rounded at the top and slanted diagonally at the bottom to fit into a skull, narrowing into a stemlike protuberance running toward the spine, like a power line.

In the diagram, in protective layers, I saw the mind's labeled hemispheres and coupling systems. The action centers, the awareness centers, the biological structure. The cingulate gyrus looked like a snake curled around the deep recesses: the ropelike hippocampus, the egg-shaped thalamus near the bottom and, extending from it, a round small point looking like a drop of water, a speck labeled "amygdala," at which I stared.

This was the part Ray Teaks had talked about in Maryland. But so far most labels were meaningless to me.

"Have you ever heard the old saying that the human brain only operates at ten percent efficiency?" Dr. Whiteagle asked, glancing from face to face like a good lecturer.

"Sure," I said. "That humans would be supermen if we could only access the unused ninety percent of our brain."

"It's bullshit. The truth is, the brain is so efficient, it only *needs* ten percent at one time. But five minutes later, you might be using a different ten percent. We use our brains well."

"So?"

"So I'm guessing, based on what you told me, and on your disk, that when it comes to this drug of yours, don't think of it as something that helps access areas of the brain never used before. What's more likely and thrilling—theoretically, of course—is that it might help the brain do what it does when, say, the genius German composer Werner Lutz writes a symphony."

"Who?" I said. "What symphony?"

"Look at these brain scans," said Dr. Whiteagle, flipping excitedly to another page in the book. "They were taken inside an fMRI machine, in Berlin last year, at the Institute of Human Cognition. It's Lutz's brain."

More engrossed by the second, I found myself looking at top-down views of a human brain, superimposed over a grid, as if on graph paper. Numbers at the top and side of the page enabled a researcher to identify a brain part by where it sat in the grid, as if the brain had latitude and longitude numbers, like maps.

In each scan, most of the brain looked whitish, with a few areas showing small gray dots or blots like Rorschach images. Some of the scans included many of these shadows. In the last, I saw only one pinprick of gray near the bottom.

"You are actually looking at mental activity in Lutz's head," explained Dr. Whiteagle with relish. "He agreed to compose music while lying inside an fMRI machine, to help doctors try to track creativity in a brain. The fMRI measured blood flow to different parts of his brain before he started working, and also while he worked. Blood flow in an fMRI—represented by the gray shadows—tells us that a particular part of the brain is being used at that moment."

He pointed to a dot in the topmost photo. "This mark means he's using his eyes, looking around inside the fMRI machine. He's just gone in. He's checking it out. He has not yet begun the creative process, has not yet accessed his amygdala, where intuitive and creative impulses begin. The amygdala is clear."

"What about this other scan?" I asked excitedly, pointing out the picture that included the most activity: shadows all over the grid. "Is he working here, and we're watching his brain light up as he feverishly writes?"

Dr. Whiteagle smiled as if I had fallen into his trap. "On the contrary. He's failing to write. The doctors told him to compose, but instantly started making noises and flashing lights. All this activity means he's aware of that. He's tuned in to his surroundings. His activity is diffused. He's distracted. He can't work. But *here*," Dr. Whiteagle said, indicating the photo where only one tiny spot of gray showed, "he's composing. He has shut everything else out. What I'm suggesting is that your drug may not *heighten* any part of the brain at all. It may simply shut down everything that's not relevant to intuition, and allow intuition to act unrestrained. For a limited time it may give an average person the concentrative, intuitive powers of a special person. The intuitive genius of a true empath."

"Are you saying everyone has this power naturally?"

He shrugged. "Abilities differ in each person. Einstein actually had a large brain. I'm simply giving you possibilities based on what you told me. You *said* the researchers in Maryland work with the amygdala, yes?"

"Yes."

"Well, the amygdala always lights up during mind-reading experiences. . . ."

I said, bolting upright, *"Mind reading?"*

Dr. Whiteagle quickly held up his hands. "I didn't mean that like it sounded. Personally, I don't believe in ESP, Mike. All those claims about thought transference, or telepathy, those news stories in the early nineteen hundreds? They turned out to be hoaxes. The Creery sisters in Scotland fooled people for fifty years with hidden signals. Sixth sense? Hooey. Tricks!

"And the ESP tests at Duke University in the thirties never proved a thing. It was just a bunch of people sitting around, trying to guess which playing cards other people held in their hands. Flawed situations. No conclusive proof. No one could ever duplicate a good performance."

"Then why say 'mind reading'?"

"Because neuroscientists today use the term scientifically, to describe the complex series of signals that humans send one another when communicating. For instance, right now you're hearing my words, but you're also analyzing my expression, to see if I'm serious. My eyes, to see if I look believable. My voice. My posture. A thousand things . . . And it took your whole life to learn to do it. That's why parents are so good at knowing when small children are lying. Small kids are bad liars. They haven't learned how to lie yet."

"So when you say 'mind reading,' you mean average communication skills," I said.

"That's right, Mike. A thousand muscles in our face, combining to send a thousand variations in messages. Do you know that sometimes when doctors ask a stroke victim to smile, they can't do it?"

"Sure. Because their muscles don't work."

"Ah," Danny's cousin said, smiling himself. "Then how come, five minutes later, when they hear a joke, they smile broadly? The answer is, it's because a phony smile and a real smile require the use of totally different muscles."

"Oh."

"Which means *reading* those smiles requires special skill." Dr. Whiteagle nodded, clearly loving his work. "In autistic kids, who lack the ability to understand obvious signals—a smile, a frown—there's no activity in the amygdala when they interact with people. They have to be taught in a classroom what a smile means. Danny says I should accept what you tell me as valid, so I'm guessing that it all boils down to this: Either your 109 drug goes straight to the amygdala and empowers it, or it cuts off the amygdala's competition—the reasoning brain—when you swallow it."

"But how, if it even works that way at all?"

Dr. Whiteagle nodded approvingly. "You'd make a good scientist, Mike. Keep hammering at the premise until you can't find a hole anymore. Good for you. I think that's why those chimpanzees are being cut open in Maryland. To find out what the drug does once it hits the brain. But whatever it does *chemically*, it makes you the equivalent of a super-empath for a while. I think, when you ingest 109, your natural ability is enhanced enough or the rest of your brain shuts down enough so you can 'mind read' other adults as well as a practiced parent reads a very young child. A small child's emotions seem obvious to adults, yet the child is amazed that adults read them. By the way, have you heard that our new President is on his way to Beijing for a summit conference tomorrow, on nuclear issues?"

"Yes."

"I bet he'd like some 109," Dr. Whiteagle said as I glanced at my watch and realized it was almost time for Gabrielle and me to head for Rye, and Keating's party, for my best chance to find Schwadron and Keating in the same place. "If the drug acts like I think, it would enable any negotiator to tell if the other side is bluffing. An unbelievable tool."

"So you *do* need to be close to whomever you're 'reading'? Or watching?"

"That's my guess."

"If what you're saying is true," I said, "how come when I was under the influence I didn't have a sense about *everyone* around me? Only certain people?"

"I expect because, as with any sense, you tune out what you don't need. Every time you walk down busy Mercer Street, you block out sights, smells, voices. A hundred people in your field of vision, but your brain filters out the unimportant stuff. That's why oftentimes people who use hearing aids have problems with too *much* sound. Hearing aids don't filter out unwanted sounds as well as the brain does. Everything can flood in at the same level.

"And as for your headache, Mike, you said it spiked whenever you used your new intuition, and lapsed a bit the rest of the time. But that it hurt *all* the time tells me that it was still active, just less so unless you needed it.

"By the way," he added quietly as we got up to leave. "You wouldn't have a bit of this substance left over? Just a tiny bit, of course. I have a couple of students in my intro class who I think are cheating. But I'm not sure."

There was a shine in his eyes now. Greed. I knew what was coming, and it chilled me. His was the first voice in a chorus that represented 109's future.

"I wonder if it would help me know if they're lying," he said.

O utside, we retrieved our cars from a parking garage. Gabrielle and I would take her white Saab to the party, after stopping to buy clothing and a mini-recorder for me. Danny and Kim would return to the beach. They'd make copies of the disk.

While Danny and I finalized plans, Kim moved off to use a pay phone, probably checking on her son, Chris, in Vermont. Gabrielle dabbed on perfume from her purse. Just a whiff produced a tingle in my groin. She smelled great.

"You'll check in every hour, Mike," said Danny.

"And you'll try to find Hoot," I said.

"Remember, treat those guys like drug lords. Addicts and drug lords. And let me know whatever you learn, the second you learn it. No waiting this time," he said as Kim headed back toward us. I did not like the frown on her face.

"I promise," I told Danny.

"If you can't reach us in Rockaway, try my cousin Laura's in Brooklyn. We'll keep moving. Kim, what's wrong? Is Chris all right?"

She came up to me and touched my arm, drawing Gabrielle's quick glance toward the point of contact.

"He's fine," Kim said. "But Mike, something has happened, I'm afraid."

On the street, people passed all around us, oblivious to our problems, plans, intent. Using their evolved five senses, as Dr. Whiteagle had described, to unconsciously block out unnecessary stimulation as they shopped, conversed, worried about lovers, listened to cell phones, considered which restaurant to choose, whether to eat pizza or Chinese.

"What happened?" I said.

"I called the *Key West Citizen*," she said, "to check the investigation. The police identified you from fingerprints just fifteen minutes ago. There's an APB going out for you in Florida. I have to figure they'll alert New York."

They were all looking at me, to see what I would decide about the party.

"It may be my last chance to talk to those guys," I said, tapping the place on my chest where I'd hide the recorder.

"Keating hires lots of security for his parties. If he knows you're wanted for murder, you won't get out," Gabrielle said.

"Look at the bright side. If he knows I won't get out, maybe he'll talk freely," I said, and sighed. "Hey, just how exclusive *is* this party anyway?" I added, trying a joke, aware that I was using Dr. Whiteagle's "false expression muscles" to fake a smile, which fooled no one.

Gabrielle took my arm. Kim's fingers dropped away. I finished my bad joke. "Do they let murderers in? Or are they not considered appropriate people, *people like us,* suitable for receiving Oblige?"

FIFTEEN

The grief finally hit her when we were driving to the party. She gave no warning it was coming until the Saab started to weave. We'd just passed the George Washington Bridge on the Cross Bronx Expressway, heading north toward suburban Westchester. She'd been running down names of guests I'd meet at the cook-off, sketching personalities, giving tidbits of information I might find useful in the confrontation ahead.

"You'll try to talk to Keating and Schwadron separately?" she'd asked.

I shrugged. "Depends on time. At the Bureau, we worked guys who operated as a team separately, to find differences in their stories. But Keating and Schwadron hate each other. That they joined up to screw over Dwyer in business, I buy that. That they *both* ordered the hit? Less possible. Maybe they'll turn on each other if I question them the right way."

"Unless they *were* both involved."

"It's a gamble, I know. But it's hard enough for a single person to order a killing. I'll play it by ear."

She'd continued her rundown of guests I'd meet, including several familiar names from the news: supporters of far-right-wing causes and candidates, men and women who even the *Wall Street Journal* had called oligarchs who'd like to push the country back a hundred years.

Then abruptly she stopped talking and the Saab drifted over the broken white line, into the right lane, which was fortunately empty. I glanced at Gabrielle. She was crying.

"I'm sorry he died," I said.

She eased the car into the breakdown lane and brought us to a stop—a smart move for traffic safety, but one guaranteed to attract attention from any roving squad car that appeared.

Traffic slowed, passing. Gabrielle and I had become a roadside attraction.

She stared straight ahead, then lowered her head onto the steering wheel. I laid my hand on her shoulder. Heat seeped up through the light cotton fabric. She was trembling so slightly that I'd had to touch her to feel it.

"I was so angry at him, even at the funeral," she said.

Let it come, I thought.

"He was a selfish, controlling asshole."

I rubbed her shoulder. My hand touched the flesh of her neck.

"He only thought about himself, his whole life. So why am I crying?"

I kept my hand there and she leaned into the comfort. I don't know whether she was even consciously aware of it, or whether her body had simply responded automatically. The AC hummed. I heard the light chop of a traffic copter overhead, and hoped the pilot wasn't notifying the police of a broken-down vehicle below.

Give her a couple more minutes.

She wept softly, her black hair fanning over her face and the steering wheel. I'd take over driving and get us out of here in another minute. Even a random traffic stop might put me in jail. But then she straightened, her face red. I dug out a linen handkerchief from her cocktail purse.

"Why did you help my father and stick your neck out?" she said, checking her face in the rearview mirror, wiping away tears. "You could have just stopped."

"I trusted him. He helped me believe in things when I got disillusioned. There was a clearness to the way he ran his world. At least I thought so," I said.

"Nobody's that pure."

"Now you tell me."

She smiled and readjusted the mirror to reflect the road again. Her hand moved back to the gearshift.

"Stupid of me to stop, Mike."

"It wasn't. Want me to drive?"

The Saab rolled back onto the highway, crunching over broken glass and asphalt bits in the breakdown lane. Gabrielle eased into the flow of traffic. Her hand sought mine across the gearshift. Fingers clasped, we drove in silence, both our hands resting on my lap.

It was a private moment and another border. I've always found something deliciously promising in the first brush of a woman's hand on my leg. But this touch signified trust, comfort, friendship. Nothing more.

The wild child was transforming herself into a woman who seemed less mysterious, less dream and more real. And I realized that in an odd way, a mere six hours ago the opposite had happened with Kim Pendergraph, on the beach.

Kim—my old pal—had begun taking on the allure of a lover. Gabrielle—the fiery sex bomb—was showing aspects suitable for a wife.

I had an odd thought then. I wondered whether a drug had helped me see parts of both women that I'd missed previously. Or had it been some natural spurt of understanding that had spurred a rebirth of hope.

We passed out of the Bronx and rode into Westchester. The road became better paved and the large buildings and factories dropped away.

"Do you even like chili?" asked Gabrielle, sounding normal again, even flirtatious.

"If Keating's making it, probably not."

Her hand disengaged and she downshifted, swerving us up an exit ramp off I-95 and into the oceanfront town of Rye. What remained on my thigh was a hint of coming happier moments, and possibilities that had nothing to do with profits, prison, murders, lies.

K eating's property couldn't have been more danger-ously situated. We weren't even on the grounds yet, but the twisty roads and large estates in his exclusive neighborhood would make escape more difficult if Eisner or the police showed up.

This could be even more of a trap than Danny thought.

"The border to Canada's only nine hours north," Gabrielle joked, slowing the Saab before a couple of guards in ties and jackets at the foot of Keating's long driveway and within view of a big house ahead. The men checked guests' names off a list. They had the clean look of off-duty cops, and authority in their stance. They were probably Rye town cops moonlighting on a weekend—armed, trained, hooked by radio to headquarters. Just what I needed.

"Remember, Gabrielle. If we're on the lawn and get separated, we try to keep sight of each other. And we never go into the house at the same time. Someone's got to be outside to watch for police."

Following the guard's directions, she parked the Saab in a line of cars hugging a grass traffic circle inside a cul-de-sac at the foot of the driveway.

The setup was getting worse. The property occupied a promontory jutting into the Atlantic, at the end of a peninsula. Which meant the entire neighborhood narrowed in a half-mile wooded funnel to end at Keating's house. The charming countrylike lanes we'd driven through meandered so badly that at times it was impossible to see who was coming toward you from around a corner. The nearby properties had lawns big enough to accommodate a coordinated foot assault—a line fanning toward the waterfront like beaters driving game—or to allow landing assault copters and aerial surveillance of a fugitive on foot.

In other words, easy for us to get in, harder to get out.

"Take the spare car key," Gabrielle said, parking behind an eggshell blue Mercedes convertible. But almost instantly a Honda Odyssey filled the rearview mirror, wedging us in. She sighed. "Not that it will do much good."

"Leave your key in the ignition, ma'am," the guard said as we got out of the car. He checked off Gabrielle's name on his list and did not ask for mine. I was clearly her guest. "Don't worry about your vehicle. It's safe."

"That makes me feel so secure." She smiled, dazzling the man with her appearance. Gone was the grief that I now knew she was hiding. Good actress, I thought, impressed.

She took my arm as we strolled up the curving driveway with other casually elegant partygoers, under the blazing noonday sun. A live jazz band was playing behind the house, offering up an uninspired rendition of "Take the A Train," the sort of restrained version that would appeal to stodgy dancers. I smelled grilling meat, dusky beach, salty ocean. The odor of freshly cut grass carried a paraffin whiff from hidden, anti-mosquito coils.

"I could use a drink," she said. "But don't worry. I won't give in to the urge."

The gray-shingle "cottage" was built to resemble an 18th-century French stone chateau. Two perfectly identical three-story wings jutted from the central hallway, with its huge window flanked by ivy. Identical balconies adorned twinned third-story bedroom windows. Oak copses flanked both corners of the house. Balance was the key component. Beauty was contained and coordinated, like Keating, the appeal in geometric mastery and control. This place had cost a fortune and would require another fortune to maintain.

Even though it looked nothing like the Bureau's mock-up "assault village" back at Quantico, I flashed back to my training days in that town of dummy storefronts, mock theaters, fake subway tunnels and mall-like parking lots filled with seized wrecks. The place was a Hollywood-style back lot used by law enforcement to train agents—how to break down doors or shoot terrorists from rooftops, assault a house, or theater, or parked hijacked plane with the least loss of innocent life.

I'd spent two weeks at Assault Village for training while assigned as a vacation replacement to the Bureau's Special Assault Force. The lessons I'd learned there might prove helpful now, although chili cook-offs had not been covered in the course.

My training had been largely tactical, involving how

to read landscapes, identify attack routes, anticipate ways that a bad guy might elude an agent, trick an agent, flank you or ambush you.

In a worst-case scenario today, with me being the bad guy, back to the sea, I'd have to squeeze through a closing cordon driving at me down a narrowing finger of land, with plenty of cover for anyone waiting for me to come.

Gabrielle remarked, "I know a great Japanese restaurant in Montreal. You sure you don't want to leave?"

"Do they serve chili?"

The banter hid our nervousness as we reached a pair of white-coated attendants—smiling college-age kids—offering iced drinks at the top of the driveway.

"Welcome to the big cook-off, sir. We have apple juice, vodka tonics or coke."

"Juice for me," Gabrielle said. "Honey?"

"Me too."

"Would you like a program?" asked the other attendant, a cute blonde. Her tray held neat piles of white cards embossed in gold script.

"Program?" I said.

"Recipes," the kid said. "Chef Keating versus Chef Schwadron. The score's three to three after the last six years. Today's the playoff. You vote on a card. All votes will be kept secret. The winner picks the charity of his choice. The loser donates five thousand dollars."

The attendant looked hot and silly in her red vest and white shirt and cowboy hat. Gabrielle took a card off the tray.

"Hmm," she said, reading. "Texas Chainsaw Hot Chili, by the honorable Tom Schwadron. Sounds yummy. Oklahoma Tornado Killer Chili, by our venerable host. Darling, I can never decide between those two."

"We need to know more," I agreed.

"Vegas is giving four-to-one odds on Mr. Keating," the attendant said with more grimace than smile, clearly speaking from an orchestrated script. "Atlantic City likes Mr. Schwadron."

"Which contestant is National Intelligence backing?" asked Gabrielle. "That's what we really want to know."

The kid laughed with real feeling, sensing mockery of her employer in the question.

"Gabrielle, let's go cast our vote," I said.

As we continued around back, my senses ratcheted up. The only hint of tension in her was the tight way her fingers gripped my biceps beneath my new jacket, a light-weight three-button British model I'd bought on the way here, during a quick side-trip in Manhattan. My khakis were new too, and I'd chosen lace-up rubber-soled Pradas, better suited for flight. Gabrielle was still in white.

The sun felt strange on my face. I'd not been beardless for years. The mini-recorder taped to my chest felt warm.

"What do you know? That's Alicia Dent," whispered Gabrielle, indicating a diminutive redhead in a long yellow sundress, thirty feet ahead. She turned as if sensing scrutiny. It was the famed Washington journalist, all right. Then she went back to talking to her companion, a chubby and dowdy-looking young man who simply kept nodding. We rounded the house and the back end of the property opened up.

"Ask her about the resignations, Mike?"

"Keating and Schwadron first. We won't have a lot of time."

Groups of guests were scattered on a meadow-sized lawn sloping down toward the shore. The adults stood chatting and sipping drinks. Kids in bathing suits splashed in the water. Teens were grouped near the dock, beneath a haze of rising blue cigarette smoke. The live band played in a green-and-white-striped tent open at the sides and filled with tables of refreshments. Shingled guest cottage to the right. Boathouse by the dock. Sandy strip beach ahead, on which at least a dozen people sunned themselves. One couple was pushing sea kayaks into the boulder-lined cove.

"There's Keating," I said, spotting the man who had fired me two days ago, talking intently to an athletic-looking middle-aged stranger whose tall profile and stiff bearing struck me as vaguely military. The man was in a light-blue summer suit. Jet black hair combed back. Olive skin. Drink in his hand. "How come Keating's not cooking?"

"That happens the day before. The chili is laid out in samples in the tent. But there's also usually lobster, clams, corn on the cob. Nobody comes expecting just chili."

"Silly me," I said.

I grew aware, as we approached Keating, of guests watching Gabrielle and whispering, maybe out of curiosity, or maybe they thought it bad form for a grieving daughter to be clinging to a date at a party.

Keating was all in white, like a 1920s tennis player. White short-sleeved shirt. White pleated trousers. White shoes. Blue sunglasses.

The man with him glanced toward us, and although I did not know him, his eyes narrowed slightly when he saw me. I didn't like it. He turned away.

"Mike," Gabrielle said as we closed on them, "thanks for having the guts to just sit there, in the car."

* * *

My strategy to shake up Keating and Schwadron had
seemed bold when I'd proposed it. It felt desperate
now. Stepping across the soft grass toward Keating gave
me an exposed feeling, like charging a door in an assault.
Gabrielle's heels sank in the lawn, making her wobble.

"Montreal is starting to sound better," I said.

"Bill Keating! Ter-rific party," Gabrielle said, inter-
rupting conversation between the men as we walked up.

Keating's sunglasses swung toward her instantly. His
host smile turned to sympathy. The other man's gaze returned to me, frankly interested.

Keating clasped Gabrielle's hands, removed the glasses
to show sympathetic eyes. "I'm so happy you came, so
sorry that . . ."

He broke off, having realized who I was, beardless or
not. Gabrielle drew me close as if I were her lover and she
was proud to be introducing me to family for the first
time.

"You know Mike," she said, looking at me adoringly.
"He's been terrific during a bad time."

"He's the reliable type," Keating responded, as if his
smile would erase his firing me, his pretended dumping
of a sample of HR-109. His hand, closed over mine, was
firm and welcoming and there was no sign that he knew I
was wanted for murder. He grasped my upper arm like a
delighted host greeting an unexpected guest. "I'm glad
Gabrielle has someone she can rely on," he said.

"My dad had *you* to rely on," she said.

Keating nodded sadly at both of us. As her date I was
being treated like an equal, at least on the surface, as
she'd predicted. I wondered if Keating knew about Asa
Rodriguez's death yet.

"Gabrielle Dwyer, Mike Acela," he said, turning to introduce us to the other man, "this is my good friend Colonel Alonzo Otto of the National Intelligence Director's office. Al, the whole country is grateful for the work you have been doing, keeping us safe."

The colonel exuded a crisp, athletic attentiveness. His eyes were black, his handshake firm, his teeth white and even when he smiled. I wondered what kind of smile it was.

"I believe I met someone who works for you," I told Otto, fishing on impulse. "Major Carl Eisner."

"I'm sorry, I don't know the name. Quite a few people work for me." Otto sipped an amber-colored drink in a highball glass. It had ice and a sprig leaf in it.

"Relentless officer, I'd say," I said.

"That's necessary sometimes."

"Which times would those be?"

The split-second eye contact that passed between Otto and Keating held hidden meaning. The colonel excused himself, saying he had to get back to DC. Watching him walk off was like hearing a starter pistol fire in a high-stakes race. The question now was whether I'd get off the property before Eisner or the police showed up.

Keating sighed, turning to go also. "Well, have a great time, you two. I see another old friend by the tent. Gabrielle, you and I should talk about a couple of things coming up on the Board. May I give you a call next month?"

"I got a package in the mail," I said. "From Dwyer."

That stopped him, all right, yanked his attention back to me as if I'd just pulled on a chain.

"With a disk in it," I said. "And memos. Potential formulas for HR-109, or should I call it *Enhance*?"

He put the sunglasses back on and I saw myself

reflected in them. "Did you bring the disk?" he asked evenly, and I saw I'd completed the transition from underling to threat. He handled surprise well, but then again, what else should I have expected from the new chairman of Lenox Pharmaceuticals?

I told Keating that actually there were now several disks, as I'd made copies, and he suggested that all three of us continue the conversation in the house.

"There's less distraction there," he said.

Of course, I'd be unable to see whoever else arrived on the property while I was inside.

"Actually, I'd prefer to talk to you and Schwadron together." With Otto moving farther away I felt time moving faster. I'd go for my two main suspects at the same time.

"Him? Why him? I'm the chairman."

He doesn't want me to talk to them together. Good.

"I have the disk," I said, meaning that no further explanation was necessary.

"No problem, then," he said, shrugged and added, "In fact . . ." as his head rose and he gazed over my shoulder. Following his gaze, I saw Tom Schwadron walking toward us, dressed nattily in a blue seersucker jacket and signature bow tie, even in this heat. His trajectory seemed to have originated from a spot on the lawn where Colonel Alonzo Otto stood, watching him zero in on us, like a missile Otto had fired.

"Gabby," Schwadron said, hugging her like an uncle and this was a family occasion, not a confrontation. His smile and warmth felt so genuine that even under the circumstances, I felt a tug of liking for the guy.

"I'm so happy to see you here. And with Mike Acela." He shook my hand, then turned to Keating. "See? I told you he was a fine young man," he said. "If Gabby likes him, that's the best recommendation there is."

Keating didn't reply, merely tolerating the older man's courtliness. Then Gabrielle said she'd stay outside while we had our conversation.

"I'm hungry," she said.

As if anyone was fooled.

What she *would* do, we'd decided, was be our lookout. If she spotted incoming police or DI, she'd call my cell phone, let it chime twice and hang up.

"One if by land, two if by sea," she'd said when I proposed it in the car. "Just like Paul Revere. But he got to ride a horse at least."

We turned toward the house, and Schwadron told her, "Why not try my chili, dear. And vote for me. Not Bill."

'm proud of you, Mike," Schwadron said.

Like most Americans, I doubt the existence of conspiracies, at least inside the country. I believe that a lone gunman killed John Kennedy, not a crew of CIA and the mob. I laugh when someone tells me that a cabal of bankers controls the government. After years working corporate crime, I found that usually, when a company went crooked, the problem originated with a single person. Crimes involving lots of people evolve from simple beginnings. Put the right pressure on participants and they fight to sell out one another. Criminals tend to be stupid, greedy and selectively moral. Very few are evil all the way through.

"You see, Bill?" Schwadron said. "Mike came to *us*

with the information, not the papers and not the police, even after you fired him. If that's not loyalty, what is?"

"Thanks for giving us the opportunity to talk with you, Mike," Keating said through gritted teeth.

The launch point of my gamble was the likelihood that only one of the men before me had been directly involved in the Chairman's murder, even if they were partners in something else. I doubted that Dwyer could have been *that* wrong about *two* friends.

Besides, Keating didn't want Schwadron in here.

Keating said, "Tell us, Mike, more about the disk."

Schwadron occupied a plush sitting chair in a corner, looking casual and proud, urging me on. He'd declined a drink, like me.

Keating had poured himself a glass of iced Perrier, but he wasn't drinking and the ice was melting. He sat on the couch to my left, far from Schwadron. I couldn't watch them both at the same time. I wondered if that was their plan.

"There's nothing on the disk you don't know about," I said.

The study was done in pale ash, the brocade curtains a floral pattern. The rugs were fine Italian weavings, the couches Venetian leather, and there was a trio of flat-screen TVs so the new chairman could monitor different channels at the same time. There was a loudly ticking wall clock—an antique—near a window. Each jerk of the second hand seemed to compress the passage of time.

"The Chairman sent me the story on Enhance," I said to Keating. "Or Oblige." I looked at Schwadron. "The disk contained your memos, all about Naturetech and specifics of the synthesis. Asa Rodriguez. Director Carbone." I was rewarded with the slightest stiffening from Keating.

Schwadron's smile widened as if I were a favorite student passing a test.

The clock started chiming. I added, lying, "And the Royces. The Chairman intuited some of it and figured part out. He asked me to get the disk to the press if something happened to him. He guessed he was in danger. But he thought he was going to be arrested, not killed."

"The Royces?" Keating said, frowning. He looked from me to Schwadron. "Dwyer killed himself. Who or what are the Royces?"

Schwadron nodded. "I didn't get that part either, Mike. Who did you say they were?"

"The people who murdered him. And killed Dr. Asa Rodriguez in Florida, two nights ago."

The chiming stopped, and in the room's silence I heard music and laughter tinkling in from outside, muffled levity. Keating drained his Perrier in one drink. Schwadron sat back, looking, in turn, thoughtful, sad, curious.

"Professional killers," I said, putting on my FBI face as if I were about to arrest these two instead of fearing I'd be arrested myself. "Hired to kill him and steal back what he took from Naturetech."

Keating looked at Schwadron with blatant curiosity now. Schwadron spoke first.

"You're sure of this, Mike? It's fantastic. You have *proof*?"

"They threatened me. They admitted it. I have it on tape," I lied. "Yeah, I'm sure. But I'm *not* sure," I said, hoping my recorder was working, "which one of you hired them. Which of you made a phone call after you had dinner with him. And by the way, the tape and disks get released if something happens to me. To the *Times*."

Silence. They both looked dumbfounded, but at least one had to be a superb actor. "One of *us?*" Schwadron said.

"And why," Keating asked slowly, thinking out loud, "if you have this tape, this *evidence,* are you even here in the first place? Why not hand it to the police? Proof of *murder?* Why come to us?"

It was too much to hope they'd break at the first attack.

"Because," I said, meeting Keating's gaze squarely, knowing I had to work on the timing and earnestness of the upcoming lie, "because I hoped to minimize damage to the company, and also, to be truthful . . ."

They regarded me more softly, liking the word *also.* *Also* meant that I was about to get selfish, that the pious first half of my answer hid greed or rage or self-interest, all motivations they understood. *Also* meant negotiation, not accusation.

"I want my job back. And a huge bonus. I want a share of 109 myself."

They sat back. I thought, *Let the guilty one go for it.*

I added, "I thought the decision on how to handle all this should come from the company. But if you disagree, I'll just hand the disks to the police today."

Keating stared. I couldn't tell what he was thinking. Schwadron walked to the mantel, stood with his profile to the clock, so I saw the parchmentlike quality of his aging skin, a vague concave reflection in the curved glass.

COME ON . . . COME ON . . .

This was the moment when I hoped their facade would unravel, at least enough so I'd get a hint, evidence, *something.* The carrot was on the table, and the stick.

Schwadron answered first. "You *should* have your job back, Mike," he said, eyeing Keating. "You've certainly demonstrated that your value to the company exceeds even what Chairman Dwyer considered it. Bill? Don't you agree?"

"Why are you looking at me like that?" Keating snapped. "I've never heard of the Royces. You want your damn job back? Fine."

They were going along awfully quickly, I thought.

Schwadron's brows rose.

"I imagine," he told me delicately, "*if* someone made a call after that dinner, like you think, they did so to alert legitimately concerned authorities, who needed to recover what had been taken by Dwyer, not to hire killers."

"Who did you call?" I asked him.

"Bill and I were assured that all company property was recovered quietly, that Dwyer was despondent afterward and killed himself."

"We never heard of any Royces," agreed Keating.

"Who did you call?" I asked again.

Their amazement seemed genuine, their acting astounding if this was some orchestrated lie. This was not a scene I'd anticipated. It struck me that they'd both wondered all along if Dwyer had been murdered, but had not wanted to pursue the question because it was better to keep it closed.

Later on, I'd realize that I should have been warned by how freely they were talking in front of me. But at the time I was following the way Keating and Schwadron seemed to be trying to piece the truth together between themselves.

Keating said, "Eisner?"

"That man scares me."

"Carbone?"

"Pshaw! They were college roommates! And Carbone is gone."

"So what? Dwyer gave some to Carbone, who swore to keep the secret. You know this, Tom. The whole dinner was about this! After it worked in the Mideast, Carbone wanted *everything for Washington.* Dwyer threatened to destroy the supply, formula, everything."

"Because," I said, drawing their attention back to me, remembering what Gabrielle had said about Dwyer, "he didn't mind screwing over a few hundred million people as long as he controlled 109. But he hated the idea that decisions would be taken away from him."

Schwadron nodded. "National Intelligence offered *a million dollars a dose.* Unbelievable profit. But Dwyer refused to surrender control. I don't think he really would have destroyed it. He was just mad. I could have talked him out of it. He made a threat, that's all. He would have seen reason in the end."

"But he was murdered before he had a chance to destroy the supply, and neither you nor Keating cared who did it because the death benefited you somehow."

Schwadron looked sad now. He had the face of a great actor, and the bearing. No wonder he was effective in hearings. "Of course we care what happened, Mike, but you don't destroy a miracle," he said gently. "God only makes miracles once in a great while. Penicillin. Antibiotics. Wonders that change the world. Worth trillions. You protect a miracle like Oblige, and nurture it. You use it for good. I know you see that, Mike. It takes a special kind of strong person to ignore a smaller evil—even a hateful and despicable evil—to protect a greater good. I think you're that type of person, and you've proved it by coming here today."

The door opened and my heart sank when two strangers walked in. A black guy and a white guy. G-style haircuts. G-style suits. G-style attitudes. The familiar dull look of impending arrest in their eyes.

"You're a popular fellow in Florida," Keating said as the frisk started, and the tape recorder was taken away. "Your photo's all over the place. You killed Asa Rodriguez. You killed Dwyer too, we understand. Florida's got the death penalty. And you've broken several espionage laws."

"You know that's not true." I looked at the two strangers. They didn't seem to care if it was true or not.

Schwadron told me, "I think you're the type of man who understands sacrifices, Mike." He turned to the others, moving the agents back with the gentlest wave, with his natural authority. Their hands fell away.

"This arrest may not be necessary. Give Mike and me a second alone, will you, please?"

I realized I'd never gotten Gabrielle's signal. My cell phone hadn't chimed while I'd been here. Did that mean she hadn't seen them coming? Or did it mean she too was involved?

"You like poetry, Mike?" asked Schwadron after the men had filed out, Keating too. They'd be right outside the door, and the window. There was no way out. Everything had backfired. They'd known all along that I was acting. I'd never had a chance today.

"Poetry," I said.

"Robert Frost, for instance, was a genius. He'd take the smallest bit of truth and expand it in a way that made it apply to humankind's greatest, most powerful choices."

"You're giving me a choice?" I asked.

"You know Frost's poem about roads, Mike? Two

roads on a snowy evening? The farmer sits on his sled, in a storm, eyeing two paths. Which will he take? Yes, a choice, if you agree. I don't want to hurt you. I want to help you. This may be the most important choice of your life."

SIXTEEN

"How would you like a lifetime supply of Oblige? And the freedom to enjoy it?"

The curtains remained drawn, the door shut, although for all I knew a dozen people monitored what went on in this room. Schwadron waved me onto the couch, content in the quiet to let me take in the offer, underlined by the wealthy setting—the collector's furniture, the address book on Keating's antique desk, filled with private numbers of powerful people, the whole protected cocoon of the privileged around me. The world I had once aspired to join, and that he offered me now—for, I knew, a price.

I said, "What about the murder charges?"

Schwadron shrugged. "New witnesses show up. Alibis. Favors. Certain provisions in the Patriot Act. I can't guarantee a hundred percent. Is ninety-nine point nine enough?"

"Why?"

He looked surprised. "Because you're *innocent*. I do have a conscience, you know. And I'm not offering a bribe either. You're too honest for that kind of cheap deal. But a just and proper reward for work well done, loyalty well placed and a responsible attitude that is exactly what we will need in the people who will receive this drug.

We're going to be drawing up lists. I'd feel honored if you were on the first one."

"The synthesis is complete, then? You worked out the flaws?"

He nodded. "Final tests are going on at the moment. Fifty years from now, when our country is safe and strong and protected by the right people, history will look back at this as a turning point."

"You don't intend for history to even know about this turning point. Trusting you was the Chairman's mistake."

"His *mistake* was refusing to see the possibilities in Oblige. Shall I go on, or are you closed to making a fair, objective deal?"

"I'm listening," I said, thinking that Gabrielle had been right. The Chairman had not known who his friends were. He'd kept himself so aloof from people around him that, in the end, he'd been wrong about them too.

From the side, standing at an angle to me, Schwadron was stooped slightly like an old man, but his voice was as young and vibrant as a visionary's. And I was the prisoner allowed a few last moments of luxury as a temptation of a better fate.

"The twenty-first century," Schwadron began, spreading his arms as if to encompass a hundred years. "And the United States. The greatest, most powerful empire in history. Our economy is the biggest. Our armies protect the world. Our citizens enjoy the highest standard of living, and yet . . ."

"It's endangered," I said, completing his thought.

"*Yes,*" he said fiercely, and in his face I saw the political warrior he had been in his youth, as an ambassador, as a friend to Presidents. "Our democracy is in jeopardy everywhere. Terrorists plot against us. The Europeans are coalescing into a new unified force. The Asians take our markets, and try to build nuclear bombs. *One nation under God, Mike.* That's what every school child recites. I believe God himself gave our corporation and our government this drug to maintain gains we fought to achieve over three centuries."

"You're bringing God into this?" I said, astounded.

"If we use His bounty in the right way."

"Are you out of your mind?"

He laughed, a delighted, merry sound. He slapped the mantel. "Oh, Mike," he said, pouring Perrier in a fresh glass. "I like you. You don't mean that. Was Tom Jefferson out of his mind? Was Salk? No, they just understood the power of new ideas to transform society. And so do you."

"What do you want from me?"

"The disk. The copies. A promise of silence from you and your friends. Nothing that you wouldn't want for yourself if you thought about it more. I want you to be one of the people who will, from now on, safeguard the security and happiness of the nation. Anticipate the moves of our enemies. Protect our industry and leaders. I want you as one of the responsible few privileged to take Oblige."

"I thought you said Washington was going to control it now. How could I even get it?"

Schwadron shrugged. "Dwyer's death changed the dynamics a bit. No one wants the story to get out. People flew off the handle at first. Part of the value of Oblige is the fact that its use remains secret."

"So a deal was worked out between the company and Washington. You'll get some Oblige yourself, I bet."

"That would be the right thing, I believe."

"And the Royces? Remember them? The people who killed Dwyer?"

He nodded. "No one intended for Dwyer to be hurt. If he was, these people will be found. Quietly. I promise."

I thought about it. The moral blindness that his offer represented was not so different from the sort I'd provided for Dwyer. The stakes were bigger, but not the principle. The Royces would never be punished, but I could choose to believe that they would. I could pretend, and in exchange I'd be given safety.

I said, "And who decides exactly which people get the drug? Those semi-fascists eating chili on the lawn?"

"Don't be naive, Mike. We both know these kinds of important triage decisions are made every day in corporations, government, even families. Who can be trusted with a key formula? Access to a bank account? Who will be included in the secret White House list of those to be housed underground if nuclear war breaks out? Now we add a new question. Who will partake of Oblige?"

"You're saying the White House was involved?"

He sipped his Perrier. He smiled. He said, "There are some things, Mike, that even I don't know. But over the next few weeks, lists will be drawn up. Reliable people working together, choosing who gets initial access in Washington, industry, academia. There'll be a small supply when synthesis begins. After all, we only have a single laboratory and the process is slow."

"What about the resignations in Washington over the last few weeks. The President. The Supreme Court Justice. Is 109 involved?"

"We're not discussing that."

"Did the Chairman know that 109 was being used to investigate people who have nothing to do with security problems? That it's being used to carry out a drug-fueled coup?"

I laughed. "It's appropriate, I guess. The most drug-dependent society on earth ends up being ruled by pharmaceuticals."

Schwadron looked genuinely pained. "Don't exaggerate. And I had nothing to do with Dwyer's death. Dwyer threatened to destroy the drug, Mike, eradicate the greatest discovery in democracy's arsenal in the last century. There are certain trade-offs you accept when the reward is so meaningful. And there are always a few kinks to be worked out when a new system is put in place."

"You call trying to take over the government a kink?"

"*It will be worked out.* And anyway, Mike, if the people who quit their jobs had nothing to hide, nothing would have been discovered. Isn't that right?"

Schwadron seated himself to my left, on the couch. He patted my knee, gently, like a grandfather would.

"Question, Mike. If you had the formula for making a nuclear bomb, would you publish it in a newspaper?"

"Of course not."

"Exactly. Oblige is the same, except its existence is *part of the secret.* When the President sits down with the Chinese Prime Minister in Beijing tomorrow to negotiate a nuclear treaty, theoretically, what do you think the effect would be on negotiations if the Chinese knew that the President was enhanced when it came to seeing their position on things, no matter what they say to his face. *Everything is changed when you can't lie.*"

"So the President *does* know."

"I said 'theoretically.' " Schwadron moved to the mantel, always keeping the left side of his face averted.

"The point is," he said, "it's to no one's advantage to

have a dispute over Oblige spill into the courts or newspapers. It's in everyone's advantage—yours, in particular—to work out an agreement that distributes it safely, without fuss. Dwyer's death—the possibility that the secret could get out—made the arguing parties more inclined to see parallel interests. To share it."

I thought about it. His offer tempted me. I was innocent. I was scared. My friends were in danger. And even if Schwadron's negotiated arrangement fell apart after a few weeks, I could change my life if supplied with HR-109. And not only financially. I'd finally be a full-fledged member of Dwyer's world. A superman when dealing with people who didn't have the drug. I remembered how clear my flashes of insight had been in Key West, and knew what that power could do if applied to business, love, a thousand daily questions. Oblige would make its users giants. It would make me one.

"Just say yes," he said, sensing my temptation. "We can all work together for good."

But I heard myself ask, "This is why the New York police were pressured to call Dwyer's death a suicide?"

"Suicide was considered a real possibility, so we let the conclusion lie there."

"Why did Eisner keep coming at me, then?"

Schwadron sighed in a way that made me think that for him, also, Eisner was an unpleasant subject. "He was investigating the contract before the death occurred. He's a maverick. He decided you're crooked, Mike. He saw Dwyer's list and figured you took the disk to sell secrets. But you've put that fear to rest today." Schwadron glanced at the door, as if to let me know that the men out there worked for Eisner. "But I can keep Eisner's people away from you. It's up to you. How we'll be able to help people, Mike!"

"Little people."

"Don't be petty. Strategic decisions are difficult. Sometimes the world is gray, and even Dwyer knew that when the greater good at Lenox meant breaking laws. You went along with it for him. What's so different now?"

When I hesitated, he moved closer, still holding his head at an odd angle. He sensed my reluctance and said more softly, "There are personal advantages too, you know. Not that they're the primary reward, but why shouldn't special people get extra for a job well done? In finance. In love."

In his seersucker jacket, he looked at that moment like some elderly, dandified Mephistopheles. His features seemed more elongated, his chin sharper. He said, "I saw how you looked at Gabrielle, out on the lawn. When it comes to women, some men like a chase. I prefer to take uncertainty out of things. Oblige is such a help. Who needs games? Mastery, that's the key."

"Gabrielle can be difficult," I said, and smiled.

"Good! So you'll give back the disks. And also, we'd like to offer the same arrangement to your loyal friends. Mr. Whiteagle and Dwyer's secretary. Where are they, by the way? Do you know?"

My heart plunged.

"Why don't we phone them now," he said, smiling, and suddenly I realized why he'd been averting his face. I didn't need HR-109 to see the truth.

I'd never had a chance in here. I'd been a fool.

I said, "Do you mind looking at me straight-on? Turn your head."

He sighed, but he did it.

Sure enough, the purple rash was on his neck. It rose out of his shirt collar, and up the bulge in his throat, the small irregularly shaped dots grouped like a series of tiny bunched triangles, a winding snake.

"Keating's rash appeared on his back, and Dwyer's on his knee," Schwadron said. "I had to get it on the neck." He shook his head at his bad luck. "I see you know what it means. There are no copies of the disk headed for newspapers at the moment. You don't have details of the synthesis either. It's funny how Oblige works, at least in me. It's like heat rising in my head when someone says something untrue. Like a little lie detector in here," he said, tapping his skull. "I had to pay attention to it at first. I didn't believe it. But the signal got pretty darn strong after a few hits of Oblige. We really need to find your friends."

"It's no use for me to say I'll help you, then," I told him. "Is it?"

"See?" he said, patting his head. "No heat this time. No flash of intuition. You're telling the truth now, and I'm sorry about that, because you really are the kind of person I'd prefer on my side."

"You'll hand me over to the Key West police?"

"Mike, you still don't understand. You're on tape, in front of witnesses, threatening to release classified secrets to newspapers unless you are paid a bribe and get your job back."

"I was lying."

"I know. Also, your fingerprints are all over Dwyer's apartment. You held off calling the police after his death while you removed evidence from the premises. You've been identified by eyewitnesses as the murderer of a Lenox scientist in Florida. Under the Patriot Act, crimes committed against persons employed in key defense industries make you, legally speaking—"

"An enemy combatant," I completed. The room reeled.

"*Also*, you lied to enter Naturetech, where you obtained blueprints of security arrangements at a lab working on a sensitive Defense contract.

"So no, Mike," he continued. "The only chance you'd ever even *go* on trial in Florida—where you'd lose, by the way—would be for you to get away from the place you're going now. I tried to help you avoid this, but you refused. I *would* have helped. Think of what's going to happen now as a sacrifice for your country."

"I was never going to get Oblige, was I? It was all a lie so I'd give you my friends."

"I would have made a reasonable deal. I'm not evil, Mike."

"You look the other way when evil things happen. Am I going to kill myself too?" I asked. "Or don't you want to know that? Like with Dwyer?"

The door opened again. Schwadron said as the men came back in, "Believe me, I'd hoped for a happier outcome. I admire you, whether you believe that or not. I'm truly sorry that things didn't work out."

SEVENTEEN

The black man snapped the cuffs on. "Tell me if they're too tight, sir," he said. He was very dark-skinned and soft-spoken and he moved with a slight bowlegged gait. Ex–college athlete, I figured, and lean. I made him for a tennis player or runner.

The thinner, pale man's nose had a mashed look, as if it had been broken more than once. His emerald tie clashed with the muted gray of his out-of-date three-button suit. He had the grip of an ironworker, the widow's peak of a country singer, and old acne scars pitted what otherwise might have been a handsome face. I guessed Appalachia—Kentucky or Tennessee.

The pale guy draped a handkerchief over the handcuffs, so when we got outside, Keating's guests wouldn't realize I was being escorted away.

I felt a brief sharp pressure at my hip, and looking down, saw a small black twin-pronged box in the athletic man's hand.

He said. "If you cry out, if you fight, if I get the notion you're even thinking about running, it'll feel like someone threw a radio in the bathtub with you."

"Where's Eisner?" I asked. "In the car?"

Schwadron had opened the book *The Age of Jackson,* and, back to us, pretended to scan pages. The men moved me into the hallway and hustled me out a side door and across a strip of lawn, into woods, abutting Keating's property on the landward side. It was classic extraction technique. I'd learned it at the Bureau: how to remove suspects from public places with a minimum of fuss.

I didn't see Gabrielle when we left the house.

Maybe she's still at the party. Is she arrested also? Or is she cooperating with them?

"Where are we going?" I asked.

"Shut up, you fuck," the black man said, rougher now that Schwadron wasn't there. The box pressed against my side, but he didn't set it off.

He shoved me forward. I heard the band playing. To a restrained version of "Mood Indigo"—another slow retirement-home rendition—the men pushed me along a seaside path, past stumpy pines that clung to rocks, their exposed roots like clawing fingers. The path avoided Keating's driveway and the town cops guarding it. We emerged abruptly onto another quaint curvy street. A new white LTD idled there. I couldn't see if it had a government license plate. The driver getting out wasn't Eisner, but a hard-faced woman in a business suit, blue-tinted sunglasses and the bulge of a shoulder holster under her jacket.

"Aren't you going to read me my rights?" I asked the black man. If the arrest was legal, they'd have to do that, I knew.

Instead, a blast of pain erupted in my left shoulder, driving me into the pale man on the right. Razors sliced my nerve endings, exploded like claymore bits to rip from arm to hip to belly. Dizzy, I lost the edges of vision. I smelled meat grilling. It was me.

"For Christ sake, Boat Man," the pale man told his partner. "Warn me when you're gonna do that." He pulled me back to my feet. I'd been wrong about his origins. He spoke with a long Chicago "A."

I was already missing those little rules that used to annoy me at the FBI. Like having to inform an arrestee of his protections under the law.

"*Rights,* you piece of shit?" the black man said as the driver opened the rear door, and I saw the mesh wall sealing off the back. "You have the right to get shot while escaping. You have the right to shut your mouth when I tell you to, eat when I say, piss when I say, and frankly, to do everything we order the first time we say it. Marty," he said to the pale man, "did I miss any of Osama's rights?"

"I'm not who you think I am," I said.

He must have turned the taser dial up when I wasn't looking, because this time the pain made me cry out and bite into my tongue. My head slammed into the window. My elbow caught fire where the prongs had touched. Needles scraped bone, sliced synapses and tore into nerve endings. The jolt must have closed down my throat muscles. Suddenly it burned to breathe.

"I knew I forgot something. You have the right to as many volts as you can take, asshole."

This time I didn't answer.

"That's better. See, I'm the Boat Man and you're the passenger," the black guy said, putting his face so close that I saw sweat shine in his pores. "Boat Man's brother was in the World Trade Center when the first plane hit. CBS showed him over and over, jumping out of a window, on fire. So when I get a chance to meet a traitor raghead sympathizer like you, I want you on my boat."

I didn't want to know what *boat* meant. My breathing slowly subsided back toward normal. I still felt vestiges of electric current jumping around my heart, spinning like sparks in my veins.

The pale man got in the backseat beside me, and told me to turn my face away. "Look out the window, at the fucking trees."

"Can I ask a question?"

Light disappeared as he blindfolded me.

"No. All aboard," said the black man's voice. "You're on my boat."

They tuned into talk radio while we drove, conversing little, grunting approvingly whenever a caller—and there were lots of them—ranted against the retired President, the United Nations, protesting students who had been gassed in Boston last night. The host announced a news bulletin. Superb intelligence work had uncovered a terrorist money-laundering operation in the Bahamas, and all enemy accounts had been seized. Tremendous victory! Colossal coup! Funding that would have paid for bombings had been traced back to sources in Vienna and Islamabad.

"God bless our Intelligence services," the host said.

"Think about my brother burning up," the black man's voice said from the front.

I don't know how long we traveled. It seemed like hours, but time doesn't speed by when you've got a blindfold over your eyes. The commercials began repeating themselves, many for paranoia products: gasoline generators in case a hurricane hit your house, home alarms in case a burglar tried to get in, computer security systems, gas masks, first-aid kits, water-purifying tablets.

"If office workers have nothing to hide," a caller was

asking, "why should they object to taking regular lie-detector tests to screen out bad apples?"

"I have to go to the bathroom," I said.

The black man held up the stun gun and tapped his finger against it. "You might want to reconsider and hold it in."

I shut out the voices coming from the radio. I tried to remember any dents or markings on the LTD. Had the driver spoken, so I could place her accent? No. I pictured the green-and-black-checkered pattern on the upholstery, knowing that federal agencies often equipped their vehicles differently. Maybe later, if I got the chance, I could match the pattern with a particular order number.

Try to stay optimistic in a kidnap situation, my old instructors at the FBI used to say.

The hum of highway traffic changed to the coarser drone of tires on rural tarmac. We slowed, and the car turned left sharply, rolling me into the pale man. From the bumpy movements I imagined the LTD driving over dirt or grass.

Through forest. Deserted woods.

We're not murderers, Schwadron had promised. But he'd lied about so much else, so why not this too?

The car stopped so sharply that it pitched me forward. The radio shut off and I heard the hum of automatic windows rolling down. A wash of hot summer air brushed my face. I envisioned the LTD parked in a field, and heard the front door slam and felt the chassis rise, meaning someone had gotten out. The *chuk-chuk* sound of a helicopter was coming closer. The back door opened beside me as the copter sound grew loud. The rushing air now carried the tart smell of fuel.

I tried to fight off fear. *Is that copter coming to take me away? Or bringing someone here?*

From close to my ear the black man's voice said, "I met a guy once, Raghead. A copter pilot who flew for Saddam. I had the guy on my boat, see? He and I talked quite a lot. He told me about one of Saddam's favorite hobbies. Know what it was?"

I smelled breath mints and cologne and sweat. His silence told me that I was supposed to answer this time.

"What was it?"

"To take an enemy up in a copter, over water. To ask 'em a question, and if the answer wasn't right, push 'em out and watch 'em fall, from way up high."

"And if the answer was right?"

"You got me, Sand Man. They'd push him out anyway."

I will not be scared.

They dragged me out and shoved me toward the roaring copter, which sounded like it had landed. I tripped but stayed up. The black guy said, "Take that piss now, Mike, here, so you won't mess up the copter." I had to go badly, but afterward they didn't let me zip up. I guess they thought it was humiliating to make me stumble around with my dick stuck between the prongs of a metal zipper.

They were right.

This is a fear problem. Not an adrenaline problem.

Someone shoved me hard and my chest rammed into the copter. My manacled hands came up and smashed against the hull. I told myself not to show the men how much I hurt, to use my pain to give me resolve.

I will not let them get to me.

"My brother's name was Landon," the black man said, from behind me, as I felt hands grip my shoulders and haul me through the door of the copter.

My knees slammed into steel as they dragged me across the floor. The copter was shaking. I felt webbing at my back as they pushed me against the wall and ordered me to stay there.

"Landon worked on the ninety-first floor, north tower," the black man said. "He was a broker. He liked to play softball on Sundays, and grill bratwurst in his backyard. He always burned those links. They'd get this charred stink. That's the way he looked after he fell."

I said, "Whatever it is you think I did, I didn't do it."

"You a good swimmer, Sand Man?"

"He has handcuffs on, Corby," the pale man shouted over the rotor. *Corby,* I thought. *A name.* But even without it, I'd recognize the voices as long as I lived. The pale man added, "Corby, no one can swim with handcuffs on."

"Hey, asswipe, do you think it's possible to swim with handcuffs on? We could try an experiment."

I felt the copter lift off.

They're bluffing. If they intended to kill me now, they wouldn't have involved so many people. The driver. The copter crew.

But the truth was, I didn't know.

Minutes later, the copter was buffeted by an updraft and swept violently sideways. I tried to turn and grab the webbing. I heard the hatch slide open, and suddenly the wind was inside the helicopter, not just out, carrying the unmistakable salt-humid odor of the sea.

I imagined gray, heaving ocean far below.

At the FBI, in Hostage class, instructors had told us, "Try to exert some control in the situation. Try to befriend your captors."

They yanked me to my feet. The black man shouted, "Bye-bye, Sand Man."

I tried to fight but couldn't see anything. They pushed me toward the blasting wind. My manacled fists whooshed through thin air. I kicked out but hit nothing. I clawed at a shirt. I heard buttons pop.

I screamed, "I'll take you with me."

The blow came from the right, slamming into my kidneys and arching me back and left and I was falling—plunging—but then I hit the floor, not air, and I was crawling away from the wind. My head hit the hull. I spun, back pressed against webbing. I flailed blindly, screaming that I'd kill them. I reached to remove the blindfold and something hard slammed down on my right shoulder. I heard a crack.

The copter seemed to be spinning, or maybe I was the one spinning, blind.

The attack stopped as suddenly as it had begun.

"Hey, Corby, he pissed himself," the voice of the pale man said.

He didn't sound angry. He sounded amused.

"I *told* you to get it out before, Raghead, and not mess up the copter."

They didn't throw me out of the copter.

They'd never intended to, I realized.

"Don't try to escape again," said the one named Corby. He was letting me know what their story would be if I complained about the treatment. "Next time we'll get rough."

We landed, and as the rotor sounds died I heard, in the distance, a sound I recognized from my days at Quantico. Male voices counting calisthenics. Drilling. I told myself, *I'm on a military base.*

My blindfold was still on when they brought me into a building, but I instantly recognized the sound of sliding steel gates and the prison smell, that institutional mix of oiled steel, testosterone, steamed meat, open plumbing and lingering sweat. But this jail lacked other sounds I remembered from the times I'd interviewed suspects in penitentiaries, county jails, drug houses, halfway houses. There was no cacophony of noise—no screams and curses, no blasting music, no never-ending barrage of talk, murmurs, prayers, threats, bowel-moving, water-trickling, lock-clicking insanity.

"That's because this is no ordinary prison," Corby said. "This is my boat. Your new home. I'm Charon. The Boat Man. The old Greek guy who takes the newly dead down the River Styx to eternity, Mike. To hell."

They let me take a shower with the blindfold off, in a long, empty, shower room. I was alone there except for the pale man, who watched me soap up and rinse off.

The next time the blindfold came off, I was in a cell with no window. The door was black steel and the room small, ten-by-nine roughly, with cinder-block walls and a steel view plate in the door, movable only from the outside, so someone could look in. The single creaky bed came with freshly laundered sheets and a new, thin, gray wool blanket. The open toilet shone, polished, but on the floor by the tank I saw pelletlike droppings, so I figured there were rats.

I hate rats.

I spotted another, long, wide slot on the bottom of the door for food trays.

Where the hell is this place? Whatever they want, fight them.

They had taken my belt and my shoelaces. They'd

given me gray tie-on lightweight pajama bottoms, with an elastic waistband, a matching button-up pajama top and backless terry-cloth slippers that were too big for me unless I walked with my toes curled. The wound on my shoulder oozed blood that stuck to the fabric. There was no chair in the room, no TV. No books or shelves. No mirror, of course, to be broken or used for simple reflective companionship, and the bright lone bulb was recessed three feet—out of reach—into a ceiling shaft.

It was so humid that condensation collected in pit holes in the cinder blocks, and ran down the walls and dampened my pajamas. Vaguely, through the thick walls, I heard the faint, regular sounds in the distance of men close-order drilling. I smelled a chalky, salty odor that reinforced my guess that this base was by the sea. I felt like I'd been traveling for hours, but there had been no way to measure time or distance on the way here. Florida I wondered. Cuba? There was only the tropical heat as a clue.

After a while the portal opened and a steel tray slid in, covered with a brown puddle of lumpy food. I forced myself to use the plastic spoon and swallow bland-tasting chili.

I wondered if Schwadron had been sadistic enough to have arranged this particular meal.

Halfway through the meal, the light went out.

Plunged into darkness, I groped to the bed. A high-pitched squeaking started inside the walls. I heard scurrying and tiny slurping noises from the toilet; a splash; small, sucking noises coming from the direction of the food tray on the floor.

Go to sleep.

I closed my eyes.

The light came on. I saw the rat—brown and thickly

haired and gigantic—running toward the bed. Its pink tail disappeared under the bed. I guess that's where the hole in the wall was.

I sat on the bed and tried to control my thinking. I remembered the way Mets pitcher Al Fooze had shut out the Cubs last September, during the playoffs. I remembered how great Kim Basinger looked in *The Natural*, seducing Robert Redford under a pier, leaning back, head tilted against a piling, mouth open, eyes soft. Then I remembered kissing Kim Pendergraph on the beach, and the way her mouth had tasted of cinnamon, and the soft way her small breasts had felt against my chest.

I remembered Christmas last year, and taking Danny, Hoot, Kim and her son, Chris, to the Odessa Room, a Russian restaurant in Brighton Beach, where the waiters served vodka bottles encased in ice and chopped liver mixed with sweet browned onions, and the veal chops had been as thick as steaks from Argentina, and we'd gotten so drunk that a Lenox car service had taken us home because we were all too pissed to drive.

The light went out again and I felt dizzy. A loud, warm buzzing filled my ears.

Did they drug me?

The light went on. It had only been off a few minutes this time. Five at most.

Eisner will show up tomorrow, I bet.

I heard muffled noises in the corridor and groped to the door and pressed my ear to steel. Sound carried better this way. Dogs barked and I heard a man screaming. Then I heard another man singing and recognized the long, high notes that an imam cries out each night from minarets around the world. The notes of Muslim prayer.

Am I in a prison where terrorist suspects are held?

* * *

I was banging on the door and shouting. I figured, why not? Maybe my friends were here too. "Hoot," I cried. "Gabrielle? It's Mike! Danny?"

Maybe no one could hear me out there.

The lights went off as another wave of dizziness enveloped me. My throat was parched, my sinuses dry.

"Danny!"

I went the wrong way in the dark, trying to get back to the bed. My center of gravity was off. Something soft and alive scurried over my bare foot. I was falling, trying to break the impact with outstretched hands. Pain exploded in my wrists. I lay on the floor, breathing hard, and felt something warm walking on my leg. I shook my leg to scare it off. Inches away, on my chest, I saw two small red beads, disembodied orbs in the dark.

Am I hallucinating?

The barking sounds grew louder from the hallway.

Had more than a day passed since I'd gotten here?

The black man's words came back to me.

He'd ferried me to hell.

Night became day and days lasted for minutes. I heard the Muslim man praying. I heard a woman screaming. I heard a pack of barking dogs. The panel in the door slid open and I knew someone was looking at me, but I only saw eyes.

I saw rat footprints in my spinach.

The next time the light came on, the rat didn't bother to run away. It stayed in the room, looking back at me—mean, curious, lonely, unafraid.

* * *

Where's the disk, Mike?"

"I told you, I don't know."

"Did you kill Asa Rodriguez because you had a falling-out with him? Were you working together to sell the disk?"

"Why don't you listen to me? I never even had a conversation with him."

"Where are your friends, Mike. Tell us where they went. They didn't just disappear."

Don't tell them about Danny's cousins.

"I want a lawyer."

After the laughter stopped the pale man said, "I *am* a lawyer. *Your* lawyer. Are your friends still in New York?"

"I need to sleep."

"Where is Danny Whiteagle? Where is Kim Pendergraph? How did Gabrielle Dwyer know to leave the party when she did?"

"She got away?" I felt a flash of exuberance. *Maybe she spotted them coming and slipped away into the woods.* And then I realized something else. "You're not on 109," I told the pale man. "Why not? If I'm so important, why didn't they give you the drug before you questioned me?"

The black man spoke up. "One real answer, Mike. Just one. One *true* answer, and you can go back to bed and sleep for as long as you like. So tell us. Is Danny Whiteagle in Washington?"

I felt a surge of hope. "Schwadron lied, didn't he? You *haven't* synthesized the drug yet. You're running out! That's it, isn't it? Or you *are* out until you synthesize more!"

"Take him back to his cell," the black man said in disgust.

* * *

I pushed the breaded chicken cutlets away, but I was too hungry not to eat them. I crawled back and took a few more bites. The salted meat made me thirsty. I drank all the water from the plastic bottle on the tray, feeling the metallic aftertaste in my throat. Like copper pennies being absorbed into my veins. Rust.

I was planting tomatoes in my garden. Using my hands to scoop out dirt, smelling loam on my fingers, knees filthy, elbows black, cradling the baby plants and smoothing over the ground, spraying the plants with a fine arc of cool, fresh water. My son was helping me, bringing in a wheelbarrow piled with more dirt.

I looked at his face. He was Chris, Kim's son.

"You didn't want us," he said. "Why not?"

"What if you ended up in a wheelchair too?"

I saw then that the garden was not mine but my father's. I saw my parents gazing at me from behind Chris. My father held the arms of Mom's wheelchair. He seemed content, robust, glad to be with her.

"I was afraid of obligation," I told them.

I looked at myself. I'd turned back into a boy. From the edge of the garden my father said, "Love isn't obligation. And obligation that comes with love is God's gift, Mike. It's purpose. James Dwyer wasn't your father. He was just a scared old man. Is that who you want to be?"

Then Chris interrupted us. "That rat is biting your ankle." The dream disappeared. The rat was running off the bed. My ankle was bleeding.

Corby and the pale man stood looking down at me.

"Good news, Mike, you're out of here. Sign the release and you can go home."

They laid a lapboard on the bed and handed me a ballpoint.

They smiled. Any fights earlier had been a mistake.

"Give me your hand, Mike. Sign the paper. See the line at the bottom? Sign it just like you'd sign a check. One, two, three. You'll be free."

"This isn't a release form," I said.

"Oh, don't bother figuring out the legal terminology. That's bullshit for lawyers. There's no need to read it. See your clothes hanging on the door? There's a car outside waiting for you. Home sweet home, Mike. Sign."

"This is a confession," I said, my head hurting. I had a fever. "I didn't say these things."

"You're making the Boat Man angry, Mike. You're pissing Charon off, and that's not a good thing to do. Sign the paper. Sign the fucking paper. Put the pen in your hand and write your signature, because, frankly, we have people who can copy it just as well as you can write."

"Then why don't they do it?"

"Play him the tape, Marty."

Suddenly I heard myself saying, "I killed Dwyer . . . and Rodriguez. . . . The drug is worth so much money."

"I didn't say that! You mixed up the words!"

"Bring in the dog, Marty."

It was a German shepherd. I curled backwards, pressed into the wall. The dog strained and snapped at me and its toenails clicked on the concrete floor.

The man I heard screaming this time was me.

* * *

You win, Mike. You toughed it out. You get a deal."

"Liar."

"Admit you killed the Chairman. Admit you were involved in the death of Tom Schwadron. You'll be out of here by nightfall, in a regular prison, with other people, exercise—movies, man. Real movies. Real prison is a breeze. And that rat bite is infected, Mike. You're running a fever."

"Schwadron is dead too?" I was terrified. It was getting harder to think. "But I thought . . . he was *behind* everything. He . . . he died?"

"That private plane crash didn't fool anyone, fella. It was no accident. The big Indian's prints were still on the fuselage."

"You're getting rid of everyone who knew about HR-109!"

"Tell the Boat Man. Did you plan the attack before we took you in, or are you getting messages to your friends?"

"How could I do that? You're . . . you're screwing with me. If I sigh the confession, you'll kill me."

"Danny Whiteagle has relatives involved in the radical Indian movement. Hoot attended meetings of the Iranian American students' movement."

"I'm sick," I told them. They were going in and out of focus now. My head was burning. I didn't remember being brought into the interrogation room.

"Tell us how you planned it, Mike. Sign this paper."

"Planned it . . . I planned it . . . we splanned, tranned . . ."

"Shit. He's babbling. Take him back to the cell."

* * *

The light came on and I was on the floor, near the toilet, lying in a pool of vomit. My head was throbbing. I heard raspy breathing and realized it was me. I wasn't sure if drugs had done it. I didn't remember coming back here after the talk.

The door was shaped like an hourglass. The room looked trapezoidal. The walls were crooked, and the rat was running away even though I was harmless, fleeing under the bed as it had when I was new here, even though I couldn't move anymore.

"This is disgusting," a new voice said.

I saw a pair of white Rebocks and jeans cuffs by my face. I tried to look up but it was difficult to move my head. The voice seemed familiar. It was a man's voice. An angry voice. It was saying, "You've had him for eleven days and you haven't learned shit!"

I shielded my eyes. The bright light made it hard to make out the man's features. His white face seemed to blend in with the cinder blocks. Even light hurt now.

The man growling, "Where did you learn to interrogate prisoners, Captain? At Miss Smith's School for Little Girls?"

"He's been tougher than we figured," said Corby's voice, except it was respectful for a change. Corby must fear the new man.

"I'm taking him with me. Now," the first voice snapped.

It's Eisner, I thought, horrified.

Corby saying, "I'm not authorized to release him. . . ."

"Can you read, Captain? Can you see the *signature* on this page? Do you know what *anything I want* means? *All* cooperation? Frankly, you two have screwed up and the colonel is furious. And now you want to make it worse for yourselves."

I felt hands at my collar, at my elbows, roughly pulling me up. Eisner's angry face went in and out of focus. The words that spewed from him seemed out of synchronization with the movements of his mouth.

"Traitor," Eisner said. "You think it's been bad so far for you? So far has been a vacation compared to what's going to happen now. No deals for you. Nothing to sign. Just you and me now, and you'll tell me everything I need in the first fifteen minutes. Where are your friends?"

He hit me in the face, knocking me back. My legs crumpled against the bed. I was weak as a doll, but dolls don't hurt. You can bounce a doll off the floor and it feels nothing. You can tear its arms off but it lacks synapses to register what it has lost.

I clawed at the steel frame of the bed to try to keep him from dragging me away. The one conscious fact of my existence was that I must avoid going anywhere with this man.

I couldn't believe I wanted to stay with Corby and Marty, that things could get worse.

Eisner's face came close. "These pansy bastards don't know how to converse with a hard guy like you. I do."

I think an argument started. Corby and Marty wanted me to stay. They were threatening to make a phone call. I hoped they would. My fever was spiking and words seemed to come from far away. I heard from the corridor the singsong Arabic prayer again.

Eisner was telling Corby, "You want to call Washington? Here's his personal number. What would you prefer for your next assignment, Captain? Afghanistan? Or Korea?"

Corby and Marty didn't call the number.

"Have him clean in fifteen minutes," Eisner ordered. To me he spat, "You better not throw up in my car."

The sun was dazzling and I squeezed my eyes shut. The natural light seemed to erupt from not just the sky but the land, and sea, to drill into my brain. The air was cloying, humid. I squinted out and saw, as Eisner half dragged, half carried me across a parking lot, that we were by the ocean. I saw barracks and moss-covered trees. I saw a shark gray cruiser on blue water in a bay. I saw a dozen guys in gray gym clothes playing basketball, and an olive green copter angling in over boats bobbing at anchorage.

Help me, I thought. *Help me get away from him.*

"South Carolina," Eisner said as we reached his car.

He came for me alone. There will be no witnesses.

My teeth chattered. It had to be ninety degrees out here, but my body was freezing.

This had to be my record month for the most rides taken in LTDs. Eisner's had white government plates and a tall radio antenna. There was no cage in back, just a normal cloth-covered seat. He strapped me in back, cuffed me to the passenger-side door. But even if he hadn't, I couldn't have fought off an angry eight-year-old if I had a stick.

We started driving. It seemed to take a long time to get to the base's fence. The exit road was flanked by dunes. At a guard shack, men saluted Eisner and peered in at me. "Help," I croaked. Eisner spun the car out onto a rural road and accelerated past piney woods and roadside shacks. COX'S BARBECUE, UNCLE GERARD'S FURNITURE, BIG FURIA'S BAIT 'N TACKLE, hand-scrawled signs read.

He drove fast and the rocking motion made me throw up in the car, spattering the front seat and windshield.

I figured he'd start hitting now, but he just kept checking the rearview mirror. Twenty minutes later, he grunted and turned off the road and we lurched down a logging track that ended at a boarded-up trailer. He drove around back and I saw an old green Dodge parked by the busted-in side. He was going to kill me now, I knew. Right now. Right here.

"Sorry I had to hit you, Mike," he said. He unlocked my handcuffs. "Rub the wrists. It'll help circulation."

I braced for the blow. He talked fast, ignoring the vomit on his hands as he helped me out of the car. He sounded different now. Not angry. Gentle. He didn't rush me, but he seemed in a rush.

"Those guys would have murdered you," he said, "the second you signed that paper."

"I won't help you find my friends."

"They'll check with Washington. They'll figure out the story I told was a fraud. They'll be coming for us, Mike. *I'm not going to hurt you.* There's food and water and clothes in the trunk. They were drugging your food."

I think I passed out, because when I woke we were on a rural two-lane road, passing farms and hamlets in North Carolina, and then Interstate 95 took us north. I opened my eyes again later and we were on another rural road. I saw corn growing. I saw rolling land and woods and a man on a tractor. I understood Eisner's trick then.

"You just driving around, Eisner? Trying to get me to tell you things that way? I do that and I'm back in prison?"

"What are you talking about? Drink some water. We're in Virginia."

At dusk he turned off the rural road—it looked like tidewater country—and onto a long dirt driveway. In the distance, getting closer, was a two-story antebellum ole-time Virginny farmhouse—white, pillared, with a gray roof and a front porch. I saw a blackwater river, and pecan trees, and a tire hanging on a clothesline. I saw geese overhead. They honked madly as they flew south.

It was an idyllic scene, but inside the house would be a torture chamber, I knew. There would be no one within miles to hear the screams.

"Is this where you do it?"

People came out of the house and walked toward us—tentatively at first—like zombies in a horror film. Tell them nothing, I told myself. You can't protect yourself, but shield your friends.

Then I realized who the people were, and my heartbeat picked up.

I'm hallucinating.

It was Kim, looking fine, unhurt, unbound, healthy.

And Hoot.

Danny.

Gabrielle.

"You're . . . *together*?" I asked Eisner, through the fever. I felt myself losing consciousness. I felt tears in my eyes.

I thought I heard, "You have good friends. I was wrong about you. And I need your help, Mike."

I passed out again.

EIGHTEEN

The demons came for me then, howling and shrieking and tearing at me with their sharp claws and teeth, eating into my brain and riding in my bloodstream. Free as banshees. Loud and inescapable as ghosts.

It was cold in that room. The walls dissolved like water. Voices merged into a screeching, steady chorus as faces above me changed and elongated or floated like talking balloons on different necks. Faces familiar. Faces dead.

The Chairman lay murdered in his office beneath his open safe, which had been rifled. I needed to warn my friends that they were in danger, to escape the executive suite, but my feet moved too slowly and soldiers—the ones from the brig—closed in on me. I stumbled into Keating's office. It turned into the chili cook-off. Guests guzzled liquor as Asa Rodriguez floated in the water, murdered, bleeding, close to the house.

Then I realized the guests' eyes were glowing. They were eating HR-109, not chili, spooning it as if it were Rice Krispies. They had purple spots on their necks.

The sun became the bright light of my prison cell. Corby and Marty reached for me as Schwadron hung on the cinder-block wall, arms out like Christ's, and Keating's voice said, "Eisner, trick Mike. Fool him."

In the dream the cell had a window, and in the distance I saw a line of people walking slowly, like slaves, heads bowed. They were my old friends and teachers, parents, fellow agents. None of them had the purple rash. Keating stood with soldier guards, watching. He pulled his face off. It was a mask. Underneath was Eisner's face.

"Tell me what you learned, Mike," Eisner said.

I opened my eyes.

"You're awake," Gabrielle said, from beside the bed.

She sat in an old stuffed sitting chair. The temperature must have dropped since I'd arrived, because she wore a thick green sweater under a flannel shirt; wool pants; felt boots. Her face was scrubbed and her eyes were red. The hand that took mine was soft. Her voice trembled.

"We took turns sitting with you."

The window was open and I saw ice coating green leaves on a tree outside, as if summer had been frozen. I smelled mold in the house, and river and mud. The bed was large and soft beneath an old-fashioned canopy. There was a woodstove burning and a rifle rack, but the weapons were gone, and I saw a Civil War–era photo of a Confederate soldier leaning against a split-rail fence, smoking a corncob pipe. I thought, *It can't be winter. I can't have slept that long.*

"Mike, you were running a hundred and five fever. The news on TV is horrifying. . . . Riots. Firings. Terrible things."

"What month is it?"

"Oh. It's just a freak August ice storm, crazy out there. You slept six days. Eisner brought a doctor, a friend of his, to take care of you. The house belongs to the doctor. It's been in his family since 1845. Weekend place."

So Eisner *had* brought me here. It hadn't been a dream. Gabrielle was babbling. Tears collected in her eyes.

"The rifles," I croaked. "Where did they go?"

"I'm sorry I didn't see those men at Keating's party. They must have come in from the front."

"Not your fault," I said.

"If Eisner hadn't found you, I wouldn't have forgiven myself. And not just because I couldn't help at the house."

She was overwhelmed, yet I understood her declaration. I was too exhausted to respond or even know how I felt. My body throbbed with pain that made the room barely real.

But the needle in my arm was real, as was the hanging bottle at the bedside. I smelled rubbing alcohol and disinfectant, wood polish and freshly cut flowers, which almost masked evidence of bodily struggle here: a whiff of bile, urine, disgorged food and disease sweated onto sheets.

The lights flickered in the room.

"There are power outages all over Virginia, Mike."

"Where's Eisner?"

"Downstairs. He saved us, but says we can't stay here long. The people you escaped from are looking for you."

I tried to sit up, but it was impossible. I remembered Eisner in my dream, trying to trick me. I said, "He just wants the drug, like everybody else. Bring Danny here. We have to get away, get the news out about what's going on."

HR-109 was a horrible perversion. It was worse than anything I'd fought at the FBI. It corrupted everyone who knew about it. It should be called Enslave, not Enhance.

She leaned down and kissed me on the forehead. Her lips were cool and soft, and they moved to my cheek, my mouth. I must have tasted awful. She didn't seem to mind. The touch was light and she tasted of oranges. Her lips withdrew but a promise remained.

I need a gun, I thought.

"I'm with you, Mike. From now on."

* * *

Eisner came in first, the others following. Gabrielle rolled her eyes to let me know that her efforts to keep him away had failed. Everyone was smiling, offering tea, orange juice, cookies, words of relief. I watched Eisner.

Kim saying, "Drink slow, Mike. It's hot."

I hurt with a kind of pain that exceeds the physical. I felt hollow, as if organs had been scooped out. I felt old.

"Why did you get me out?" I rasped at Eisner.

In civilian clothes, he looked big as a lumberjack, wearing a black knit sweater, Levi's and chukka boots. Eisner the woodsman. Eisner my new best pal.

"Where should I start, Mike? A forty-million-dollar contract overpayment. A dead CEO and a scientist killed. I was yanked off the case when I decided you might be innocent. And then there's you. Tortured. It was my fault. I'm the one who told Keating you'd gone to Washington. I didn't know you were working against him then."

"What do you want?"

"What I always want. What *you* want. To put away scumbags who take all the privileges Uncle Sam gave them and turned them against our own people. Tell me what you learned about HR-109. Tell me who else knows."

"You're one of us? Then give me a gun."

"I see. You don't believe me."

The others crowded close, not letting confrontation spoil reunion.

I fell asleep before anyone could say more.

Trust him. He came for us all by himself," Danny said when I woke the next time. We were alone. A TV was in the room but the sound was off. The picture showed street riots above the caption "Los Angeles Rally Turns Violent." A line of police advanced on protesters waving signs.

"Maybe I will," I said, signaling for pad and pen.

"Eisner went AWOL. He *helped* us, got us out before the FBI came. They're looking for us now too."

"Maybe he *is* with us, then." But I wrote, "Microphones?"

Danny shook his head. He said, "The country's going crazy. Generals fired. Resignations at the Justice Department. A judge here. An undersecretary there. Extremists moving into key positions. I've been stationed in other countries where this happened. I never thought it could happen here."

I wrote, "Agents in the woods?"

"The President is introducing a martial-law bill so he can use federal troops against riots. Hell, Eisner brought a whole arsenal. His own stuff. Bobcat BW5. AR-15. Glocks. We're patrolling the grounds with them at night."

I wrote, "The Chairman said to stay away from him."

Danny grabbed the pencil and paper. He wrote back, "Someone's using that drug to take over. Tell him if you know who."

The river was iced over and meandering and there was an old wrecked landing that jutted on splintery pilings into the water. I saw a derrick-shaped cell-phone tower in the distance. It was the next morning. I was well enough to walk for a little while. Eisner and I were alone as far as I could see. But he carried a Bobcat assault rifle and I was still unarmed. He didn't trust me either.

I figured, *His agents could be in the woods.*

"Who exactly is after us, Eisner?"

"The guys who arrested you belong to a special new domestic anti-terrorism unit. Handpicked from what I can tell, but from the bottom of the barrel. Leavenworth guys. Guys who like to hurt people. Guys with very particular political points of view. I think they work for the same boss as the Royces. Danny told me about those two."

The land glittered with ice, over frozen cornstalks and fields that had once been brown with pungent tobacco, the Colonial-era drug of choice. The rutted road bumping down to the river had been cleared centuries ago so slaves could roll casks onto ships bound for England. Clouds floated over unmarked Civil War battlefields, woods and wildflowers killed by freak ice.

"That brig you were in, Mike, is a secret place for terrorist suspects," Eisner said grimly, his breath frosting. "Like the roach motel. They go in. They don't come out."

"If it's so secret, how did *you* find it?"

He curbed his impatience to learn things. He knew I'd been through a lot. We sipped coffee and moved at my sick man's pace, our shoes cracking ice glaze covering long-buried bones of Confederate dead.

"Gabrielle said you'd been hauled from the party. No one saw you go, but I worked it, Mike. It turned out Keating's neighbor had called the police to complain about a car in front of her house. I traced it to an officer stationed at that brig. Suddenly I'm shut down by a colonel in Washington, Alonzo Otto. The same guy who'd stopped my investigation after Dwyer died, ordered me to stay away from you when I started thinking you might be okay."

I remembered Otto from Keating's party, the black eyes

fixing on me. I said, "Gabrielle just *told* you this? You're leaving out how you even found her. Found all of them."

"You're getting better fast, Mike. Strong."

"I'm persistent. So answer me."

I froze at a *chuk-chuk* sound as three army helicopters appeared, flying low over the fields to our north, flying fast and low and with purpose.

"Maneuvers," Eisner said, maybe lying, covering for his men. "There's a base nearby. Look, Hoot triggered the firewall in the DI data system. When I picked her up, she told me about Danny. Danny's Rolodex gives me the address of the Rockaway house. I figured I'd have to fight through his cousins to get in there, but they fell back when they saw my ID. They were there to protect him from someone else, not me. That was point two in your favor."

"What did you do to Danny's cousins?"

"Nothing. But they're probably under surveillance now. All your friends are. Probably mine too." He smiled. "Technically, you're under arrest. I'm just taking you in the long way."

"Why did Hoot help you in the first place?"

He shrugged his powerful shoulders. "She did the same thing that she did two years ago, when you tracked her down for hacking into Lenox."

"Told everything."

"Military prison is pretty damned frightening. I let her know exactly what it would be like."

Gray frozen woods lay massed a hundred yards away, like a Confederate army. We stepped over trip wires and a tin-can alarm system Eisner and Danny had set.

Eisner stamped his feet to keep warm. "Hoot told me what you'd asked her to research. Me. Keating. Diseases. Up until then I was sure you'd stolen things from Dwyer."

"But when Hoot told you what I'd asked her to do, you decided I was investigating, not selling. Is that it?"

"You weren't acting like a guy marketing secrets. You were lying like a cop on the job. You didn't trust me. You'd seen Dwyer's note. 'Stay away from Eisner.' You *still* don't trust me, eh?"

I felt dizzy, sick. I needed to process all he was saying. "But I *heard* you talking to Keating."

"No, you heard *him* while I questioned him over the phone. He was hiding something. *You'd* just reported to him. You'd been avoiding me. I thought you were a team."

"Yeah, Keating and me." My coffee had gone cold. Eisner made sense, but that didn't mean he was truthful. Truth and logic don't always go together. I'd made too many mistakes and couldn't afford one more.

"Why did Dwyer write, 'Stay away from Eisner'?" I asked.

"I was investigating the new contract."

"Who's *behind* the brig in Carolina exactly? How high does it go?"

He smiled grimly. "That's what we need to prove, Mike. Special counterterrorism unit, my ass. I think they're someone's private army. The greatest transfer of power in history—without an election—has occurred in Washington over the last month. *Who's behind it?* Do you know?"

"What happens if you find out?"

"If we know who to avoid, we know who to go to with proof. There are still good people in Washington, *most* of them are, but *nobody is going to believe us without proof.* You're like me, Mike. I had you wrong. You're Don Quixote. You didn't quit the FBI for money. You quit because you got disillusioned. Do you really want a few bad apples to destroy everything you love?"

"You don't know what I love." I looked at the fields stretching off toward freedom. The horizon looked far away.

"Don't even think about it," he said.

"Give me a weapon," I demanded.

He nodded slowly. "All right. When we get back. And after dinner you'll participate in tonight's escape drill too. There's an old Underground Railroad tunnel in the basement. I'll give you a weapon. Will that make you feel better? Will you trust me then?"

The tunnel started in a downstairs linen closet and led down to a hidden storage room, and under the river, to come up in the woods. Eisner had stocked clothes down there in case we had to leave fast, and extra handguns and ammunition. He'd also moved the farm's vehicle, a Ford SUV, to an equipment shed on the next property.

We timed how long it took to get to the car. It was important in the cold that the car start right away.

I couldn't sleep that night after the drill, even though I was exhausted. I told myself to trust him. And my friends had urged me to do it when we were alone. But I wasn't ready yet.

I went into the hallway. I left my Bobcat BW5 semi-automatic by the window. Eisner had been right. It made me feel slightly secure, but not much. I was famished and needed energy. I'd have to fight Eisner soon enough, or someone's private army. That much was clear.

The plank floors creaked and moonlight sifted through the window to illuminate the washbasins and antique pine dressers, and the sketches of tobacco fields and Colonial-era Native Americans on the walls. It was cold in the house. I smelled ashes and smoke from a hearth fire. Danny was outside somewhere, mud on his face, AR-15 in his hands, moving through the woods the way he used to in the Philippines, looking for crack labs.

Danny the guerrilla, taking a turn standing guard.

I wish I had some 109 to tell me if Eisner's lying or not.

I went downstairs and opened the refrigerator. I made a sandwich of salami and cheddar cheese. It tasted like cardboard, but I felt calories going in, drifting as energy into my bloodstream. I needed strength for tomorrow's conversation. Debriefing. Interrogation. Possible fight if Eisner turned out to be a clever liar like everyone else who had anything to do with HR-109.

When I got upstairs I saw lights on, glowing out from beneath two of the bedroom doors.

Kim's. And Gabrielle's.

The door was ajar at Gabrielle's room. Kim's was shut, but I had a feeling it was unlocked.

I envisioned them in strangers' beds, reading or lying there, maybe even hearing my footsteps. Seeing the lights made me remember the taste of Kim on the beach, and the way her hip had felt against mine, the curve of it, the heat. Then I remembered the feeling of being kicked in the stomach each time I saw Gabrielle. And I recalled other times when other women had given me that same electric sensation, and the sourness that remained, the sense of waking from a dream, which had replaced the gut-wrenching excitement later on.

You made it pass, Mike, I thought. *You picked women who would guarantee it would pass. That was what you wanted.*

I remembered the orange citrus taste of Gabrielle, that brief and indelible branding of intent and desire. My lips tingled where hers had touched.

I also felt the patience in those strips of light, and the invitation. I saw through my illness that second chances come when you don't expect them. Second chances are often as obscure, yet more important, than firsts. Second chances don't necessarily come with signposts or vigor to make them. They can slip off into the past so quickly, like a dream you can't remember, like a town you drove through in the dark.

This time Eisner and I both carried automatic weapons in the woods. My Bobcat was a delayed throwback-operated model. Epoxy-coated, with a 16.5-inch stainless-steel barrel and a fluted chamber. I'd fired it last night in target practice. It worked.

Eisner had risked mutually assured destruction by letting me carry it. Or maybe he figured he was faster. If one of us made a sudden move, we'd shred each other apart.

He walked at my speed, bulky in tight Levi's and hiking boots and a zip-up leather flight jacket and stocking cap. I wore white Levi cords that fit despite being one size too small for me. An Eastern Mountain hooded parka covered a soft checkered red and black flannel shirt.

The temperature was still plunging. We'd lost power around dawn, but had gotten it back.

"These are your private weapons? What are you, some gun nut?" I asked.

"The right to bear arms just might save your life, Mike. The people after you might come here to arrest you, or they might come the other way."

It was twenty minutes after sunrise and we walked parallel to the river. I tried to memorize landmarks if I had to run. Slopes. Boulders. A cell-phone tower. Our breaths smoked and a fish jumped in mid-stream—the arc of its trajectory, the spraying water and normalcy of geometry a miracle to me. I wanted to weep from seeing a fish.

"Tell me more about Alonzo Otto," I said.

"He's assigned to the National Intelligence Director's office. Liaison stuff. There's always a dog in the house, running errands. A deniability guy. Every agency has 'em. If they do the job, their careers go golden. If they're caught, maybe they go to prison and come out a talk-show host. Ollie North was one. Gordon Liddy. Otto—rumor is—handpicked the guys who arrested you, guys to the right of Attila the Hun."

"But why?"

He nodded. "Someone with clout is behind him, but unless you know already, or Otto tells, we'll never find out. Carbone? He quit. Keating? No influence. My turn. Did Schwadron say anything at the party to give you an idea who controls Otto? That's the thread we want to follow, Mike."

"We again." The Bobcat felt heavy in my arms.

Eisner said, "As long as we're free, we can hurt them. There are still honest journalists, legislators and a million good people in the armed forces. Tell them the truth, give them *proof*, and we turn things around."

I went back over what I knew Danny and the others had already told him. I said 109 was being used for legitimate security interrogations, but afterward privately too.

"The Washington resignations? You take a pill. You sidle up to Senator X at a party and turn the conversation in directions you want to investigate. You let intuition guide you. *Hey, Señator, did* you *ever take an illegal contri-bution? You don't have any sexual skeletons in* your *closet, do you?* Believe me, if you know where to hunt for dirt, it's easier to find."

I kept back from him what I'd figured out in the brig.

"You actually *took* this drug?" he said.

"It's how I got out of Key West, past the cops."

He leaned forward, shiny intensity on his face. He seemed to be turning implications over in his mind.

"Mike, if you were under the influence now, would you know what I'm thinking?"

"It's not like I hear thoughts. More like I'd know if you're lying, what you intend. Like when you get a feel-ing about someone, except it's a thousand times stronger than anything you've ever felt before. And it's right."

"That explains why the Defense contract was inflated. The purchase price is buried inside. Hell, it's worth it to find terrorists. That would make 109 the greatest security tool ever invented."

"If it were used for that only, sure," I said. "But the pill has only been in existence a month, and already peo-ple are killing each other over it."

Eisner got the angry look that I'd seen when I'd first met him. "Personal use violates the law."

I laughed. "The drug can't be controlled. It makes people crazy. Everyone wants it. Even if you use it for le-gitimate reasons, you take the effect home."

Eisner looked at that moment like an artillery spotter eyeing a faraway target, adjusting angles of fire. He stared into my eyes, probing with his normal unenhanced intu-ition.

"That's all you found out?"

"Where are your guys? In the woods?"

He looked astounded and then angry. I realized he was actually hurt. "If you don't realize by now whose side I'm on, fuck you, because you can't see an ally in front of you. Maybe you *need* a goddamned drug to appreciate a friend. I'm not just talking about me either. The sexual tension in that house is so real you could cut it with a knife."

"You're a jailer, Eisner. You said so yourself."

"*And you're a liar.* You know what my daddy used to say when I was a boy, in Kansas?"

"I told you, I don't read minds."

"That the hardest choices in life are between good and good. That's you and this whole sorry mess. Bring back the old days, when choices were clear."

"I don't know you, Eisner."

"Did you know Dwyer? He got you into this. Not me."

We had another escape drill after dinner. I counted steps between trees in the dark, and recognized landmarks as more ice fell. Later I dreamed of sex hard and constant, sweaty and uncomplicated. One dream after the other, as if memories were being purified, jettisoned, rearranged to make new points. Gabrielle took me into her mouth and the sweetness was overpowering. Kim looked up at me in the dark, her small body clothed in silk, the folds of her robe falling away to show white. My body was as hard as iron. Desire lifted me. I saw faces of old girlfriends, faces I knew. Powered by testosterone, I felt my hips bucking. I was wrapped by legs that contracted like an animal's. I smelled sex when I awoke alone at four A.M., the blood coursing through me hot and eager. I felt at some fundamental level renewed.

I got out of bed and walked into the hallway. The effect of the sex dreams made it hard to think.

Firelight glowed from under Kim's door.

And Gabrielle's.

Two doors. They looked the same. They were both of heavy oak, with brass knobs, and slanted floors beneath them, as the house canted in accommodation of its idiosyncrasies, and made noises in the dark, its inanimate components straining toward subparticle life. A breeze filled the hall, bringing a chilled promise of new seasons.

I felt a stirring below my belly, above my legs. A stiffening of muscles and a catch in my throat. A wave of weakness almost bent my knees.

I've known what I was going to do since that kiss on the beach, I thought, my blood flowing faster, carrying life, oxygen, promise, desire.

I took a step toward a door and it opened and Gabrielle stood there in a terry-cloth robe, naked beneath, it seemed, barefoot, eyes locked on mine, breasts rising and falling, skin a slash of V at the chest. A clock ticked in the house.

She said nothing. But she took a step toward me.

Kim's door opened and she came out with Hoot. Both women wore light flannel pajamas. Kim's were blue with small yellow monkeys imprinted on the sides, grinning animals with goofy smiles. Hoot's legs looked chubbier than I would have guessed. Her pajamas were pink, and showed slices of fruit pies on plates—blueberry pies. Her pajamas were a child's.

Hoot said, "How come everyone's standing around in the hall? Are you all right, Chief?"

"Oh, he's all right," Kim said.

We went back to our rooms. I lay in bed thinking.
I'll tell Eisner tomorrow. I'll take the chance.

At breakfast Gabrielle made butter pancakes from pre-mixed batter and Kim cooked omelets with thick chunks of cheddar cheese, from scratch. I ate it all. Hoot babbled about computers. Eisner remained quiet, look-ing tired. I knew he'd stayed up in case I ran. Danny glanced with curiosity around the human points of my love triangle, me and Kim and Gabrielle. He still had mud on his face.

As I ate I measured risks. I'd get Eisner away from the house so that if he was tricking us, when the Bobcat went off my friends would hear the firing. Eisner would be fast, so how could I surprise him? How could I hide intent?

Even as I planned, I recognized that he was a strange and likable man, loyal to his dead wife, brave to be here alone, even if he had backup. I had no illusions about his forcefulness. But if he'd been acting, I'd fight.

We walked away from the house and into the woods, out of sight of the others. The cold was so bad, my teeth hurt. The news shows said Virginia hadn't experienced end-of-August temperatures this low in 196 years. The river was now glazed with ice.

I need to get close to him. I'll tell him what I figured out, but I'll watch his eyes. If they change the wrong way, I'll swing the Bobcat like a club.

"I didn't share everything with you, Eisner."

He took a step away from me. He was no fool. "Big surprise."

I told him that 109 had still not been synthesized as of

a week ago. Naturetech was working frantically to do it. It was where proof would be stored. Formulas. Samples.

"What else?"

I told him that journalist Alicia Dent had been at Keating's party and I thought she was being supplied with 109 to help her drive from office powerful people in Washington. She had access to them. She could ask any questions she wanted during interviews. She was passing on answers, I said.

Get ready, I told myself.

I told him everything Schwadron had admitted as I watched his eyes, waited for them to change the wrong way and end what was left of my hope.

But when I was done he stared at me a moment, then nodded slowly. He laid his AR-15 on a boulder. He moved back, away from it. He spread his arms.

"Are you always this difficult to deal with, Mike?"

I put my weapon beside his. I could see us reflected in ice on the river. Our faces were indistinct. The sky was white as smoke over the trees.

We decided it would be best to send everything to the press immediately, to put Hoot on the Internet back at the house. She'd contact CBS, CNN. We'd send out the Chairman's disk and story—minus the formulas—to websites, the White House, news organizations, watchdog operations, Senate offices. . . . There was one *Washington Post* reporter Eisner knew personally and trusted. A man named Harris.

"Someone will run it," I said with hope as we hurried through the woods, around fallen branches. "They have to."

"We send it and head for Canada," Eisner suggested. "We wait till the news breaks. Then we come back when everything is public. You'll be safe then."

A branch crashed behind us, weighed down by ice. The ground was slippery. Eisner almost fell.

For the first time, I dared to think that things might work out.

But as we reached the house, the power went out again, so Hoot couldn't use the Internet. Driving would be impossible. We'd wait out the storm. By one P.M. we'd lit fires in all the rooms. By six, the world outside was a sheet of ice. Eisner said he'd take the first guard shift. Danny would come on at eleven. I offered to take a turn too.

"We send the message the second power comes back," I said.

We should have gotten out at that moment, though, ice storm or not. We didn't.

The grandfather clock downstairs chimed midnight. Ice battered the window and the fire had died in my room. I left the Bobcat by the bed. I padded into the hall.

I saw the flicker of firelight under the doors to Kim and Gabrielle's rooms.

I paused, filled with deep abiding certainty. It might be my last chance. I reached for a knob, feeling like a man watching the sun come up after too much rain, and I knew that either one of the women in the house—had the other not been in my life—would have set my heart pounding.

But the choice had been made on the beach in Rockaway, when my lips met Kim's, and true knowledge of who we were passed between us. That knowledge had been more important than the momentary feel of her small, lithe body pressed against mine.

Schwadron had talked of two roads. But it had taken

me all my life—until now—to learn that in some things, two are too many. I wanted one road now, with curves and surprises, where the journey itself constituted the destination, and the precise view behind the next bend would matter less than the person who rounded it at my side.

My two fates. The one I knew better and the one who had mystery. The one who set the blood boiling and the one who set it simmering and added sweetness to the flow. The troubled and passionate one with undefinable extra, some inexplicable recognition, who had told me she feared intimacy as a way of creating it. And the one who had stood back from love along with me as a partner in self-deception, understanding me, thinking like me that love is something you can put in a box and retrieve, unvarnished, if it pleases you. Learning with me at the same moment that no box should ever be thought big enough to hold love.

I opened the door. In shadow Gabrielle sat up in bed.

I smelled the wonderful mix of women smells—perfume, sleep, fresh linen—and even the ice on the pane was a drumbeat of possibility. I walked toward the bed. The floors groaned like waking muscles. She moved the covers back. She wore pajamas tonight. We looked into each other's eyes. Shadows etched her face like tears.

When I stopped short of the bed, I heard her long, slow exhalation. Then:

"When did you fall in love with her, Mike?"

"It built up over a long time."

"You're a good man to come here first."

"It's the least I could do."

She laughed ruefully. "I would have preferred the most. But listen to me: *Go in there. Do this right.* If I'm going to lose out to Kim, it better be to the biggest grand explosion of passion. I'll know people are getting what they deserve tonight. You'll make it easier, believe it or not."

"Thanks."

"We won't be friends, you know. With me it's everything or nothing."

"Your father was a fool," I said.

"I was too. I stopped trying with him." Now she was trying too hard, but I was grateful. I felt regret that comes from passing up opportunity, but the soaring freedom that comes from making a choice. We held hands, but the touch wasn't electric anymore. It didn't set my heart pounding. It was the same skin, the same hand. But Gabrielle was already, in some way, in my past.

I turned away. Behind me her breathing was strong and audible. Sometimes you can't explain limitations, or hope. Just be happy that it's there.

NINETEEN

I tapped on Kim's door lightly and her voice said, "Come in." I pushed the door open and saw the fire dying. In its glow she was dressing, pulling on a sweater over her tight jeans. Her hair looked mussed, which was unusual, as if each individual strand was in a rush to get out.

"Musical rooms?" she asked. But she didn't pull off sarcasm. She was hurt and getting ready to go outside, to walk in the storm.

"I needed to tell Gabrielle before I came in here."

That stopped her. "Why?"

Fair question. She was asking if Gabrielle and I had been lovers. It was Kim's first demand as a partner, a voice from my future, representing my willing surrender and passage over a line. I shook my head. "No. It's just you and me now. That is, if you want."

"Oh." She softened. "Then maybe *we* should go out." Now she was taking Gabrielle's feelings into account, which is one of the reasons I loved her. Sound carried in the house. But Gabrielle had been right when she said tonight was not for niceties. Tonight might turn out to be the only one Kim and I might ever have.

"No need," I said, stepping closer. "She and I talked about that too."

"You got a lot in, in five minutes." Kim's voice caught. "I'm having trouble breathing."

"Me too."

On the sheet, by the rumpled covers, lay her burgundy-colored nightie, no cute pajamas for Kim tonight. The fabric looked soft and silky. Some unconscious signal passed between us and we started undressing, watching each other, watching our slow ceremony of life together begin. I was engorged. She looked hard at me. She said, "Do you know why I chose this color tonight? I wanted you to come in here and I thought it would be," she whispered, touching me intimately for the first time, with one finger, "the same color as you, down here."

We started kissing while standing. The kiss went on a long time. Her back was small and warm. Her bare leg slipped between mine and the soft feel was electric. She was lovely in the firelight, pale and lean, breasts fuller than I'd envisioned, hips jutting, belly flat. I'd never stood naked before a woman I'd known as a good friend first. I'd always imagined such an encounter as comfortable but not exciting. I hadn't counted on experiencing more, not less, and now I felt as if some unknown reservoir had shattered inside me, and the accumulated passion held back let loose. It rushed in an emotional cataract to lift me. Constraint fell away. My body seemed to melt. The intensity, the *focus* contracted all my will and life force into the physical point of contact between us. It was more than pleasure. It was pleasure distilled. It was more than physical. It started from that.

Mike Acela had finally allowed himself to experience love.

We were on the bed but I'm not sure how we got there. The fire popped and flared. Her fingers were in my mouth. Her knuckles gripped the sheet. Her nostrils flared like a pony's. Her eyes reflected light. I saw that we'd moved the bed to a different location. The night table looked farther away and the window—with its coating of ice—was close.

"Again," she said, a few minutes after we were done.

They say the second time is slower. That's a lie. It was faster and more passionate. She was under me and on top. I watched the dark V of her pubis, bouncing. I kneeled at the bed and she reached back and I felt the sharp rake of long nails against my thighs. The throw rug was soft beneath my knees. The cool floor smooth on my toes. "Ram me," she said. We were straddling the sitting chair by the window. Her hair was so wet with sweat that she might have just come in out of the rain. I filled with love for her, and fear for her.

"Again," I said hoarsely, half an hour after that.

This was the slow time. The no talking time. The fire had gone out but the storm must have ended, because moonlight was in the room now. I let my eyes rove over her in pieces. I was Picasso breaking her into individual images to be savored for the rest of my life. Her arms were lean and smooth with muscle. I saw a bit of raised knee, a tapered ankle, a curve of arched foot, a rounded white shoulder. Our hips moved in perfect rhythm. Her body smelled of musk and sweat. I think we'd done a fair job of keeping our voices to a whisper, our cries into our knuckles, or into the mattress, the sheets.

But I didn't know. I'd lost track of time, space, sound, effort.

I was sore with sweetness. We gasped for air, breathing like surfacing divers. We'd been trying to ensure a future with intensity. To jettison pasts.

Three A.M.

"I wouldn't mind doing this a few hundred times more," she said. "Over the years."

"Kids," I said. "Well, at least a brother or sister for Chris." I heard my own words and wanted to laugh. Until now those words would have sent me hurtling from a woman's room.

"Mike, want to hear something funny? Chris asked me over the phone if this had happened yet. I guess everyone else saw the thing we ignored."

"You still want to move to Vermont? I'll go if you do."

"You have a nice house, Mike. Big, with that garden. A house for a family. Or are we imagining what we want to see in each other?"

We lay in bed, her head on my shoulder.

"Maybe that's how you make a life," I said. "You imagine it and do it. Now that I'm getting around to it," I said as she snuggled closer, "it doesn't seem hard."

The room didn't feel like a stranger's anymore. It was part of our history, where we'd created something special—or rather, recognized what had been there all along.

"Why didn't we do this before?"

"We weren't ready for it to work, Mike."

Our dreams cushioned us, but we both knew on some level that comfort was an illusion. Unless we figured out what had happened at Lenox, and who was after us, there would be no future for anyone in this house except one of pain.

"Mike, remember when I asked you not to stop looking into Dwyer's death, no matter what happens?"

"Reconsidering?"

"I still mean it, more than before, even though Dwyer turned out to be a fraud—a scared, selfish old man. I'm proud of you. I'll help any way I can. I want to fight those bastards. No matter what happens, we did the right thing."

I woke at four-thirty to find the house silent, cold, still dead of electrical power. I went to the window and looked out at the gleaming treetops. I heard a vague rhythmic crunching out there, and a moment later my heart seized up when I saw white forms—*men in camouflage parkas*—moving in the forest, creeping forward and stopping, crawling and stopping.

Moonlight gleamed on steel out there.

Soldiers.

I screamed, *"They're here,"* to wake the others, as a figure in black, *Danny,* burst from the tree line, heading for the front porch across a strip of gleaming ice-covered lawn.

We never sent the story out on the Internet last night, I thought. *Now it's too late.*

Kim jerked up behind me. The attack coming faster, the forms outside standing and running now, rushing the house behind Danny, who was weaving as bursts of snow kicked up at his feet. Suddenly it sounded like the old FBI shooting range out there. I was hearing automatic assault weapons. Eisner had said men might come legally, to arrest us.

These attackers had come to kill.

Practice drills are never like the real thing, no matter how many times you repeat them. Still naked, I ran into my bedroom and grabbed the Bobcat. I smashed out the window and suppressed the trigger and glimpsed attackers slowing, falling back, as I heard Danny's footsteps on the porch below.

Heard the door slam. *Danny is in.*

But the window exploded beside me, glass blowing out to pinwheel into pine furniture, converted kerosene fixtures, shredding wallpaper. I fired again, wildly. I couldn't show myself at the window. Ducking, I ran, remembering to shut the door behind me. That way if they used gas, it would stay inside the room. Suddenly floodlights were gliding over the walls, shining in from out of the other bedrooms. Lit blue, Kim stood in the hallway barefoot and robed and holding out pajamas to me. I waved them off. There was no time to put them on. Eisner and Gabrielle were already halfway down the stairs, in pajamas, their flashlight beams bouncing, and from outside I now heard men shouting, issuing instructions.

Automatic-weapons fire erupted from inside the house, inside the living room below.

Danny. Danny was shooting, and screaming, *"Wake up!"*

As if anyone could sleep through this.

No helicopters, at least, I thought.

The ceiling splintered apart. Crockery shattered. Holes ran up the walls. Plaster and wood chunks flew in my face. Frames holding old Matthew Brady Civil War photos flew in the air. I imagined men on their bellies shooting the hell out of the porch and house.

From the bedrooms came sounds of more glass breaking and the whine and smack of bullets. My flashlight beam bounced across the sitting room. We fled past the kitchen, toward the tunnel that had hidden fleeing slaves 150 years ago. There would be warm clothes down there.

"Move! Move!" Eisner was yelling, a flashlight in one hand, his AR-15 in the other.

"They're all over the place out there," Danny shouted from the living room. I ran to join him while the others kept going. We took up positions on either side of the shattered main window. We only needed to stall the attack while our friends reached the tunnel.

"Thirty guys, easy, Boss. Dressed like Rangers."

"Are you hurt, Danny?"

"Whaddaya, kidding? I heard them drive up. They parked off the property. I heard 'em whispering. It's your Carolina crew. Corby, right? Someone called someone else Corby."

Eisner was shouting, "Mike? Danny? Where are you?"

They'd break in wearing night-vision masks. They'd come as I'd been trained to do in the FBI, through front and rear doors at the same time. They'd enter in pairs so one man could cover the center of each room while the partner checked corners. They'd come in firing. Shooting to kill.

I told Danny, "Give me a minute in the kitchen. Then come."

"Midnight snack? Or looking for some trousers?"

"The gas line," I said.

I emptied my magazine out the window and heard someone scream. I rushed for the hall but halted when I saw Hoot frozen in the den doorway. Hoot amid the wreckage in her cute fruit-pie pajamas, screaming in Farsi, the language on which she'd been raised. She'd been sleeping on the couch by the beloved computer. She was injured or in shock. Just standing there, screaming.

I pulled her toward me as a vase disintegrated beside her. Her face was streaked with the black kohl she used under her eyes. She stared at my naked body. It was just one more disorienting factor to her.

"Hoot? Can you hear me?"

I pushed her along the hall, toward the back of the house. Her eyes focused. We ran.

Less than four minutes had passed since the attack started. In the hallway we passed a kicked-away throw rug and a raised wooden trapdoor to the cellar. The others had stopped to open it, then continued toward the center of the house. In drills Eisner had made us stomp around in the dirt cellar, to leave recent footprints.

That was because the real escape tunnel was *not* in the cellar but beneath a linen closet down the hall.

I heard automatic-weapons fire from the back of the house now. That would be Eisner, holding off a rear assault.

Turning toward the kitchen, I glimpsed the women down the hall, clustered around the open linen closet. Kim and Gabrielle on their knees, pulling at a wooden box, which was nailed down as part of the trapdoor. What I was about to do was *not* part of Eisner's drill. The kitchen was untouched, for a few more seconds, at least, filled with hanging pots and a butcher-block table. I reached behind the stove and found the propane line. I twisted it hard. I pulled off the spigot, to the soft hiss of gas escaping as I moved quickly to slide open a pantry door. We'd kept candles here during the blackout, and matches. Lighting a candle, I imagined gas seeping like water toward the tiny flickering flame.

Then I ran for the tunnel. Danny was retreating out of the living room. Eisner was backing into the hall, reloading as he moved. Ahead, the women still had not opened the trapdoor. *Is it stuck?* Through their clustered bodies I saw shelves stocked with towels, sheets, brooms, cardboard boxes—a mishmash of supplies.

Then the women pulled up the box of cleaning supplies and the *second* trapdoor. No seam in the floor to show it. The craftsmen builders had designed the cellar to fool slave-hunters. And I hoped it would fool the men outside.

Kim saying, "They're out on the porch!"

Gabrielle went first, breath starting to frost as she disappeared into the basement. Kim's bare feet were white as she climbed down the ladder. Then Hoot. Danny. Eisner. I was last, carrying the Bobcat, shivering, now pulling the door shut behind me as I heard splintering wood—doors breaking. With the trapdoor closed, the sound grew muffled.

Come on, gas, I thought. *Blow.*

"Nice and toasty down here," Danny said, as the others stripped off their robes and pajamas and we all reached for the clothes and shoes we'd stocked here, in case we had to leave fast. We pulled on long underwear, socks, gloves, jackets as I heard a new noise overhead. Heavy and rhythmic.

We grabbed a cloth bag holding extra magazines of ammunition for the assault rifles, as well as two 9mm Glocks and a Sig Sauer. There were holsters, but no time to put them on. I jammed a Glock in my waistband, stuffed a Swiss Army knife in my pocket.

I whispered, "I cut the propane line."

I envisioned soldiers upstairs, whispering into mikes or communicating by hand signals, splitting up, checking closets, living room, bathroom. . . .

The tunnel narrowed to a crawl space. We scrambled on hands and knees. In the flashlight beams, roots hung down from the dirt roof. I heard a rat squeaking. I smelled water and dust and dirty boots. I followed Eisner's boots to sounds of labored breathing.

If the gas blows, will the explosion reach the tunnel?

My Bobcat scraped the ground. The cold seeped through my gloves. We must be beneath the river, I thought as Hoot began to hum anxiously, not a tune I recognized, something Mideastern, I think. Eisner's boots went up and down in front of my face. He said, "Just a little longer." I blanched at a quick rumble overhead, but it wasn't an explosion. We were beneath the road. Kim's voice said, from ahead, "Danny. Your face. Is that *blood* on your face?"

"Makeup," he said.

"Blood," she said.

"I'll look at it after we get out."

We kept moving, sucking in dank air. *Why hasn't the gas blown?* I imagined gas pouring from the severed fuel line. Had the men heard hissing? Had they stopped the leak or blown the candle out?

The tunnel seemed to go on longer than I remembered. We were still descending, not even halfway through.

I whispered, "Did you see Oliver Royce, Danny?"

"No, but I heard the name."

"But how did they *find* us?" Hoot asked from ahead. She'd stopped humming. Her senses seemed to be returning to her.

Eisner's voice floated back, sounding disembodied through all the huffing. "They must have checked my friends, *all* of them. Hit their houses, phones, computers."

Hoot saying, "Who *are* those guys?"

It was, of course, the real question. After all that had happened, I *still* had no idea who was directing the hijacking of HR-109, the murders and takeover. Keating?

No way. Colonel Otto? It was possible, but he was a mere colonel. I was missing something. What was I missing? Every time I had a good suspect, they died—or quit and disappeared.

"We made it! I can't believe it!" Kim said.

I stopped, last in line, waiting for the people blocking my view to open the door to the icy woods up top. I was too angry to be frightened. I wanted to fight.

I don't believe in conspiracies, but I thought, *How high does this one go?*

Then I heard, "The door's iced over. *Stuck*."

I envisioned Corby and Marty. They were functioning as someone's private army. Someone high enough to form a secret military unit. Someone able to control troops outside of normal military channels. Someone with access to soldiers' psych reports and records, able to put together specific types. Someone audacious and connected, trying to pull off one of the greatest power plays of all time, helped by a drug.

"The door won't budge," Eisner gasped. "Mike, can you squeeze over here and help?"

It was hard to maneuver. In the cramped space beneath the trapdoor, we three men pooled our strength. We pushed. We pressed our backs against the tunnel and kicked at the door. Danny groaned, in pain. I smelled the sour-sweet odor of blood. I dug the Swiss pocket knife out and chipped at the area around the trapdoor's edges. Bits of frozen dirt sprinkled down.

"Push!"

In the flashlight beams, faces seemed elongated. Emotions heightened. Hoot's face was smeared with snot and tears. Kim's flashlight went out.

I envisioned men on the other end of this tunnel climbing down, crawling after us.

"One . . . two . . . !"

We grunted, pushed, and the door broke free. Eisner reached to haul himself out.

Suddenly he slid sideways, down into the tunnel, crashing into the wall.

Gabrielle's flashlight flew from her hand. It smashed and shattered. The bulb went out.

Dirt blew into my face. Kim smashed her head against a protruding rock and fell onto my chest, limp as a doll. I thought I'd heard a *snap* inside her. The laws of physics seemed askew. Our bodies were in motion but we weren't willing it. The tunnel shook as a *BOOM* rolled toward us—simultaneously coming down and through the open door from outside. The shock wave dislodged ice from the trees.

"Kids, don't leave the gas on at home," Danny said, after a pause.

"Kim? Are you . . . ?"

"I'm fine."

I pushed her up, pushed Gabrielle out, saw them scramble away, thank God, and Hoot was out, and Danny. I rolled away from the opening. Behind me, Eisner slammed the door down. Now all I saw was ice-covered grass. Above us the moon was full. Our breaths rose. The normally clean air was fouled by chemical after-taste.

To the east I saw the glow of fire, through the woods.

"Bye-bye, Corby," I said.

"You hope," Danny said.

"Our footsteps," Eisner said, frowning, "will show on the ice."

Danny rubbed ice on his face, wiped away blood. An orange corona smeared the sky. I told myself that all the attackers had been in the house. But then I heard engines starting back there in the woods. Revving. There came a second, smaller explosion. The concussion dislodged more ice, which sprinkled down on us like glass.

Eisner looked toward where the SUV was hidden. "Canada's fifteen hours' drive. We walk across the border. We bypass immigration. We access the Internet from there."

Danny was favoring one leg. "Old basketball injury."

"Anyone else hurt? Kim?"

I remembered the crack I'd heard.

"Old gymnastics injury." She smiled, rubbing her neck.

Hoot said, "Those people are worse than the Ayatollahs."

"I'm not running to Canada," I said as we started moving again, up a slope. "You think we'd be safe there? We just blew up a house full of soldiers. We'll be extradited, or they'll come after us."

Eisner nodded like he understood. But he said, "We get over the border. We send our proof, *send it to every journalist, website, every Senator, and let the shit hit the fan.* That will buy us time while things get sorted out. What just happened was self-defense. We can prove that."

Hoot made a strangled noise then, in the back of her throat. She halted, trembling like a shell-shocked soldier, "I . . . I . . ."

Kim put her arm around her, but Hoot didn't seem to notice. I could tell I would not like whatever she was trying to get out.

"I was scared," she stammered. "I heard shooting. I ran. *I forgot to take the disks.*"

Hoot started to cry.

"They're *back* there?" Gabrielle said in a tiny voice, as if hope had gone out of her. Each of us had been assigned jobs in escape drills. Since Hoot slept in the room with the computer, her job had been to take the disks.

We should have been moving now, but Kim sat down in the snow. She made a heavy noise in her throat, as if air had been forced from her. The energy seemed to have left her. We all have a breaking point. Kim had reached hers.

I told Hoot, as the engine noises grew louder, "We'll figure something out."

"Like what?" Gabrielle snorted. "Inventing *another* drug that will make people tell the truth?"

We were all thinking the same thing. Our evidence was gone. The disks were captured or burned. There was no proof to send over the Internet, not even a hint of wrongdoing, a place for someone to *start* an investigation.

Hoot kept saying, over and over, "I'm sorry."

I saw blood on the snow beside Danny. It had soaked through his groin area to run down his pants to the ice.

I heard shouting in the woods. Troops coming.

"Run," I said. We did.

The bright moon meant better visibility. We hurried up the slope and broke from the trees, Danny limping slightly. A hundred yards ahead I saw the neighbor's cornfield and two-story saggy barn where Eisner had hidden the brand-new Ford Explorer—the vehicle belonging to the owner of the house we'd just escaped.

Kim seemed dazed but her feet were moving. Eisner unlatched the door of the shed. Inside it was dark and cold and the white Explorer sat amid immense farm machinery. It had maroon-colored leather seats, seat-back screens so passengers could distract themselves with videos. Little cup-holders. Dual airbags.

In the interior light Kim pulled the medical kit from among the sleeping bags and extra gas cans we'd stacked in back, beside gallon jugs of now frozen water.

"Pull your pants down," Kim ordered Danny, opening the medical kit.

"Sorry, I'm married, miss."

"You're losing blood."

Hoot gagged when she saw the wood chunk jutting from Danny's groin. It was a two-inch-long splinter, driven in during the gun battle at the house. When Danny yanked it out, blood oozed but didn't gush. No artery was severed. Eisner kept the pressure on, on both sides of the wound, as Gabrielle smeared on anti-bacteria ointment. Kim pressed the bandage down, breathing hoarsely, half in shock herself.

"Canada," Danny said. "I have some cousins north of Montreal who can put us up."

Gabrielle said, "How many cousins do you *have*?"

"It's a clan," I said, getting into the driver's seat. Everyone squeezed in except Eisner, who waited to close the shed door after we got outside. I scooped the ignition key from under the front mat. In the crisp air, sound seemed magnified, but perhaps the soldiers' Humvees would mask any engine noise we made. Tinted glass made visibility more difficult, but I didn't want to use the headlights yet. The heating system blessedly worked. Eisner climbed back in and we drove off by moonlight, down the icy dirt road on which—even under four-wheel drive—we skidded as we headed for the paved two-lane highway two miles ahead.

Hoot beside me. Eisner at the front passenger window with his AK-15, and a Glock on his lap. Danny in back with the Sig, wincing silently from pain when we hit bumps. Kim and Gabrielle side by side, next to Danny in the backseat, their faces wan in the red glow each time I pressed the brake.

"Oh Canadaaaa, oh Canadaaaaaaa," Danny sang softly. He had to be one of the worst singers I'd ever heard.

I looked back. "I didn't mind the shooting, but stop singing."

"That hurts, Boss."

"Keep the GPS system off," Eisner ordered as I reached for it. "They can track us by satellite if you put it on, and if they know we've got this car."

"You think they have access to satellites?"

"Gee, let's see. Would high-up guys in Washington, covert op guys, have access to satellites?"

It was just before dawn, but the glow in the sky was on my left, south, not east, so it wasn't the sun but the fire. Wheels churned on black ice. We slid toward the trees. I couldn't stop. The trunks loomed and I took my foot off the accelerator and at the last second felt a collective exhalation as the wheels gripped the road.

Paved highway half a mile away, I hoped.

We made it.

Then we rounded a bend and the soldier stood directly in front of me, ninety feet ahead, turning toward us, as surprised as I was to see him. White parka. Hood up. Hand going for his sidearm. He'd been staring at the glow in the sky, and now I saw the idling Humvee in the trees, and a second man, in the driver's seat. They had not heard us coming because of their radio and engine. It was too late to change direction or back up. Time seemed to slow. Eisner's window was going down; he'd been level-headed enough to know it was quicker to roll it down electrically than smash it.

Everything happening fast and slow at the same time.

The soldier's sidearm coming up.

The moonlight falling on a face I recognized, a pale face pitted with acne scars. *It's Marty, from the brig.*

I slammed my foot down on the accelerator, praying the car wouldn't slip.

Danny firing behind me. *Crack-ack-ack* . . .

The noise immense . . .

The wheels caught and the engine screamed and there was the pellet assault of rocks hitting chassis. Flame erupted from Marty's hand. He was gutsy or stupid, standing there. When we struck him he lifted off the ground and I felt the crunch of body on fender. His face flew toward me. Just before it hit glass there was a thump as Marty flew sideways, off the car.

Eisner letting off shots now too.

The Humvee driver staggering, falling by his car.

We rounded a corner and the highway lay ahead, plowed and salted, black flanked by white. I bumped onto asphalt. I switched on the headlights. I kept my foot hard on the accelerator. On this road traction was fine.

My hands on the wheel were shaking. The shots still sounded in my head, made hearing difficult. Someone's hand was on my shoulder, and Kim was saying, "We're past them. It's okay. Slow down."

Kim massaging my shoulders, trying to calm me.

After a few moments Gabrielle even tried a joke.

"Mike, when I said to make the biggest explosion in history with Kim, this isn't what I had in mind."

There was an instant of silence and then everyone started laughing. It was relief, not hilarity. The joke hadn't been that funny. But we felt alive. Kim blushing. Hoot giggling like a kid. Danny roaring. Eisner slapping his leg like a fraternity boy.

"Naturetech," I said. "Not Canada."

That quieted them quickly enough.

"Forget it," said Eisner.

"The proof is at Naturetech."

"So are more soldiers, Mike."

There were no other lights on this road, no sirens or movement. Just a white line running toward Canada. I heard the throbbing engine and hum of tires. Eisner said, "Canada." So did the others. They said it like it was Switzerland. Fantasyland. But at best it would be a mere respite.

The road seemed to plunge into nothingness. The trees looked like sentries. There would be no refuge in Canada, or anywhere else, I knew. We'd be harder to find, but ultimately people would come for us.

Get Kim to Canada. Go back to Naturetech on your own.

There are times when reality needs to catch up to consciousness. When you step beyond boundaries that have tethered you to the world. The rim of the sky brightened to the color of fire. Black seeped out of the night. At dawn I drove through small towns. A few pickup trucks were out. Outside of Isaacville, my heart started hammering when, behind us, a state police car pulled out from beside a barn, where it had been idling, its lone trooper waiting for speeders, or sleeping or drinking coffee.

The squad car fell in behind.

Five minutes later, it peeled away, the trooper having run our license and found nothing amiss.

My glance met Eisner's. Maybe whomever was after us did not know about the Ford. *Or maybe they're coming after us privately. They don't want publicity. They don't even want a real arrest.*

On I-95 we joined the stream of type-A early commuters heading for Washington, and big semis on the highway. We passed the exit for Quantico, where I'd attended the FBI Academy. Traffic thickened. We crawled in the great anonymous mass, past sleeping suburbs filled with people who had no idea that the government had been turned upside down by a drug. They probably wouldn't even believe it if they heard it. Sound barriers flanked the road like blinders. I was exhausted but I let my friends sleep. I turned on the radio to hear that a "terrorist bomb factory" had been assaulted by a special army anti-terrorist unit at a farmhouse in Virginia. The "bombs" had gone off during the fight, destroying the house and terrorists just before dawn.

The cold front had never reached Washington. The air here was suddenly warm. My friends dozed on, and at ten A.M., too tired to drive farther, I pulled into a new rest stop north of Baltimore. We'd change drivers. Buy machine coffee. I'd take a turn in back, go to sleep.

Gabrielle got out and stretched. Hoot headed for the bathroom. Danny roused himself and rubbed his hip and leaned over Kim, to shake her awake.

"Kim?"

Her head rolled left. She slid down in the seat, now that Gabrielle wasn't on her other side to prop her up.

"Kim?" Danny sounded alarmed now. It was not a tone I recognized in him.

There were only a half-dozen cars in the rest stop, as there was no gasoline or hot food to buy here. People strolled in and out of the bathroom and vending machine area, while inside the Ford, Danny pounded on her chest. I pushed him aside, filled with terror. She was cold and still and her lips had long gone blue.

I was screaming inside my head for her to wake up.

I checked her airways with my finger, remembering the way she'd hit her head in the tunnel, her dazed look after that, the way she'd just sat in the snow after Hoot's confession, the way she'd fallen asleep first in the car.

I was just driving while she passed out, less than three feet behind me.

I felt as if my organs were tearing out of my body. There had to be a way to save her, revive her. We would take her to the hospital. Doctors would work on her. Just because she was unconscious, just because Danny didn't feel her breathing, was no reason to . . .

"No hospital," Eisner said.

I grabbed the car keys, but Eisner and Danny wrestled them away from me. I tried to fight them in the grass, in that far corner of the parking lot. They held me down. The Ford shielded us from view. When I stopped struggling, Eisner rechecked her temperature and told me she'd been dead for hours.

"You know, Mike, if there were any chance for her . . ." Danny said.

But the blood was already draining to her feet, her thighs, we saw when her pants were off. She was blue down there, white on top. Cold marble.

"She died sleeping," Eisner said.

I don't know how I kept from screaming. Gabrielle

and Hoot just stood frozen, watching. They'd come back to the car, carrying candy bars for all.

Eisner was the most professional about it. And why not? He'd known her the least amount of time. "We have to go," he coaxed. "People are starting to look. Mike? Get into the Ford. I'll drive."

"You mean just keep her with us in the car?" Hoot said.

"She wouldn't have wanted you to get caught, Mike," Eisner said. "She especially wouldn't have wanted her death to be the cause."

"Don't tell me what she wanted," I snapped.

But he was right. She *had* told me what she wanted, and only hours ago. She'd held me in bed. I'd felt her warmth and passion. She'd been quite certain of her wishes. She'd said, "Keep going, Mike, no matter what. I want to help any way I can."

Kim.

I was in the backseat now. I guess Eisner had started driving. I don't remember him getting behind the wheel, but we were moving at the speed limit, and he told us that it would be better, smarter, if we forced ourselves to eat. I don't know what he was planning. I didn't know if, in his mind, we'd keep going north with Kim. I couldn't have stood that, for hours. I knew that much.

Eisner started in about Canada again. "Mike, I know how you're feeling, but—"

"Stop the car," I said.

"Mike . . ."

"Let me out. I'll walk. If you want to go to Canada, I don't blame you. I'm going back to Naturetech. I'm going to find those sons of bitches. I'm not running away from them anymore. I'm going to stop this thing."

I heard Danny blow out air. Then, "I'll go with you."

"Me too," said Gabrielle softly.

"Oh, Christ," Eisner said, but there was an exit sign for Aberdeen coming up, and he put on the blinker. "What the hell do you think you can do at Naturetech?"

"Watch it from the park. Follow Teaks when he leaves. He'll know what's going on."

"Shit," Eisner said. He hit the dashboard with his fist.

But he turned us around. He got off at Aberdeen, the old Army Ordnance grounds. It was grassy here, rural, and he crossed the highway on an overpass and swung south again onto I-95, back toward Washington. He didn't seem to want to go to Canada anymore himself.

We didn't speak. Kim's head was on my lap. In a funny way I felt as if she approved of this. But I also knew I needed a plan. By the time we reached the Baltimore beltway, a logical one had come to me, but it was so upsetting, I pushed it away.

It came back.

Fifteen minutes later, when we were in the Baltimore tunnel, I told it to them. It horrified them.

But we agreed to try it anyway.

Eisner sighed. "It's the best we can do."

TWENTY

The cottage was small, neat, gray-shingled, and located on the back side of a wooded half-acre lot off River Road in northwest Washington, by the towpath and the Potomac, up a long driveway, shielded by oaks from heavy traffic below.

"He's an honest reporter," Eisner said, pulling the SUV behind the house. "I worked with Harris on the helicopter scandal. He trusts me. His wife works at Treasury, so no one's home during the day. I hate what we're about to do, but Mike is right."

"Leave a body on a reporter's doorstep," I said, "and he'll write a story, that's for sure."

There were wind chimes by the porch, and a hammock near a flower bed. My heart was breaking. I made myself remember what Kim had told me in Virginia. If she hadn't said it, I never could have followed through on this.

I want to help, Mike, whatever it takes.

People say death makes you look peaceful. But it makes you look as if you've never lived. We left her on the porch, protected from the mosquitoes—at least, zipped into a sleeping bag. Eisner had phoned the *Post* to make sure Harris was in town.

I'd composed the note we'd leave with Kim, but Eisner wrote and signed it. The reporter knew him, not me.

It started, "Eddy, I wish there were another way to alert you to an urgent story. Meet Kim Pendergraph, friend, and former executive assistant to ex–Lenox Pharmaceuticals Chairman James Dwyer. Both were murdered to protect a secret."

The note described HR-109's discovery, its power and its misuse. It named Naturetech, Keating, Schwadron, Otto.

The note also sketched out my personal story, and details of the explosion in Virginia this morning. We included information about the escape tunnel and brig that only someone who had been there would know. We named Asa Rodriguez and the Royces. We admitted setting the explosion to save our lives. We said we'd phone in a day or so.

"Eddy will show this to his editors," Eisner predicted. "The story is too huge to ignore."

He wrote, "Trace the forty-million-dollar Pentagon overpayment to Lenox. It will lead you to HR-109."

"Yeah, but when he traces it," Danny said, "what will happen to *him*? Will they even run the story? There have been resignations at the *Post* too."

"We can hope. Mike? Write your postscript."

I did not want to leave her. I took the pen. Italians believe that dead people can communicate with loved ones, and I felt Kim urging me on. Or maybe I only wanted to believe. I wrote, "I love Kim. It is a measure of our desperation that we're leaving her here. Be kind to her. We're not abandoning her. We're entrusting her to you. We'll be back to bury her like she deserves."

I signed my name under Eisner's, and as we drove off I looked back at the rolled-up form on the porch. My chest hurt. I'd kept my promise to Kim. The edge of the envelope poked from the sleeping bag, a macabre card accompanying a corpse. We were gambling that Harris would write the kind of story we needed.

Eisner left a message on the reporter's answering machine at the paper. He did not identify himself but said "an important document, a huge story" waited on the reporter's doorstep at home.

"That'll get him here fast," Eisner said. "No beers for him at the Post Pub tonight."

Thespian Land is a cheap costume store in northeast Washington, a mile from Union Station on a block including a liquor joint, a Goodwill, an Army-Navy store and a Boston Chicken. Gabrielle and Hoot did the shopping, Hoot coming back in a blond wig, floppy hat and nonprescription glasses that made her cheeks look fatter, her chin shorter. The nose ring was gone, the tattoo covered. I'd never seen her in a flower-print dress before, or footwear that wasn't sneakers. She looked like twenty thousand secretaries in town.

Gabrielle was still brunette, but the wig flipped up at jaw level. Her blouse/dress combo was loose and frumpy and she wore flat heels, the kind she'd never be caught dead in any other time. The sunglasses made her face angular. She smelled of a different perfume when she climbed into the car.

"Smell different, you act different," she said.

For the guys, Hoot and Gabrielle brought back Goodwill gray suits, Washington's unofficial uniform. Wingtips and white shirts, bland ties and tan raincoats to go over our arms in case it rained, or we hid firearms. We looked like accountants or lawyers. Half a million men dressed like us walked the capital today.

"I still have my Lenox ID, Boss," Danny said, fixing his tie. "You?"

Eisner had recovered it, with my wallet, at the brig.

We men had our pistols in shoulder or belt holsters. The assault rifles were hidden in the Ford's cargo area. The women—neither of whom had ever used firearms— were unarmed and had bought two pairs of binoculars at the Army-Navy store.

Spend your life trying to avoid something, invariably it catches up to you. I'd spent my years avoiding loss that comes with commitment. I'd thought I was having fun, but saw now I'd been protecting myself. Now I'd suffered the loss anyway. I fought off grief and felt Kim's presence as we drove to Union Station, Washington's Amtrak terminal. From the passenger drop-off zone, the Capitol dome was visible in walking distance, above treetops. It was the familiar shot opening films, symbol of my country; a view that, when I was a kid at Lowes Theater, made me dream of working for the FBI.

But now that dome seemed fragile, calcified, about to collapse in on itself.

"Remember," I told the women as they climbed out amid a stream of arriving or departing passengers, "get off at Ticonderoga. Do *not* take the train into Canada. Danny's cousins will meet you at the station, take you up Lake Champlain in a boat. They'll hold a sign saying '*Roberta.*' We'll check in with you every day."

"I've never been on a reservation," Hoot said, with real curiosity.

"Fresh air. Woods. It beats that East Village dump of

yours," I said. "The second you reach the reservation, get on the Internet. Can you still hack into Lenox?"

"What do you mean, *still*? I used to collect people's passwords, or stand behind their backs when they signed in. You can even *record* the sound of keyboards. Each key makes a different noise when it hits."

"Well, use the passwords to find any connections we might have missed between Lenox and Colonel Otto, Ray Teaks, Ralph Kranz. . . ."

"That Nazi!"

"Also Keating, Dwyer, Carbone. Check stock awards. E-mails. Board memos. PR. Gabrielle? Make sure that Hoot—"

"I'm not going to Canada," Gabrielle interrupted, folding her arms. "I've changed my mind. I'm staying in DC."

I started to argue. Gabrielle turned to Hoot.

"You don't need a babysitter, do you? How old are you anyway? Twenty-five?"

"Twenty-two."

"Then you can take a train by yourself. You won't talk to anyone. You're certainly not going to turn yourself in, are you, after what's happened?"

"You think I'm crazy?" Hoot said.

Gabrielle turned to me with a satisfied air. "See? She'll remember what to do without me."

"Don't talk about me like I'm a baby," Hoot said.

"You're a social retard, dear," Gabrielle said. "And Mike, you don't need to protect me. I'm a big girl."

I pretended that her reversal had nothing to do with last night, and my choice of Kim over her. The last thing we needed was a squabble.

I argued, "If a fight breaks out, you've never fired a

gun. You'll be safer in Canada. Come back and testify later, if things work out."

She pressed her index finger to my mouth, silencing me.

"If," she said, "is a big word. This isn't about you, Mike. I own nine percent of Lenox. I spoke to Senator Lark Petrie at Dad's funeral. Lenox has factories in Ohio, Petrie's home state. Thousands of employees. She told me, 'If you have a problem, call.' "

"I don't think she was referring to 109."

"I'm not consulting you. I'm informing you. Senator Petrie's on the Armed Services Committee. She's supposed to know about weapons like 109. Want to bet she doesn't? Let's *use* my connections. If you can gamble on a reporter, I can gamble on a Senator."

"We don't know who to trust."

"They killed my father," Gabrielle said.

"Yeah," I snapped. "Who you didn't even talk to before that."

The rage on her face told me we were back where we'd started when I'd met her. She spun away from the Explorer and stomped toward the escalator to the Metro line. I started to go after her. Eisner pulled me back. He called after her, "Check in every hour."

"You check in," she snapped back. "You have my number too."

To me, Eisner said, "It might work, Mike."

"We shouldn't split up."

"Not your choice."

I heard myself say, "I couldn't protect Kim."

Danny put his big hands on my shoulders. "Boss, you're the only reason there's any chance of stopping this mess at all. Look, we'll go to Naturetech and wait for

Teaks to leave, like you said. We follow him, grab him. He's the weak link."

Danny got a hard look on his face. "Then I'll have a talk with him the way I used to talk to guys in the Philippines."

Eisner agreed. "You called it, Mike."

I kissed Hoot on the cheek like a parent sending a child off to college. She looked small against the marble building, disappearing toward the Amtrak line with most of our remaining cash. "Remember, Hoot, don't use credit cards," Eisner warned. We piled back into the Ford and drove up Massachusetts Avenue, toward Maryland. I still smelled vanilla—Kim's scent—in the car. We headed north along Embassy Row, passing a security roadblock near the Vice President's residence. Fortunately, the soldiers worked only the inbound side of the road. I don't know if they were looking for us.

"Little detour before Naturetech," Eisner announced, eyeing the roadblock. "We've pushed our luck too long in this car."

The mechanic's shop was off Park Valley Road, near Sligo in Chevy Chase, squeezed between an auto parts store and an Italian bakery. I could barely wedge us into the narrow entrance. Inside, two men in jumpsuits painted a civilian Hummer, changing the color from red to blue. They looked up nervously at our arrival, but relaxed when Eisner got out of the car.

"My good friend!" cried the fatter man, pumping Eisner's hand enthusiastically. He was pale, oily-looking, and practically foamed at the mouth eyeing the Explorer.

"A ve-ry nice car, Lawrence," he said, checking the bodywork for dents.

Fifteen minutes later we drove out of the lot in back in

a seven-year-old champagne-colored Acura, worth far less than the Explorer Eisner had traded in for it, plus six hundred dollars in much-needed cash. The car's pickup was excellent. The Acura held the road. The interior smelled of air freshener and cigarettes. We'd transferred our assault rifles to the trunk without anyone having seen. Eisner said the garage was operated by a Belarussian ring stealing soldiers' vehicles—altering records, diverting cars shipped under government contracts, burning off ID numbers and sending contraband abroad on big car carriers headed for Poland, East Germany, Latvia.

"Who's Lawrence?" I asked Eisner.

"He thinks that's my name. I was looking forward to arresting the shit heel myself. The bust is scheduled for the twenty-fourth. Surveillance was called off two weeks ago."

Five minutes later we reached the Beltway. Traffic moved swiftly along the turnoff to I-270, the research corridor lined by companies servicing the government, sat outfits, think tanks, military-hardware sales groups, lobbyist firms.

We turned on news radio, our HR-109 warning system. We heard no bulletins naming us, even when the explosion in Virginia was mentioned. The search for us was wide but private.

"Colonel Otto must think we've still got Dwyer's disk," I said.

Just now a commentator was going on about another security coup overseas. Thanks to information supplied by US Intelligence, Russian investigators had seized a ship stocked with stolen anthrax, bound for sale in the Mideast.

I remembered Kim, how surprised she'd looked when I walked into her bedroom last night, and how strong and soft she'd felt. I remembered the cinnamon taste of her, and the salt on her breasts and belly. I remembered the hollow where her arm joined her shoulder. I remembered the momentary glazed look in her eyes after she'd smashed her head on the tunnel wall. That was the moment she had started to die, I knew now.

I was happy when she closed her eyes while I was driving. I thought she was tired, asleep.

I felt my rage bubbling up.

Last time Danny and I had been on I-270 we'd been unsure whether Chairman's Dwyer's death was linked to Naturetech. Now I turned off the highway into a transitional zone—part rural, part suburban—a mix of old horse farms and new condo developments. Half a mile north of Naturetech I made a sharp left into Deer Run Park, Montgomery County's newest recreation area. The park occupied a low plateau overlooking the lab. Anyone leaving Naturetech for Washington would have to pass this way to reach the interstate, I knew.

It was four o'clock, almost quitting time at most businesses, but who could tell what work hours scientists kept at a lab racing to synthesize a world-changing drug?

A quarter-mile-long driveway took us up a grassy hill, past a new playground and basketball court. In August, I saw kids and day campers playing b-ball, picnicking, kicking soccer balls, running in the woods.

"Our suits and binoculars will sure blend in here," Danny said, eyeing the picnickers as I parked. "Maybe the moms'll figure we're professional soccer coaches, checking out talent. You think?"

"I think when Washington kids see suits they couldn't care less. I think the trees will shield us and you don't have a better idea."

"Me?" he said. "I don't have any idea."

I was right about the woods, at least. A clearly marked footpath took us to a fenced-off overlook beyond which was a horse farm, foals running, then—beyond a low barn—the barbed wire and electric fences surrounding Naturetech. The binoculars gave us a decent view inside the property: the jagged donut of lawn around the actual three-spoked brick building; the thickly forested strips at the edges of the property, to keep farmer or satellite-company neighbors from seeing in; the guardhouse in front and the parking area for staff; the soldiers patrolling; the loading dock behind the animal experimentation lab area, C wing. The whole facility looked quiet below.

"Gabrielle must have reached the Senate by now. How come she hasn't called?" I said.

Eisner tried to reach her. She didn't answer.

"Look. Keating," Danny said.

I raised my binoculars, moved the O over Naturetech's roof. Three men stood by the loading dock, looking happy, gazing into the back of an unmarked panel truck. Keating was snappy and stylish in a cream-colored summer suit. To his right, sweating in the heat, gesturing animatedly, Dr. Teaks wore lab blues, and beside him stood a darkly handsome man in uniform, nodding and smiling.

"Alonzo Otto," I said.

"So *that's* what he looks like," Eisner said. "I've only spoken to him on the phone. Cuban mother. Dutch American father. See the limp? He was shot in Iraq."

Danny grunted. "What's that? *A body?*"

Now white-coated technicians had appeared on the loading dock, carrying a gurney covered by a sheet. At first I thought there was a fat person underneath because it arced up so high. But then I realized it was lumpy. A long hairy arm fell out from beneath the sheet.

"Chimps."

The techies slid the gurney into the panel truck. Keating shook Teaks's hand. Otto glanced up toward the loading dock, but following his gaze, I could only see a fourth person's shoes. Shiny brown lace-up shoes. A man's.

Otto looking respectful. Otto nodding as if receiving instructions and saying, "Yes, sir."

"If those guys are happy, I'm not," Danny said.

Move out from under the roof, I urged Mr. Shoes in my head. It was clear from Colonel Otto's expression that the hidden man was someone of importance, a higher-up.

Who the hell is he?

Mr. Shoes took a fraction of a step forward. Now I could see a brown ribbed sock and the fringe of a tweed pants cuff, brown on white. He stopped moving.

Danny grunted. "Addicts."

"Excuse me?" Eisner said.

"I looked at scenes like this in the Philippines a dozen times. It doesn't make a difference if they're manufacturing heroin down there or 109. I don't care how prominent they are, or if they work for the goddamn Oval Office. You're looking at people enslaved by a drug, and there's only one way to beat them. Take it away for good."

The brown shoe lifted and the cuff moved forward and *he looks familiar,* I thought. The stranger coming into view was of average height, pale and unremarkable, chubby and dweeby, even, in a dark boxy suit and matching glasses. Lawyer, maybe. Think-tank guy. His shirt was white and his striped tie a bland moss and brown. His gray-black hair was thickly curly, cut close to his skull. His posture was that of a man who spends lots of time at a desk, none at a gym. He looked like someone who comes home at night with sweat rings on his shirt.

"Who's that?" Eisner said as Teaks flourished a bottle of scotch and four drinking glasses.

"Shit. They're celebrating," Danny said.

Where have I seen him before? I thought.

Considering the collective power of the group, it was striking how the others deferred to the stranger, in the way they paid attention when he gave the toast. Snobby Keating, ramrod-straight Otto, intense Dr. Teaks didn't lift their glasses until *he* did, or drink until *he* did.

Mr. Think Tank–type jabbing at his watch, as if emphasizing time. Maybe he was saying *time* was important, or it was time to stop drinking and get back to work. Maybe time was running out. I hoped that was it, but I doubted it. He'd looked too pleased a moment ago.

I asked myself, *Have I seen him on TV? Newspaper photo?* Nope.

Maybe I recognized him from Lenox or Naturetech. I played matchup in my brain as Teaks tossed the empty bottle into a recycling bin. I'd learned this association technique at the FBI. I ran through venues in my head, starting with the night Dwyer died. Had I seen this man on the street outside his house? With cops *in* the house? Among the crowd of reporters?

Uh-uh.

How about Gabrielle's neighborhood? The airport?

The men were splitting up now—Mr. Shoes and Otto conferring, Keating and Teaks going back inside.

I remembered the Senate hearings where I'd met Tom Schwadron. I switched to Keating's chili party.

"That's it," I said, blood rushing in my brain as the connection came through.

In my mind I saw the stranger dressed casually, sipping a drink on Keating's lawn. And next to him was journalist Alicia Dent, who'd broken so many big stories in DC recently, wrecked so many careers, jabbering away while he nodded. I'd pegged him as unimportant, an escort awed by his celebrity date, happy to have a pretty girl on his arm.

"Are you *spies?*" a kid's voice suddenly said from a few feet behind us.

I whirled. Two boys in soccer uniforms stood there. Gangly, curious kids of 12 or 13, who eyed the binoculars, then squinted at the scene below, trying to figure out what we were watching.

Danny told the kids, "We're worse than spies."

The kids didn't move.

Danny pointed at the sky. "We're Antarean invaders, earth children. Our planet is very far away."

One kid laughed. The other rolled his eyes.

"I told you they wouldn't say shit," the kid said.

The boys ran off.

Below, the panel truck pulled away. Colonel Otto got into a black Caprice. He'd come alone. The stranger was suddenly looking up toward us, but he couldn't know we were there, could he? Could he *sense* surveillance?

Could he be on HR-109?

I stepped back involuntarily. The drug wasn't supposed to work at this distance. I looked back and he was cleaning his glasses with his fingers. He strolled to the parking area and a shiny new blue Cadillac. He walked around the car, carefully wiping spots off the finish with a handkerchief. He spent three minutes compulsively rubbing one spot. Dr. Evil seemed pretty anal about his new car.

"We follow him. Not Teaks," I said.

The sun was sinking at five o'clock, but hours of daylight remained. We headed back toward the Acura, and down the long driveway. At the end we pulled over and idled within view of Route 355. If the stranger headed for Washington, he'd come this way.

If he went the other way, we'd miss him.

Five minutes passed. Eight. He must have gone the other way. Shit.

"He drives like an old lady," Danny drawled from the back as the Caddy appeared and crawled past, the guy on his phone. Danny added, "Hallelujah. His right brake light's out."

I fell in behind the STS, keeping back. The man was a preoccupied or methodical driver, staying in the middle lane on I-270, moving at a steady fifty-three miles an hour. He used his brake often and defensively. The busted light made it easier to stay back and keep him in sight. Eisner used the binoculars and recited numbers on the DC license plate. Usually, important guys in Washington have drivers. But important guys on private missions, I'd learned at the FBI, often prefer to drive alone.

"You'd think one of us would know someone who can still run a license," Eisner said.

"Me," Danny said.

"Not another cousin."

"Little Sparrow's in the New York Motor Vehicle Bureau, not here. But the bureaus cooperate, twenty-four hours a day."

We stayed with the STS onto the Beltway and up the exit for Connecticut Avenue. Gabrielle still hadn't fice. She's out of the country. Her staffers got all weird when I told them who I was, and then her aide excused himself and I saw him making a phone call and—"

"Slow down."

"I got out of there fast. Maybe I'm imagining things. I panicked. You're right. I don't know who to trust. I wish I had some 109. Are you still in Washington?"

"Where exactly are *you*?" I said, alert, suddenly not liking talking on the phone, even though mine was encrypted.

"I've just been riding around. I can meet you. Tell me where to go. I'm sorry I snapped before," she said, jumping from one subject to another. "Kim was right next to me, in the car. Her head was on my shoulder. I thought she was sleeping," she added, voice cracking.

"I did too."

"I don't want to be alone. I'm sorry I went off."

I told Gabrielle to take trains, switch trains, move round, try to see if anyone stayed behind her. I said to get Florida Street near 13th, and a small Mexican restau-nt, La Taqueria. It was dark and private, with small ooths; and it stayed open late. I'd spent lots of nights there hen I was at the FBI, with an old partner, Justo Vasco. u never saw government types there, just immigrants, st of them illegals, Vasco said. They minded their own iness and spent their evenings moving between the aurant and the Internet/long-distance phone shop next r. From there they contacted their families abroad.

I'll go, Mike, but isn't there something I can do to while I wait?"

Vhich gave me another idea. I told her to go to the In-t shop and do a Google search on Paul Ludenhorff. I her his address. Description. The license of his car.

called, or answered our tries. I was worried about her. We followed the guy into the District and pulled over while he ran the STS through a Connecticut Avenue car wash and went through the inspection routine again when it came out. Danny's encrypted cell phone buzzed while we watched.

"Thanks, Little Sparrow," he said, after listening for a few moments. He hung up.

He announced, "Our friend's name is Paul Ludenhorff with two *f*s. He's got a Georgetown address up on N Street. No other drivers listed at his apartment. Maybe he's a bachelor. I hope so. It makes things easier."

"Eisner, ever hear the name?" I asked.

"No."

Ludenhorff followed Connecticut to Macomb Street and Macomb to Wisconsin. He pulled into the Safeway supermarket, parking his car protectively in a corner of the lot, to keep it from getting dented, I suppose. Danny followed him in to make sure he was shopping. Eisner learned Ludenhorff's home number from Directory Assistance. The answering-machine message mentioned his name, no one else's, but that didn't mean he didn't have a family. Danny came back and reported Ludenhorff had bought frozen dinners, Raisin Bran, Bumble Bee tuna, milk.

"Bachelor food. He must be heading home. That crap he bought better not be for a date."

I knew that N Street was narrow and even an idiot would spot a car following, so I took a chance and went ahead to the house. His block was charming, tree-lined, cobblestoned. There was a tiny park across from the house with a bust of John Adams in it, and benches. The bust's proportions were off. Adams had too small a head.

Ludenhorff occupied the first two stories of a redbrick Federal-style four-floor townhouse, divided into two condos, if the JUST SOLD sign out front was to be believed. The lights were off in his apartment, on in the one above. I parked on 36th Street so the Acura would be hidden. Dusk had fallen. Streetlamps glowed. Ludenhorff's neighbors came home from work. It was a nice neighborhood to live in. Georgetown homes tended to come with lots of strong locks and security. No windows were open in his apartment, and silvery wires built into the panes told me there was an alarm.

"How do we get in?" Danny said, thinking aloud.

I risked going up Ludenhorff's steps and peering through the window of the outer door, which was locked, of course. The apartments shared a foyer and had separate doors, with double locks. PROTECTED BY ZEUS-ALARM said a sticker on his door, showing a muscled man holding a sword and shield. Electrical bolts shot out of the helmeted guy's head.

Mail lying on the carpet was addressed only to him.

He should have come home by now. *Where is he?*

I got away from the foyer. The last thing I needed was for him to see a stranger standing on his top step. "Ah, here's Dr. NASCAR now," Danny said as I reached the bench in the little park. The blue Caddy had appeared, moving at a crawl.

He drove slowly past the house, signaled and turned right, either looking for a parking space or heading for a lot. *Maybe this will be the big break,* I hoped.

Between Danny, Eisner and me, we had plenty of experience lying our way into strangers' apartments, bullying our way in, coaxing our way in. But if Paul Ludenhorff

knew our names and faces, getting in would require a different kind of trick.

"We hit him while he's going in, as he opens his door," I said as my phone chimed.

I ignored the phone, because Ludenhorff was coming up the block, carrying a leather briefcase and plastic Safeway bag.

But lots of other people—witnesses—were suddenly on the block too: student types from the university, and a private uniformed street guard from neighborhood watch. Ludenhorff's upstairs neighbor came out, greeted him and held his shopping bag as Ludenhorff searched for his apartment key.

Chime. I didn't recognize the incoming number, had a Washington, DC, area code. Could it be Gabr

Inside, I screamed with frustration. The caller ga The security guard leaned against a tree and w Ludenhorff. What was so damn fascinating abou looking for keys? Then, through the glass, I saw Lu open his apartment door. The door shut behind hi sioned him clicking those double locks.

He was safe inside.

The guard strolled off, toward M Street. T neighbor rushed off toward Wisconsin Avenu

Lights came on in Ludenhorff's apartm peared at the window, drawing the curtains, ol

My phone chimed again, and this time I

"Mike?"

"Where are you, Gabrielle?"

"I'm scared," she said, talking fast, her into each other. I heard a public intercon echo in the background, something abo Red Line. "I'm in the Metro, Mike. I

His car, I thought, as another idea hit.

"We'll pick you up later, Gabrielle. Call in every hour." I hung up and saw Danny looking at me. I grinned at him. "The *car,*" I said.

Danny smiled back. "Of course."

Minutes later, I was back on Ludenhorff's top step as Eisner lounged below and Danny called the house from the park, and signaled that the phone was being answered. He said he was a DC cop. He asked if Ludenhorff owned a dark blue STS, license number blah-blah-blah. Telling Paul that, sorry, his Caddy had been involved in an accident, explaining when Ludenhorff protested that the car was *parked* that Danny *knew* that, but *another* car had just rammed it.

Danny flashed a thumbs-up as he broke the connection, which meant Ludenhorff was rushing out to see the damage to his car.

I heard pounding footsteps in the house, even through the foyer door. The apartment door swung open. Ludenhorff looked so panicked he didn't register the presence of another person on his steps. The instant he opened the outer door I shoved into him hard, pushing him so powerfully into the foyer that he crashed into his apartment door, lost his balance and fell. He said, "Whaaaaa." I heard Eisner racing up the iron stairs behind me. I bulled ahead like a linebacker, towering over the man on the floor. Ludenhorff said, "Who the hell do you think—"

He froze as the sight of my gun registered. His keys lay on the carpet, on a chain.

"No noise," I said.

He thought I was a robber, but then he focused on my

face. He looked startled, not so much from fear as comprehension. *Do I see admiration there too?* I thought.

"I guess there's nothing wrong with my car, Mr. Acela," he said in a normal voice as Eisner scooped up the keys and demanded of him, "Tell me the alarm code."

"It's off. I was in a rush, as you know," Ludenhorff replied dryly, pushing himself up on one elbow, rubbing his shoulder where I'd rammed him.

I raised the Glock. Pointed it at his stomach.

"It's the truth," he said, and even smiled a little. He saw the irony of it. After all, the ability to tell lies from truth lay at the heart of why we were all here.

Eisner opened the apartment door. The alarm keypad was right inside and the system light glowed green, all right. Unarmed.

"I'd worry more about myself than my car," I said.

"But nobody hit it. Right? I just bought it."

He stood.

I was impressed at the speed with which he'd composed himself. You form gut impressions of people in an instant, with or without HR-109. His body was flabby but his personality came through as hard and calm. The eyes were pools of intellect. Thought crackled behind those glasses.

"Major Eisner too," he said. Danny arriving now. "The three musketeers. And where are the women?" Ludenhorff squeezing his shoulder where I'd struck him. His gaze was a tractor beam. What he said next surprised me. "Well, I have some warm strudel inside, gentlemen."

"Strudel?" I must not have heard right. I was doing all I could to control myself. I wanted to start hitting this man and never stop. He was talking about cake.

"My stepmother made it. I'll warm it up. Come in. Let's talk."

It's funny the things that set you off.

It was the arrogance that did it. My knee moved by itself, burying itself between his legs. The air went out of him. Ludenhorff fell backwards, into his apartment. He struck the carpeted floor with his side and rolled into a ball. He clutched himself, choking.

I heard someone close the door behind me. I couldn't stop myself. My friends let the silent beating go on. Ludenhorff trying to cover himself. Ludenhorff tucking his head, grunting as my blows fell. Ludenhorff the human turtle, absorbing punishment that would never be as severe as his crimes.

I stood back, drenched with sweat. And Ludenhorff began to breathe again.

"I want answers, Paul," I told him. "Now."

Strudel.

TWENTY-ONE

Danny and I duct-taped him to his study chair, a Venezia model, of Italian leather. The room was on the ground level, so his ceiling and second story would muffle his cries from his neighbors upstairs. There were no windows in the interior room. And the chair was so heavy he'd never move it, slide it, bang it up and down, inch it across the floor to the phone or one of the two computers—a wireless laptop and a top-of-the-line secured Macintosh, both on—on the mahogany desk.

Eisner was upstairs, going room to room, searching for anything that might help us.

Ludenhorff was a silvery, chubby mummy, head jutting above the chair.

Glasses askew. Face and mouth puffy where I'd beaten him. Hair tousled. Blood crusty beneath his nose and mouth. But the eyes had regained intensity. I had to admire the force in him. He looked more furious than scared. Tough.

"Who are you?" I said.

He hissed at me, "You can't imagine what you're screwing up."

"Tell me how high this goes."

He gasped for air. "Save yourself. Make a swap. Me for you. The disk for life. Safety. Money."

"Tom Schwadron said that. Look what happened to him."

The rest of the downstairs had looked as bland as he did when we'd dragged him through it. Modern furniture. Wall-to-wall carpeting. Unremarkable paintings of nature scenes—waterfalls and canyons—the kind of art sold at shopping malls, not auction houses. Glass coffee and dining room tables, all light and reflection and sharp angles. Apartment filler that bachelors buy in a single rushed day of shopping—to get the task out of the way.

But the study was different. The study was love. "A man's study is his state of mind," Barney Birnbaum at the FBI used to say. And *this* study was dark wood and leather furniture, pipe smells, Iraqi Shiite throw rugs, three solid walls of overstuffed, floor-to-ceiling, well-thumbed books. Hardbacks, not paperbacks. Cataloged and arranged, hundreds of volumes, mostly history and politics, from what I could see. Arranged by subject. *Security in the Age of Terror. Democracy and Safety; strange bedfellows. The US in Decline.*

And on the fourth wall, the trophy wall above the bar, bits of personal history in which he took pride. The University of Chicago Ph.D. in Government. The photo of Ludenhorff with former National Intelligence Director A. J. Carbone at a Senate hearing, Paul beside Carbone. A shot of Paul in the Mideast somewhere, in a Humvee with army officers— Ludenhorff goofy-looking in a business suit and combat helmet, the army guys bareheaded, as if no danger existed except for the kind in Ludenhorff's head. I recognized the type of picture. You see them in homes of Washington desk drivers. It was an I-was-in-danger-for-five-minutes picture. Paul had probably spent two hours in a war zone before being flown quickly out.

"Why were you in the Mideast?" I asked.

"Because he's Deputy Director, NIA," Danny said. He'd been rifling the desk. He held up an ID from Ludenhorff's wallet, showing Paul's face beneath black letters.

Ludenhorff groaned, from pain or anger. He couldn't even move a hand, but ordered hoarsely, "Get away from the computer. You're breaking the law just looking at it."

"*I'm* breaking the law?" I said.

Danny shrugged. "Is it my fault you left it on while you ran out of the house? And what's *this* on the side of the desk, Mr. Director? A hidden safe, *left open*? A *gross* violation of security. I'm shocked!" The panel was slid aside. Danny wagged his finger at Ludenhorff like a first-grade teacher. "He's signed onto *Sipranet,* Boss."

"Turn that off," Ludenhorff raged.

"Sipranet?" I said.

"Closed-loop Internet, encrypted and protected. We used it in the Philippines. He can send e-mails to anyone else in the loop, safe as the Air Force Cheyenne Mountain bunker. Hmm. Here's an interesting-looking site. Alphasitesecurity.army.mil. Let's click on it."

"People like you, people who try to stop progress, are the first to die in revolutions," Ludenhorff said. Cheery guy.

Danny told me as he waited for information to swim up, "He's got a removable drive like ours at Lenox, and a great big 'Classified' stamp on his files."

I blocked out a sudden image of Kim, in the Explorer, looking as if she were dozing in the backseat. I saw Kim wrapped in a sleeping bag, lying on a stranger's porch. "Tell me about Naturetech," I said to Ludenhorff, trying to control myself.

"Nature what?"

I stepped up to him and hit him, snapping his head back. I jammed my gun into his mouth and felt teeth crack against steel. His glasses flew off. His eyes, even without them, remained dark and focused, and he reminded me of a rat I'd caught in a glue trap years ago, in a Manhattan apartment. The rat had been unable to move, but unlike a mouse, which would have been trembling with terror, it had glared with antagonism, waiting for an opportunity to lunge.

His face was so lumpy from blows that he looked like he had the mumps. Blood oozed from his lips.

"Naturetech," I repeated. I turned away from him, I ejected the Glock's magazine and spun back and jammed the gun into his mouth, driving it in. I pulled the trigger, heard the *snap*. He screamed and screamed but he didn't answer.

Through tears, he smiled, as if daring me to fire.

"All my life people made fun of me," Ludenhorff said when I pulled the gun back. " 'Fat boy.' 'Four eyes.' 'Blimpo.' Go fuck yourself."

Well! He certainly didn't act as mild as he looked.

Danny called over, "Alphasite *is* Naturetech, Boss. Here's an e-mail from Teaks. They completed synthesis at three this afternoon. They're shipping the first batch in the morning."

I felt a hollow throbbing in my belly. *So that's what the celebration was before.*

"And *here*," Danny said, "we find a list of people who will get our wonder drug . . . but shit, it's in code. Twelve doses to 'Washington.' Forty to 'Jefferson,' 'Betsy Ross.' 'Revere.' Hell, I thought they were dead. Guess they got over it, huh, Paul?"

"Who are these people?" I demanded.

Ludenhorff's eyes shifted between Danny and me. "Make a deal," he said, like a broken record. Maybe he thought if he kept repeating it, I'd do it. "I'll call your prevention off."

"My *prevention*," I repeated. I never tire of Washington euphemisms. *Prevention* meant murder.

"You can stop the Royces?" I asked.

He hesitated. He nodded. He knew them.

"And the troops from Carolina. You have the power to tell them to leave us alone too?"

"I can phone someone," he admitted.

"Someone in the White House?"

He went blank. I had no idea what he was thinking.

"Someone in the Pentagon?"

Not a twitch, grunt, tell of any kind. I wouldn't want to play poker against this man. But I was.

I switched subjects. "How come you went to Naturetech alone today?" I asked. "Guys at your level get full-time drivers. Didn't want a witness?"

"I toured the installation. It's part of my job."

"Yeah, you look pretty powerful to me," Danny said, "taped up like a new microwave oven in a box."

Ludenhorff swiveled to him. His voice was raspy. The gun must have damaged his vocal cords but not his resolve. "Your wife's caught a cold on that Canadian reservation, Danny. Your son's learning hockey. Still think they're safe?"

"I'm just a dumb aborigine." Danny shrugged, giving away nothing, but he had to be terrified for his family. He ran two fingers down his cheeks, as if smearing on war paint. "We never learn."

Danny went back to scanning files, the blue laptop light reflected on his face. He was a crackerjack at his job.

"Here's the access list for Naturetech tonight, Boss. Everyone allowed on the grounds. Fifteen guards. Shift times. Captain Robert Van Tries is in charge. Hell, here's the name of a dog patrolling the perimeter—Schnowzie."

Ludenhorff said, "All you have to do is go along. Leave. Go home. Live." His eyes flicked toward the open safe. I saw extra computer hard drives there, metal boxes the size of old eight-track tapes. I saw manila folders.

Eisner was upstairs, going room by room, searching for anything that might help us.

Danny read the labels out loud. " 'HR-109 in Military Interrogations.' 'Synthesis Progress.' 'Alicia Dent.' And we open that one, and hey! it's a list of payments to the journalist. She's not his girlfriend. He just pays her. And *here's* a news story she did—unpublished—about former Director Carbone's wife. Alcohol abuse. Detox center visits. Screaming sessions at midnight. What did you do, Paul, threaten to release this if Carbone didn't resign? You're pretty loyal to your ex-boss, you scumbag."

"An alcoholic wife is a liability for someone in Intelligence. He hid her problem from the White House. He *should* have resigned."

"So someone in the White House *is* involved."

Ludenhorff didn't answer. I demanded, "Who is Revere?"

"A dead patriot."

"Is Alicia Dent Betsy Ross?"

"Find her attractive, do you?"

I hit him again. I reversed the gun and smashed it into his shinbone. His scream went on. But his hatred was stronger than his physical pain. He gasped, "Once in a while . . . something comes along that . . . changes history. Gunpowder. The nuclear bomb. *Enhance.*"

"Oh. History killed Dwyer and Kim."

"Dwyer tried to ride the tiger and it ate him. It will eat you. You don't have the talent to break me. You don't have the instinct. You don't have enough knowledge to know if I'm lying. Killing me won't help you. It's too late."

Then Eisner walked into the room, dangling a small plastic Baggie in his hand. The light caught the sheen. In the Baggie lay an inch of herblike substance, like marijuana. It jiggled as Eisner shook it. There wasn't a lot of 109 in there. But there was enough for three or four doses.

I said, "Is that what I think it is?"

Ludenhorff froze at the sight of it. He stopped looking as confident as Dr. Kissinger.

"That's mine," he whispered.

He made a welcome sound then.

He screamed with rage.

He was right that I'm not a torturer. We made a strategic decision, deciding to interrogate him after the drug kicked in. But we put the time to use. We ransacked his house, going through his safe, bills, closets, photos, clippings.

"Look at this," Danny said, scrolling through Ludenhorff's computer files. "He's like every other high-level shitheel I ever put away. Naturetech's a total covert op. He diverted funds from Homeland Security for the brig in Carolina. He's got a backdoor communication link here to Otto and the security desk at Naturetech. He can monitor their memos, reports, e-mails. They can't see his. He can send instructions straight to the lab if he wants."

His other files involved legitimate security issues: nuclear weapons development overseas, secret ops in Europe, surveillance reports on foreign charities suspected of operating as terrorist fronts in the US.

Outside his house, as we worked and Eisner went upstairs again, a summer block party started up on the street. Music. Beer. Friendly neighbors. Now we couldn't take Ludenhorff to our car even if we wanted to. Great.

At length, Danny said, "I thought 109's supposed to kick in after three hours. I don't feel a thing."

Hoot hadn't called, and I was growing worried about her, but at least Gabrielle checked in from the Internet shop, to report that she'd found references to Ludenhorff on Google. The earliest one was about an essay he'd written as a poli-sci professor at the University of Chicago, urging full-scale military strikes against Colombian drug lords and even street gangs in the US. Later his name popped up in relationship to the "Six-Thirty Club," an exclusive breakfast group on Capitol Hill that *Washingtonian* magazine mentioned in a wrap-up piece titled "Power Brokers You Don't See. Informal Groups with Big Clout."

"Read what it says out loud," I told Gabrielle.

"Okay. 'The Six-Thirty Club—as secrecy-obsessed members call it—reportedly meets at staggered times for breakfast and consists of ultra-right-wingers so militant they've been shunned by better-known neocon groups. They are rising stars in Washington, teaming up to further personal agendas and careers.' "

By ten-thirty, chilled by Gabrielle's words, I found Ludenhorff's Ph.D. thesis from U Chicago in his library: "Small Groups That Changed History." The subject matched titles lining one section of shelves. I opened a few books.

The Jacobians was about "the men who engineered the French Revolution." *Between Midnight and Six* told the story of the night the Bolsheviks completed the takeover of Russia, combining legal maneuvering with murder behind the scenes. *The Colonels* took readers step by step through a coup in Greece that, the book said, "saved that country from communism." And *The Daring* lauded American revolutionaries: Washington, Ross—names assigned to people in Ludenhorff's secret files.

Danny scratched his arm. "I'm feeling like I've got ten thousand mosquito bites. Was it like that for you, Boss, before 109 kicked in?"

"Not that bad."

"It's almost eleven o'clock. How come I don't feel anything except this damn itching?"

"How do I know," I snapped, and went back to Ludenhorff, who was relaxing more by the minute as the drug failed to take effect on us. "You seem to have revolution on your mind," I said.

"Order," he said.

"Murder."

"Safety."

"Is that what you call killing Kim? An act of safety?"

He hesitated. I think he hadn't known Kim was dead. But he rallied. "I haven't harmed anyone. I'm sorry if she got hurt. But even during benevolent transitions, a few people suffer."

His eyes flickered to the book in my hand, *The French Revolution*. For an instant his face assumed a benign, even academic air. Duct-taped to a chair, he actually lectured. "Robespierre engineered the Reign of Terror but saved France for democracy. A thousand discontents lost their heads, yes, but after that, centuries of culture, strength."

"Don't forget warm croissants," Danny said.

Ludenhorff looked like an irritated professor glaring at a heckler. "Better a little suffering during transition than total failure and collapse."

"Transition to what?"

"A peaceful world cared for by those with the intelligence and capability to do so."

I was tired of this kind of talk. "You're the third guy I've heard say that," I snapped. "Dwyer wanted to limit Enhance to people like him, Schwadron too. Now you. It's funny. No one ever feels unworthy of 109. It's always the other guy who can't be trusted. Let's get back to the code names in your files. Are they in your Six-Thirty Club?"

Thoughts clicked like abacus beads behind his eyelids. He seemed surprised that I knew about the group. "It's a study group, Mr. Acela. Nothing more. We meet once in a while and read books and talk politics. It's what people *do* in Washington. Talk."

I was wondering, *Why hasn't the drug taken effect?* "You're a fanatic," I said.

"Eye of the beholder. Christ was a fanatic to the Romans. By the way, Colonel Otto will be calling soon, and if I don't answer the phone, he'll come. If I were you, I'd be gone by then."

"Then why mention it? I'd think you'd want us here if that happened."

He shrugged. "Not if I'm caught in a fight. I can't exactly move if bullets start flying. I'm telling the truth, which you'd realize if Enhance were working. But the drug has an expiration date. It's useless after that. *That* was the synthesis problem. You took it four hours ago and it still hasn't kicked in. Worthless."

He smiled broadly. "Sorry," he said.

I hit him because I was afraid he was right. Because Kim was dead. Because he was tied up, and still winning. I hit him for wrong reasons and right ones. I couldn't stop, and Danny let it go on. I felt helpless. But I wasn't a torturer. Through my fury I became ashamed of myself. I saw myself hitting a man in a chair and I stopped.

A failure at this, even.

Danny said, "Leave the room, Mike. I have no problem with beating the living shit out of this turd."

Ludenhorff said, "Otto will be at the door."

The clock chimed. The phone rang, as he'd predicted. Colonel Otto's familiar voice floated from the answering machine. "Where are you, sir? Is something wrong?"

"Twenty minutes," Ludenhorff said.

There was a sudden scraping sound from the corner. I spun to see that Danny had shoved his chair back so hard it fell. I thought he'd finally been goaded to lose control. But he was staring at his wrist, openmouthed, eyes enormous.

To Ludenhorff he said, with growing wonder, "You're not as confident as you look."

Danny extended his wrists to me. The purple spots were thick and bright. In awe, Danny whispered, "It's like a voice shouting in my head. Was it like that for you, Boss?"

And suddenly it hit me too, with the force of a mental sledgehammer. *No one is coming for Ludenhorff.*

This time the certainty was beyond merely powerful, exactly as Schwadron had predicted. If last time had felt like a voice crying out in my head, *this* time was a choir, a crowd, a single-minded mob burning up my synapses.

He's lying.

"A study group, huh?" I said.

Ludenhorff looked from Danny to me. His bluff had failed. His confidence disintegrated into a jumble of conflicting emotions, as if his facial muscles were having trouble arranging themselves. He didn't know what to do. He didn't know what role to play. He was realizing he couldn't play *any* role but a real one. I felt this. I *knew* it.

"Twenty questions, Paul," Danny said.

Ludenhorff looked terrified. Stunned. Trapped.

And then suddenly he did something that astounded me.

He started singing.

Well, shouting, actually. Shouting a Christmas carol.

Danny gasped. "What is he . . . 'Jingle Bells'? Whaaaa?"

I stared at the incomprehensible scene.

It was insane. Lunatic. He'd just opened his mouth and the words came out—high, loud, frantic, off-key. Screamed and barely intelligible. A tune for happy people, bursting from a man covered in blood, bound to a chair.

"Dashing through the snowwww . . ."

He's gone off the deep end, I thought.

But then my enhanced sense smashed into me. I saw what he was doing, and it was logical, all right, so logical that it filled me with hope and wonder.

He's not crazy! He's blocking us out on purpose.

". . . a one horse . . . la la laaaa . . ."

The singing made sense now, lots of it.

He's trying to drown out his own thinking and hearing. He knows that otherwise 109 will give it away.

And I also saw something else, crystal clear now.

He's been bluffing for hours.

"Gag him, Danny."

I swung a wooden chair so I could sit directly in front of Ludenhorff. His eyes were huge above the gag. Sweat popped on his forehead as he breathed through flared nostrils like a frightened horse. He swung his head away, squeezed his eyes shut. He was afraid to look at me. He knew what could happen if he did.

"Just a couple questions," I said.

There's an art to interrogating while under the influence of 109, and we stumbled onto it quickly. You ask yes-or-no questions. That makes it easier to read intent. You avoid questions requiring explanations. You narrow down answers in the drive to reach the truth.

"How high does knowledge of the misuse of 109 go? Is the President involved?"

He didn't respond out loud. He didn't have to. I sensed the answer.

Ludenhorff did not seem to know.

"The White House Chief of Staff?" I asked. He had no idea. I tried the name of an ultra-right-wing political strategist who had the new President's ear.

He shook his head no, trying to fool me, I saw, because the real answer boomed into my skull, as concrete as the room around me. *Yesyesyesssssss.*

"Do you know the real names of the people getting the drug tomorrow?"

Yes.

"Is Colonel Otto making the actual deliveries?"

Yes, came the voice in my head.

"Holy shit," Eisner suddenly gasped, entering the room. He held his head in both hands. He had an openmouthed look of awe on his face that I recognized. "So *that's* what it's like," he said. "Can I ask one?"

He stepped up to Ludenhorff. "You and Otto work with the same people, then. Are these people in the Six-Thirty Club?"

Yes.

"Oh, baby. I *love* this," Eisner said. "Most people have something to hide. You use HR-109 to find it out. Is Alicia Dent a member of the Six-Thirty Club?"

Yes.

"So," I said, reasoning out loud, pausing at the end of each fragment, waiting for the surge of certainty or hesitation that would direct me further. "So, the old President and A. J. Carbone were driven out because they didn't agree with some agenda, some big plan. . . ."

Yes.

"They must have done something pretty bad for them to resign without a fight."

Yes.

I felt giddy, majestic, at least for a moment, before realizing the scope of what I was hearing. I focused on his face the way I'd never looked at anyone's before. Not as a mass of coordinated muscle, but a thousand signposts and twitches, hints of truth. Schwadron had been right: Last time 109's effect had been foggy compared to this. I saw what questions to ask, what connections to make, what assumptions to use. His fear and terror were like arrows pointing at truths.

I was a god looking down at humans, who could never hide what they thought, believed, desired, sought to conceal.

A drug-fueled palace coup.

Eisner asking him, testing our theories, "Did you first

learn of the existence of HR-109 from your boss, A. J. Carbone?"

Yes.

"Were *you* brought on board originally for a logistics purpose? Maybe sent to the Mideast to bring the drug overseas and report back to Carbone on its effectiveness?"

Yes.

"Did you bring in Colonel Otto?"

No. The person in the White House had done that.

"Is Colonel Otto the one who did the interrogations overseas, so the secret would stay hidden?"

Yes.

"Did you later give the drug to Alicia Dent, so she could dig up dirt on people and get them to resign?"

Yes.

"Did you and Colonel Otto set up a separate unit of the Army, answerable to you, to help safeguard the secret?"

No.

Eisner frowned, thought, rephrased the question. "Was the counterinsurgency unit already in place when you found out 109 exists? You run the Royces, Colonel Otto controls the troops?"

Yes.

"Did you tell the Royces to kill Dwyer and get back the item he took from Naturetech?"

"I didn't," Ludenhorff shrieked.

Yesssssssss, went the booming certainty in my head.

It was so easy, as easy as getting truth from a real friend. Normally, interrogations are conducted over weeks, at special locations. The subject is studied and probed by experts. Barney Birnbaum had trained me in rudimentary debriefing and interrogation. Taught me how to ask the same question a dozen ways, to catch an error or lie. To employ strategies designed to trick, cajole, befriend, frighten.

Take your time—rush and screw up, Barney had said. But we had to rush now.

"Did you order Schwadron killed?" Eisner asked.

Yes.

"Will Keating be murdered too eventually?"

Keating's being blackmailed, so there's no need, I realized. *Ludenhorff also uses 109 to force lots of people in Washington— important people—to go along. Once you know their secrets, you're in control. Another few months of this, fueled by Enhance, and there will be no turning back.*

"Does Otto take orders from you?"

He swung his head wildly. He made noises under the gag, tried to drown us out. Tears of rage ran from his eyes, but the certainty in my head—the sense of him scheming even against Otto—was clear.

Ludenhorff expects to be appointed the new director, I thought. *Otto will take orders from him then.*

I asked if the reporter we'd contacted at the *Washington Post* was involved.

No.

"This'll really stand up in court," Danny remarked. "We testify that he admitted nothing but gave off guilty vibes. That ought to go over big with a jury."

But my own excitement was rising. "Why were you celebrating at Naturetech this afternoon, Paul?"

His eyes widened as he realized we knew about it. I picked up strong emotion, fear, but not facts.

"Ask yes-or-no questions, Boss," Danny reminded me.

"Were you celebrating because the drug has been synthesized finally?"

Yes.

"So tomorrow's shipment will be the very first one of the fully synthesized drug?"

His panic was growing. I was close to a key point, but what was it? I felt vulnerability in him.

Ludenhorff twisted in the chair and tried to loosen his bonds. It was impossible. His face was a mask of hate. All intellect gone. The mouth a feral line and the eyes small, as his chest heaved with emotion. In a normal interrogation *maybe* we would have uncovered this. If we were lucky. If we were good. If we believed him. If we had time.

Eisner stepped up beside me. His voice went quiet with emotion. "This drug could have been so beneficial."

Ludenhorff nodded. He seemed to want the gag off, so we complied, with a warning that he'd better not scream again. He licked his lips to give them moisture. He said, "Yes, beneficial. To help people!"

Panicked, I thought.

I stared into his face, the key to answers. I saw the pores in his skin moving as he breathed. I tried to reason out his plans, but remembered I didn't have to. Not under 109. I only had to ask the right questions.

I asked, "If the drug is being shipped tomorrow, where is the supply tonight?"

"Ask yes-or-no questions," Danny said again, sighing.

I cursed and started again. "Was the drug at Naturetech?" *Yes.* "All of it, except what we found here?" *Yes.* "What about records and formulas? Were they at Naturetech too?" I asked, bearing down, my own pulse roaring.

Yes.

"Are there duplicate records *outside* Naturetech? Or is everything in the facility, copies too? Total covert op."

"You won't get in," Ludenhorff croaked, looking horrified. "They'll stop you."

And now I saw the only chance to stop what was about to happen. *Danny was right. Take away the supply.*

Danny returned to the desk, to the wireless encrypted laptop. He started typing. After a minute, he turned the screen around so I could see what he'd called up.

"The access list at Naturetech. Remember?" he said.

"Nonononono!" Ludenhorff cried.

I ignored him and asked Danny, "Even if we put our names on it, what's our excuse for showing up there at two A.M.?"

But I answered my own question. "Spot security check."

Danny grinned and opened his wallet, to his old Lenox ID. Eisner shrugged, hunted in his back pocket and produced *his* wallet, his Department of Defense card. I had my old ID also, identifying me as head of Lenox Security.

"Help us out with the long odds," Danny told Ludenhorff. "Have the guards been informed of our names? Or are they just plain old grunts, who never heard of us?"

"They'll kill you!"

Danny gagged him again, more tightly this time. Saliva dripped past the cloth. The answer was obvious.

The guards don't know our names, I thought.

I asked Ludenhorff, "Can we put ourselves on the access list from your computer, by pretending to be you?"

He shook his head, but the answer was yes.

"Does Colonel Otto also have access? If we make the change and he calls up the list, will he see our names?"

We could never try this in a million years without Enhance.

Eisner sighed. "It's the middle of the night, Mike. Otto won't call up the access list. There's no reason to. He's probably asleep."

"You hope," Danny said.

I was thinking that Danny and I had already walked through Naturetech's security system. I remembered the layout, the electrical and alarm wiring, the lab's location. The lab was filled with chemicals that could explode, burn, eat away metal and plastic. Destroy.

Worry about proving what you did later. First destroy the fucking drug.

"You'll walk us through the process, Paul."

He was gagging.

Danny sat at the computer like a happy secretary ready to take dictation. It was time to risk everything, I thought.

"Give it to us step by step," I told the frothing, struggling man duct-taped to his chair. "Now, access. Step one . . ."

TWENTY-TWO

When we walked out of that house an hour later, Ludenhorff's block looked the same on the surface, but it felt like a different planet. The trees were still there. It was summer. But for me the world had divided itself into two sorts of people. Intuitive giants and everyone else.

At one A.M. most of America is sleeping, but Georgetown is one of those cosmopolitan areas where people stay out late. In my enhanced condition, I was like a psychic who could suddenly see beneath the facade that humans put on. An elegant, proud-looking man strolled toward me, wearing a tuxedo, walking a sleek saluki on a leash. But when I concentrated on the man, desperation came off him in waves, like flies off rotted food.

Is he having trouble at home? Or on the job?

Two students—on opposite sides of the street—walked casually toward the university, seemingly oblivious to each other. I turned my attention to them.

They're excruciatingly aware of each other. They want to talk to each other. Why doesn't one of them make a move?

A limo pulled up to a townhouse and dropped off a woman in a silky white gown. She looked to be in her early fifties: platinum hair, slim legs, strapless sandals. She blew a kiss to the person inside, waved, flashed a big smile.

She can't wait to get away from him, I knew, walking past. It wasn't speculation, but certainty that came without being summoned. These strangers might well have been dogs, telegraphing their mood with wagging tails. I couldn't read their thoughts, of course. But their raw intent was clear.

"Cathy Ann Pratt," Eisner said wistfully as we walked to retrieve the parked Acura. "I had a crush on her in sixth grade. But I never figured out how she felt about me. I never had the guts. I used to wish she had a light-bulb over her head—y' know, glowing red if she liked me, green if she didn't. Dumb, huh?"

"Red and green. Was this a girl or a traffic light?" Danny asked.

Eisner eyed a Domino's delivery car pulling up across the street. "Let's test if we're in sync. The pizza guy."

We turned toward the kid who'd gotten out of the car, carrying a Domino's warm-up bag. He passed us beneath a streetlight, a pimply teen with bad posture and a vapid expression. But I felt the kid's mind going a mile a minute. I felt him concentrating on something that had nothing to do with pizza. A wave of cold distraction washed over me. Of focus and brilliance.

Danny said, "Science or math. It's not personal."

Eisner said, "This is one serious guy."

I stopped the guy by calling out, "Hey! Kid!"

He turned, neither fearful nor curious. Simply waiting.

Eisner went obnoxiously tipsy, as if he were drunk. He slurred his words, "My buddies and I were in the bar, see? We made a bet. A telegraphic . . . ha-ha . . . *telepathic* s'periment. I'll give you ten bucks to tell us what you're thinking. I say you're thinking about a tall redhead at the beach. Getting laid."

Danny rubbed his forehead theatrically, like a bad medium. "You're thinking you're hungry," he said.

I shook my head. "*Casablanca*! The movie, right?"

The kid pocketed the bill Eisner held out.

"You're all wrong. I'm thinking about a paper I have to write on recombinant DNA."

Bye-bye, pizza guy, I thought as he carried his hot pie up the townhouse steps.

We looked at one another. "I'm not sure I like this," Danny said.

Eisner sighed. "I wonder if I'd still be living in Indiana if Cathy had had the hots for me."

We reached the Acura and drove off toward the all-night lot where Ludenhorff kept his precious Caddy. We'd taken his registration, keys and card to exit the lot. His wireless laptop too, and his files. I imagined Naturetech as it looked from Deer Run Park. The one-story facility would be starkly lit, atop the highest ground in the compound, surrounded by, in jagged concentric areas, thick trees, electrified fence inside the outer barbed-wire fence, 150 yards away. Beyond that would be the neighbors: the horse farm, the corn farm and a satellite company.

Situated on the grounds would be floodlights turned on at night, and roving guards.

Inside, as the electronic security had not been changed since I'd been fired—according to Ludenhorff's files—we'd find Lenox's standard array of interlocking precautions: motion detectors that triggered alarm systems, LED cameras monitored by guards, card access for the lab and a four-digit Moseler safe inside. Its combination had been in Ludenhorff's files too.

"Fifteen guards," I said. "One at the gate. Two at the

security station. The rest floaters. If the duty officer checks out names with Alonzo Otto while we're there . . ."

Danny said, "Relax. We may not even *get* inside."

He looked calm. He always did. But I sensed his heart beating like a snare drum. "You're not as confident as you look, Danny."

"Don't start with me."

But I couldn't help it. I wasn't just picking up what strangers felt, but friends too. Then it occurred to me that Danny and Eisner would sense my feelings also.

Eisner spoke up in the silence. "I know, Mike," he said. "Pretty weird, huh?"

We'd stolen a pocket camera from Ludenhorff's house, flashlights, a thick blanket to lay over a fence and a Sony miniature recorder. We'd record as much as we could inside Naturetech. Along with Ludenhorff's disks and files—minus the synthesis formula and bit of sample remaining in the bag, which we might still need tonight—we'd pass all evidence to the FBI and the press.

If we get in and out alive.

Eisner drove the Caddy, Danny and I the Acura. We headed down Q Street toward 13th, hoping Gabrielle would still be at La Taqueria.

Danny laughed. "My favorite part was telling Ludenhorff we were taking his car. Beating him up didn't bother him half as much as that."

We fell silent, mentally preparing, feeling the wash of chemicals inside. I was aware of solid support from the man beside me, kinship and trust beyond a level previously experienced.

I remembered Dwyer on his last night, staring at me, telling me he trusted me.

"I didn't know you cared, dear," Danny said.

"Turn on the radio," I snapped. "See if there have been any developments."

The itching had stopped but the drug should stay in our systems a few more hours, hopefully long enough to get in and out of Naturetech. I stopped at a red light, and saw a Metro squad car idling beside us. The cop glanced at us, expressionless.

He's exhausted, I thought. *No threat.*

"Shift's up, I bet," Danny said as we started off.

Next time we halted, at V and 13th, a pretty young prostitute sauntered up to my window. Waifish figure. Stiletto heels. Short gold dress that showed off coltish legs. She had to be no more than 17, young enough so her face still showed her real age, innocent-looking although she wasn't. She smiled. "Want a date?" she asked.

A wave of revulsion washed through me.

She feels dirty. Sick. Diseased.

There was no doubt of this. It was fact, as real and obvious as a tank coming down a highway.

"See a doctor," I advised gently. Startled, she backed away, eyes huge, lip trembling as she retreated into the darkness between parked cars. I imagined her face shrinking into hollows, the hollows dissolving into bone. A whiff of corrupted perfume lingered.

Danny punched in 911 on his encrypted cell phone. "Just to be safe," he said. "I live on V and 13th," he told the police operator. "There's a prostitute outside my house. Pick her up. She looks sick."

His phone buzzed as our two-car convoy reached Florida and 13th, and I parked outside La Taqueria.

"Danny," he said, answering. He listened and frowned. "I agree. Go home," he said, then hung up.

"Hoot never got off the train, Boss," he said. "At least not at Ticonderoga."

"You think she was taken?"

That's why she never called in. If Hoot's been captured, if she talked, that would wreck the whole plan.

A wave of futility hit me. I envisioned Hoot in a cell, trembling and blurting out information, saying the word *Naturetech.* And the name Alonzo Otto. She would not have known about Paul Ludenhorff. But if Ludenhorff's people had her, they'd be trying to reach him right now.

Maybe she simply panicked and got off the train.

"I'll understand if you want to quit, Danny."

"If we do that we'll never stop distribution."

La Taqueria was the only store on the block still open. The neon sign flickered, and the Latino music washing out was fast but muted. No one here wanted police showing up. The Internet joint next door was dark. Eisner and Danny waited in our respective cars as I went in to get Gabrielle.

I was so concerned about her and Hoot that I'd not prepared mentally for what was about to happen. I'd always found La Taqueria a friendly place. Now a wall of fear smashed into me the second I strolled in. I practically staggered back from its weight. No one was moving, but the crash of emotion might as well have been men running for exits.

They're afraid of me, I thought.

My eyes adjusted to the dim light. I looked around. Small dark men wearing tractor caps sat in pairs or threes in booths, before long-necked beer bottles and plates of papusas or enchiladas. No one looked at me. They didn't seem to notice me.

They think I'm with Immigration, I thought, my headache worsening as if I were absorbing all this emotion.

Gabrielle was weaving toward me down the aisle, from a vinyl booth in back.

I wanted to tell the men that there was nothing to worry about, but that would make things worse. I needed to get control of myself. I realized that with the intuitive part of my brain heightened, my emotions had more free rein than usual. My indiscriminate power was disgusting to me. I'd violated these men. I didn't want the responsibility of knowing their fears. Their collective scrutiny was a sourness in the pit of my stomach, a bile in my throat.

So I focused on the lovely woman walking toward me, and a second blast of certainty flowed into me. It must have shown in my face. She halted a foot away, puzzled.

She loves me. I don't want to know this. Not after what happened to Kim.

I wiped sweat off my forehead. The headache was spiking, as if the intent of others—their fears and desires—had weight and collected inside me, except there wasn't enough room. The pain throbbed between my eyes, clutched at the base of my brain.

No way to deny what I felt or even suggest that I might be wrong. Dr. Whiteagle had guessed that humans selectively used 109, to zero in on subjects, but the effect was more rampant tonight. Maybe the second batch was producing a stronger effect. Maybe, as Schwadron said, the power grew with usage. Maybe I was so keyed up that the drug put its stamp on everyone around me. I wasn't a fucking scientist. All I knew was that I wanted this to stop.

"Mike, why are you looking at me like that?"

The words calm, the face coldly beautiful, but I saw through the mask to her vulnerable center. I had power over her that I didn't want.

She's afraid for me. More for me than for herself.

"Nothing's wrong. Let's get out of here," I said.

I didn't tell her we'd found more 109 at first. None of us did. It was an unspoken agreement as we sat in the Caddy and made plans. Later I'd think back and see this as the first moment the drug gained power over me, but at the time I told myself it was more important to concentrate on Naturetech. I felt my rage extend sensation out like antennae. I burned energy at a fantastic rate. A fire raged inside.

I heard Gabrielle saying, "Danny, is that a purple rash on your neck?" She was staring at him—eyes boring into him.

"Um, yeah. Um . . . we found some 109."

"You mean you *took* it?"

"Um . . . yes."

"All of you?"

"I was going to tell you," I said. "I was. Really. We're keeping it in case we need it later."

She went red. Her eyes probed us one by one and settled on me. I didn't need a drug to see the fury. "And what is 109 telling you about *my* intent at the moment, Mike? That I want to punch your face in? That you left me alone in a goddamned restaurant while you gobbled down drugs?"

"Something like that," I said.

"Give me some! Right now. If I'm coming with you, I need it too."

I produced the bag reluctantly. I didn't want to share it, especially now that I'd felt the new stronger effect. But the three mental giants had been reduced to the status of cowed four-year-olds. Danny actually hung his head. Ah, the power of angry women.

"I can't *be-lieve* you," she said, cupping her hand, tossing the last of the Enhance into her mouth. Her delicate white throat tipped, while she drank the drug down with water from a plastic bottle.

"Don't you *dare* guess what I'm thinking," she said.

"I didn't use it on you," I lied.

"What a considerate gentleman you are," she said. "I suppose you think I should thank you for that."

It was a relief to go back to planning.

I told Eisner and Gabrielle what Danny already knew, that with Hoot missing, the guards at Naturetech might know we were coming. I felt obligated to offer them another way out. Perhaps it would be better for them to slip away and hide, to hope the *Washington Post* got the story out the right way.

But I didn't want to hide. I'd been pressured so much, I'd crossed a line.

Eisner shook his head. "It'll take weeks for the *Post* to confirm the story," he said. "If they even can. If management's not in Otto's pocket, threatened or resigned by then."

Gabrielle agreed. "Do you really think Ludenhorff's going to just sit on his ass once he's out of that chair and he finds out a reporter is asking questions? He'll come after the reporter too, any way he can. Besides, you said the drug will be shipped tomorrow. After that, it's permanent. A permanent part of the world."

"Gabrielle, about not telling you before about, you know, taking 109 . . ."

"Don't go there, Mike. Don't even start."

So I explained the plan. She would take the Cadillac to Deer Run Park, and send a last-minute message to Naturetech on Ludenhorff's encoded, wireless laptop. Instructions from the great man himself to go with the updated access list we'd sent out from the house, an explanation that in exactly fifteen minutes a surprise security alert would begin at the lab. No live ammo to be loaded by either side, either "attackers" or "defenders," to avoid an accident. Duty officer to cooperate fully with Major Carl Eisner and Lenox Security's Michael Acela, who would arrive soon. Hitting SEND would shoot the message out via a private loop, trigger a buzz alarm at the Naturetech Security office, alerting the officer that an important message had just been sent.

All this knowledge thanks to Ludenhorff.

Never, in a million years, could we have tried anything this audacious without the drug in our systems.

"The key to pulling this off is to throw as many last-minute decisions as possible at the duty officer," I said.

Unfortunately, I also knew that Gabrielle's message would be visible to *anyone* eyeing the access list. Our gamble was that, hopefully, late at night no one who knew our names would be looking.

"After you send the message, get to the perimeter of the park and stay glued to the binoculars. If anything goes wrong . . . troops show up, or police . . . ring my cell phone once and hang up. Then get out immediately. Get to Canada if you can. Send Ludenhorff's files over the Internet, to Congress. CNN. *New York Times*. Your friends."

"Why not send it now?"

"Because if they know the news is out, we'll never get into Naturetech, and like you said, Gabrielle, once the drug goes out, there will be no way to stop it, even if we stop Ludenhorff."

Gabrielle burst out, "I can't believe you didn't tell me you had it, Mike."

"Danny will hit the back fence and set off the alarms," I said. "That should trigger the alert. If everything goes well afterward, we'll just drive off the way we came in. But if something goes wrong, we'll retreat out the loading dock, into the woods, to the fence. We can shut off the electricity from inside. Danny will leave the blanket by the fence before setting off the alarms. We toss the blanket over the barbed wire. We climb out."

"Yeah, a cinch," Danny said. "Can't you think of anything harder?"

What I was thinking was that in a few hours, Gabrielle would be high on 109 herself. It gave me a funny feeling. I didn't want her using the effect on me.

"Be careful," she said, relenting now that we were leaving.

"We'll be fine," Danny soothed. "We're young. We're pure. Well, maybe not young."

I tapped my rash. "Besides," I added, "we have a secret weapon."

Gabrielle sighed. "I'd rather have plain old luck."

The lights of Ludenhorff's Cadillac turned into Deer Run Park. They receded as Gabrielle drove up the hill.

A mile ahead was the glow of white lights bathing the grounds of Naturetech.

My headache was in my neck and shoulders now, pulling like ropes against my muscles. As I drove the Acura, Eisner checked our guns, sliding in clips, checking triggers, weight, heft. Contrary to our own "instructions," we'd keep live ammunition loaded during the alert, unless Van Tries objected, in which case we'd remove it.

"What if he takes our guns?" I said.

"Then we won't have them," Danny said from the back.

"We tell Van Tries," Eisner said, "that if our attackers have one of his men in their gunsights, and shout 'lay down,' that soldier will be assumed killed."

I told Eisner, "I'll need fifteen minutes in the lab. I have the combination to the safe, so fifteen minutes should be enough to get in, pour the acid, wreck the supply and computers. I'll keep the Minicam to shoot the contents of the safe. You hang on to the pocket recorder in case the guards have knowledge of the drug."

Danny reminded us, "The dog's name is Schnowzie."

Eisner sighed heavily. "Mike, those guards are going to be regular soldiers. American soldiers. If shooting starts, if things go wrong, will you be able to fire at them?"

"I don't know."

"My own people," said Eisner.

I asked myself, *How can this possibly work?*

Be careful what you ask for, the old saying goes. As a boy back in Brooklyn, reading books about the FBI, I'd dreamed of taking on enormous odds, fighting evil, saving my country. FBI agents don't usually end up thinking about their job that way, but it's generally how they start out.

What a jerk I was, I thought.

I pulled over by a pasture and split-rail fence a quarter mile from the Naturetech turnoff. The back door opened. Danny's big form drew off into the dark cornfield. The dead stalks didn't rustle. How the hell could a man move like that?

Eisner and I drove off again, and a minute later I was actually turning onto Naturetech's driveway, then slowing as we approached the guardhouse and bright lights.

WARNING, DEFENSE DEPARTMENT FACILITY. UNAUTHORIZED VEHICLES TURN AROUND, said a sign.

"Costa Rica is lovely this time of year," Eisner said. "With no extradition."

"Smile for the cameras, Carl."

My hands were wet on the steering wheel. A guard walked toward me, gliding around the headlights, speaking softly into his neck-mike, M-16 aimed at me. I tried to concentrate on what he might be intending, tried to aim my senses, but I was unsure suddenly how to do this. If I sensed recognition, it would mean he'd seen photos of us.

I picked nothing up.

What if the effect's stopped working? It's been hours.

I rolled down the window. The air smelled of grass and carried a chemical whiff that reminded me of seaweed. I thought, *They're making Enhance in there.* Then I saw the security camera aimed at me from on top of the gate, over the soldier's left shoulder. It would be broadcasting my face to the control room. I fought off an urge to back up the car. I heard Eisner's steady breathing. I had my wallet and Lenox ID out as the guard came up. Young guy. Thai or

Indonesian American. Alert and professional. Ludenhorff would not have entrusted such an important job to drones.

I hope Gabrielle sent the security alert.

"Can I help you, sir?"

I feel wariness, suspicion. But not recognition.

The black eyes flickered to Eisner's lap and back to my face. Our hands were exposed, our sidearms hidden. My words would be broadcast back to the control room through the guard's powerful mike.

"We're here for the drill," I said.

"Drill? What drill?"

Uh-oh.

"Defense Intelligence," Eisner said, holding up his wallet too as the guard frowned at our civilian car. Eisner said, "Where *is* everybody? Don't tell me you guys are just sitting around in there, on your asses?"

The soldier looked more closely at me. "Please remove the ID from the folder, sir."

He stepped back and held it up. He read my name out loud, into his mike, Eisner going irritated, ordering the guard to call the duty officer right away. Time was important, he said. He demanded to speak to Captain Van Tries immediately.

"Sir, I'm sorry. No one is to be admitted unless their name is on the access list."

"I suggest you *check* the access list."

Was Hoot captured? I suddenly wondered. *Are we still on the damn list, or were we taken off?*

The soldier retreated a few steps and spoke again into the mike. I couldn't hear what he was saying. The muzzle of his assault rifle started to rise. I resisted the urge to grab for my Glock.

Then I realized that he was spelling our names into the mike.

My back was sweating. My armpits were wet. I envisioned Danny working his way toward the fence through the cornfield. If Eisner or I sensed a problem, we'd hit the RING button on our cell phone. We'd tell the guard, "That's Colonel Otto on the line." We'd try to turn the car around.

Who are you kidding? I told myself. *If they're waiting for you, snipers have you in their sights right now.*

"Major Eisner?" the guard said, returning our wallets, "Captain Van Tries will meet you at the front entrance. Sorry to hold you up."

Thank you, God.

I put the car in gear, imagining Gabrielle in the park, watching through binoculars. The building grew closer. In the glare of floodlights a trio of uniformed men waited for us just outside the door. Officer out front. Two specialists behind, with M-16s.

"Ah, you didn't want to turn around back there, anyway," Eisner said, smiling. At that moment I actually felt a wave of *happiness* coming off him.

"Admit it, Mike," he said, as if monitoring my thinking. "Aren't you a little happy also?"

He was right. A rush of adrenaline hit me. "Commit yourself and just do it," my father used to say. The exhilaration that filled me—the sense of purpose—had nothing to do with 109.

The officer—Captain Van Tries—was in his late twenties, bulky with muscle, blond and hook-nosed, and he wore silver wire-framed glasses. Hands on hips. Posture perfect. Lit by headlights as he stepped up to the car.

"I just got the message about you, sir," he said. He had the accent of a slum kid from the Bronx.

High-ranking visitors show up unannounced at military facilities late at night for two reasons. The first is emergency. The second is surprise. Captain Robert Van Tries looked ready for both, examining our IDs, listening as Eisner verified that a drill would start imminently. The captain nodded at the no-live-ammunition part, but he kept eyeing the Acura.

Curious but not suspicious so far. Cooperative.

"Something wrong with our automobile?" Eisner asked.

"I'm wondering, sir, why you came in a civilian car."

"And *I'm* wondering," Eisner said, prepared for the question, "*since* it's a civilian car, why the guard at the gate didn't approach with more caution, especially in the middle of the night."

Van Tries colored.

"Don't you teach your people about car bombs?" Eisner said. "That guard should have issued instructions by loudspeaker. He should have stayed back and not approached, alone, on foot. What has all our experience in Iraq been worth, Captain, if we make the same mistakes over again?"

"I'll talk to that man, sir."

Easy so far, I thought. So easy.

Eisner pushing hard, trying to make Van Tries pliable. Telling him we were here to monitor his crew's response. Explaining as a command that he and I would split up. Eisner would stay with Van Tries during the alert. I would head for the main lab.

This, of course, was the big moment. *Go for it,* I urged.

"The lab, sir?" Van Tries asked.

He's just gotten a little suspicious.

"It's not a request, Captain," Eisner said. "It's an order."

"Yes, sir. It's just that no one is allowed in the lab. We don't even have cameras there. We're not supposed to see what the scientists are doing."

His suspicion is growing. Do something, Eisner, I thought.

Almost instantly Eisner changed his harsh tone to one that was more conspiratorial. "Captain," he said, as we waited for Danny to hit the fence and trigger the alarm. "Mike Acela is one of the men who set up the original security system here. This highly paid civilian expert maggot insists he's found a hole in your defenses, that *his* men can get past *yours.* I assured him that would never happen."

"No, sir," Van Tries said, responding better to the us-against-them approach.

"I not only expressed this thought to him verbally but backed it up by wagering my personal hero, General Ulysses S. Grant, a great fighter and brave man."

I imagined the picture of Ulysses Grant on a $100 bill.

Danny, hit the damn fence. What are you waiting for?

Captain Van Tries eyed me with polite condescension. He addressed Eisner. "You'll be one hundred dollars richer, then, Major."

"That's what I told the civilian maggot," Eisner said, grinning as if he and I were friendly rivals. "But he insists that his rent-a-cops will get into the main lab."

"The lab is locked. I don't have access," Van Tries said.

"I do," I said, holding up Ludenhorff's key card.

Van Tries's expression didn't change. We had the proper identification. He'd been instructed to help us. But *still* a small tick of warning started up in my head.

DANGERDANGER...

Where the hell is Danny?

Van Tries said, "Do you mind if I make a call, sir? Just to verify my instructions?"

I broke in witheringly, to stop him. "Captain, how many hours have you spent studying the air-vent systems in this facility?"

"Not many," he admitted.

"How many have you spent studying the layout of the old utility-company tunnel *outside* Naturetech, on that farm?"

I had no idea whether utilities had built tunnels there.

"Tunnel?" he said.

An alarm went off: shrill, insistent, coming from the direction of Deer Run Park.

"Amateurs," I shouted over the noise to Eisner, with a self-satisfied air. "I told you. Put this place back into the hands of my guys. *Professionals.* Send the clowns away."

From out on the grounds, I heard men shouting, dogs barking. Van Tries reacted to the noise instinctively. His performance was on the line. He had no time to make a call.

"All right. You can get into the lab if your key card works."

Eisner asked him quickly, "Aren't you forgetting something else?"

"Sir?"

"Is this a live-fire exercise?"

"I already took care of that when the alert came in."

Van Tries got on his radio. He sent out a message that a "drill" had started, not a real "attack." He reminded his men to remove live ammo from their weapons. He ordered, if they "apprehended attackers," to bring them in handcuffs to the security room. He gave them the exact instructions Gabrielle had sent over the Internet, about playing dead if they were "shot" by intruders.

Easy, I thought, moving down the hall alone, unwatched, toward the lab area.

All I had to do now was destroy the place in minutes.

I exulted, It's about time something was easy.

I should have known it was too easy.

I heard footsteps running after me. Sirens were whooping. I saw a soldier closing on me, assault rifle up.

"Stop!" he cried.

| TWENTY-THREE |

"Sir, you forgot to take a radio!" the soldier called out, running toward me.

I almost staggered with relief. The guard caught up with me ten feet from the heavy vaultlike door blocking off C wing, the hallway lined with labs. The kid looking more helpful than dangerous, 18 or 19 years old maybe, with an eager-to-please boyish face and air of excitement, as if the drill were a welcome diversion from boring night duty. BURGOYNE, read the stitched name on his shirt.

"You can talk directly to Major Eisner on this set, sir, and hear what's going on all over the grounds. It's got three channels."

His boots echoed on linoleum as we walked. His M-16 smelled of oil. His keys and radio equipment jangled, and he was so close, I could smell the garlic on his breath.

"Thanks," I said.

Go away now, I thought, reaching the door, aiming Ludenhorff's plastic key card at the slot.

But I heard him say, behind me, "Captain Van Tries said I'm to go into the lab with you."

I didn't let him see my face, but it was burning. The card went in and I held my breath, eyeing the red light that should be changing to green, but wasn't. How in

God's name could I possibly destroy the most important part of the laboratory with a minder watching me?

The light turned green.

I heard steel bolts moving inside the door.

I pushed it open, sweat dripping under my armpits, and pretended to misunderstand what he'd said, "No need to come along. I know where the lab is."

"Captain Van Tries said not to bother you."

"Aren't you needed elsewhere during a drill?"

"He said watch everything you did."

There was no time to argue. I started down the windowless hall tracked by a security camera overhead, with the kid beside me. I racked my brain for a way to make him go away. If he saw what I planned to do in the lab, and if he saw me photographing the contents of the safe, it would take him half a second to figure out this was no drill.

The lab door came up now, just beyond a grille inside of which lay the wiring, I knew, to the electrical alarm and lighting system for the west fence. I envisioned Danny outside the fence, circling, setting off alarms, making it seem like a whole team of "attackers" were breaching or probing defenses. I'd instructed him to let himself get caught entering the grounds after fifteen minutes. And we'd told Van Tries to have his men bring any prisoners to the control room. The plan was to have our assault fail. Danny would report that the tunnel outside was blocked. The Lenox team would have been thwarted. Van Tries would look victorious.

The three of us would drive off.

But the whole plan depended on speed, surprise and deception. With HR-109 to help us monitor reactions of the soldiers. And with me getting into the lab alone.

How did I come up with this stupid plan? I thought.

I tried one last time to keep Burgoyne from entering the lab with me. "You don't have clearance," I said.

"The captain said not to bother you, but not to leave you alone. We can stay out in the hallway together instead of going in, sir, if you want."

Great.

I cursed inwardly and slid the card into the slot, simultaneously punching in a three-number combo I'd memorized off Ludenhorff's file. The reader hummed electrically. The second access light glowed green.

I was in.

But so was Burgoyne, with his rifle and radio and ammo magazines.

"Wow," he said, looking around the bright, long room, as impressed as a seven-year-old during a first trip to the museum. "What *is* all this stuff, sir? You know, the guys joke about this place, call it a secret lab and all. Carver says it's anthrax they're working on here. Gonzales says it's engineered germs."

I grabbed the opportunity to try to scare him off. I said "Well, we probably *should* be wearing surgical masks for protection." His eyes widened. But he didn't leave.

Damn.

From inside the lab the alarm outside sounded muffled. Then a second alarm started going off inside C wing with a *whooooop-whooooop*. The lab was shiny clean, bright from banks of super-lights overhead. I'd been designing security for Lenox labs long enough to recognize some equipment. On the stone-topped tables were fractionaters to break down compounds and microscopes where researchers pored over Asa Rodriguez's dried rare fish. The workstations had "hoods," large metallic scoops equipped with lights and fans, to suck away fumes from solvents. The glass cabinets contained five-gallon brown glass jugs of chemicals, and rows of beakers with reagents mixed in them to try to reproduce Enhance. The microwaves and Bunsen burners were where researchers cooked compounds. The cyclotron was where they mixed them. The room seemed larger than I remembered, with only two people in it. It smelled of ozone and graphite, alcohol, linoleum polish and a hint of a warmed-over rancid American cheese sandwich wafting from a trash can no one had emptied today, below the AC vent. Everything was steel and glass and the walls were pastel green.

If Burgoyne gets on that radio and tells anyone what I'm going to do, the whole plan is over before it starts.

"This equipment is delicate and costly," I told him, racking my brain for a way to immobilize him. "Sit at a desk. I may move around a bit."

I could feel the clock ticking, the second hand on my watch moving as if it scraped my wrist. In one corner were desktop computers, each with a rectangular hole in its side, the entrance point for the metal cassettes containing removable hard drives. The drives and supply of synthesized 109 would be in the Moseler safe in the north corner, built of steel, bolted to the floor, toughest damn safe in the world, I knew. I'd been responsible for choosing Lenox's safes.

But thanks to Paul Ludenhorff's files, I knew the four-number combo, at least as of a few hours ago. It was 1775, the year the American Revolution began.

Asshole, I thought.

"What do we do now, sir?" Burgoyne spoke up from a corner chair. "Just wait to see if anyone gets in?"

We, I thought. *Me and Burgoyne. The team.*

"How many guys do you have trying to get in here anyway?" he went on. He was a talker, no matter what his instructions had been.

"Oh, I'm not supposed to tell you that," I said.

"Last time we had a drill we used paint guns."

That gives me an idea how to handle him, I thought.

The radio he'd handed me crackled and Eisner's voice came through so clearly, he might have been in the room. "Are you in the lab yet, Mr. Acela?"

"Yep. We're *both* here, Major. Private Burgoyne and I," I said, letting him know there was a snag, knowing that anyone on the security staff could be monitoring our conversation.

Eisner pretended to goad me. "So far our security team seems to have kept *your* people out," he said, letting me know that Danny was still free. "Want to double the bet? Your probes are setting off alarms. That's all."

My eyes flicked to the glass cabinet and brown jugs, their labels reading, "Sulfuric Acid," "Hydrochloric Acid," "Acetic Acid." I'd seen the kind of damage they could do, once, when a Lenox supply truck overturned outside one of our plants near Paris. The acids had eaten through the truck. They'd left smoke where tires had been. They'd left the glass windows unharmed. At the moment, I was looking at fluids you never wanted touching your skin. Hell, you didn't even want them within a hundred feet of your house.

"In ten minutes you'll change your mind about my team," I said, promising him to be finished by then.

Because if the alarms keep sounding and no attackers show up, Van Tries will get suspicious. And once Danny is in custody, all activity outside will stop.

Meanwhile, Burgoyne was staring up at the air vents,

looking puzzled. He was trying to figure out how attackers could get into the lab.

"Nobody could squeeze through that," he said. "Even a little guy."

"You'd be surprised." I walked toward him, to immobilize him, keeping my voice friendly.

"Even a *midget* couldn't."

When I reached within four feet of him I brought my Glock out and aimed at him. But I smiled.

"Bang," I said. "You're captured. Give me your handcuffs. See? I *said* there was a way in."

His mouth dropped open. But under the rules of the "drill," he'd been ordered to surrender. "Aw, sir," he said, lowering his rifle, hanging his head. "You tricked me. The captain will be furious. That isn't fair."

"Burgoyne, a terrorist wouldn't be fair either, would he?" I said, staying friendly. "I'd say your captain was in a bit of hot water. We have to conduct these drills realistically." I took his assault rifle and ammo magazine away from him, and his plastic cuffs. My armpits were drenched and I was still smiling. I moved him to the air vent, locked him to it.

"Aw, you don't have to do that, sir."

"Don't feel badly," I said. "Your captain is probably captured too by now. You did nothing wrong. You followed orders perfectly, I'll report."

He sighed and grinned but his smile turned puzzled when he saw me unlock the glass cabinet and reach for a graduated cylinder, a long beaker with red markings to show the amount of liquid poured inside.

"Sir, Captain Van Tries told me not to let you touch anything."

I reached for the acids. I lined up the five-gallon jugs on the long stone-topped table, by an empty beaker.

Burgoyne was growing worried, "This *is* a drill, right?" he said.

I had to gag him. I couldn't help it. I made sure he could breathe through his nose. "I can't have you screaming when I'm on the radio. I won't hurt you. I'll be gone in minutes. You'll tell this story to your grandchildren."

But he didn't believe anything I said anymore.

My fingers tingled as I reached for the lock on the Moseler. I slid the dial right, left, right.

The alarm in the hallway stopped ringing suddenly. I wondered if that meant Danny had allowed himself to be caught.

I turned the knob to the fourth number and heard no responsive click, but when I pulled, the heavy door slowly opened. I wanted to shout with triumph. Inside I saw three shelves, and on them, a bonanza. The portable hard drives lay beside an index-file-type metal box, which I opened to see the plastic disks inside. The backup files.

Paper files lay stacked on the middle shelf.

Stoppered plastic sample bottles labeled "HR-109" sat on the bottom. They were filled with small blue capsules. The drug was clearly ready to be shipped.

My radio crackled to life, clipped to my shirt pocket. Eisner's voice echoed inside the safe as I turned the hard-drive boxes on their sides, exposing the holes, the joiner spots where the cartridges went into computers—the vulnerable areas where acid could wash in.

"Mr. Acela? Are your men inside the lab?"

He wanted a progress report.

"Not yet," I responded testily, as if irritated that my team had not yet arrived. I snapped a few quick photos of the contents of the safe. I moved back toward the row of jugs. In the far corner, Burgoyne was making muffled protests. He was too far away for the radio to pick up the sound.

Eisner gloated over the radio, acting for Van Tries, who would be standing next to him. "Captain Van Tries caught one of your people coming over the fence. He's being brought in now."

Meaning, *We're running out of time. Hurry.*

"Care to up the bet, Eisner?"

"Two hundred," he said.

"Three," I said.

If something went wrong on either end, the code sentence would be "Looks like a wrap, podnuh." If someone needed help immediately, the alert words would be "I'll buy you a beer." Which meant the other guys better come running.

And in a worst-case scenario, where we were to try to get out in any way possible and leave the others—if someone was captured or hurt but could still communicate—he was to say, "Buy you a Bushmills."

Which would mean, Run. Now. Alone. Get out.

I clicked off. With Danny caught, all "attacking" activity had ceased, but the security crew would be waiting for another probe. I quickly but carefully unscrewed the top of the acetic acid five-gallon jug.

The fumes made my eyes water and burned the back of my throat. It was advisable to wear a lab apron and thick gloves when working with this stuff, but I hadn't had time to look for them. I upended the jar and watched a stream of clear thick acid gurgle into the graduated cylinder.

Coughing, feeling the rake of fumes in my lungs, I replaced the cap and moved on to the hydrochloric acid in the next jug.

It sloshed as it poured into the same cylinder.

I'm mixing the most powerful cocktail, to destroy everything in that safe.

Over the radio, I monitored Van Tries's crew checking in from different parts of the compound, sounding more confident than they had ten minutes ago. East fence secure. North fence too. They still thought a drill was on.

Hurry, I told myself.

"A wing empty," a voice said.

"Cafeteria secure."

I finished pouring the sulfuric acid into the mix in the cylinder. My eyes watered like crazy. I carried the cylinder at arm's length to the safe.

And then a last-second twinge of doubt hit me. The hesitancy came from the last place I'd expected. Myself.

Do you really want to destroy the whole supply?

Yes, I told myself, staring at the Enhance.

All of it? Every gram?

Of course. I eyed the sample bottles of capsules on the lower shelf. HR-109 had killed friends. It might bring down the government. But at that moment it tempted me like the devil's whisper, working on my desire, logic, any emotion it could leverage for success.

You'll never feel that power again if you destroy it. You'll never experience that certainty. Are you sure that you won't need a bit of 109, just a little?

I watched my hand reach out and touch it. I ran a few capsules through my fingers.

What are you waiting for?

I put a few capsules of HR-109 in my pocket. Just a tiny bit.

I'll get rid of it later, I thought.

I turned on the overhead exhaust fan. Then I stepped back and upended the beaker, splashing mixed acids like a pyromaniac splattering gasoline on a house.

Immediately there was a hissing and white-gray fumes erupted. I saw paper curling and discoloring, and the edges of the manila folders disappearing. My eyes burned. I threw in the whole cylinder, and it shattered and acid ran down shelves and soaked into holes in the metal casings of the portable hard drives. The plastic disks were melting, their segments pulling apart. The vials of HR-109 were dissolving, smoking. I was driven back by fumes, throat burning, nostrils aflame, vision doubled from tearing, the rampant smell of chemical destruction obliterating any other odors in here.

Throw the last bit of 109 in there too.

But I felt a fierce and sudden burning atop my left foot.

I looked down. Acid had splashed my shoe, only a *drop,* mind you, but already it had eaten a hole in the leather and the pain felt like a hot nail digging into my flesh.

I saw a couple of brown spots on my cuffs also, widening, and at the same time realized that all alarms had stopped ringing.

Get out of here. Now.

But I hadn't counted on the way I looked. I started dry heaving from the fumes. I was supposed to stroll out of here and smoothly shake hands with Van Tries and drive off the grounds, so I could not very well stumble from the lab like a toxic spill survivor. I wiped tears away with a paper towel. My eyes were veined pink, reflected in the silver dispenser. I looked like a drunk, or a sick man. Mucus ran out of my nose. I blew my nose but it did not stop running. The pain in my foot was worsening. I imagined that drop of acid eating through cartilage and bone.

To hell with it. I'd check it later. Burgoyne watched everything, terrified eyes huge over the hanky I'd stuffed in his mouth.

He was farther away from the fumes but still panicked. I started to leave but his terror hit me in a throat-gagging wave that stopped me in my tracks. *He's afraid I'm leaving him to die. Afraid I've released a biological agent, or an explosive.*

I could see his chest going in and out like a piston. I went over to him and removed the hanky so he could breathe better. It would only take a second or two to reassure him. "Burgoyne, there's no fire, no germs. I'm no terrorist."

His eyes were wild, staring at the gray-white smoke rising from the safe. He wasn't even looking at me.

"Burgoyne, nothing is going to happen to you. The stuff I just destroyed was . . . Oh, hell, I don't have time for this."

I retched again. My mouth tasted of chemicals.

Eisner's voice came over the line, boastful now, but he was letting me know I should get out of here. "Looks like your attack's been called off." He sounded proud, like we'd practiced, like a man who'd just won a big bet.

Eisner saying Danny was caught. The tunnel was sealed. My other attackers had melted away without ever penetrating the grounds. It was a stunning victory for Van Tries and his security forces. A humiliation for the civilians who'd mocked Uncle Sam's troops. Van Tries—

who was probably right beside Eisner—had done a perfect job.

"I'll be right there," I said. "You win."

"Yep, it's a wrap, podnuh," Eisner added. "I'll buy you a Bushmills."

That's the code sentence.

My heart started galloping. Since there were no windows in here, I could not see outside. I had no idea what had just gone wrong.

"I'd rather have a beer," I said, making sure of his meaning.

"Nah. Bushmills was always better," he said.

He clicked off.

They've been caught.

I made sure my radio was still broadcasting and switched to the band that the security team should be monitoring. I cried out, "Burgoyne, I *told* you not to touch anything. Clean up that spill! Catch up to me in the office later. I'm going to talk to Van Tries."

Playing games, trying to fool them. But a voice came back at me now over both our radios. A man—an officer of some kind—was calling Burgoyne, asking him to report in. Demanding to know why he wasn't answering. "Burgoyne? Code A. Where are you? Burgoyne?"

I didn't know what *code A* meant, but I was sure I would not like it.

And now I heard a new sound from outside, muffled by the walls, but unmistakable after my recent adventures, steady, growing, mechanical, coming closer. It filled me with rage and terror. It was a helicopter.

Alonzo Otto is here, I knew.

I grabbed Burgoyne's rifle. Eisner had just told me to leave him and Danny and head out of C wing through the rear door, as we'd planned to do together, and run across the strip of lawn toward the fences.

If Otto's here, so are troops.

My fear fell away. I had a sense of all the forces I'd been dealing with over the last few weeks converging on Naturetech. I didn't need the key card to get *out* of the laboratory; I only had to turn the knob. The copter sound was getting louder. I jammed one of Burgoyne's ammunition magazines into the rifle. I clicked the safety off. The rifle was light, its feel familiar. I hadn't used one in years, but remembered training with assault weapons at the FBI. I'd gotten decent scores.

Well, four years ago, that is.

I might have had qualms about fighting soldiers on the security force, but I'll have no problem shooting at Alonzo Otto and the guys he'll bring.

At the door I paused, turned the knob, kicked the door, and spun into the hallway, keeping my back to the wall.

The hallway was empty.

The copter noise had stopped. *Meaning it's landed.*

Now there was a small, shrill chiming in the hall and it took me an instant to realize it was my cell phone. *Of course, Gabrielle is in the park and can see everything going on outside. She'll be able to tell me.*

I rushed toward the security camera, used the butt of the assault rifle to smash it. I was ten feet from the vault-like door to the main hallway. If people tried to get in, I'd hear a buzzing sound accompanying the use of the access card.

I have a few seconds to find out what Gabrielle is seeing. It's better to know what you're up against.

"Gabrielle!"

"Get out, Mike. All of you. I see troops coming, a helicopter landed!"

"How many?"

"Fifteen, twenty maybe. Some of them look . . . injured."

"Are they inside the building yet?"

"The regular security force is leaving, getting into Humvees. The new troops are replacing them! My God. Their faces are painted black. Body armor. Helmets. Assault rifles. Some kind of weird-looking opticals on their faces . . ."

Night vision, I thought.

I repeated, *"Are they inside the building?"*

"Not yet. They're spreading out around it. Splitting into three groups. But they're only in front so far . . . moving carefully . . . and one man's limping. One has bandages on his face . . ."

These must be the people we hurt at the farmhouse this morning. Otto's special unit.

Gabrielle said, "I see a civilian man in a baseball cap. Not a soldier. Oh, Mike, you can still get out. Run to the fence! You have a few seconds before they cut the whole place off!"

"A baseball cap, you said."

"And a woman with him. Disable the electric fence, like you planned!"

"The woman, is she blond?"

Gabrielle cried out, "What are you waiting for?"

It's Otto and the Royces. What's left of Ludenhorff's special counterinsurgency unit, his private army, here to wipe us out in secret. They must have caught Hoot. I hope she's all right.

I glanced down the long hallway toward the locked doors at the far end, leading to escape: the loading dock and parking area, the strip of lawn and woods beside the fence. Gabrielle had just told me the way out might be clear for a few more moments. But Eisner and Danny were somewhere in the main building, I knew.

Otto's strategy was clear and obvious.

They'll try to get into the lab. They'll want to eliminate witnesses. They'll say terrorists attacked Naturetech. They have to protect themselves.

"Mike? *Are you there?*"

Every alarm in the place seemed to explode at once, into an earsplitting cacophony of bloops, whoops, electronic screams.

I didn't go out the back doors to the fence, as Gabrielle had wanted. I went the other way.

My hand was steady. There was no question of leaving without my friends. Instead of unscrewing the grate to cut the wiring, as Eisner had wanted, I punched in *1775* at the keypad and watched the green light come on and I hit the door leading *into the main rotunda* with my shoulder, spinning out of C wing, into the central lobby connecting all wings of Naturetech.

Nobody was there. Just alarms screaming. Either the security staff was elsewhere, or they'd withdrawn.

The security office would be a hundred feet across the lobby, just beyond the main entrance and the door to A wing. In it, I hoped, I'd find Danny and Eisner.

Then I was sure they were there, because firing erupted from corridor A, behind the door.

But I realized that I was hearing the stacatto bursts made by an M-16 rifle firing on automatic.

Neither Eisner nor Danny had brought assault rifles into Naturetech.

I didn't know if they'd just been shot.

I TWENTY-FOUR I

The shots died away, and in the silence the lobby remained empty. I needed to find out what had happened to my friends. I forced myself to move, hearing the sound of my own footsteps over a loudspeaker that had switched on outside. A voice was advising us to come out, hands up, you won't be harmed, blah, blah, blah.

I recognized the flat, harsh intonations. I'd heard them at Keating's lawn party. It was Alonzo Otto. All my fates were converging on the grounds.

Danny and Eisner may still be alive if Otto's trying to coax us out. He can't yet know I've destroyed the lab. He'll want to capture us alive, for interrogation.

But we would not stay alive after that, I knew.

I stayed low as the message continued, envisioning Otto's troops—pissed off after this morning's battle in Virginia—taking up positions around the building. I slipped behind the unmanned guard desk, using it as a shield as I passed Naturetech's glass-front doors. I slid past visitor exhibits: posters of jungle plants, a chart showing steps needed to develop plants into drugs "for your medicine cabinet," blowup photos of researchers in tropics, a display case of softball trophies won by the "Naturetech Sharks," pictured in the case.

Colonel Otto gave us ten minutes to surrender.

"If you don't, we'll come in."

I reached the door to A wing and pulled it quietly open. Ahead, corridor lights were lit, the hall empty, but the security office itself, twenty feet up, looked dark.

Maybe Danny or Eisner turned off the lights to keep anyone from seeing in.

Then Danny's voice floated out at me, from the office. He must have heard footsteps in the hall. "John? Fred? I have the grenades."

He's bluffing, thinking Otto's guys are in the hallway.

"You're a bad liar, Danny," I called out.

"Mike?" he cried with relief as I burst in. Eisner stood in the semidark at the far end of the room, beside the window, wielding an M-16 obviously seized from one of the lab's security staff. He'd done the shooting to keep the attackers away. Danny's face was mud-smeared, from the "drill" earlier. Van Tries glared up at me from the floor, cuffed to a desk leg but unhurt as far as I could see. Humiliated. Enraged.

I instantly felt a powerful wash of emotion: relief from Danny, calm from Eisner, bafflement from the captain, who was staring at Carl.

"How did you know what Colonel Otto told me?" Van Tries asked Eisner. *"How did you know I was about to arrest you?"*

Danny studied my face with a glance. "You have redeye, Boss. Been smoking marijuana in the bathroom again?"

"Lab fumes," I said.

"Then you got into the safe?"

"What safe?"

Danny smiled grimly. "At least that part's over."

Van Tries groaned. He didn't know what I'd done in the lab but knew it was bad for him.

Eisner spoke up from beside the window as he monitored the lawn outside, but he had a limited view. He had to stay back. "Van Tries got a phone call and I felt him *change* inside. The Enhance did it, Mike. I took him down. Told his guys we'd kill him if they didn't leave. Why did you come here? Didn't you understand my message? I told you to run!"

"Would *you* have?"

Otto announced from outside, "Eight minutes. There are only three of you, and I have fifty guys out here."

"More like twenty," I said, remembering Gabrielle's words. But the depleted, vengeful unit would be out for blood. They'd be trained for this contingency, attacking a building seized by "terrorists."

Terrorists. That was us.

I realized suddenly why Danny and Eisner had remained in the office instead of running, and it choked me with emotion. They'd stayed intentionally—fired shots—to draw Otto's attention in case I hadn't yet finished up in the lab.

And now I felt the wall of reciprocating emotion coming back at me, thanks to the Enhance we'd taken. It was embarrassing. Unmanly.

Girly men, that was us.

"Emotional retards," I said.

I also remembered the bit of 109 still in my pocket.

No need to mention it yet. Get everyone concentrating on the fight or they'll sense you're hiding something.

I told Eisner, "We can still get out. Otto doesn't have enough people to cover the grounds and come in after us at the same time. He lost too many guys before."

"Get out how? Lenox's new invisibility drug?" Danny said.

We needed to stay in the security office—at least for a few more minutes—to figure it out. The equipment here might help. The console contained built-in TV screens, showing soldiers moving around the side of the building, staying just inside the tree line, dark gliding forms.

C wing is sealed off now, I thought, watching. *There's no way out that way.*

I tossed my encrypted cell phone to Eisner and told him to call Gabrielle, to stay on the line with her in case she saw something useful. The east-wing screen showed a man aiming a rifle at it. It went blank. The north-wing floodlights went out, creating pools of black to mask the assault.

Maybe attackers were coming already. Maybe Otto had lied about that too.

"Otto has to finish this as fast as possible," I said. "He can't risk media attention, or police."

Eisner signaled that Gabrielle was on the line.

I flicked on the switch controlling the intercom system. When I'd toured the labs with Danny weeks ago it had broadcast Muzak while scientists worked. "Tie a Yellow Ribbon." Burt Bacharach stuff. Now I used it to address Otto in a strong, confident voice.

"I got into the safe, Alonzo. I took the disks, formulas, files. If you come in, I'll destroy them."

"Five minutes!" he responded.

"Well, that worked," Danny said.

Moving fast, I cut electricity to the fences so we could get out if we reached them. I hit the switch controlling rooftop floodlights, and they came on brightly to illuminate figures on the ground, frozen on their bellies. They'd been wriggling out of the tree line, directly toward us, rifles held in front of them, night optics flipped down.

Bathed in light, they wriggled back.

Then I heard quick shots outside and the roof lights went out.

"I'll stay here. I'll distract them," I said. "You guys go out the back, try for the fence."

It wasn't worth an answer, apparently. Danny sat at the duty officer's desk, feverishly scanning a computer on which he'd called up Naturetech's blueprints. He traced lines with his finger, looking for a hiding place. An ambush place.

"Employees' cafeteria? Nah," he said.

I drove my palm into the red button on the console, the silent alarm connecting Naturetech to the county police emergency system, as Otto's voice came back at us. "Mike. White flag. Bring me what you took from the safe. Let's talk."

"Give me a few minutes to think about it. I don't trust you," I said.

What a laugh. That we would fight—we both knew at some level—was a foregone conclusion. We were poker players, playing out our hands—Otto lying, me stalling, while what was left of his unit took up position. Danny poring over blueprints and Eisner talking with Gabrielle, who reported that before the lights went out she'd seen a handful of soldiers outside the back doors to A and C wings, but only two guys behind corridor B. Otto was keeping three reserve guys by the main entrance, to be dispatched if they were needed, or to keep people out of the grounds.

B was the weak link. They wouldn't be coming in from that direction.

"Otto's gambling the fight will start elsewhere. They're probably behind B in case we run out," I said. "Or maybe that's where they *want* us to come out, when they burst into the other corridors through the back doors."

"There, and the front entrance too," Eisner said. "I'm guessing three-way attack. Five soldiers in each team. Hurry."

I got on the sound system again, making Otto a phony offer while Danny switched the image on the screen to B wing blueprints. I spoke lines I remembered from role-playing at the Bureau. I demanded that Otto provide us with a helicopter, offered to trade Enhance for escape. I told him I wanted to be flown to Costa Rica. In the old FBI games, the terrorists always lost, but negotiations took time.

Danny muttered, "There's a crawl space under B wing's storage room. But it doesn't lead anywhere. It's for maintenance."

I announced over the intercom, "I'll provide the *website* where I hid the synthesis formula. That's right, Colonel. Your secrets are on the Internet now."

Danny said, "The equipment room? The animal-containment room?" He explained to Eisner, "The lab's in C but they keep the chimps in B away from the surgery area, so they don't freak out. We could hide behind those cages, fire when they come in. The animals will make plenty of noise."

Otto countering my offer with his own. Come out and talk. "Three minutes."

I wish there were a way to use 109. But we need to be close to someone for it to work.

Van Tries spoke up from the floor. "If you give up, I'll tell them you didn't hurt me."

"It won't help, but thanks."

"Two minutes left, contestants!" came a new and happy voice from outside. It was Oliver Royce doing his Regis Philbin act again, playing the cheery television

MC. Actually chuckling over the loudspeaker. Everything a game to him. Especially fights. I guess Otto figured the Royces would scare us into coming out.

"Seventy seconds, sports fans," Royce called.

"Forget the blueprints. Let's get out of here," I said.

But I should have known they wouldn't wait for the full countdown to be over. It was clear we weren't coming out.

"Incoming!" Eisner shouted, already dropping toward the floor. A tremendous explosion shattered windows even though the impact point had been against brick, not glass. RPG.

I was thrown off my feet. I saw Danny in the air, slamming into the wall five feet up and crumpling, limp as a six-foot doll. At least he was moving. His hand crabbed around on the floor, searching for a weapon. The TV monitors had shattered, plaster was falling. Chairs were turned over and pictures had fallen off the walls. Didn't this stuff ever stop?

They're rushing the building right now.

I pulled my Glock from my waistband and aimed at the broken window as I rose. I fired so the attackers would hear shots at least. Maybe that would slow them. But I realized I heard nothing. No gun. No explosion. No screaming. *The gun doesn't work,* I thought. Then, *No, that's not it.* I couldn't hear *anything,* not even my gun firing. Danny looked like he was shouting at me. He *must* be shouting, because his mouth was moving, but no sound came out. Reaching for the M-16, I saw a crumpled body in the corner. There was no face on it, just meat and an eye hanging, and I realized that one arm was gone. Blood spurted from the stump. I thought it was Van Tries, but saw Van Tries out in the hallway, crawling.

The dead man was Eisner.

A wave of grief hit me.

DANGEROUSDANGEROUS.

Only seconds had elapsed since the explosion. I didn't hear actual words, but Danny's intent broke through my shock and grief. I picked up a dust-covered assault rifle and ran, wobbling, into the hall. The walls accordioned in and out. The floor tilted like the deck of a ship. With sound gone, so was my balance. The buzzing in my ears was more a hideous vibration than noise.

I reached the main lobby just as soldiers burst in through the front doors.

I didn't hear my assault rifle fire when I pulled the trigger, but it bucked and leaped and I saw orange bursts at the muzzle. I was filled with adrenaline, beyond fear. I was screaming, I think. I stood in plain view, firing.

Men flew back. They slid down the wall. Men spun and returned fire and must have missed me, or I was too filled with adrenaline to realize I was hit. Then hands pulled me back by the shoulders, yanked me behind the cinder-block corner, but not before I saw two soldiers turning and running out of the building, into the dark, onto the grounds. One of the men fell.

My ammunition must have run out. I didn't feel the gun bucking now.

We fought them off, for the moment. Is it possible?

Danny's face loomed, close to mine. He was shaking me, gripping my shoulders, and his mouth was moving, and suddenly there was sound in the world again.

". . . fucking crazy?" he was screaming as he shoved a fresh magazine toward me. "Load!" he yelled.

We'd responded so quickly to the initial assault that the A and C wing attackers had never reached the lobby. We'd probably have a couple of minutes before the second attack came. Danny eyed the closed door to C wing, waiting for it to burst open. I covered the door to A. I figured right now Otto's troops would be securing their corridors, going room to room and making sure none of us was hiding there. Checking the lab. The lab had been their main objective. They'd be regrouping. There would be no more bargaining now, bluffed or otherwise.

We were past bargaining. We'd been that way for weeks.

I saw Van Tries on the floor, crawling out of the building.

We couldn't run into A or C. We couldn't stay in the lobby. If we backed into B wing, we'd be trapped there.

"Hmm," Danny said.

"Eisner was right," I said. "Three-way attack."

I smelled fire. Smoke curled out from under the door leading to the security office, and from a vent in the lobby. Fires starting . . .

Maybe Otto's plan all along had been to obliterate the whole place and blame it on us.

I heard moaning. I saw an injured soldier outside crawling down the steps. Three more troops had been knocked sideways by my bullets, inside the lobby and to the right of the entrance. They lay bloody and motionless in places where they couldn't be seen from outside. I checked the bodies quickly. They were dead. I grabbed ammo belts and a rifle and tossed it to Danny.

So this was the legacy of Enhance. People who should be on the same side, shooting at one another.

My own people, Eisner had said.

Lights plunged off in the lobby, which meant the fire had reached the wiring, or Otto's guys had shut off power. Visibility was twenty feet in here, and outside, through the front doors, I saw a vague pink glow at the edges of the dark. Night was ending, dawn approaching. But smoke made it harder to see. I wished I had night-vision opticals, flip-downs, like Otto's guys.

Wait a minute. The opticals and mikes are on their helmets!

Danny jerked up beside me. "You figured something out?"

"The sound system," I said, reaching out and jamming a fallen soldier's helmet onto my head. Now I had night vision too. The goggles used ambient light. I'd practiced assaults with them at the FBI. And Otto's voice instantly filled my ears, coming from the built-in communication system. He was positioning his guys in A and C wing, all right, as we'd thought—securing the lab, as we'd thought. He was checking casualties.

Otto asking someone, "How many?"

"They killed the lieutenant. And Sergeant Miller."

Of the force in front, we learned, four were dead and the fifth injured, on the steps outside. Attack teams five soldiers strong were inside A and C corridors, securing rooms, checking closets and making sure they wouldn't be ambushed from behind when they drove into the lobby minutes from now.

At least we have a few minutes, I thought.

The rear guard outside B wing, the two guys, were still there, they reported. Everyone else was on the driveway, ready to be dispatched at a moment's notice, or to keep anyone—civilians or police—from getting onto the grounds.

We don't need to beat Otto, just fool him long enough to get out of the building, past his men. That would give us a chance to try for the fence. What was it that Danny said about the animal containment room?

From what I was hearing, Otto was a pretty good tactician. His problem was that I heard all his orders going out. B wing guys were to sit tight out back, with their perfect kill view of the rear door. A and C contingents would send two men each to replace those killed in front. When everyone was in place and A and C corridors secure, the three larger groups would hit the lobby simultaneously, killing us in a cross fire or driving us into B wing, trapping us. If we were already *in* B wing, they'd hunt us down, room to room.

Yes! The animal room! But we need time to do it.

Now Danny had a helmet on too, as the voices in my earpiece said state police had arrived at the main gate. Otto's men were keeping them off the grounds but calling for him to talk to them. The police were threatening to come in. It meant Otto had to delay attack while he went to meet the cops, to show ID and order them to let "proper authorities" handle the "terrorists."

Otto sounded furious over the delay.

That will give us a couple more minutes. Move! Now!

I made sure the on/off switch was off on my microphone. I said, "Danny. Help me carry these guys."

We couldn't afford to leave a trail of blood.

We slung the rifles over our shoulders. We hefted the first man across the lobby, into B wing, as fast as we could. The animal-containment room was second on the right, and inside were five chimps in cages, panic-stricken, screaming, rattling bars. The blood smell and smoke drove them even more wild.

Hurry, I thought.

Still monitoring communication, we rushed back to the lobby and brought the second man back—leaving the lobby door ajar behind us—as Otto's argument with the cops ended with the police agreeing to stay back.

Of course they did.

I could see smoke oozing from the vent at the back end of B corridor, rising by the exit. The smoke was seeping through the ventilation system. Soon it would be coming out of all the grates. The night-vision goggles would not help see through smoke.

Otto was back to coordinating his men now. "Ready, everyone?"

But someone seemed to be arguing with him, urging him to call off the attack, with police witnesses out front.

Otto reassured the officer. "Don't worry. I can squelch any inquiry. There are terrorists inside."

My heart fell. *So it does go that high up.*

I reached down for the dead soldier at my feet and began unbuttoning his shirt, trying to change clothes as fast as possible. The dead men were bloody, the smell in the animal-containment room of smoke, feces, urine, bananas. The uniforms would make us look like soldiers. And as for the blood on us, well, I figured guys out there had blood on them too.

Someone out front reported thick smoke in the lobby.

I got the shirt on. The trousers wouldn't snap up.

"No more peach cobbler for you, Boss," Danny said.

A soldier in my earpiece reported to Otto, "Ready in A wing."

"Ready out front, Colonel," another voice said.

Danny had his pants on. With the electricity out, the sprinkler system would be too.

Smoke began drifting from the air vents in the containment room. The animals were screeching—a steady, unstopping wail.

Danny saying, "If this doesn't work . . ."

"Yes?"

"I told you so."

"One minute," Otto told his guys over the helmet communication system. "No prisoners."

"You're fired," I said, coughing from smoke.

For what I planned to work, the animals and attackers had to reach the lobby at the same time. Danny ran into the hallway, turned left and stopped.

"Scare 'em into the lobby," I called.

I moved to the cages, reaching down from behind, one by one, pulling the latches, raising the wire doors. The animals inside didn't need any help to get moving.

The first chimp—the biggest one—jumped out and began running around the room, hooting in terror. The animal disappeared into the main corridor, turned left, changed direction as Danny shouted and waved, and headed for the lobby. The spider monkey leaped down from its table, and followed as if it had been told what to do.

The baby chimp sat in its cage, trembling.

In less than thirty seconds, all the animals were free.

I chased them from the containment room, joining Danny, herding them down the hall. I shut the lobby door behind them after they fled through it. I heard them running on the other side of the door, shrieking, screaming, their high-pitched cries adding to the cacophony that would erupt in seconds when—

BOOM.

The attack began with the sound of a rocket or smoke or gas bomb going into the lobby, as we ran back to the containment room. I heard shooting from the front of the building. Lots of it. They were raking the lobby from the outside.

"Am I really fired, Boss?" Danny said, puffing as we reached the room. "I'll lose my dental insurance."

I left the Enhance in my pants pocket.

I reached for the trousers I'd discarded and retrieved the last capsules of the drug. Danny, adjusting his uniform, didn't see. It was crucial for us to wait until the moment was perfect to leave. In my earpiece I heard progress reports from incoming soldiers. They were entering the front entrance. The team from C wing hit the lobby.

"Watch out for ambush," someone was saying.

Danny's eyes were hidden under goggles, his forehead a quarter-inch slit of dirty white under his camouflage helmet. His barrel chest looked bigger with the armor vest over it. He looked taller in military boots. His trousers were too short for him. With all this smoke, who'd notice, I hoped. Maybe the chimps would distract the soldiers out there.

And then a voice was screaming, "There! Behind the security desk! Running! It's them!"

Thank you, God, I thought.

Shooting exploded in the earpiece. Someone was screaming, *"It's a goddamned monkey!"* I imagined the wild scene, soldiers firing, animals hooting. Utter chaos amid the smoke and . . .

Now, I thought, envisioning the two soldiers that Gabrielle had reported stationed outside the back of B wing. The guys who were to do nothing except if Danny and I showed up.

I turned on my mike. It wasn't hard to sound panicked. I pitched my tone to sound like one of the men I'd heard. A Brooklyn accent was easy for me to do. Just summon back Devil's Bay.

I shouted, "Ambush! Everyone back to the lab! They were hiding *in the lab! We missed them before!*"

I fired my rifle so they'd hear shooting. I shouted, "That's everyone, and I mean everyone! The lab! The *lab!*"

I heard commotion. Lots of voices at the same time. A voice was saying, "I didn't say that!" The smoke was thickening and Danny and I were coughing but I'd heard no confirmation of my order from Otto.

Maybe it hadn't worked, but we had to leave anyway.

Goggles on, we charged down the hallway, toward the rear exit. If we ran into soldiers coming in, if they entered through B wing instead of going around the side of the building, we'd shoot.

"The lab! He said get to the lab!" a new voice shouted in my earpiece.

It was working!

Then Otto's voice broke in. "We're *in* the lab, but no one is here."

Danny and I reached the exit. Reached for the knob.

"A wing! They're in A wing!" Danny shouted into his mike.

We opened the door. Otto sounded clear in the earpiece, furious at whomever had jumped the gun and panicked. He demanded to know the name of whomever had just sounded the alert.

I looked out. Dawn was still not up. There was very dim gray light, no soldiers, but that didn't mean someone wasn't watching from the tree line, not fooled by us.

Trust the Enhance.

Otto suddenly figured it out. He shouted over the earpiece, "They can hear us! They have helmets! It's *them!* Shut off your mikes!"

I stepped outside, holding my breath. I remembered how, in Key West, my senses had warned me when a detective had even *looked* in my direction. I winced, exposed, waiting for the surge of certainty.

I felt nothing. Nothing at all.

I hissed at Danny, *"Let's go."*

We took one last precaution, pretending to hold each other up like injured soldiers as we staggered from the doorway. The floodlights were off. The main lights were off. Gabrielle was supposed to be waiting by the fence, but God knows where she'd gone.

The fence . . .

The voices in my earpiece had stopped.

And then there was another burst of shooting from inside the building. The troops must be firing at the animals or one another in the smoke. I had no way of knowing which. We were less than a hundred yards from the inner fence, on the lawn, exposed to anyone wearing night-vision goggles. We stepped across the grass. Thirty yards would bring us to the woods, thirty more to the fence.

I held my breath. The trees were a dark welcome line ahead. Protection.

We made it to the trees.

We broke into a trot, avoiding low-hanging branches and staying as quiet as possible. My breathing sounded as loud as shooting. I heard blood rushing in my head. I heard Danny's heavy limping boot-falls behind me.

The fence coming up.

I was reaching for it, thinking, *We made it.* But at precisely that moment a voice seemed to erupt in my head, a scream of *DANGERDANGERDANGER*, and it came from my right so I was already swinging, pulling the trigger before I even saw the shadow there, the baseball cap in the air and the man wearing night-vision goggles flying back into a tree, a tangle of flailing arms and legs.

More firing came from right behind me. *It's Danny.*

Our shots mixing with the sound of more shooting from the building. I felt a white-hot stab in my side. It spun me sideways, into a tree. I was falling.

I was down.

I couldn't move for a moment. Then the pain started up in my side.

I lay on cool grass, cheek against the ground. I saw smoke drifting from the muzzle of my M-16, mixing with morning mist on the ground. The smell of cordite tingeing the loamlike odor of grass. The pain came harder now. I saw, five feet away, Oliver Royce. He was dead, no question about it from the way his limbs twisted. His goggles had risen off his eyes, and his eyes were open, staring.

I wouldn't have seen him without Enhance. I would not have even known he was there.

"Mike? Mike!"

Danny knelt beside me, assault rifle at his side, and I saw a silvery Sig Sauer jammed in his waistband. Beyond him, Abby Hayes Royce lay four feet off, on her side, blinking, gasping, coughing up blood. I heard a sucking sound in her chest. She was mortally wounded, and wearing all black: black jeans and a tight black T-shirt, black sneakers, black cap, black soot on her face.

Her wedding ring reflected a spot of cold white light from the sinking moon.

She was the one who'd shot me.

I felt pain sweep up and seize me from my side. I burned inside. I felt something hard scrape against my ribs.

Danny reached down, helped me up. It hurt.

"They probably heard the shots, Mike. The cops too."

I tried to stand. Pain shot through me. But the fence was right here. I gripped the strands with my fingers.

I can do this, I told myself.

I heard Abby's baffled whisper float out at us from behind me, her dying tones of surprise. "How did you know we were *there?*" she said.

Danny helped me. I made it over the smaller fence. But ten feet ahead was the barbed-wire fence. I doubled over, dizzy. I straightened and reached for the fence, and a steel band cut into my side. *Lie down for a minute,* I thought. But then I saw a thick blanket lying over the wire, and someone on the other side coming out of the trees.

Gabrielle. Saying, "Oh God, Mike. God."

Gabrielle steadying the blanket while I reached and Danny pushed and I sweated with pain and told myself, *One step up at a time.*

Danny dropped over the fence at the same time I did. He was saying, ". . . .to a hospital."

But I remembered Colonel Otto in my earpiece, saying, "*I can squelch an inquiry,*" and I knew that he, or Ludenhorff, or someone above them—someone influential—*still* had the power to keep secret all that had occurred. If that happened, there would be no hope, not for Gabrielle, not for Danny or Hoot, if she still lived, or their families. Not for Kim's son, Chris.

I know exactly where to go, how to end this. Just give me one more hour. Just let me reach the car.

"We have to go somewhere first," I got out. "Before the hospital."

I told them where we had to go.

Gabrielle answered, "I left the engine on. Hurry. The car is close."

TWENTY-FIVE

"I don't care who you used to work for. I don't care whose daughter Gabrielle is. This story is total bullshit," the bald man said.

The *Washington Post* occupies a nine-story yellow brick building at L Street and 15th, in downtown Washington. It sits across from the Mayflower Hotel, home-away-from-home to diplomats, Presidents, Kings, movie stars. At six-thirty A.M., the grate protecting the main entrance is up, the overnight crew gone and type-A reporters begin trickling in, coffee or notebooks in hand, suspicions abloom over whatever stories they plan to work on that day.

"Are you sure you don't need a doctor, Mr. Acela?"

"It's a bad flu," I said.

I sat with Gabrielle, Danny and a handful of *Post* editors in a glassed-in conference area on the periphery of the big City room. The curtains were drawn both in the direction of the City room and out to the street. I wore a makeshift bandage beneath my shirt, but I was bleeding. I could feel the warm, sticky blood spreading. Running out of me.

"There's blood all over that uniform, Mr. Acela."

"It's not mine."

"Oh."

On one end of the table sat Harris, the reporter, an

exhausted-looking man in his early thirties, with a receding hairline, khaki trousers and a yellow crewneck sweater against the AC, over his thin chest. The *Post's* executive editor was a WASPish, bald 50-year-old in a crisp white shirt and tie, with a tan that didn't hide the liver spots. The managing editor looked about 60, with curly white hair and the elegant manners of a Southern plantation owner. He was black.

"You're telling us that our own columnist was driven from her job by this drug?" he said. "Blackmailed?"

"So was the President, the Chief Justice, the head of the FBI," I said.

The deputy managing editor, a former investigative reporter and Pulitzer Prize winner, sat across from me, sipping Starbucks hazelnut vanilla blend and breakfasting on a power bar. She'd come in wearing spandex workout clothes, having been summoned on the way to her gym. She looked cute, and skeptical, like she thought I was a nut.

"Can you tell me what I'm thinking?" she said.

"Only that you feel guilty," I said, as Gabrielle nodded agreement. "I'm guessing one of you called the FBI before the meeting, probably when Harris told you we were coming. Is that why the curtains are closed to the City room? Is someone already out there? Or maybe your security guards are out there, making sure we don't leave. Don't worry. We have nowhere else to go."

"That's quite a story," the woman said, and blushed. "Ha-ha."

Of all of them, Harris seemed to be the one who wanted to believe us. He said, "I was up all night after finding Kim's body, checking your claims. NIA denies involvement. Defense Intelligence says Carl Eisner is

AWOL. Homeland Security wants you arrested. Hell, you admitted causing the blast in Virginia. And Naturetech's all over the morning news. . . . Terrorists hit their lab."

"I told you, we're not terrorists."

I'd never been inside the *Post* building, but our phone call to Eisner's reporter friend had resulted in this dawn meeting. I'd wanted to hold it in a public place. A newspaper. When the FBI showed up—when *whomever* they'd called showed up—I wanted witnesses. Lots of them. *Journalist* witnesses with journalist friends working in TV and magazines and radio.

"Where's Carl?" Harris had asked when I'd reached him.

"Dead."

Glasses of water sat before us. We hadn't touched them. The room felt freezing even though I was sweating, and I leaned to the right, moving as little as possible, fighting off waves of pain. I pitched my appeal to the editor-in-chief, the final decision-maker. "Look, we gave you three sources on the story, right? Harris said you only need two. You have Ludenhorff's disk—"

"Which could be faked," the managing editor interrupted. "Like the Hitler diaries. You say you took photos? What will they show? Some beakers with labels on them? That's not proof."

"And if it's *not* faked, it's classified," the Pulitzer Prize winner said. "You told us you stole the disk. You admitted tying up the Deputy Director. Beating him up. You want to make us a party to breaking the law?"

"I thought Pulitzer journalists had more guts," Danny said.

"You have to run the story!" Gabrielle burst out.

"Oh, we will. A responsible one. The question is, what story is the real story?"

"We'll look like idiots," the Southern guy said. "I say we call the FBI right now."

"Stop that. You already did," I said. "And we're staying anyway. Doesn't that convince you we're serious?"

I couldn't stand up. I was losing peripheral vision and the temperature seemed to be dropping into the arctic zone. From the confident feeling I picked up in the journalists, I was pretty sure security guards were outside the office. The FBI would crash in soon, depending on whatever deal the editors had made with them. It didn't matter. We'd left our weapons in the car. We weren't going to convince anyone of anything by brandishing weapons, and next stop after the *Post* would have been a prison hospital anyway, for me at least.

"Run," I'd told Danny and Gabrielle in the car when we'd pulled up, outside the paper. "I'll talk to them alone."

"Go to hell," Gabrielle had said.

Now the editor-in-chief said, "There's still one part I'm not clear on. . . ."

Danny said, "Is that the part where Mike hangs himself in his cell in military prison? When they stick Gabrielle in Guantánamo and it takes the Supreme Court five years to find out she's even there, except by then she died of disease?"

"Hell of a story, either way," the Pulitzer Prize winner remarked.

"Well, what do you *expect* us to do," the managing editor said. "We've confirmed that Naturetech was sabotaged and work destroyed on chemical-weapons antidotes there last night."

"The drug was not an antidote!"

"My *question* is," the editor-in-chief resumed with interest, "how do you know *we're* not in on this terrible plot to undermine the country? You're so sure that so many others are."

I felt blood soaking out of me.

"Yes, this *conspiracy,*" the managing editor said, as if conspiracies were impossible and never happened, as if Danny, Gabrielle and I were three psychopaths escaped from St. Elizabeth's, and they would humor and stall us until authorities arrived to safely get us back in our cells.

Gabrielle said, "We know you're not part of it because we would have sensed if you were. We told you, that's why we came in person. To sit with you while we talked."

"Oh, right. Because you're under the influence," the managing editor said, "this very minute."

Danny held out his wrist to show the purple markings. Gabrielle had them beneath her chin. But a child could buy paint that color in a shop. The editors gazed at the spots like they were Halloween makeup. I would have done the same thing a month ago.

The voices sounded far away. The cold left my body and suddenly I was sweating profusely. I smelled cinnamon.

"If you don't print this story today, you'll be stopped from printing it later." I barely heard my own voice now. "They'll use force, or threats, or the court, but they'll do it."

The men and women at the table sat back. They smiled knowingly at one another. They were among the most powerful journalists in the world and it was clear to them that I did not truly understand this. That if they wanted, *when* they wanted, nobody could stop them from printing anything they could prove. They weren't afraid of lawyers or jail. They weren't afraid of the President, God or country. They were only afraid of looking foolish.

I roused myself, sensing the time was right to make the final point. I said, "What if we could prove to you, now, that 109 is real? That everything we claim about it is true. If you believed that, if you *knew* that, would you print our side of the story today?"

The executive editor said, after a pause, "Well, of course."

"*If* you proved it," added the managing editor.

I glanced at Gabrielle and Danny. Simultaneously, we reached out and pushed forward the untouched glasses of water in front of us. The glasses now sat in the middle of the conference table, like three cards arranged by a monte artist. Three shells. Three peas.

I took my hand out of my pocket and showed the editors the synthesized 109 that I'd taken from Naturetech.

I was starting to collapse. I couldn't see anymore.

I said, "That's the other reason we came in person. Drink up. Any three of you. Now."

| TWENTY-SIX |

On a hot August day exactly one year later, I was enjoying a quiet afternoon picking tomatoes in my garden. It was a clear day, smog free for Brooklyn, and I had the Bose sound system on inside the house, loud enough so I could hear it out here. I was listening to NPR as I puttered around. The sky was blue. I heard kids in the street, going by on bicycles. I smelled earth and fertilizer and plum tomatoes ripened on tended vines. I figured I'd cook a sauce tonight, nothing fancy . . . just homegrown roasted tomato and garlic. Brown the garlic. Slice the shallots. Add freshly grated Pecorino Romano from Freddy's, and a touch of golden virgin olive oil.

I'd be dining tonight with Chris, my adopted son and Kim's real son. He'd come to live with me, from Vermont.

"And now today's news," the radio voice said.

It was odd having a son, even an adopted one, odder since we'd never lived together with his mother. But he reminded me of her, in the way he talked, the way he read books all the time. In his kindness. In his righteous temper. It was good to have a teenager in the house. It brought life.

Chris was at the beach at the moment, with new friends in the neighborhood. Devil's Bay had embraced him after hearing on the news how his mother died. He received constant invitations to parties, dinners, ball games. He liked the rhythms of the place even as he grieved for Kim. He didn't miss Manhattan. He'd even told me one day, when we were at the cemetery together, "When I was younger, I used to dream you were my father, but not exactly this way."

From the open kitchen window the radio announcer said, "Sentences were handed down today in Washington in what will undoubtedly go down as the most famous conspiracy trial in the nation's history."

I leaned down and felt for ripe tomatoes to break off the vine. Bending was still painful. The wound in my side had never entirely healed, even after a month in the hospital, and rehab after that. Bones had been clipped, muscles ripped. I exercised hard every day.

Maybe I was just getting old.

The announcer said, "Former National Intelligence Agency Deputy Director Paul Ludenhorff and Army Colonel Alonzo Otto were sentenced to be executed for treason and murder."

I plucked tomatoes off the vine, one by one. I'd make the sauce extra rich tonight.

The announcer continued over the sound of a car door slamming, in front of the house, probably Chris coming home.

"Sentences were also handed down against Sebastian O'Hayes, disgraced political strategist for the White House, along with three other members of the now defunct and notorious Six-Thirty Club, including Alicia Dent, former star journalist . . ."

Who took the easy way out, I thought. Like all of you.

"The White House announced that the President will not seek reelection, although he was not personally involved in the activities of the Six-Thirty Club. The

President said, quote, 'It will be healthier for the nation to put all aspects of this shameful episode as far from public life as possible.'

"Critics claim that the President is gracefully bowing out of a losing situation, distancing himself from appointees who caused his approval rating to drop to a dismal nine percent, even after the administration's much-touted victories against terrorism. Several other prominent Washingtonians have also quit or been fired in light of revelations about blackmail and the so-called Intuition drug. And spokesmen for the FBI confirmed that the suicide of Lenox Pharmaceuticals Chairman Bill Keating came hours before he was about to be arrested. Wall Street is rife with rumors that Lenox will be broken up, and acquired by other drug firms."

I heard footsteps coming around the flagstone path that I'd installed beside my house. They were light and quick, a woman's. It was probably my neighbor, a pretty divorcée named Cindy Castro, asking to borrow salt again, or milk, or bringing me a cheesecake, angling for a date.

She was sexy, and kind. I liked her. But I wasn't interested in involving myself with any women just now.

I didn't think I would be for a long time.

The radio announcer said, "Meanwhile, scientists and navy divers off Florida continue to scour reefs in a mad search for the fish said to carry the Intuition drug. No findings have been reported. It is feared that the fish is extinct."

I hope so, I thought.

"Reached for comment, Daniel Whiteagle, current head of Lenox Security, said of today's verdicts, quote, 'Finally Washington got something right.' Mike Acela, reached at the FBI in New York, where he is an agent again, refused to comment, and the third member of the team whose testimony brought on today's convictions, heiress Gabrielle Dwyer, is said to be out of the country, vacationing in Costa Rica."

"Wow. Costa Rica looks just like Brooklyn," Gabrielle said, from twenty feet away.

She was standing inside the white picket gate, beside the herb garden, beautiful in white shorts, tennis shoes and a tight emerald-and-white-striped sleeveless pullover. Gabrielle smiled with warm hesitancy, as if unsure whether she should have come here or not.

"I'm happy to see you," I said.

"Well, you know, with the verdicts in, I thought I'd drop by."

We sat on a stone bench in the garden, by a fountain I'd installed. Peasant or aristocrat, Italians dream of Michelangelo. The water gurgled pleasantly. The radio announcer went on to detail other resignations, a chain of them, a whole ripple effect of hirings, firings and deaths that were linked to HR-109.

"Funny thing is," I said, "in the end, every group that had an opportunity to keep the drug was just as bad as the others. Dwyer. Defense. Political people. Everyone."

"I guess there are some things people want so badly, there's no way to peacefully keep them in the world," she said.

"If it hadn't been this trial about 109, there would have been another, sooner or later," I agreed.

I could smell the ocean from blocks away, and for an instant, suddenly and powerfully remembered kissing Kim on the beach. Feeling the crush of her lips on mine. Her slim feel. Her small body. The strength in her arms.

"I made you think of her," Gabrielle said.

"Most things do. Tell me, how are you?"

"I travel a lot. I went to Argentina last month. Patagonia has beautiful mountains. Ever been to Argentina, Mike? The mountains . . . I already said that, didn't I?"

"I heard they have good steaks in Argentina."

She laughed as if I'd said something witty, but of course I hadn't. Seeing her brought on a wave of memories. I remembered the cold of that house in Virginia, and the underground tunnel. I recalled the moment when Kim hit her head. The images accelerated in no particular order, as if Gabrielle's presence had released the flood. Usually I kept them at bay during the day. But now they rushed in with all the reality of the present.

I saw Kim's head on Gabrielle's shoulder, in the car. I saw myself walking into Kim's bedroom that last night, as if my choice had determined her fate. Sometimes in my dreams her bedroom door had bat wings folded in front of it, like protective hands. I'd walk toward it and the wings would unfold. The room would be black inside, like the mouth of an old person, a mouth without teeth.

Inside the room, I'd know in the dream, was death.

Gabrielle was asking, "What's it like being a father?"

"I should have done it earlier," I said. But I did not want to share with her. I did not want to relive these things. They were my business. All those years when I could have been with Kim.

"Much earlier," I said angrily.

She blinked, feeling my resistance. She gazed over my shoulder as if she'd spotted something interesting, but she was just keeping from looking into my eyes.

"It's more important to do it right," she said. "Father-hood, I mean."

"How about you? New boyfriend?"

"Several."

"Well, this feels like one of those Enhance situations," I said, wanting her to leave, surprised at the tide of disquiet she brought on, having no idea what she was thinking and not wanting to know.

"Nothing is ever an Enhance situation, Mike."

"Yes. Of course. I know that. It was a joke."

A pause. A breeze came up, bringing a garbage smell from the neighbor's kitchen, a whiff of burnt popcorn and a hint of dark chocolate. I felt that so much time had passed. I didn't really know this woman. We'd shared the intensity of an episode. There was more to life than that.

"Well," she said, standing, "I remembered you lived in this neighborhood. I thought I'd take a chance and drop in."

"Glad you did."

There didn't seem to be more to say but we chatted a minute or two longer, to ease the awkwardness. Once I'd sensed so much between us. Now the quick exit seemed like driving away from a steep drop. We kept smiling, but it was Dr. Whiteagle's phony smile we were using. She admired my garden—the basil coming up, and the thyme.

"Take some home with you," I said.

"Nah, I always eat out," she said. "I'm a terrible cook."

The radio had switched from news to advertisements as I walked her back around the house. An announcer was going on about a new miracle drug to make hair grow fast and thick.

"Be younger. *Look* younger. You'll know what she's thinking when she looks at you *now*," the announcer said.

Her car was a BMW convertible, same model as the

one leased to me when I'd worked for Lenox. It was red, and the top was down. The upholstery was leather. She looked as perfect as an advertisement, sitting in the car. I didn't miss mine. I wished her well. She started the engine.

I went into the house.

I was glad at that moment that Chris was out. I sat in the living room, as if out of breath, feeling my heart beating. I smelled vanilla, Kim, but I smelled Gabrielle too—the perfume that had emanated from her car. I did not want that. It made me furious. There are times in life when people are open to possibility, and times when opportunity constitutes nothing more than added weight. There are boundaries in life, I now knew too, beyond which, once you cross them, you can yearn and yearn but all the yearning in the world won't reverse your path. It's like my garden. In winter, plants die. They never come back the same. They only look that way.

I sighed and felt hot. I'd been sitting here a while. I went upstairs to wash my face, glanced out the window from the bathroom and was surprised to see Gabrielle still sitting in her car.

Just sitting as I had been sitting, staring straight ahead.

At that moment my hands moved by themselves, lowering themselves, and by the time I slid the drawer out I was looking at a small blue capsule, the last bit, the tiniest reminder of a chemical that could take a human brain and make it more special. I was looking at the last few grams of Enhance that I'd saved and stuffed in a knothole outside of Naturetech, while Danny and Gabrielle brought the car. After my stay at the hospital, after my interrogations by half a dozen security agencies, I'd driven back one night and retrieved it, alone.

It was enough for one dose.

One hit. Or one donation to any government, any lab or scientist who might use it to re-create the synthesis formula.

Gabrielle sitting out there now, not moving . . .

What, I wondered, was she thinking?

I opened the toilet and broke the capsule and watched the powder drift down into the bowl. It floated on the surface like leaf bits in a pond. I flushed the toilet and the powder circled on top with the water, as if it were alive, refusing to go under, trying to save itself, as if asking me to pluck it from danger. The water level lowered. The water rushed faster. I could still reach some of the drug.

The last 109 in the world disappeared.

I went downstairs barefoot, opened the front door, watched her look over, watched her eyes meet mine as I approached the BMW. I didn't know what I was going to say. I wasn't sure how I felt, or what was going to happen, or even, I guess, what I wanted to happen, but I felt a great weight gone. I felt the 109 gone. Sometimes the biggest issues can be triggered by the most mundane questions.

"Want to stay for dinner?" I said. "You can even help make it."

"Now, *that's* trusting me," she said, and smiled.

We didn't touch, not then, not yet, walking toward the house. But I felt something I had not experienced in a long time, and without any drug inside. I felt bigger. More alive.

I felt my blood flowing.

I felt enhanced. Without any help.

ABOUT THE AUTHOR

BOB REISS is the author of sixteen books of fiction and nonfiction, including the best seller *The Last Spy* and the critically acclaimed Conrad Voort series, written under the pseudonym of Ethan Black. He is a former *Chicago Tribune* reporter and former correspondent for *Outside* magazine. His magazine articles have appeared in publications including the *Washington Post Magazine*, *Smithsonian*, *Rolling Stone* and *Parade*. He lives in New York.